THE
STAR
RUNNER

ROB J. LABELLE

Library of Congress Control Number: 2021912309

ISBN: 978-1-7373440-1-8
eBook ISBN: 978-0-578-58416-4

Book design by Rob J. LaBelle
Cover illustration by Ethan Shaw

This book is dedicated to my beautiful wife, Melissa.

Thank you for putting up with my insane amount of nerdiness.

I love you!

Author's Note

I have always been a huge fan of science fiction, specifically aliens and otherworldly creatures. And I hope that you all are too.

But, the main reason why I'm including this little blurb in here is to let you know that while you're reading, you may find some grammar and punctuation mistakes. Why? Well, for one, this is my very first book. And two, as a self-published author, I had to do *everything* myself. It was challenging but enjoyable work. Plus, I'm not perfect. No one is.

Now, as far as the science behind everything in this story goes, I can guarantee you that it may or may not make sense. I mean, let's face it, I'm not here to win any writing awards or take home a trophy for scientist of the year. I wrote this for you and everyone else to simply read and enjoy. It's a story that hopefully, by the very end, you'll think to yourself, *Wow! Now that was entertaining.* If so, then my job as an author is complete.

So, just sit back, relax, and enjoy the story for what it is... pure entertainment. Nothing more, nothing less.

Anyway, I thank you for listening. And, as always…

Happy reading!

Prologue

Huh? Oh, uh, hello.

I assume that you're here to listen to what I have to say? Just by looking at you, I guess you are. Well, I hate to break it to you, but by the time I'm done telling you what I need to tell you, you're probably gonna think I'm nuts.

So, in that case, why don't you pull up a chair, listen to what I have to say, and please, hold all of your questions until I'm finished. Deal?

Okay then. Let's get started.

First of all, let me ask you something... do you think that aliens really exist? Now, I know you must've asked yourself that question at least a million times in your own head, right? I mean, come on. Is Earth really the only planet in all the farthest reaches of space to host intelligent life? Seriously though, think about it.

All the little green men that have supposedly been spotted over the years, Area 51, and even UFOs in the sky... some people claim that it's all a product of government testing or merely a cover-up. If you were to ask someone about it, they'd tell you it's complete bullshit. As for me, well, I'd tell you something completely different.

Now, I know what you're thinking. You're thinking, *This man already sounds like a crazy lunatic.* Well, I can tell you one thing, I'm not crazy, and I'm definitely no lunatic.

Okay. Technically, that's two things. But who's counting?

Anyway, I will say this... they do exist. And so do a lot of other mythical creatures that you wouldn't believe either, like vampires and fairies. But we'll get into that a little bit later.

Shit. Where are my manners? You have no choice but to sit there and listen to my story, so allow me to introduce myself. My name is Samuel Watson. But everyone I know calls me Sam. Unless I was in trouble, then it's Samuel. But I digress.

Look, I know that you don't wanna be here listening to my bullshit any more than I wanna be here telling it to you, but we have no choice. You're stuck here listening to me, and I'm stuck here telling it to you. So get comfy.

Anyway, where was I? Oh yeah! Aliens...

Like I said, they *do* exist. And they're not as bad as everyone makes them out to be. Actually, they've been visiting our planet for tens of thousands of years. And, you could say that we're a lot alike. How do I know this? I'm glad you asked. So, sit down, strap in, and we'll get started.

Technically, it all started two days ago...

Chapter 1

With it being a beautiful, sunny July Saturday, I decided to go down to the river and do some fishing. After I cast my pole out into the water, I took out some suntan lotion and slathered it all over my pale skin.

You see, when I go fishing, I always like to fish in nothing but my swim trunks, just in case I feel like going in the water. Also, if I'm out in the sun, I'm one of those people where I either stay white or turn into a tomato. There is no in-between. Plus, with my dark hair and brown eyes, I'll wind up looking like a human pepper.

Anyway, I was there with my best friend, Darius, whom I've known since the sixth grade. I was always jealous of him because he was so much better looking than I was. And because he had the muscles and the looks, he got the girls and got invited to all of the parties. I felt like I held him back, though, because most of the time, he wouldn't go anywhere or do anything without me. He always stuck up for me and was always there for me.

"Why do you always gotta put so much of that shit on your skin?" Darius asked.

Now, he didn't really need any suntan lotion because he already had dark skin.

"Look at me," I said as I continued to lather it on. "I'm as white as a ghost."

"Yeah. You're white now because you put all that shit on you. You need to use less of that and get more sun."

As you probably could've already guessed by his comment, I stayed in and played a lot of video games. Again, he was the popular one. I wasn't. And, with him being my only real friend, when he wasn't around, I had my video games to keep me company. But again, I digress.

"Maybe I like lookin' like a ghost," I said.

"And that's why you're also single," he jokingly added.

He knew that my sex life was an issue for me and realized what he had said after the fact.

"My bad. I didn't mean that," he said.

"No worries," I said. "Besides, I'm not interested in anyone right now."

"You know what? You should come to Alice's party later."

Alice is his girlfriend, and they've been going together for the last two years. Now, I'll admit, when I see them together, I do get a bit on the jealous side.

See, I'm 30 years old, and up until that point in my life, I've only had sex a handful of times with two different women. However, he was right. I've been single for way too long. I mean, maybe I should go? Maybe I'll meet someone there, who knows? The sky's the limit, right?

"What time does it start?" I asked.

"Holy shit!" he excitedly said. "Are you actually gonna go?"

"I'm thinking about it."

As you could've also guessed, I wasn't really much of a party animal either. But, every once in a while, I'd make an effort and go.

"Yo, dog," he said. "If you're gonna go, then you need some new clothes."

"What's wrong with the ones I own?" I asked.

"I love you, bro, but you really need to upgrade from nerds-r-us."

Sadly, he was right. Every piece of clothing that I owned ranged from ripped jeans to video game t-shirts to converse sneakers. Although, he never did seem to have an issue with my sneakers. I mean, come on, everybody loves those shoes.

"Alright," I said. "I'll go."

"Well, it's about damn time!" he replied. "It's been *way* too long since we've gone to a party together. It's gonna be off the hook!"

Nah. He wasn't excited for me to go at all.

"As a matter of fact," he continued. "I'm gonna go meet up with Alice and tell her that you'll be showing your face later. She's gonna be psyched!"

I figured I would at least go and make him happy. I mean, he does a lot of the things that I like to do, more often than me doing the things that he likes to do. So, I figured that I owed him a few. And, for some strange, odd reason, a party didn't sound too bad.

"So, the party starts at ten," he added. "But you and I are goin' shoppin' for some new clothes around seven."

"Want me to meet you at your house?" I asked.

"Nah. I'll come pick you up."

"I'll be waiting."

We then gave each other our usual bro-hug.

"Remember," he said. "I'll pick you up at seven."

He then left the river bank and ran up the hill to hop in his car.

Once he was gone, I just stood there, thinking about how much I was actually looking forward to going to that party. So, I just continued fishing there for the next few hours until my skin felt like it was on fire and ready to burn right off.

After I packed everything up in my 2017 red, four-door sedan, I then went back down to the river, just to make sure I wasn't leaving anything behind. And, after a thorough sweep of the area, it was as clean as a whistle.

Now, I didn't have a towel with me or a change of clothes. And I don't know whether it was the hot sun or because I just felt like it, but I decided to take a quick swim. So, I dove into the river and had at it.

After a few glorious minutes of floating too far out, I started swimming back to the shore, but not before I noticed something blinding me from underneath the water.

It was silver in color and looked like it was jammed under a rock. Now curious about what I was looking at, I took a deep breath and swam down to get it. Once I had it dislodged, I swam back up to catch my breath before swimming back to the shore.

I held this tennis ball sized metal object in my right hand and just stared at it for a bit. I had never seen anything like it before. Of course, I would eventually figure out *why,* but we'll get to that a little later.

After examining it a little further, I tried to see if there were any openings or buttons or anything on that sphere that would tell me exactly what the hell it was. But, five minutes later, I still had nothing. So, I just shrugged it off and took it with me. Besides, I now had to go and get ready for a party.

• • •

Now, I won't bore you with the details of shopping in a small town like Laconia, New Hampshire, and Darius making fun of every single outfit that I picked out, so I'll just skip straight ahead to the party.

There had to be at least a hundred people at that thing. I don't think Alice could've fit another body onto her property, even if she tried.

I was hanging out with Darius, who was wearing a black, silk, button-down shirt, along with his black dress pants and somewhat comfortable dress shoes. I, myself, had on a navy blue, silk, button-down shirt with black dress pants and my black converse sneakers. I totally decided against the dress shoes.

Also hanging out with us was Darius's girlfriend, Alice.

Her breasts were practically popping out through her tight, white t-shirt, while her black, leather mini skirt accented her long, smooth, silky legs. Along with those two features, her long, flowing dark hair and her mocha-colored skin completed the full, gorgeous package. I envied him big time, and I think he knew that. However, as much as I did envy him, he knew that I would never try anything with her. That's not how we were. Also, as best friends, we had one golden rule: neither of us would ever date each other's exes. That would just be too weird.

"You enjoying yourself, Sam?" Alice asked me.

"I am," I said. "This is a great party."

"I'm glad you made it this time."

"It's like pulling teeth to get him to go anywhere," Darius added. "Hey! I'm not a total nerd," I replied.

Having said that, I looked at Darius, and he looked back at me before we both just started gut laughing.

"Okay. Maybe I am," I said.

"Don't worry, bro, we still love you," he said, smiling at me. "We're gonna go get some more drinks. You want anything?"

"I'll take another hard iced tea."

Now, everyone who also knows me knows that I've never liked the taste of beer. Instead, I always drink those hard lemonades or hard iced teas or anything fruity. Yeah, everyone always gave me shit for it, but I didn't care. I knew what I liked, and those made me just as drunk as everyone else. Besides, in my opinion, only a real man can handle those drinks.

"Another girly drink, coming up," Darius joked.

"Ha-ha. Very funny," I replied.

"Just messin' with ya. We'll be back."

I then moved off of the dance floor and stood against the wall, watching as both of them zigzagged through the crowd.

As I stood there waiting for them to come back, I watched the crowd dance and move while "Poker Face" by Lady Gaga blared over the stereo system. I also couldn't help but think of that sphere I had found earlier down at the river. *What was it? Was it a cannonball of some sort? Was it some kind of an alien object? Or was it just simply a melted-down hunk of metal?*

I just continued to stand there and think about it until out of nowhere, a woman came crashing right into me. After she did, she immediately turned around to face me.

"Oh my god! I'm so sorry," she said.

As I stared and practically drooled at her long, blonde hair and her beautiful brown eyes, I could only muster up a high-pitched, "That's okay," before she giggled.

I then quickly cleared my throat so I could muster up a more low-pitched, manly tone.

"That's okay. Don't worry about it," I said.

"I didn't hurt you, did I?" she asked.

"I'll survive," I replied as I continued to look over her incredibly fit body.

Like I said before, I've only been with two women until that point in my life, and as I was standing there talking to her, I could feel the sweat starting to seep out of every pore in my body. My heart started pounding, and I was so nervous that I felt like I was about to stand up in front of a big crowd to give a speech.

"Hi! I'm Sam," I said, hoping she would give me a response.

"Nice to meet you, Sam. I'm Nicky," she said.

Holy shit. I couldn't believe I managed to get her name without making a complete ass of myself.

"Nice to meet you, Nicky," I said. "Are you here by yourself?"

"I initially came with some friends," she replied. "But for some reason, they all took off, and now I can't seem to find them."

"That's too bad. If you were with me, I wouldn't leave you alone for a second."

And there it was. The *ass* came around full circle.

Thankfully, though, she just laughed it off. However, I wasn't prepared for what she said next. She said the one thing that I never thought I'd ever hear someone like her ask someone like me.

"You're cute," she said. "Do you wanna get out of here?"

Again, holy shit! She wants to leave with me? What do I do? What do I say? I mean, I came here with Darius. I can't just leave him here with his girlfriend while I suddenly split with this incredibly hot-looking...

"Let's go," I said.

Hey, I'm no fool. But, since Darius drove me to the party, I felt awful for making this girl drive me back to my place. It should've been my job to drive her. Luckily, she understood the situation and didn't seem to mind.

• • •

After we arrived at my building in her black, two-door SUV, we both got out and immediately hightailed it up to my fourth floor, one-bedroom apartment. I opened the door to go inside, and we never even made it to the bedroom. Instead, I couldn't help it and just laid her down right there on the couch.

She knew what she was doing, though, because before I could even do anything else, she pushed me backward, only to climb on top of me and start kissing me. A few seconds in, however, she stopped and looked at me.

"Hold those lips," she said. "I have to use the bathroom. Don't go anywhere."

And with that, she climbed right off of me and made a b-line straight for the bathroom.

I just sat there on the couch with a gigantic smile on my face, almost as if *that* was gonna be my first time all over again. But, unfortunately, the magic moment was cut a little short.

As I was sitting there waiting for her, I happened to peer into my bedroom and take a look at the metal object I found earlier. I was still curious about what it was and why it was sitting on the bottom of a river. How did it get there, anyway? With many questions racing through my mind, I decided to get up and make my way in there to get a closer look. But before I could even take two steps, I heard her yell something out from the bathroom.

"I'm almost done!" she shouted.

Curious, though, because I never asked her anything to begin with. "I didn't say anything," I replied.

I then heard the toilet flush, followed by her coming out of the bathroom.

"You didn't say anything just now?" she asked.

"No," I replied.

"You didn't just ask me if I was almost done?"

"No. Why?"

Neither of us said a word as we both just stood there awkwardly for a moment. I honestly thought she was gonna think I was nuts and take off. But because of what she said next, that thought quickly dissipated.

"What are you waiting for, hot lips?" she asked before turning and heading back toward the couch.

Holy shit. This was it. I was finally gonna score woman number three! However, this is where my story officially starts to get a little weird.

Now, I know what you're thinking. You're thinking, *Why did you ask me if I believe in aliens and other creatures if they aren't even in this story?* Well, they are. Just be patient. I wanna make sure you get the whole story before I'm judged.

So, anyway, as she was walking back to the couch, I shit you not, I heard a man's voice that wasn't my own, as clear as day, say something that blondes *definitely* don't like to hear.

"Damn!" the mysterious male voice said. "I guess blondes really are that stupid if they'll sleep with anyone."

After hearing that, Nicky stopped dead in her tracks and slowly turned around, only to give me the dirtiest look that I have ever seen someone give another person. My own jaw was now hitting the carpet because I just couldn't believe it either.

"What did you just say?" she asked me with a slightly angry tone.

I could now tell that she was pissed off beyond belief. I mean, how do I respond to that?

"I did *not* say that," I said, ever so shockingly.

"What the fuck's wrong with you?" she asked.

"I swear to god. That wasn't me. I don't even know where that came from."

At that point, I was just praying to god that one of the neighbors had their TV turned up really loud.

"You didn't just say that?" she asked.

"I don't know who said that," I replied. "I've never said anything like that to anyone in my life."

She didn't say a word and just looked me right in the eyes to determine if I was being truthful or not. Sometimes, you can just tell.

"I think someone might have their TV up too loud," I responded.

It took her another second, but she could see that I wasn't lying.

"Okay then," she said. "What are we waiting for?"

She turned back around to head for the couch when suddenly, it happened again.

"There she goes," the mysterious male voice said. "I guess it is true. Blondes really are that-"

"You son of a bitch!" she angrily said, interrupting the mysterious voice mid-sentence.

Before I, myself, could even get a word out edgewise, she walked right up to me and just gave me the biggest slap in the face that I've ever had. Thankfully, it was the *only* slap in the face that I've ever had. She then followed that up with a dirty look and immediately stormed out of my apartment. I was now left standing there alone in my living room, holding my numb, stinging face, wondering what the hell just happened.

With her now gone, I immediately decided to put myself to bed so I could reflect on what went wrong. But I couldn't sleep. I couldn't stop thinking about what was said and the fact that I didn't say it.

While I was lying there, I checked my text messages to see that Darius had messaged me multiple times, asking where I was and what the fuck happened? I responded to him by letting him know to meet me for coffee in the morning and that I would explain everything to him then.

I eventually managed to fall asleep, and a few hours into my siesta, I was awoken by a strange sound coming from within my room. I opened my eyes and picked my head up to quickly peruse the area where I thought the noise was coming from. Unfortunately, I didn't see anything and simply decided to put my head back down on my pillow. A few seconds later, however, I heard *another* noise coming from my bedroom.

It sounded like someone tripping over something, followed by a groan, almost as if they had just stubbed their toe on a bookshelf. Instead of picking just my head up, I sat up and turned on the light. I perused my room real slow to try and see or hear anything. After a few minutes, though, I just chalked it up to noisy neighbors and fell back asleep.

· · ·

The following morning, after a very rough and sleepless night, I got up and quickly got dressed. I threw on my vintage Batman t-shirt (circa 1989), a pair of blue jeans with both legs ripped at the knees, and instead of my black converse sneakers, I threw on my red ones before meeting Darius at the coffee shop, which was located just two blocks from my house.

After we grabbed our drinks, Darius and I both sat in a corner booth, far away from everyone, so that we could speak in private.

"Dude, what happened to you last night? Why did you bail on the party?" he asked while taking a sip of his coffee.

"You wouldn't believe me even if you were there in person," I replied.

"Try me."

I shrugged. "If you insist. Well..." I began.

I explained everything to Darius about my night from the moment I met Nicky and left the party, all the way up until she slapped me and took off. Of course, after I finished telling him what had happened, he didn't say one word. Instead, he just stared at me like I was mental or something.

While I waited for him to respond, I just slowly sipped my coffee. He did the same, until finally, instead of saying something back to me, he just busted out laughing. My only friend in the world was now laughing at my failure. But because I know him better than the back of my own hand, I expected that kind of a reaction and wasn't really all that upset.

"She slapped you?" he asked. "Damn, man! That's a new one even for me."

"It was the first time I've ever been slapped, too," I replied. "I gotta say, though, it hurts a lot more than people make it out to be."

Again, he didn't say anything but just continued to laugh for the next few seconds.

"Go ahead," I said. "Get it all out now."

"Alright, my bad. I apologize," he said. "But, you said you heard a strange voice?"

"Yeah. I mean, I thought it was just the neighbors, but it was so well-timed that it couldn't have been."

"Maybe you got a stalker?"

"I don't know. But if it happens again, I'm calling the cops."

"Yeah, right. What are you gonna say? That the invisible man is haunting your apartment?"

As stupid as that sounded, he was right. I mean, what was I gonna say? That would definitely come off as crazy to anyone. However, rather than press the issue, I just shrugged my shoulders and immediately changed the subject.

We sat in the coffee shop for the next hour or so, just chatting about how the party was last night and about how he and a couple of other dudes had to escort a couple of drunk people out of there. After we were done, we went our separate ways, as he had a few things to take care of and, well, I didn't. So, I just decided to go home and watch a movie.

• • •

When I got back, I didn't even bother to take my shoes off and just stormed in to turn on the TV. I then popped in the Blu-ray of the original 1933 classic *King Kong,* my all-time favorite movie, before plopping my lazy butt down on the couch.

Believe it or not, I actually had a hard time focusing on the movie. I just kept thinking about Nicky and all those rude, mean things that I never said to her. Many thoughts continued racing through my mind about who that was or what it could've been. Did someone really have their TV turned up that loud? If that was the case, the muttered lines were said at such a precise moment that it would've been a bizarre coincidence.

Nah. It couldn't have been that. Did I really have a stalker? Plausible, but highly unlikely. The only other thing I could think of was that someone watched us leave the party and then followed us back there, only to be a dick when the time was necessary.

Nah. That couldn't have happened either. I was up on the fourth floor. They would've had to climb all the way up the fire escape to do it. Plus, my windows were closed and locked.

Anyway, about an hour into the movie, and still thinking about Nicky, I was interrupted by a knock on my door. I just stared at it for a moment and thought to myself, *Who the hell is that?* I wasn't expecting anyone.

Okay, so that moment right there was pretty much the end of my life as I knew it.

Now, I know you were waiting for the story to get good. So I can assure you, *this* is where it gets interesting. Or weird. Or just downright stupid if you wanna believe that I'm crazy. But again, I assure you, I'm not.

So, not wanting to leave my mystery guests waiting, I paused the movie and got up to go over to the door.

"Who is it?" I asked.

Of course, there wasn't any answer. I then looked through the peek hole in my door to see if anyone was out there. There wasn't.

Now, even though I've seen almost every horror movie that's ever been made (and like a moron), I opened the door to look out into the hallway. When I did, I didn't see a soul. I then went back into my apartment, closed the door, and just shrugged my shoulders before going back over to the couch.

I picked up the remote and was about to hit play when I heard another knock on the door.

"Are you fucking kidding me right now?" I said out loud before pausing the movie again.

Once again, I got up off the couch and went over to the door. But this time, I didn't even bother to ask who it was (although I definitely should've). Instead, I just opened the door, thinking that no one would be out there. When it flung open, I saw, well, I don't know what the hell I saw.

There were three *people* or whatever, who stood at least seven feet tall, standing out in the hallway. They all had bright red skin, red eyes, dark hair, pointy elf-like ears, two squid-like tentacles that came down from their jaws (one on each side), and they were all dressed in some sort of battle armor that looked reminiscent of what someone would wear in the *He-Man* cartoons.

At first, I thought it was some kind of early/late Halloween prank. So, I decided to compliment them on all of their costumes.

"Holy shit! Awesome costumes!" I said.

But, my compliment was for naught, as they didn't reply back. Instead, the one in the middle pulled out a small, metal device, which kind of resembled an old Walkman.

The device itself had a couple of knobs and buttons on it and a small computer screen on the top half that displayed alien languages. For them, it was some kind of intergalactic translator.

The one in the middle then looked at the screen on the device and tried speaking to me. Of course, I had no clue as to what the hell he was saying. I didn't even think that kind of language existed. Well, not here on Earth, anyway.

"I don't understand," I said.

He then pushed a couple more buttons on the device before attempting to speak to me a second time. However, I still didn't understand them.

"I'm sorry. I still don't understand you," I repeated.

Once again, he pushed some more random buttons on the device. But when he spoke to me for the third time, I understood him as clear as day.

"Give us the sphere," he said in a deep, threatening voice.

The sphere? How did they know I had that thing? I never even got a chance to tell Darius that I found it. And, not knowing who those guys were or the fact that they were even aliens, I decided to mess with them a little bit.

"Can you guys understand me now?" I asked.

"Give us the sphere," he said again in the same threatening tone.

"What sphere?" I asked, knowing damn well that I had it on the shelf in my room.

"We know you have it. Now, give it to us!" he demanded.

Were these guys for real? Standing on my doorstep, threatening me over a small metal ball?

But, not yet knowing who they really were, I did the only thing I thought was right at the time.

"Look," I said. "I don't know who you are or what kind of game you're playing, but I'd leave if I were you. And don't come back. If I see you again, I'm calling the cops."

And with that, I just slammed the door on their smug, red faces and locked it.

How did I know they were aliens, you ask? Well… I didn't. At least, not at the time. I wouldn't find that out until a few minutes later. But, first things first.

After I slammed the door shut, I went back to the couch to resume watching my movie. Again, I didn't even get a chance to hit play when I heard what sounded like an electrical charge building up. That lasted all but two seconds before my living room door had exploded into a million pieces.

I screamed at the top of my lungs. "Holy shit!" Before all three of those things came walking right in.

Instead of one gun being pointed at me, all three of them had their guns pointed at me. I then heard that same electrical charge before realizing that was my cue.

I immediately ran from the living room and into my bedroom, only to hear a discharge, followed by pieces of my couch, hitting my apartment's walls and floor. I quickly peeked into the living room, only to see that my couch had been replaced by a giant cloud of dust and debris. That's when I knew that these weren't everyday, ordinary people. I still hadn't figured out what they were or why they were so hell-bent on getting the sphere.

So, I quickly reacted and did the only thing that I could think of. I closed my bedroom door and grabbed a few of my personal items: my wallet, my keys, my phone, and of course, the sphere. I then opened my bedroom window and quickly jumped out onto the fire escape. When I got out there, I looked back into my apartment, only to see them completely disintegrate my bedroom door.

"Jesus Christ!" I yelled out.

Those guys definitely weren't messing around.

Without thinking twice about it, I made my way down all four stories of the fire escape ladder until both of my feet were planted safely on the ground. I then ran around to the side of the building, hopped in my car, and burned some serious rubber getting my ass out of there.

• • •

While I was driving and escaping for my life, I thought about calling Darius and telling him about what had just happened. However, I decided against it because, yeah. Who in their right mind would believe that kind of a story? I mean, I could always tell my parents, but I don't think they would've believed me either. Plus, they were in California on vacation, and I definitely didn't feel like ruining their fun.

I now needed some time to think and reflect on what just happened. But where do I go? What do I do? How the hell do I explain any of this? However, after some serious thought, there was only one place I could go to where no one would bother me.

• • •

After I pulled into the parking lot that overlooked the river, I quickly got out of my car and ran down the hill to the water's edge. Once I was safe, I stopped and hunched over, as I was now panting and breathing really hard from everything that just happened. And, in my moment of panic, I started talking to myself.

"Get a hold of yourself, Sam. I don't know what you just saw, but none of that was real. It was all just a big illusion, brought on by your weird imagination."

Was it, though? Was all of that really in my head? Was I really going crazy?

So, to try and wake me up from any type of dream that I might have been having, I immediately knelt down on the grass and splashed some of the cold water on my face. After it hit me, I just closed my eyes, shook my head, and took a couple of deep breaths, hoping that when I opened them, I would be back in my apartment, sitting on my couch, watching TV. I then took one more deep breath and opened my eyes. Nope. Still at the river and still freaked out.

Shit. It wasn't a dream. That really happened. I really did almost just die at the hands of whatever the hell they were. What was I gonna do now? And more importantly, why were they after the sphere?

"The sphere!" I said out loud.

I had put it on the ground to splash some water on my face. So, I picked it up and quickly started to analyze every single inch of it. After a few minutes, however, I couldn't find a damn thing.

And, apparently, that's when I started thinking out loud too.

"What do they want with you? What makes you so special? You're just a ball of metal."

But my mind was blank. The more I thought about it, though, the crazier my thought process became.

"Maybe I should just give it back to them," I said out loud again. "Then they'll leave me alone. No, I can't do that. I'll give them the sphere, and then they'll kill me anyway."

Yeah, I definitely watched one too many movies.

So, deciding not to add any more fuel to my already fiery brain, I took a seat right there in the grass to try and calm myself.

As I sat there, I couldn't help but think about my parents and how they always supported me no matter what I did. They always told me to do what makes me happy and to earn a good living while doing it.

You see, my dream was to own my own video game store. I worked as an assistant manager at the one in town and was up for a promotion soon. Then, I would be one step closer to achieving my dream. I mean, yeah, being an owner of a video game store isn't the most glamorous job, but the market for video games nowadays is insane. They're more popular than ever. And that's also what I studied in college.

No, not video games, but business. I got my Bachelor's degree in business so that one day I would understand everything that comes with owning my own store. It's definitely helped me out so far, and the CEO of the company I worked for knew that. He knew how smart I was and had faith in me that I would one day succeed. He also purposely transferred out the current store manager just so I could get the job.

But as I was sitting there, thinking about my current situation, I thought, *Hey, it could still happen.*

I then took out my phone and checked the time.

"Eleven am?" I said.

It wasn't even lunchtime yet, and I've already been chased out of my apartment by who knows what.

However, I only had a few more seconds to think about everything because no sooner did I check the time, I heard footsteps behind me. I quickly put my phone back into my pocket and stood up to turn around, only to see the same three whatsits from earlier.

Great. Now, what do I do? I had nowhere to run. Even if I tried swimming for it, they could easily pick me off in the water. So, I did the only thing I could. I manned up and just stood there, holding my ground. Of course, they just pointed their guns at me. But for some reason, they didn't fire. I knew it had something to do with the fact that I was holding the sphere in my hand. Maybe they didn't want to shoot because they thought they might hit it. I had no idea. But it didn't take a genius to figure it out.

"Hand over the sphere, and we'll let you live," the ugly one in the middle said.

"We won't hurt you," the one on the left said.

"We promise," said the one on the right.

Yeah, right. I thought to myself. *That's the biggest crock of shit I've ever heard in my life.*

But I still had to know why they wanted that thing so badly.

"Why do you want it so badly?" I proceeded to ask. "Who are you? Where are you from?"

All three of them just looked around at each other before looking back at me. The one in the middle opened his mouth and looked like he was gonna say something to me, but then stopped. I was now wondering what they were thinking. And before I could even ask them myself, all three of them were looking up over my head and out toward the river.

Curious as to what they were now looking at, I turned around to see nothing. So, I then looked back at them. And sure enough, they were still looking in the same direction. Of course, I turned back around to look out over the river again and still saw nothing. That is until I saw what looked like two yellow balls of light appear out of nowhere and blast those guys.

"Holy shit!" I screamed, quickly hitting the ground.

I then turned around to see if those three were still alive, only to now see three big piles of ash sitting there on the ground. They were completely vaporized. I couldn't believe it. I blinked a few times just to make sure I was seeing it correctly. I was. They were dead. But who shot them?

I immediately stood up and quickly turned around to look out over the river again. And that's when I saw something I never thought would ever be possible.

I had only seen it in the movies and knew that this kind of technology didn't exist. A spaceship, hovering over the river, had just de-cloaked itself.

A spaceship? Here? I thought to myself. Now I know I had seen it all.

The silver ship's cockpit was about 20 yards from me and was now staring me right in the face. The ship itself went back about 50 yards and branched off to the left and to the right, making the whole thing look like a giant capital letter *T.* I could also see flames shooting out from the back of both of those two branches and from underneath. Just behind the cockpit, I could see two laser cannons sticking out. They kind of reminded me of those machine guns they have on Huey gunships. Except that those obviously weren't machine guns.

I just stood there, watching this thing, waiting for it to shoot the lasers at me and blast me into oblivion. But it didn't happen. Instead, the ship started to turn sideways and lower itself over the water. After it was done positioning itself, it stopped and was now hovering about three feet off of the river. *What was gonna happen now? Was I gonna die? Would there be an army of intergalactic androids that come out and take me hostage?*

No sooner did I think about that, I noticed a door located about ten feet behind the cockpit start to open. It rose up, just like the doors on a DeLorean, and when it did, a retractable metal platform extended out and was now resting on the shore, just a few feet in front of me. Someone, or something, was actually coming out to greet me. But who? Or what? Again, I just stood there and held my ground.

I waited for what seemed like an eternity for something to come out of there. But nothing on this Earth could've ever prepared me for what actually did come out. In the doorway of the ship appeared a woman. Not just any woman, mind you, an actual *alien* woman.

Except for her long, flowing purple hair, her bright, violet-colored eyes, her shiny, amethyst-colored skin, and some skin-tight clothes that I've never seen before, she was a couple inches shorter than me and looked just like an Earthling. She walked on two legs, had two arms, five fingers on each hand, and I can only assume five toes on each foot. She also had a beautiful set of normal-looking pearly whites.

Okay. Now, I was really seeing things.

My face now looked like a cartoon character, as my jaw was hung low, and my eyes were bugging out. But before I could react or do anything else, she started walking toward me. Now, what do I do? Do I run for the hills? Do I piss myself right then and there from being too nervous? Of course not. I just kept on staring.

When she finally did get over to me, she looked me right in the eyes before looking down at my left hand, where the sphere was currently residing. She then took a look around at the surrounding area and didn't even flinch. It's almost as if she wasn't even fazed by being on another planet. I mean, come on. Who was I kidding? She was already an alien from outer space. There's probably nothing that she hasn't seen yet.

As I stood there, unsure about what to say or do, she took one more look at the sphere before looking back up at me and speaking.

"You need to come with me right now," she said. "You're in serious danger."

Chapter 2

She just continued to stare at me, waiting for me to give her an answer. Of course, I didn't. I mean, how could I? I was still in shock.

Before that day, I definitely thought that anyone who believed Earth was the only planet in all of infinite space to host intelligent life had to be a complete moron. Well, as it turns out, they were.

Anyway, with me standing there, still not saying a word, she tried speaking to me again.

"I know this is a bit of a shock," she said. "But we have to get going before more of them show up."

She had the softest, sweetest voice that I've ever heard. At that moment, I thought to myself, *Did I really just think that?*

"Come on!" she said in a slightly louder tone. "If we don't get out of here, then we're both dead!"

I wasn't dreaming. This was for real. Those other guys that hunted me down and tried to kill me were actual aliens. And so was she. A beautiful, purple-haired, amethyst-skin colored alien who was so hot. Also, how the hell does an alien from outer space speak perfect English?

"Hey!" she said even louder before slapping me across the left side of my face.

"Ow!" I said, now holding my numb, stinging face.

I couldn't believe it. Before yesterday, I've never been slapped in my whole entire life. Now, that's twice in two days. I was on a roll.

"Why did you slap me?" I asked.

"Because you were off in la-la land," she replied. "And if we don't get going, we're both gonna die."

"Forgive me if I seem a bit out of line, but you're a fucking alien!"

"Not true. To me, *you're* the alien."

Up until she said that, I never even thought about it like that before. She was right. In her eyes, I was the alien, which I now know definitely goes both ways.

"So, you want me to just get on your ship and fly away with you?" I asked, making a sliding motion with my right hand toward the sky.

"You have to," she said. "We need to return the sphere."

"What's this *we* stuff? Why can't I just give you the sphere, and then you bring it back yourself?"

"Ugh," she groaned. "We don't have time for this. Just come with me now, and I'll explain everything on the way."

Explain everything on the way? What the hell does she mean by that?

"The way to where?" I asked.

"To Morgide,"[1] she said.

"What the hell's Morgide?"

"It's a planet located about one hundred light-years from here."

"A hundred light-years!" I shouted. "That's way beyond our own solar system!"

"Yeah," she continued. "We have a long way to go. And if we don't hurry, the Morgidians will catch us."

Okay. Now I've heard everything.

So, apparently, those three aliens were from the planet Morgide, as she called it, and they were after the sphere that I found. According to her, I couldn't stay here, or I was dead. On the other hand, if I did go with her, I'd have a chance to see space and everything in it. Of course, there's always a strong possibility that I still might die. Now, what person in their right mind would actually turn down a chance like that? Definitely not this guy.

"Take me to your leader," I jokingly said, using a robotic voice.

She definitely didn't seem to find that funny and just gave me a dirty look before turning around and leading me across the retractable bridge. Once we were inside the ship, she didn't waste any time and immediately pointed toward the cockpit.

"Get to the cockpit and sit in the passenger's seat," she ordered.

---

[1] (Pronounced *More-guide*)

She then pushed a red button on the right side of the doorway, causing the retractable bridge to pull underneath the ship, kind of like one of those loading ramps you would see on a moving truck. The door then slid shut from the top down to the bottom, sealing itself with a hissing noise after it was closed.

She turned to look at me, and I could now see the look on her face, almost as if to ask me why I was still standing there. So, I immediately turned to my right and made my way toward the cockpit.

The short corridor that I walked down to get there was silver and metallic in color. The shape of it was round, except for the floor, which was flat. The corridor kind of sort of reminded me of what the inside of the *Millennium Falcon* looked like. The cockpit... not so much.

The cockpit itself was about a 20-foot by 20-foot room, with two chairs set up in the front middle, both of which looked like a mix between those black gaming chairs and an office chair. The front dash of the cockpit had a bunch of weird-looking buttons, switches, and levers, most of which were on the driver's side.

I sat down in the passenger's chair, and when I did, a harness, almost like the ones used in jet planes, automatically came down over my shoulders, from around my sides, and in between my legs, to secure itself right around the middle of my chest area.

"Holy shit!" I said. "How awesome was that?"

She didn't say a word but just looked at me as she sat down while her harness did the exact same thing. The moment her butt touched the chair, a small, three-by-three area of the dashboard came right up off the panel and was now directly in front of her. Both the left and right side each had a small, glowing half orb, in which she placed her hands. When she did, those two areas separated from the small panel, and she could now move them around however she wished.

"Are you ready?" she asked.

"I don't have a choice, do I?" I replied.

"You don't happen to get airsick, do you?"

"No. Why?"

And with that, she pushed one of the buttons in the middle of the panel, put her hands back on the glowing half orbs, and then looked back over at me again.

"Good," she simply said with a smile. "Hold on."

And before I could even ask another question, the ship took off skyward like a launching roller coaster. Only, we were going about a thousand times faster than any roller coaster.

It didn't even take us what felt like two seconds to get from the ground and break through the Earth's atmosphere to reach outer space. When we did, I think she noticed the excitement on my face because she wound up slowing down to a stop so that I could get a good look. I was now seeing what only a few people from Earth have ever seen.

Something that only astronauts see. Earth was now staring me right in the face, and it… was… awesome.

Seeing it from outer space, though, gives you a whole new outlook on just how insignificant we really are down here. The glowing blue and green planet was just massive and beautiful. Not many people get to see it like that, and it definitely was a once-in-a-lifetime opportunity. However, after I came to my senses, I quickly pulled out my phone and snapped a photo of it. She could tell how much I was enjoying it and decided to make another pit stop before we took off into deep space.

"Wanna see the moon?" she asked.

Now excited at the prospect of seeing the farthest humankind has ever traveled, I could only think of one response.

"Fuck yeah!" I excitedly replied.

And with that, she immediately turned the ship around and quickly rocketed away from Earth.

• • •

With the way the ship was built and the technology it had, we arrived at the moon after a short, ten-minute haul. She then stopped to hover above it and pointed the nose down so I could get a good look.

"Wow," I quietly muttered.

There it was. Our own moon, staring me right in the face.

And although I wasn't on its surface, I could only imagine how Neil Armstrong, Buzz Aldrin, Alan Shepard, and John Glenn must've felt when they actually got to walk down there and touch the gray, dusty surface.

Okay. I know that John Glenn didn't actually walk on the moon itself, but he was just as cool.

Anyway, of course, with my phone still out, I quickly snapped another photo. I then looked around the surface to try and disprove a long-standing conspiracy theory. *Was the moon landing real? Or did it actually take place in a movie studio?* With those two questions looming in my mind, I looked around for only a few seconds until my eyes found the answer I was looking for.

"There it is!" I excitedly shouted.

"There, what is?" she asked.

"The American flag! It's right there!" I replied, pointing down toward it. "Which means it happened. It actually happened."

"What happened?"

"The moon landing. All those conspiracy theories about whether or not we actually landed on it? Apparently, it was all just a bunch of bullshit."

Of course, the flag itself wasn't all that colorful, as it was now bleached white from all those years of radiation exposure.

She then said something to me that I wasn't prepared for, something that made me question all kinds of other things like Area 51 or any other long-standing conspiracy about aliens. Of course, I now know all of those to be true.

"I could've told you that the moon landing was real," she said.

And there it was.

I just slowly turned to her and thought to myself, *How does she know about that?* I mean, seriously. How long have the aliens really known about us, and vice versa?

However, she knew exactly what I was thinking and quickly responded.

"You're probably wondering how I knew that," she said. "Well, we have a long ride ahead of us, and once we're out of the Milky Way, I'll throw this thing on autopilot and answer any questions you might have. Until then, just sit back and enjoy the view."

Then, just like the glory days of MTV, we were gone.

• • •

Now, the next part may get a bit boring, and when I say boring, I mean that it's no action and pretty much a question and answer game. But I still need to tell it because it's part of the story.

Before we finally made it out of the Milky Way, I saw so many things that I didn't even think were possible. As far as I knew, I was the first-ever human being to see all seven of the other planets and their moons with the naked eye. And, when I say seven, I mean Mars and beyond, including Pluto. In my mind, it's still technically a planet, even though grand old science deemed it not to be.

Even though I had plenty of time (a whole day, in fact), I didn't ask one… single… question. Instead, I was just so enamored at all of space and what it looked like. I was so excited that I didn't eat or go to the bathroom. However, I could now feel that creeping up on me, and I knew that time would soon factor itself in before I pissed and starved myself.

"How much longer?" I asked, now feeling my bladder about to explode and my stomach rumbling.

She took her hands off of the controls, pushed a few buttons in the middle of the panel, and I watched as both of our harnesses instantly retracted.

"Close enough," she said before standing up and allowing the ship to drive on autopilot.

"Good," I said while doing the pee-pee dance. "Cause' I have to use the bathroom."

"Follow me."

And with that, I immediately stood up and followed her out of the cockpit.

Now, it doesn't look like much from the outside, but the ship itself had a lot to offer on the inside. It had all of the usual things that a spaceship would have: a bathroom, a galley, sleeping quarters, and of course, an engine room.

We walked down the corridor and away from the cockpit. We got just past the entrance where we first came in when she stopped and pointed to the first room on the right.

"The bathroom is in there," she said. "Please, don't make a mess, and clean up after yourself."

Apparently, she was a very clean alien.

"You won't even know I was in there," I said, dancing around like a fool.

She then pushed another button, just to the right of the door. I immediately heard a *swoosh* sound as the bathroom door lifted itself. But because I had to go so bad, I didn't even have time to ask any questions and immediately ran in there before listening to the door close behind me.

I was kind of shocked when I got in there because that bathroom looked just like a typical bathroom… sort of. To my left was a sink, and in front of me was the toilet, which looked just like a metal version of what you would find in a Sani-can.

Wasting no time, I quickly unzipped myself and whipped it out to go. Almost 24 hours of holding it in made me feel like Tom Hanks in that scene from *A League of Their Own* when he waltzed into the locker room for the first time, drunk, and took almost a minute long pee. And because I bolted in there so quickly, she never got a chance to mention one small detail.

After I had finished and turned around to use the sink, I heard the same sound you would hear on any ship when the doors opened, followed by a vacuum sucking everything out. I quickly grabbed the sink, and my feet left the ground for a split second before the vacuum stopped, and they were firmly planted back on the floor.

"What the fuck was that?" I said, still reeling from the shock of almost getting sucked out through the shitter.

After I realized what had happened, I put my hands in the sink, where the faucet automatically dispensed soap and water at the exact same time. Once I finished washing, the water turned off, and a massive blast of air shot down from the ceiling, practically blowing my hands right off. However, they were now completely dry.

I saw the button on the left-hand side of the door and pushed it. The door swooshed open, and I walked out, only to hear it close behind me. Once I got back out to the hallway, I could see the alien woman just standing there, smirking, while trying to hide her laughter. I would've asked what she was laughing at, but I already knew the answer.

"Sorry," she said. "I forgot to warn you about the auto flush."

"Well, let me tell you," I said, now slightly pissed off. "Getting sucked out into space through the toilet wouldn't exactly be the highlight of my trip."

"Again, I'm sorry."

I then realized that she probably didn't get many visitors like myself on the ship and wasn't used to explaining how stuff works.

"Don't worry about it," I said.

"Are you hungry?" she asked.

"Starving."

"Follow me."

We continued on down the corridor until we reached the sleeping quarters located on the right. She then pushed the button on the left side of the door to open it up. After it swooshed and slid open, we went inside.

The sleeping quarters was a small, square-sized room with three sets of bunk beds in there set up in a *U* shape: one on the left side, one straight ahead, and one on the right. All the beds had a mattress, a few blankets, and a pillow. That was it. Very simple and very plain. However, why she had so many beds on a ship where she was the only passenger was beyond me.

"How come you have six beds?" I asked. "You're the only one on the ship."

"It's only in case I ever need to rescue a small group of people," she replied.

"Does that happen often?"

"Every once in a while. But, not as often as you'd think."

I briefly looked around the room again before a strange and curious thought entered my mind.

"If this is where the guests sleep, then where's your room?" I asked.

"It's behind the cockpit," she replied. "But I'll show that to you later. Next up is the galley."

I just smiled as we continued on down the corridor.

When we finally got to the end, there were two doors: one straight ahead of us and one on the right. The one straight ahead of us led to the engine room. But we'll visit that at another time.

The door on the right was just a simple, open archway. We walked through that one, and when we got in there, the galley looked almost like a galley you would see on a cruise ship, except everything was silver and metallic in color.

From left to right, it had counters and cabinets in the shape of a *U,* with a little island in the middle. Just in front of the island, sitting against the wall, was a metal table with eight metal chairs surrounding it. Inside all the cabinets and counters, many cooking utensils were neatly placed and hung within them. There was also a fridge and a stove.

"Look at this kitchen!" I remarked.

"Since I knew I'd be going to Earth," she said. "I had the fridge and cabinets stocked beforehand."

"With Earth food?" I curiously asked.

"Not exactly," she said with a shy smile. "So, what are you in the mood for?"

I had no clue how to answer that. Seeing as how I was about to officially go into the realm of eating alien food, I gave her the only response that came to mind.

"Surprise me," I said.

"One surprise coming up," she replied.

While she was cooking, I took a seat in one of the chairs before pulling out my phone. Looking around and still not believing where I was, I started snapping some photos. Either way, no one was gonna believe what they were looking at. But, I did it anyway for my own personal experience.

About 15 minutes later, she finished cooking and brought over a steaming plate of food, along with a knife and fork. She then placed it down in front of me before taking a seat directly across from me. I immediately looked down at my food and thought, *Wow! This looks just like spaghetti!* It looked just like spaghetti and meatballs smothered in meat sauce and parmesan cheese. However, I knew that couldn't possibly be the case.

"This looks just like spaghetti and meatballs," I remarked.

"Yes, it does," she said. "I knew this was a popular dish on Earth and decided to make you something similar."

My brows immediately furrowed. "Something similar? What is it?"

"Just try it."

At that point, I was so hungry, I could've cared less what it was. Even if it were shit on a shingle, I'd still eat it.

I bent down and took a good sniff. Now, let me tell you, it actually smelled pretty damn good. So, I grabbed my fork, stuck it in there, and started to twirl the noodle-like stuff onto it. After I had the right proportion on there, I paused and took a deep breath before taking a bite.

Not knowing what I was eating or where it came from, I cautiously started to chew. I will say this, though, that was the best damn (whatever the hell it was) I've ever eaten.

"This is really good," I said with a mouthful of food.

"I'm glad you like it," she replied. "There's plenty more if you're still hungry after that."

But I didn't reply. And, after watching me pig out for the next ten minutes, we finally got down to business.

"So," she began. "You must have a ton of questions about what you're doing here and where we're going."

"That's an understatement," I said.

"Ask anything you want. There isn't a question that I won't answer."

I just looked into her big, beautiful, violet-colored eyes and could tell that she was truthful.

"Do you have a name?" I asked.

Did I really just ask that? I mean, of all the questions in the world, I lead off with that one.

"Actually," she said. "I was never given one."

"You don't have a name?" I asked.

She was obviously pulling my leg because I could see her snickering to herself after I asked it.

"What's so funny?" I asked.

"You're so gullible," she said. "Of course, I have a name. It's Sartia."[2]

"Ha-ha. Very funny."

---

[2] (Pronounced *Sar-shuh*)

Not only was I traveling with an alien, but apparently, I was traveling with a comedic alien. However, after hearing her say her name, I thought it was just as beautiful as she was.

Now, usually, when I watched a science fiction film, most of the aliens had names that were just about as long as the English alphabet. Thankfully, that wasn't the case with hers.

By that point, I was just going with the flow of my mind, and the next thing that came out of my mouth was something that even I didn't intend to have come out.

"Sartia's such a beautiful name," I remarked.

And there it was. I was now officially flirting with an alien. Well, at least in my mind, it was flirting. However, through her amethyst-colored skin, I think I actually saw a red hue cover her cheekbones.

"Thank you," she said, now sporting a shy smile.

"I'm sorry about that," I said. "I didn't mean to make you blush."

"That's okay."

"It really is a beautiful name, though."

And, of course, she blushed again before I realized what I was doing and quickly changed the subject.

"Anyway," I continued. "About the sphere… who's after it again?"

"What you found is a Morgidian sphere, and they're the ones hunting you," she replied.

"Where do these *Morgidians* come from, anyway?"

46

"They hail from the planet Morgide, which is at the center of the Dromede galaxy."

"Why do they want it so badly? Is it some kind of a secret weapon or something?"

"I don't know. All I know is that it's important, and we have to get it there ourselves before every bounty hunter in the universe comes looking for it."

As soon as she said that, I immediately stopped eating and slowly looked up at her with a very nervous look on my face.

"Bounty hunters?" I asked.

"Yes, bounty hunters," she replied.

"As in, find us and kill us to take the sphere back themselves, bounty hunters?"

"The very same ones."

"Wonderful," I sarcastically replied while rolling my eyes.

Now that I knew the basics, I quickly decided to change the subject, just so the thought of me getting zapped by intergalactic bounty hunters would immediately leave my brain.

"So, Sartia," I said. "Now that I know your name allow me to introduce myself. My name is-"

"Sam," she said, quickly interrupting me. "I already know who you are."

"You do?"

"I always take the time to learn about my missions and who I'm working with ahead of time."

I'm part of her mission? What does she mean by that? Was she some sort of a bounty hunter too? Was all this just a ploy to fatten me up so she could cook me and eat me later? Too many obtuse thoughts began running through my head, and I quickly had to get a hold of myself.

"Your mission?" I nervously asked.

"Don't worry, I'm not a bounty hunter," she reassured me. "I was hired by a private employer to find the sphere and bring it back to the Morgidians. When the job's done, I get a nice little paycheck."

"Umm… I'm no expert or anything, but you just described to me *exactly* what a bounty hunter does."

"Well… okay, you're right. I am a bounty hunter. But for me, my job isn't to kill you. My job is to return the sphere and make sure that you get home safely."

"Thanks for that," I kindly added.

I then remembered a question that she didn't answer before but said she would answer later.

"So, tell me," I began. "Why couldn't I just give you the sphere and have you bring it back yourself?"

"I was wondering when that would come up again," she replied. "The reason you have to come with me is so I can protect you."

"Protect me from what?"

"That sphere must've been thrown in the river for a reason," she began to explain. "Water masks its homing device, and when it's submerged, it's undetectable. When you pulled that sphere out of the river, it automatically activated. Also, after handling the sphere, you left your prints all over it. Even if you gave it back to me and stayed on Earth, they would still hunt you down and kill you just for knowing about it."

After hearing her answer, I just sat there and thought about it. I didn't really know what I was expecting her to say or even what I wanted her to say. But I was hoping it would've been just a little simpler than that.

"Well, I have faith that I'm in good hands," I said.

"You have my word that no harm will come to you while you're under my protection," she reassured me.

"I appreciate that."

After another fifteen minutes of uninterrupted eating, I was all finished. And, being the polite person that I am, I offered to clean up my own mess. Of course, she had no problem agreeing to it and pointed out where everything went.

After everything was cleaned, I made another pit stop in the bathroom. Once I finished in there, I quickly exited and waited for the vacuum to suck everything out before going back in to wash my hands.

I then made my way back up to the cockpit and took a seat in the passenger's chair. Sartia was already occupying the captain's chair and was looking over some of the instruments to make sure that we were still on the correct course. I just continued to stare at the sphere and think about how this little, tiny thing could cause such a stir. I kept trying to think about what it actually was and why these Morgidians wanted it so badly.

But, as much as I thought about the sphere, I thought about Sartia even more. *Who hired her? Where is she from? Does she have any unique, alien-like qualities? What does she look like naked?*

Okay, let's face it. That last one is because I'm a guy. Of course, I was curious.

After all those thoughts came and went, I then decided to see if she would give me some more answers. Minus the naked part, of course.

"So, uh," I started. "Where are you from, exactly?"

"I'm from the planet Arnaxia," she said. "It's also in the Dromede galaxy."

"Is it just one species on your planet, or are there more than one?"

"It's just the Arnaxians."

"Well, that's good, I guess."

"Yes and no."

"What's so bad about it?" I curiously asked.

"It might have something to do with the fact that eighty percent of the planet's population is female."

"Well, that must be fun for the men," I joked.

But before she answered, I could tell that my response had stung her a little bit.

"Not really," she said, slightly saddened. "We still believe in having only one life partner. The problem is because there are so many women on our planet, we're bound by law to marry another species."

"What's wrong with that?" I asked.

"A treaty was put into place centuries ago when, our ruler at the time, promised the Morgidians that they could come and take any non-married women for their own. In exchange, they wouldn't kill us."

I was so taken aback by that answer. And because of what she just said, I now felt horrible for even asking about it.

"That's awful," I said. "Have you ever tried fighting back?"

"We've never tried," she replied. "The Morgidians outnumber us ten to one. With those kinds of numbers, the treaty was the only option."

"I'm so sorry. You should be free to marry whoever you love, not have it be arranged."

"Try telling the Morgidians that."

After hearing the whole story, I was now officially intrigued by this woman and her species' history. Which meant I definitely had to find out some more.

"Are you promised to anyone?" I asked.

"Thankfully, no," she said.

Now, what came out of my mouth next, I meant. However, I definitely wasn't prepared for what was to follow.

"Well, I think that you're a smart, beautiful woman," I said. "You definitely deserve to be happy. You shouldn't have to marry someone because of an arrangement. You should marry someone because you love them."

Now, I don't know if it's what I said or her feeling down about that whole conversation, but it was blatantly obvious that me saying that to her definitely made her feel better.

But before she said anything else to me, she got up out of her chair, came over to me, and was now standing directly in front of me, just staring at me. She just gave me one of those smiles like you would give to someone after they've cheered you up from being depressed or sad. Then, without any kind of warning, she leaned in and kissed me on the lips. When that happened, it was like a whole fireworks display had gone off all at once.

Obviously, you already know that I've kissed women before. But, when she kissed me, I don't know. It was hard to describe. I mean, I've just met this woman, an alien woman nonetheless, and it was like the Earth had moved under my feet. How was that even possible? I barely knew her. Was it fate? Was it destiny? I don't know. All I knew was that I didn't want that kiss to end. But, unfortunately, it did.

She removed her lips from mine, gave me another smile, and said something to me that, even though I wasn't feeling sad, made me feel a lot better as well.

"Thank you," she said in a genuine tone. "I'm glad you're here and under my protection."

And with that, she stood upright and left the cockpit. I was now sitting by myself, still trying to figure out what the hell just happened, smiling from ear to ear while thinking about that kiss. After a few minutes of reflection, however, something had dawned on me.

As far as I knew, I was the first and only human to *ever* kiss an alien.

Rob J. LaBelle

Chapter 3

I continued to sit in the passenger's chair, thinking about what just happened while trying to process all the feels. At that point, I still couldn't figure out what the hell was going on. But one thing was definitely certain... I was one lucky son of a bitch.

Sartia was in her quarters or, where ever she went, for a good 45 minutes. I didn't wanna go and look for her because I knew something was wrong and thought it'd be best to give her a little bit of space. However, she did eventually come back out. But not because she wanted to. She came back out because she had to.

As I was sitting there daydreaming and looking out into the nothingness, I heard a loud bang, which caused the whole ship to rumble and shake.

"Sartia!" I yelled out to her. "I think something's wrong!"

Now, I don't know whether or not she heard the bang or whether it was my yelling, but she immediately came back out to the cockpit and sat down in her seat.

"We've got company," she said as her harness buckled itself, securing her into place.

"What do you mean, company?" I asked.

She immediately started looking over the monitors on the panel to find out who or what hit us.

"Shit!" she said. "We're under attack!"

"Attack?" I nervously said. "As in, someone's firing at us?"

"Correct."

"Who?"

She then pushed a few more buttons on the panel before the mystery ships ID signatures started broadcasting onto her screen. When she saw it, I could tell from her facial expression that we were in deep trouble.

"What? Who is it?" I asked.

"The Morgidians," she replied. "Three Morgidian warships are now tailing us."

"Perfect! I've been out in space less than a day, and already I'm getting shot at."

"Oh, quit your bitchin'. They must've dropped out of light speed shortly after we entered this sector."

"Wait, you guys call it light speed?"

Upon hearing my question, she briefly looked over at me and was now confused about why I would ask that.

"Yeah," she said. "Why?"

I shrugged. "I don't know. I just thought it might be hyperspace or warp drive or something else."

"No, it's light speed."

"Still pretty cool. See, I always thought-"

But before I could finish my own sentence, the ship took another hit.

"Shields are down to seventy-five percent!" she said. "We're gonna have to outrun them."

She then started to analyze something that looked just like a star chart.

"What are you doing?" I asked.

"I'm looking for a place to lay low," she replied. "Somewhere, they won't follow us."

We then took another hit. But this one sounded a lot worse than the first one.

"Dammit!" she shouted. "Shields are down to forty-five percent."

"They dropped thirty percent after just one hit?" I asked.

"Let's just pray we don't take any more damage."

She continued looking vigorously at the star charts, searching for any place that we could hide out for a while. At that point, I was just sitting in my chair, holding on for dear life and praying that we didn't get blown to bits. After all, I heard the cold vacuum of space is not a fun place to be without a spacesuit on.

However, our prayers were soon answered.

"I found one!" she said, touching the monitor to bring up the planet's elements. "Oxygen? Okay. Nitrogen? Okay. Well, the air is definitely breathable."

"Great!" I said. "The less chance I have of dying, the better."

She then grabbed hold of the controls and made a b-line straight for the mysterious planet.

The moment we took off, and wouldn't you know it, the three ships started shooting at us. During our escape, Sartia turned left and right, then left, then right again, trying to avoid the massive amounts of blaster fire the warships were throwing out. She even tried barrel loops and dive bombs, but they weren't enough. The ships just kept following and firing at us.

Thankfully, after a few more maneuvers, we finally hit the planet's atmosphere.

"This could get a little bumpy," she said. "Hold on!"

As we soared through the atmosphere, I shit you not; I could actually see the outer hull of the ship on fire as we broke through. We were now like a meteor crashing to the planet's surface. Once we finally made it through, the rest of the trip was smooth sailing. That is until we landed and discovered that we were on a planet I didn't even think would ever exist in modern-day space or time.

• • •

She landed the ship behind a huge mountainside, then turned on the cloaking device to keep us hidden. Thankfully, her ship's landing was nice and smooth and wasn't anything like landing in a plane.

Once we were down, I looked out of the cockpit window and noticed that that particular planet didn't have any sunlight. In my mind, I couldn't help but wonder how the air was breathable if there was no sun to grow any oxygen-producing plants.

"Do you know where we are?" I asked.

She fiddled around with the star charts a bit to try and get a more accurate reading.

"I mean, come on," I continued. "What kind of a planet has no sun and breathable air?"

"Definitely one that we shouldn't be on," she replied.

"Why not?" I curiously asked.

If you haven't been paying attention to the story so far, then I suggest you buckle up. Because, believe it or not, the planet that we were on exists. And the creatures that live there are real.

"You watch a lot of movies, right?" she asked.

Now, when someone asks you that, you know specific questions are most likely to follow. For example…

A few might be, *Do you remember in that film when so and so escaped the clutches of the villain?* Or, *Do you remember the creature's name that they fought?* Or even, *Who was the girl at the party?* But when she asked me that, I knew it had to be bad.

"I do," I cautiously responded. "Why?"

"I know where we are, and I don't think you're gonna like it," she said.

"Oh shit. Where are we?"

"Do you remember the fabled story of *Dracula?*"

Now why in the living hell would someone ask me if I knew about *Dracula?*

"Yeah," I replied. "What about him?"

"Well…" She then gave me one of those dramatic pauses before continuing on. "We're on his home planet."

Okay. Back up a bit. Did I just hear that right? *Dracula's* home planet? Was she for real?

"What do you mean we're on his home planet?" I asked.

"You know all those movies that were made about vampires?" she asked.

I definitely didn't like where this was going.

"Yeah," I responded.

"Well, they're real," she said.

"What do you mean they're real? Where exactly are we?"

"We're on the planet Vampila."[3]

As soon as she said that, I thought to myself, *What the hell kind of a name is that?*

"Vampila?" I remarked in a confused manner.

It took me a second to get it, but I finally figured out where she was going with all of this.

"So, what you're telling me is that vampires actually exist?" I asked.

"That's exactly what I'm telling you," she replied.

Still not believing her, I just had to find out the truth. And suddenly, I was in the mood for a good story.

---

[3] (Pronounced *Vam-pee-la*)

"Okay. You need to tell me everything about this planet right now," I said.

"This planet is a technology-free planet," she began, proceeding to tell me its history. "They don't have ships or cars or anything like that. They never have. They don't need to because they can turn into bats and fly anywhere they wish. But that's not the point.

"Anyway, back in the year fourteen thirty-one, a Dukian[4] freighter had landed here to recharge its shields before lifting off. Back then, this region of space hadn't been charted all that well yet, and very little was known about it. Vlad apparently slipped quietly on board while he was a bat. The freighter crew saw it but didn't think anything of it. So, when they were done recharging, they took off, not knowing what doom lurked aboard their ship.

"While they were on route, Vlad turned himself back into his human form and murdered the entire crew. He then commandeered the vessel and headed for Earth. But by the time he got there, the ship was so banged up from meteors and comets that instead of landing it, he set it to venture off into wild space while he, himself, took one of the escape pods down to the Earth's surface. The pod crashed into one of the mountains and blew up, but not before Vlad was able to escape.

"As he was wandering aimlessly around the countryside, and still very delirious from his travels, he was

---

[4] (Pronounced *Duck-ee-an*)

found by a man named Vlad the Second, who then nursed him back to health, before giving him the adopted name, Vlad the Third. It wasn't until later that he became known as Vlad the Impaler, and finally, Dracula."

As soon as she finished telling her story, I just sat there with a blank stare on my face and didn't say a word. I mean, I just heard a story that *Dracula* was a real-life alien vampire. What was I supposed to say to that? How was I supposed to respond?

So, after hearing her story and now knowing that aliens themselves were real, I merely responded the only way I knew how.

"Fuck me," I said under my own breath. "*Dracula* was real?"

"He was," she said. "But a lot of the stories that you read were fabricated and made up to keep the truth hidden."

"Well, that's just typical," I responded in a somewhat Doctor McCoy fashion.

As I continued thinking about how governments are always covering up the truth, it then dawned on me.

"Wait, we have to get out of here," I said.

"We can't," she replied. "We have to wait for the shields to recharge."

"Recharged or not, I don't wanna turn into a bloodsucker."

"Well, we can either stay down here and recharge the shields, or we can leave and get shot to pieces by the Morgidians."

"They wouldn't be stupid enough to follow us down here, would they?" I asked, thinking they wouldn't be that dumb.

"Depends on how desperate they are."

Now, if there's one thing I knew, it's that we were in a big metal tube, and nothing short of a bomb could ever get in there and hurt us. But the Morgidians were *definitely* stupid enough to try.

Just then, the ship alert monitor on the panel started beeping.

"Yup. They're that stupid," she said.

"Can they find us if we're cloaked?" I asked.

"Definitely not."

"Then how did the other three know you were sitting over the river? Cause' I certainly couldn't see you."

"With my engines running, they could tell just by the water vibration underneath my ship. With my engines completely turned off and the ship almost shut down, they'll never be able to find us."

I immediately let out a big sigh of relief. "Well, that's good to know."

"Not unless they were close behind us and tracked our last known position," she added.

Upon hearing that, I slowly turned my head toward her and just shook it in a very disappointing manner.

I mean, there we were, on a vampire-ridden world with no sunlight and the possibility of either getting turned into a bloodsucker or getting vaporized by the Morgidians. I absolutely loved our odds.

Just then, we could both hear a loud, thunderous boom, followed by a little bit of rumbling, as the three Morgidian warships came down and landed in the shape of a triangle around our current position. When we looked outside, I could now see one of their ships sitting about 50 yards off our bow.

Its design kind of reminded me of a butterfly, except that the wings went out to sharp points instead of being round. I could then see some steam coming down from underneath it as a platform slowly began to lower itself to the ground.

And, speaking of things being weird, what I'm about to tell you happened quite a bit throughout my journey. But this was the first time that I had experienced it.

As the platform was getting lowered, I could see six red legs start to appear. The second I saw them, and as I was looking at all of this take place, I swear to Christ that I could hear the "Imperial Death March" playing in my head. But the longer I heard it, I soon realized that it wasn't in my head but coming from somewhere on our ship. Upon hearing it and seeing what I was seeing, I now felt like I was living in a real-life twisted version of *Star Wars*. Unfortunately, those weren't stormtroopers getting off that ship.

Anyway, after a few more seconds, I came to my senses and stopped looking at the warship. Instead, I started looking around the room, trying to figure out where the music was coming from, before turning back to Sartia.

"Do you hear that?" I asked.

"Hear what?" she asked me back.

I listened for another couple of seconds before pointing to the ceiling.

"That," I responded.

She immediately stopped focusing on the Morgidians and was now able to hear the music as well.

"Oh, *that*. Yeah, sorry about that," she said before yelling out. "Not now!"

And with that, the music stopped. I eventually found out *where* it was coming from, but we don't get to that until the very end of my story. So don't ask.

I soon refocused my attention back on the Morgidian warship and the three ugly red bastards that were getting off it. But as they were walking off, I quickly noticed a change in their demeanor.

From what Sartia has told me about them, I figured them to be an all-powerful and frightening race. However, while they were walking on the planet's dark and bleak surface, I think I actually saw fear in their eyes. They must've already known how deadly the vampires were and didn't want to be there in the first place. It then occurred to me that, with them being on a planet supposedly as dangerous as that one, they would stop at nothing to get the sphere back.

They crept even closer to the ship and were now about 25 yards away from it. They just continued to look around nervously, almost like someone looking for a bee that was about to sting them. It was kind of like trying to find an invisible predator. But it wasn't until one of them tripped and accidentally fired their weapon that all hell broke loose.

Up until that point, we were cloaked and quiet, not making a sound or drawing any attention to ourselves. However, being cloaked only meant that they couldn't see us. It didn't mean that they still couldn't accidentally bump into the ship or find us.

When that weapon discharged, I could see a vast swarm of what looked like black gnats flying out of a hole in the mountainside about 20 yards in front of us. After hearing Sartia's story and knowing where we were, I obviously knew they weren't gnats. They were something *much* more deadly.

"Holy shit!" I said.

My eyes were now wide open, as I just couldn't believe what I was seeing. Hundreds of bats were now flying out of this hole, ready to take human form and destroy us all!

Okay, maybe I was just a tad overdramatic, but it was still pretty bad.

Sartia, now slightly pissed off about where she landed the ship, decided to sound off. "Of all the spots to land on this planet, I had to pick the one closest to a fucking nest."

"Nice job flying there, *Ace,*" I sarcastically responded.

She just turned to look at me, and I could now see that she didn't like my comment very much. However, she did have a nice little comeback.

"You're lucky you're cute," she said. "Otherwise, I'd have no problem feeding your ass to the bats."

I knew she was kidding, of course. But, damn, if I didn't like that fieriness.

We watched until no more bats were flying out of the hole. Then, it was quiet. I just waited patiently for the army of vampires to show up and wipe them out. But they never came. I also noticed that the Morgidians had stopped moving and were now looking in our general direction. I was now curious myself and thought that we might have been made.

"What are they looking at?" I asked. "They can't see us, can they?"

"No way. Not while we're cloaked," she replied.

"Then why are they staring directly at us?"

And that's when we heard it.

It sounded like a family of mice walking around on a metal plate. The sound we were hearing was coming from the top outside of the ship. We both then turned to look at each other before slowly looking up at the ceiling. We were *definitely* in trouble.

"Oh shit," she muttered.

"They can't get in here, can they?" I asked.

"Not unless there's a big gaping hole in the side of the ship."

With the vampires now on top of us and the Morgidians all around us, it was only a matter of time before someone made the first move. It was kind of like watching a Mexican standoff.

Of course, with me thinking about that in my head, the theme from *The Good, the Bad and the Ugly* started playing throughout the ship. It fit perfectly because it was just like we were watching a real-life Wild West film. Only, this one had aliens.

Again, I was curious as to where the music was coming from and decided to speak up.

"More music?" I asked.

"Turn it off!" she yelled.

Then, the music stopped.

However, when she asked to turn the music off, one of the vampires on top of the ship must've heard her and prematurely lept off to make a move toward the Morgidians. It was now an all-out war, as it only took one shot to set everything in motion. Of course, we were still cloaked and protected by the ship's shields. And with some of the laser fire hitting the outer hull, I just had to ask another question.

"All of this gunfire isn't gonna be good for our shields, is it?" I asked.

"Unless those do as much damage as the ship's cannons, we should be fine," she replied.

It's definitely true about what she said regarding history changing the way we perceived vampires and

Dracula. When we saw them on film and on TV, transforming from bats into humans and vice versa, they always had clothes on.

Think about that for a moment.

If you're a fully clothed vampire and change into a bat, where do all of your clothes go? Do they turn into fur? Wings? Part of your anatomy? Definitely not the case here.

We were now looking at hundreds of butt-naked vampires (men and women), running and leaping at those guys with their razor-sharp fingernails and needle-pointed teeth. They still had the two traditional fangs, but the rest of their teeth were regular-sized (just pointed). They were so much scarier and uglier than any vampire I have ever seen in my life.

We watched the battle rage on for about five minutes, with blood and guts getting splattered everywhere. It was mostly the vampires because they didn't have the technology that everyone else had. However, I did notice that their deaths were pretty much the same as what I saw on TV.

Many of them took shots to their legs, arms, chests, and even heads, but they just kept moving like rabid dogs. It wasn't until I saw one of them have their head fully separated from their body that it finally went down.

I had to give them credit, though. The Morgidians were definitely holding their own, taking many cuts and scrapes and bites. I did notice, however, that as they were getting bit, they weren't turning. The only thing I could think of was that they must've had some kind of immunity to keep them from becoming bloodsuckers themselves.

"Why aren't the Morgidians turning into vampires?" I asked.

"They have a special antibody in their bloodstream, which makes them immune," Sartia replied.

Well, I guess that answered my question.

However, it didn't take me long after that until I got curious about something else. Something that, while you're listening to all of this, you're probably wondering and asking yourself the very same question. So, here ya go.

"Here's a stupid question," I started to ask. "While these two races of uglies destroy each other, why don't we just fire up the engines and get the hell out of here?"

And there it was. It seemed like such an obvious thing to do. I mean, while they're busy killing each other, we could make a run for it. Problem solved.

Of course, if you ask a stupid question, you get a stupid answer.

"I'd rather wait until the shields are fully charged," she replied. "I don't wanna take the chance of running into the Morgidians again and being defenseless. But, don't worry, if cannon fire can't break through our shields, there's no way in hell that any of them will get in here either."

So, there you have it.

We just hunkered down and watched the both of them massacre each other until all of the Morgidians and most of the vampires were dead. By the time it was all said and done, it literally looked like a civil war battlefield out there. Of the hundreds of vampires that came out to defend their nest, only about 50 of them survived.

Now, you would think that watching heads, arms, and guts go flying everywhere would gross me out. Not so much. It's what came next that, for some strange reason, really disturbed me.

I watched the remaining vampires feed on the blood of the corpses, and not just the Morgidians either. They also fed on the other vampires. I knew that they needed blood to survive, but that was just wrong. Not only were they bloodsuckers, but they were cannibals as well.

It was now like watching an awful b-rated film, which I've seen plenty of. But, for some reason, I couldn't keep my eyes off of it. Plus, I think Sartia could see that I was really disturbed by the final bit.

So, she gently placed her right hand on my left shoulder to snap me out of it.

"The shields are charged," she calmly said. "It's time to go."

"Good," I said. "Let's get the hell off this bloody planet."

And with that, we both sat back down in our chairs as our harnesses buckled themselves. She then took the controls and immediately flew us up off the planet's surface and back out into space.

• • •

I must've sat there for god knows how long and didn't say a word. Instead, I just thought of my trip so far and everything I had seen up until that point. So far, I got to see aliens, spaceships, vampires, and have now been on another planet besides Earth.

See? I told you that you wouldn't believe me. But don't worry, this story gets better. Or weirder. Or crazier.

"Okay," she said. "We're back on course."

"Good. Because I have to pee," I replied.

The harness on my seat retracted itself, and I immediately got up to exit the cockpit.

I headed straight for the bathroom so I could go in and splash some cold water on my face, too, again, make sure I wasn't dreaming. I put my hands under the faucet and drenched my face about three times. After each time, I looked in the mirror, only to see that I was still there.

Knowing I wasn't dreaming and that all of it was real, I just muttered to myself. "Dammit."

After the burst of air almost blew my face off, I left the bathroom, and instead of going back to the cockpit, I decided to do a little bit of exploring.

Oh, come on. Tell me you wouldn't have done the same thing?

So, I immediately took a right down the corridor and made my way to the sleeping quarters. I pushed the button next to the door and watched as it swooshed open. I then went inside to take a closer look at everything.

Like I said before, the bunks were set up in a U shape around the room. But, just how comfortable were those things, anyway? I mean, if I was gonna be on that trip for god knows how long, and if I was gonna be hunted continuously and almost killed, I was gonna need to get a good night's sleep. So, I decided to test one of them out. However, nothing could've prepared me for how the mattress actually felt.

I sat down on the bottom left bunk first before lying down on my back. When I did, euphoria swept over me. It was like I was now lying down on a cloud and couldn't even feel the mattress. Almost like I was Superman, just hovering on my back.

I couldn't believe it. I've never felt anything that comfortable in all my life. Honestly, though, it didn't surprise me because they don't have anything like that on Earth. Leave it to the aliens to come up with something so soft.

I continued to lay there for the next few minutes until my eyes started to get really heavy. That's when I realized just how tired I actually was. I had now been awake for over 24 hours straight and needed to catch up on some sleep. So, I didn't fight it. I just let my eyes close, and before I knew it, I was having dinner with the Sandman.

• • •

Sometime later, I was awoken from my slumber after hearing a noise coming from within the corridor. I then pulled out my phone to see just how long I was asleep.

"Five minutes?" I groggily remarked.

It definitely seemed a lot longer than that. It also could've been the fact that I was utterly exhausted. Who knows?

I put my phone back into my pocket, but not before hearing another noise in the corridor. It definitely didn't sound like Sartia walking around. So, I immediately got up to go and check it out.

I got to the door of the sleeping quarters and poked my head outside to take a look. I looked down toward the cockpit and listened. There was nothing. I then looked down toward the back of the ship. Nothing, again.

I was just about to go back inside and lay back down when I heard *another* noise. But this time, it sounded like it was coming from the galley. So, I turned right out of the sleeping quarters and made my way down there.

When I got there, I stopped in the doorway and listened. Of course, I didn't hear anything. I waited for a few seconds more before turning around and heading back toward the sleeping quarters. I got about halfway there when I heard what sounded like someone jumping from the ceiling and landing on the walk behind me. Knowing that Sartia and I were the only ones on the ship, I now feared the worst.

My heart started pounding, and my palms immediately broke out into a cold sweat. Who or what was now behind me? With my legs now feeling like jelly, I slowly turned around to see what it was. At that point, however, I wish I hadn't. Somehow, one of the vampires had managed to get onto the ship.

His naked, pale-faced self was now looking me right in the eyes, just like I was the main course on a dinner menu. I instantly froze and didn't know what to do. If I moved, I was dead. If I screamed, I was dead. I looked down at his razor-sharp fingernails and then at his razor-sharp toenails before turning my attention back up to his red, beady eyes and dripping wet fangs. That thing was drooling, and it... looked... hungry.

So, there we were, staring each other down, while one of us waited for the other to make the first move. Other than having their heads removed from their bodies, did they really die just like the vampires in the movies?

Let's do a little recap, shall we?

A stake through the heart wouldn't matter because I was on a ship made entirely of metal. How about a cross? Did I have a cross? No. Because I'm not a holy man. Wait a minute, I got it! Holy water! No. That won't work either, because again, I was in a big metal tube in the middle of fucking space! The only option left was sunlight. But as I looked out the porthole in the side of the ship, there was no sun to be found anywhere. I could always grow a pair and try to fight it. Definitely not. Being a human, I'd probably lose really bad.

Well, I guess that was it. I was about to die.

I was now ready, but I wasn't going down without a fight. So, I balled up my fists and stood my ground. But just as I was about to do battle, I heard something else behind me. It had to be Sartia. She's the only one left on the ship, right?

Not really wanting to take my eyes off of Mr. Ugly, I turned sideways so that my peripheral view could now see him and whoever it was behind me. When I looked and saw *who* it was, I simply muttered the only thing that now fit my current situation. "Fuck me."

The person standing behind me wasn't Sartia. It was another vampire. But this one was a female. She had the exact same attributes as the male, except that she had female parts. Great. Two vampires on the ship, and Sartia was nowhere to be found.

However, I looked a little closer at the female vampire and noticed another big difference that I hadn't noticed a few seconds earlier. It was probably because I was too busy thinking about my own death. But this female vampire had clothes on. As a matter of fact, she had Sartia's clothes on.

Oh my god! I thought to myself. *Sartia has been turned into a bloodsucker!*

Well, that really was it. In the short amount of time that I was out in space, I got to see very few things that other people could only dream of. But now, I was gonna die. My time card was about to be punched.

Before I could even blink, both of the vampires started running toward me. I didn't stand a chance against one of them, let alone two. So, I just ducked down, put my head between my legs, and was now ready to kiss my ass goodbye. But, there was no kissing.

Instead of both vampires attacking me, the female intercepted the male and started to drag him down the corridor. I looked up just in time to see her pull him through the back door, which led straight to the engine room. I immediately stood up and ran down there to have a look for myself. That was the first time I got to see the engine room up close.

When I looked through the door, I saw four massive fusion reactors, two on each side of the room. Each one was right up against the back of the wall and were cylindrical in shape. There were also two exhaust ports on each: one underneath and one straight behind it. There was another panel between the middle two reactors, similar to the one located in the cockpit. That was the control panel for all four engines. A safety railing also spanned the length of the room, which kept you from getting too close.

Anyway, I looked to my right and saw nothing. I then looked to my left, just in time to see the female vampire grab the male in such a way that both of his arms were now pinned by his sides. She then lifted him right up off of the ground and threw him directly at the reactor. I never saw anything so awesome yet, so disgusting in all my life.

When he hit the metal plating, his skin instantly stuck to it like glue. Within seconds, he looked like a piece of playdough being stretched out. I could hear him snarling and growling as the reactor started to melt his skin like butter. It didn't take long, though, as only about 30 seconds had passed before the vampire completely disintegrated.

In my head, I cheered out loud that the female vampire had helped me out. Two vampires had now been turned into one. Unfortunately, I now had to contend with her. But in my moment of excitement, I could see her look over at me and stare me down.

"Oh shit," I muttered before turning around and bolting into the galley.

The galley was my best bet. It had all of the pots, pans, and cooking utensils in there to use as weapons. Especially the knives. I couldn't get in there before because the male was blocking my path. But luckily, I was there now.

I went over to one of the drawers and found something that resembled a kitchen knife, kind of like the one Michael Myers used in the *Halloween* movies. I then immediately headed for the other side of the island to get ready for her to come in. It didn't take long, though, as not even a second after getting myself situated, she was already in there.

I just stood there with the knife in my right hand, ready to swing at her or run if need be. She took a couple more steps toward me but then stopped. I looked at her and was now confused because, suddenly, it didn't look like she wanted to kill me at all. Regardless, I was still ready for whatever she was about to throw at me.

It only took about a second for something to happen. I didn't run, and I didn't even swing the knife. I didn't have to. Instead, I just stood there and watched as the female vampire started to change.

I could see the nails on both of her feet and hands start to retract. Her skin color started to turn from a pale white to a slightly darker shade. Her fangs also retracted back into her mouth and were no longer visible. Her skin did like a jelly-style roll to immediately take a different shape. At that moment, I realized that whoever that was wasn't a vampire at all. *That* was a shapeshifter.

After the long, agonizing minute it took this thing to finish doing what it was doing, I could now see who it was. Who *she* was.

I couldn't believe it. I closed my eyes and shook my head to make sure that whoever I was now looking at was actually there. Once I opened them, I could now see her as clear as day.

"Sartia?" I remarked, now staring at her in a confused manner.

"Hey, Sam," she sincerely said. "Did I forget to mention that I'm a shapeshifter?"

Rob J. LaBelle

Chapter 4

Alright. Let's do a quick recap of everything I've seen on my trip so far, shall we?

Aliens? Check. Spaceships? Check. Vampires? Apparently, check. Shapeshifters? Another check. Everything that I didn't think existed before now does. But that last one… that was a little creepy. I mean, it would've been nice if she had told me ahead of time.

"You're a fucking shapeshifter?" I asked, still standing there in complete and utter shock.

"I'm so sorry," she said. "I probably should've told you sooner, but I didn't wanna throw too much at you. You know, you being new to this and all."

I was now pissed. I wasn't pissed that she was a shapeshifter. I was pissed because she withheld it from me. I was also pissed at the fact that everything was all new to me, and there are certain things out there that we couldn't even imagine seeing on Earth. Ever!

But, as mad as I wanted to get at her for not telling me, she was right.

"Don't worry about it," I said. "It's okay."

"You're not mad at me?" she asked.

"No. I understand why you waited to tell me. I would've waited to tell me too."

She then looked down at my hand and noticed that I was still holding the knife.

"Were you gonna kill me?" she asked, her eyes narrowed from curiosity.

"Only if I had to," I said before putting the knife back down on the countertop. "But not now."

"Well, that's good. Because it would be a shame if I had to mess up that handsome little face of yours."

She finished off that comment by giving me a flirtatious little smile. Of course, my ego inflated slightly as I thought to myself, *Holy shit. She thinks I'm handsome? This hot, alien woman thinks that I, Samuel Watson of Earth, am handsome?*

We then left the galley and made our way back up to the cockpit. On our way past the sleeping quarters, I thought about stopping for a quick nap in one of the bunks. But after what had just happened, I was too hyped up to sleep.

When I got back to the cockpit, Sartia was already in her chair, making sure everything was going as planned. I quickly plopped down in the passenger's chair and then looked over at her.

Look at the way she navigates that control panel, I thought to myself. I literally couldn't keep my eyes off of her. It was like watching a supermodel play video games.

Of course, now knowing that she was a shapeshifter, I just had to ask her some more questions.

"Now, because you're a shapeshifter, can you turn into anything?" I asked.

"Not anything. *Anyone,*" she replied. "But I have to visually see them first before I can do it."

"Oh, I get it. That makes sense. You obviously can't turn into someone if you don't know what they look like."

"Correct."

"And, judging by how long it took you to change back into yourself, I assume that the process isn't quick?"

"The whole process takes a total of two minutes: one minute to change into someone, and another to change back."

I immediately fanboyed out. "That's just awesome!"

She continued checking out the control panel to, what I can only assume, make sure everything was still on track. It wouldn't be until later, however, that I learned how that thing actually worked. But don't worry, we'll eventually get to it.

While she was busy working, a ridiculous thought instantly popped into my head. I was tempted to ask her about it but then stopped. I knew we had a mission to complete, and I didn't want to bog her down with any unnecessary downtime. Or did I?

"Can I ask you something?" I asked.

"Sure," she said.

"If I was to show you a photo of one of my favorite actresses back on Earth, would you be able to make yourself look like her?"

The moment I said that, she immediately stopped what she was doing and slowly looked over at me with an inquisitive look on her face.

"I mean, if you can't," I added. "It's no big deal. Just curious is all."

However, I totally wasn't ready for her response.

"Seeing as how this is all new to you, sure. I'll be whoever you wish," she said. "I'll also do whatever you wish, while I look like them as well."

Was she serious? Or was she just toying with me? I looked at her as best that I could to try and tell if she was kidding or not. I had no fucking clue.

But, she soon killed my dreams when she cracked a little smile and instantly broke out into laughter.

"You should've seen the look on your face," she said, knowing she just played me. "Do you really think I would do that?"

I didn't have an answer. Instead, I just fumbled over my own words, trying to get out anything I could possibly think of.

"What? Of course not," I said. "I just thought… well, maybe… but you said… of course not. I knew you were kidding."

And because of my random babbling, while making a complete ass out of myself in the process, I think it was at that very moment she knew I liked her. But she never told me that was the exact time she knew. I could just tell. I only knew because, well, throughout the rest of this story, she messes with me quite a bit.

"You really are cute," she said. "But we have a couple of hours until we reach Jipduk[5]. You might wanna go and get some sleep."

I definitely wasn't gonna turn that down. After all, captain's orders.

"Good idea," I said.

"I'll wake ya when we get there," she added.

I then got up out of my chair and immediately went back down to the sleeping quarters. I found the bunk that I was previously on before, laid right down on it, and almost immediately passed out.

• • •

A couple of hours later, I felt my body start to shake and thought that the ship might have been hit by cannon fire again.

"Holy shit!" I shouted.

I immediately opened my eyes, and forgetting where I was, sat right up, banging my head against the bottom of the top bunk.

---

[5] (Pronounced *Jip-duck*)

"Ow," I groaned, my right hand now feeling the top of my head for bumps and blood.

That's when I looked up and noticed Sartia now standing there.

"What happened?" I asked.

"Sorry about that," she said. "But, we're almost at Jipduk, and I wanted to wake you up."

"Thanks for that."

She then left the room and headed straight for the cockpit. After a few more seconds of checking over my head, I got up to go and join her.

When I got to the cockpit, I sat down in the passenger's chair and looked out through the window. Off in the distance, I could see a bluish/gray illuminating ball. As I stared at it, I thought to myself, *Jipduk? What a strange name for a planet.* But, I would soon find out exactly what kind of *planet* it actually was.

"Jipduk, straight ahead," she said.

"That's such an odd name for a planet," I remarked.

"So is Earth."

"Touché. So, what can we expect down there? Who're the native species?"

"Jipduk is home to the Dukians."

When she said that, I instantly remembered the story she told me while we were visiting our last planet.

"Oh! They're the species that got their ship hijacked by Dracula?" I pointed out.

"Correct. Anyway, the whole planet is pretty much one, big, giant city," she said.

"Hence the reason why I can't see any green."

"Correct again. You see, the Dukians specialize in metallurgy and are the top manufacturer in this sector of weapons, ships, and anything else that's made of metal."

"Are they hostile?"

"Far from it. They're actually a very friendly species."

"Good to know."

Within the next few minutes, I could see Jipduk as clear as day. It was now as close as Earth was when I first left and got a good look at it from space.

We were now orbiting the planet, waiting for them to contact us and give us permission to land. Sartia was busy playing on the panel, and as always, I was curious about what she was doing.

"Whatcha doin'?" I asked.

"I'm transmitting the ship's ID number, so they know who we are," she said. "Once they clear us, we're free to go down to the surface."

It was literally like I was living in a science fiction film. I had a ton more questions to ask her, but I figured that I'd wait until we were alone and had a little bit of downtime.

After another 15 minutes of us floating aimlessly around the planet, I heard a male voice come through the speaker on the ship's panel.

"Arnaxian ship, ID number zero six one nine seven nine, you are now free to land at port number five," the male voice said.

Sartia immediately put her hands on the controls and said, "It's about damn time," before guiding us down through the planet's atmosphere.

. . .

Once we broke cloud cover, I was now like a kid viewing Disney Land through a car window. I saw the most incredible thing that I have ever seen in all my life.

All kinds of spaceships were coming and going. The buildings rose from the planet's surface so high that you couldn't even tell if it had a surface or not. I could see hotels, restaurants, movie theaters, grocery stores, and everything else that we basically have on Earth. It was *definitely* a sight to be seen.

It took us a few minutes to navigate through all of the other ships and tall buildings before we arrived at port number five. I wasn't sure exactly what the landing port would look like, so I started imagining all the other landing ports that I've seen in movies, just to get a visual picture in my head.

I first thought of Star Wars, where the landing platforms usually had a walkway that extended out to a big circular platform. Then, I thought of Star Trek, where the ships would dock in outer space before the whole crew would get transported down to the surface. But, since we didn't have transporters, that didn't really apply. So that just left landing on the grass or the tar or something that looks like a helipad. That definitely wasn't the case here either.

When we got down there, I just couldn't believe it. Landing port number five was about the size of three airfields and was suspended 300 stories in the air between two buildings. The buildings themselves had to be at least 500 stories tall.

The airfield had big squares painted on the ground, and each one was numbered, so you knew where you were when you needed to leave. In between the squares were painted walkways. The walkways were big enough to accommodate two lanes of traffic: one going to the ship and one going away from it. It was all neatly done and very well organized.

We landed in space number 12, and when we touched down, Sartia immediately turned off the engines, which instantly made our harnesses retract. She then looked over at me and asked me a question that I've been dying to answer myself ever since I went out there.

"Are you ready to get your first taste of an alien civilization?" she asked.

I didn't even have to say a word, as the enormous, goofy-looking smile on my face said it all.

Since I'm a huge sci-fi nut, I've always dreamed of knowing what it felt like to visit alien planets, interact with other species, sample the food, and just walk among them. Now, I would finally be getting the chance to do that, just as the great Kirk and Picard did before me. Yes, I knew they were only characters in TV shows, but after this, I would be greater than all of the Starfleet captains combined.

Sartia got up out of her chair, and I followed suit. We immediately went straight to the side door, where she pushed the button to open it up. The door slowly slid upward, and the retractable ramp came out so that we could get down to the surface.

When the door rose, a gust of wind came right into the ship. I took one sniff of the alien planet and was just stunned at how metallic the air actually was. Well, I wasn't too surprised because, after all, it was a planet known for making metal.

"I hope all the other planets smell better than this one?" I remarked, waving my hand in front of my face.

"Oh, they do," she said. "This is just a pit stop."

And with that, we walked the 20 feet down the ramp until our own feet touched down on the rough surface.

Once we were down, we didn't move. Instead, we just stood around while Sartia looked like she was waiting for someone.

Of course, being the curious person I am and never stepping foot on that planet, I just had to ask, "What are we waiting for?"

But she didn't say anything right away. It took about another ten seconds before she finally answered me.

"We're waiting for them," she said, now pointing in front of us.

Now, by that point, I had gotten used to seeing Sartia's alien presence. So when I looked at her, I didn't really think anything of it. The naked vampires were a bit of a shock, though. Even the Morgidians were weird-looking. But the Dukians, as they called them, well, let's just say that they were a welcome sight, but still just as odd.

The Dukians were a species that had gray skin, silver eyes, egg-shaped heads, and was about as tall as you and I. Their clothing almost resembled something of a fancy outfit. They wore khaki-type pants, silk-like textured shirts, dress shoes, and they all wore robes that they pulled over their heads, kind of like a poncho that you would see in the old west films. Then, it was all tied off around the waist with a fancy-looking belt. Aside from their overall look, the thing that really made them weird was that none of them had hair. Not even the women.

Three Dukians pulled up in what I could only describe as a roofless, hovering golf cart. It flew about two feet off of the ground, and I was just amazed, as I had never seen anything like that before.

"Holy shit!" I said, my eyes now wide. "Is that thing hovering?"

Sartia turned to me and smiled.

"Pretty badass, right?" she said.

Okay. Now when a hot, alien woman says the term 'pretty badass,' you know she's perfect.

"Can you say that again?" I asked.

Don't get me wrong, I knew what she said. I just wanted to hear her say it one more time.

She then looked at me, almost as if she couldn't believe I had just asked her that. But by then, the Dukians were already standing directly in front of us.

The one in the middle, a male, approached us first.

"Greetings!" he said. "Welcome to Jipduk. My name is Ronak. What is the purpose of your visit?"

"Well," Sartia began. "We're here to take in a little bit of the local cuisine and sights. And, while we're at it," She thumbed toward her ship. "Maybe give this thing a once over?"

I couldn't help but notice that all three of the Dukians were now staring at me, almost as if they've never seen an Earthling before. Either that or they haven't seen one in a really long time. But the first one was my initial thought.

"Why are they all staring at me?" I quietly asked Sartia.

But, Ronak heard what I said and decided to chime in.

"We do apologize for staring," he said. "But we've never seen your species before. Where are you from?"

With both of us being hunted, I wasn't quite sure if I should honestly answer that question. So, I looked over at Sartia before she gave me the okay to do so.

"My name is Sam," I told him. "I'm from the planet Earth in the Milky Way galaxy."

Upon hearing that, the three of them just looked around at each other in a confused manner.

"Earth?" Ronak asked. "We've heard many stories about Earth, but only a few species from this sector have ever traveled that far. You're the first Earthling we've ever seen."

When he said that, I got a little curious.

Only a few species? I asked myself. *When? How long ago?*

With those questions now running through my head, I definitely made a mental note to ask Sartia about it later. But, for right now, I just decided to be humble.

"I'm glad to make your acquaintance, Ronak," I said.

And with that, the other two Dukians immediately went to work on the ship.

While they were busy doing their thing, Ronak, Sartia, and I all hopped onto the hover cart (as I called it) and drove away from the ship toward one of the buildings the airfield was attached to.

On the way there, we passed all kinds of ships, big and small. We also passed many different types of alien races, all of which had different colors, were of a different height, and all of which I had no clue as to what the hell they were.

It took us about ten minutes to traverse the massive airfield before reaching the outside of the skyscraper.

Ronak parked the hover cart and turned it off before all of us got out.

"Is there anything else that you need before we part ways?" he asked.

But because I didn't know what to say, I thought it'd be best if Sartia did all of the talking.

"I think we're good for right now," she said.

"Here, take these," Ronak said, handing us each a small-looking disc about the size of a quarter. "Because I am your personal liaison while you are here, if you get lost or need anything at all, just push the button on these, and I will come and find you."

"Thank you," Sartia said.

"Thanks, Ronak," I added.

He then stood upright before bowing. I immediately followed Sartia's lead and bowed back. But before we parted ways, however, I offered him something else.

"Before we go, can I show you how we say hello and goodbye on Earth?" I asked him.

"It would be an honor," he replied.

Now, I was just gonna show him a simple handshake. But instead, I decided to go a little further than that.

I extended my right hand out with my fingers pointed upright while he did the same. I then grabbed his hand with mine and pulled him in for a bro hug. As we did that, I could hear Sartia snickering behind me.

We held it for a couple of seconds before we let go of each other. I could now see the confused look on his face, as he wasn't really sure what to make of it.

"What do you call that?" he asked.

"We call it a bro hug," I replied.

Again, he didn't know what to say.

"That was very… interesting. Thank you," he said.

"You're welcome."

"I do not wish to keep you any longer. Again, if you need anything, feel free to call me."

He then bowed one more time before getting back in his hover cart and driving off.

"Come on," Sartia said. "Wait until you see the inside."

We then left the airfield and immediately went through the two front doors, entering the massive building. Once we got inside, I just couldn't believe my eyes.

The street we entered onto went around the whole entire building, forming a giant square. All of the windows were on the left-hand side while all of the shops were in the center. The place was packed with wall-to-wall humanoids. Alien races of all kinds were just walking around, shopping, talking, and eating.

Now, to me, because I was from Earth and have been to a few myself, that place literally looked like one giant comic con. It was probably one of the coolest things I've ever seen. And I'm sure that later on in this story, I'll say that again when I tell you something else. But for right now, this was it.

"How long are we gonna be here?" I asked.

"Until the maintenance on the ship has been completed," she replied. "Usually about five hours."

"Good. Because I have a few more questions for you."

"Don't worry, I'll answer them. But before I do, did you wanna take a look around?"

I just replied to her with the age-old question that basically answers everything. "Does a bear shit in the woods?"

Immediately after I responded, I shit you not, she actually paused for a moment to think about that and try to decipher its meaning. I couldn't help but laugh to myself before interrupting her thought process.

"That means yes, by the way," I said.

"Nice one," she replied.

We then turned left and immediately began our walk around the concourse.

• • •

I didn't know what I wanted to do first. Of course, the floor we were on mostly had just shops. To get to anything else, we'd either have to take the elevator up or down or go visit another building entirely. However, it was a pretty big planet, and we only had about five hours to hang around.

The first thing that I noticed while we were walking around was the music. Since I couldn't tell one piece of elevator music from another, that's pretty much what it sounded like. The only difference I noticed was the tone of the instruments. So, at least, there was that.

As we started walking, the second store on the right we came across looked like a gift shop. You know, just like the ones you see in hospitals or airports. And even though I knew we would visit other places, I wanted to take advantage of every planet we traveled to and pick up some sort of a souvenir.

So, I immediately made my way over there with Sartia in tow. She didn't really try and stop me from doing anything because she understood how new this all was to me.

When we got into the gift shop, I noticed a female Dukian working behind the counter and immediately saw her staring at me. She had the same look on her face that the other three had when they first saw me. I was willing to bet that very few, or even none of those people, have ever seen an Earthling before. Regardless, it didn't really bother me if they stared.

Anyway, I decided to peruse the shelves a bit to see if anything would catch my eye. And since I was on a planet specializing in metal, mostly all of the gifts in there were made from it.

The first thing that I came across were these little butterfly/dragonfly-looking things and thought to myself, *How not original,* before moving on.

The next thing I came across was one of the many things I didn't expect to find in a gift shop. But then again, I wasn't on Earth.

It was a one-foot, by one-foot, by one-foot metal box with a hole cut out in the front center. The hole looked big enough to fit a hand or a foot through it. I was curious about what it was and picked it up to take a closer look. However, the moment it left the shelf, Sartia immediately stopped me and told me to put it down. Which I did.

"I wouldn't touch that if I were you," she said.

"Why? What is it?" I asked.

"*That* is a Dukian torture cube."

"A Dukian torture cube?"

"See that hole in the front?" she asked, pointing to it.

"What about it?"

"There's a special device in there with razor-sharp blades. If you were to put your hand or foot or something else in there, well then, you could pretty much kiss it goodbye."

"Holy shit. Why would they sell these things in a gift shop? And to just anybody?"

"You have to remember, this isn't Earth," she reminded me.

"Good point. I'll try to keep an open mind."

So, with the cube now safely back on the shelf, I walked around a little more until I found myself standing in front of the back wall. That's where they kept all of the food and drink items.

Just like home, they kept everything in a big fridge. Except there, when you wanted something, you had to tap on the glass so the panel you were touching went straight up into the ceiling, just like a window being opened. Once you were finished, the sensor would know that you were gone, and the glass would come back down again.

I was absolutely mortified at all of the different types of things they had in there. The drinks, for instance, were all kinds of different colors. Some of them looked pretty smooth, while others looked really chunky. And the food, well, I definitely won't get into what that looked like.

Fine! You twisted my arm.

The food looked like a dangerous mix of raw fish, worms, and chunks of animal liver. Of course, I wanted to hurl and didn't have the stomach to try any of it. So, I quickly moved on.

I then came across some items that were displayed up on the far wall next to the cashier. This was definitely something I never expected to find in a gift shop. I didn't know what kind they were, but I could definitely tell what they were, just by the familiar shape.

"They sell guns in a gift shop?" I asked.

"Yeah. Why not?" Sartia replied.

"Isn't that a little dangerous?"

"Only if you're not careful. Again-"

"I know. I know. This isn't Earth."

Still trying to keep an open mind, I looked up at the wall and decided to check them out so I could see how they differed from the guns back home. Of course, I already knew that the majority of them shot lasers. I also saw some which shot a weird slime substance that would briefly paralyze you when you got hit with it. However, I was more amazed to see that some of them actually shot bullets.

I then came across one gun that looked quite interesting. It was about the size of a standard-issue police firearm, and instead of shooting bullets, it shot little saw blades, as I called them. It was called a Dukian burrower. It got its name because when you fired the gun, the blades would shoot out, sticking to whatever part of the skin they touched. And instead of stopping, they would actually keep spinning, burrowing a hole deep into the flesh, causing severe internal injuries. I thought it would be a cool souvenir. So, of course, I just had to get it.

"Can I get one of these?" I asked.

Sartia's eyes quickly narrowed. "Why?"

"I don't know. I just think it would be a cool souvenir to take home with me. Plus, it may come in handy. You never know."

She didn't answer me right away, though. Instead, she just stood there for a moment, thinking if letting me get one would be okay. I mean, come on. What's she gonna say, no?

"I don't think that's a good idea," she said.

Okay. Maybe she would say no.

"Why not?" I asked. "I'm not gonna hurt anyone."

"It's not the other people that I'm worried about."

Come on. Gimme a break. I'm a grown man. I can handle myself.

And don't judge me about what happened with the vampires. I was only a little scared. Besides, what did she think was gonna happen? I was gonna shoot my eye out?

"Seriously?" I asked. "*You,* of all people, aren't gonna let me have one?"

By that point, she knew how much I wanted it. It was seriously the coolest thing I had ever seen. How could I not want one?

She just sighed before finally giving in to my demand. "Okay. You can have it."

"Bitchin'!" I excitedly replied.

She then pointed at me. "But it stays on the ship, you got it?" she said, using a stern tone.

"You have my word."

Yeah, right. Like I was really gonna keep that thing on the ship. Besides, later on in this story, it comes in handy.

She hesitantly grabbed the burrower off of the wall and brought it over to the cashier. As we walked over, I was literally like a kid in a candy store. I couldn't stop smiling, and the Dukian cashier knew it.

When we got there, Sartia placed the item on the counter, and I couldn't help but notice that the cashier couldn't stop staring at me. After thinking back to the other three Dukians' reactions, I had a pretty good idea why.

"I've never seen your kind before," the female Dukian said. "Where are you from?"

"I'm from Earth," I replied.

"From Earth?" she asked just a little too loud.

When she said that, everyone else in the vicinity heard her and immediately stopped what they were doing to look over in our direction. I took one look around, and it was right then and there that I finally understood how a fish in a glass bowl felt.

"Oh shit," I muttered.

I had to think fast. I definitely didn't wanna become an instant celebrity, knowing that the Morgidians and other bounty hunters were out there looking for me.

So, I said the only thing I could think of, loud enough for everyone to hear. "Yeah! I've never been there myself either!"

Thankfully, that worked. Everyone immediately stopped staring at us and just continued on their merry way.

"Whew! That was close," I said.

"A little too close," Sartia added.

Of course, that just made the cashier even more curious about me.

"You're really from Earth?" she asked.

"I am. But it's really nothing to get all excited about," I replied.

"Are you kidding me? Only a handful of people from this sector have ever been that far. And as far as I know, you're the first and only Earthling to ever make it out this way."

"How much is the burrower?" Sartia asked, quickly changing the subject.

"One hundred barcs," the cashier replied.

The currency out here is called a barc? I asked myself.

Sartia then placed her thumb on a little oval pad, just about the size of a teaspoon. She held it there, and after a few seconds, it beeped.

"You're all set," the cashier said.

"Thank you," Sartia said.

"Thank you," I added. "But, before I go, can I take a picture with you?"

"Sam," Sartia said before rolling her eyes and practically doing a facepalm.

"It's okay," the cashier said. "I don't mind."

I quickly pulled out my phone, pointed it at myself and the cashier, and snapped a selfie of us together.

"Wow! This is great! Thank you!" I said.

"You're very welcome," she said. "And good luck."

I then smiled at her and grabbed the gun off the counter before Sartia and I left the store. When we got back out into the hallway, she turned to face me.

"So, where to next?" she asked.

However, I didn't answer her because I was now too busy examining my new toy.

So, of course, she tried again. "Sam?"

"Huh?" I asked, now looking over at her.

"I said, where do you wanna go next?"

Now *that* was an interesting question. I mean, I'm on a planet that I've never been to before, and it's now been some time since I last ate. Where did I wanna go next? I definitely didn't have to think about it for long, as my stomach was now giving me the answer I was looking for.

"Do they have any good restaurants here?" I asked.

She didn't say a word but just looked at me and smiled before we continued on.

When we got down to the end of the street, we turned and made a right. Again, the whole floor was a big, giant square. We passed many stores on the way to the restaurant, and I got to say, I was, and I wasn't a bit surprised at what they had to offer there.

Just like any other civilization, they had everything that we have on Earth. I saw massage parlors, arcades, movie theaters, bathrooms, and even a casino. They all looked similar to the ones we have on Earth, but in many ways, they differed as well.

I didn't stop in any of them at that rest stop, but I will touch upon some of those things later on. For now, my stomach was growling, and I just had to eat something.

• • •

We finally arrived at the restaurant, and when I looked up at the sign to read it, I couldn't. It was written in the native Dukian language, but when translated, it read, The Fat Zog. Zog was short for parizog. But, you'll find out what that is in just a moment.

When we got into the restaurant, I noticed that it was set up like a typical restaurant. The tables were spread out evenly while waiters and waitresses came around to take your order. But this restaurant had separate dining rooms of all sizes, enclosed within soundproof walls so you could enjoy yourself without listening to everyone else.

We were seated in one of the private, two-person rooms in the back by a Dukian male who handed us the menus. He then left for a brief moment so we could look them over and think about what we wanted to order.

"This must be costing you a fortune?" I asked while surveying the room.

"It is," Sartia replied. "But I want you to enjoy yourself without everyone staring at you and asking five thousand questions."

"I appreciate that. Thanks."

We then proceeded to look over the menus. Of course, I couldn't make heads or tails of it because it was written in a language that looked closely related to gibberish. Plus, I couldn't read any of the alien languages out there… yet.

So, I asked Sartia what she liked.

"I can't even read this thing. What would you recommend?" I asked.

"I think you should try the parizog," she said.

"What the hell is a parizog?"

"It's kind of like a pig that you would see on Earth. Do you remember the sign out front?"

"Yeah?" I replied, remembering the name of the restaurant.

"Well, zog is short for parizog."

"Oh. The fat zog. The fat pig!"

"Correct."

"Alright," I said while nodding. "The parizog it is."

I then looked over the menu once more, this time trying to decide what I should get to drink. But again, I couldn't read it.

"What should I get to drink?" I asked.

She also looked over the menu again before making a recommendation.

"Why don't you let me worry about that," she said with a guilty smile.

Now, I've seen that look before. And, not just on her, but on any sensible person who says that right before they play a nasty joke on you. However, who was I to argue? I couldn't even read the language, let alone tell one alien drink from another.

After I agreed to let her pick out my drink, the waiter came back into the room, ready to take our orders.

"What'll it be?" the waiter asked.

But before I could say anything, Sartia took charge and ordered for the both of us.

"We'll have two orders of the Parizog, please," she said.

"And what to drink?" the waiter asked.

Sartia briefly glanced in my direction and smiled yet again before giving him her answer.

"Two Quintz ales," she said.

"You got it," the waiter replied.

He then grabbed our menus and left the room.

"Do I even wanna know what a Quintz ale is?" I asked.

"Relax. You'll like it," Sartia replied.

So, there we were, on an alien planet, sitting in a restaurant just like I would back home. The thought still had crossed my mind that it was all one big dream. And, as you're sitting here listening to all of this, you probably think that I'm crazy? Hell, even I thought I was going crazy. I mean, this couldn't be real, could it? As much as I tried to deny it, I couldn't.

Anyway, the time had finally come for me to ask the question that had been burning a hole in my brain ever since we landed. Of course, I had no idea how she would respond to it. But, I can tell you one thing, her answer… totally out of left field.

"Okay. So, I have to know…" I started to ask.

But before I could continue on, the waiter had already come back with our food.

"Holy shit!" I said. "That has to be the quickest service ever!"

"Was that not what you were expecting?" he kindly asked.

"Quite the opposite. Thank you!"

"You're welcome. Let me know if you need anything else."

Then, just like a fart in the wind, he was gone.

When I looked down at my food, the parizog looked and smelled just like pork. It was drenched in some kind of a brown sauce that I didn't even bother asking about. All I knew was that it smelled pretty damn good.

"So, what were you saying?" Sartia asked.

Because the food came so quickly, I completely forgot about my question.

"Oh yeah," I continued. "So, anyway, there's one thing that I just have to know. How is it that other species from this sector managed to get to Earth, but no one from home has ever come out here?"

It took her a few seconds to answer me. I assume it was because she was trying to figure out how to word it without freaking me out. Which, by the way, she still managed to do.

"Before I tell you, why don't you try the food," she suggested.

She only said that because she could tell that I was now foaming at the mouth. So, I just went along with it.

I took my somewhat looking knife and fork and cut a small piece right off. I then took a deep breath before shoving it into my mouth. To my utter and total surprise, it tasted just like pork. I couldn't believe it.

"This is really good," I managed to say with a mouthful of food.

"Told ya you'd like it," she said. "Now, why don't you try the ale?"

Again, you know the story from Alice's party. I never drink beer. I was always a fruity drink kind of guy. However, on occasion, I would have a beer with someone to celebrate something. And, as it turns out, I guess this was something worth celebrating. So, I picked up my ale, took another deep breath, and took a swig.

"This tastes just like beer!" I remarked.

"I told ya I wouldn't let you down," she said. "Now, to answer your question…"

For the duration of her explanation, I just continued to devour my parizog and drink my ale.

"The reason why no one from Earth has ever been out this way is because, well, they haven't," she continued. "Species from this sector and beyond have been frequenting other sectors and yours for tens of thousands of years. It wasn't until a single Dukian ship crashed on Earth in the mid-nineteen fifties that it was discovered and brought to what you now call Area Fifty-One."

With that last comment, I immediately stopped chewing and slowly looked up at her. It wasn't until then that I finally understood how our interpretation of aliens came to be.

"A Dukian crashed there?" I asked.

"Yeah. Why? Is there some significance to that?" she replied.

Is there some significance? Of course, there is! That's how we got all of our drawings and visions of little green men! The Dukians look really close to how the first picture of a little green man came to be. It all now made perfect sense.

"No," I simply replied. "Please, continue."

I then went on stuffing my face while she continued the story.

"After Area Fifty-One," she went on. "More and more species from out this way had caught wind of what happened. And since we knew that your species was on the verge of being extremely technological, we just had to investigate.

"So, over the years, we sent more and more ships out that way to study you and keep tabs on how well you were doing. There were a few mishaps over the years, but we were able to take care of it for the most part.

"To answer the second part of your question, no Earthling has ever been out this way due to one specific law: no one is to be brought off of Earth unless it's a dire emergency."

"Kind of like, someone finding a Morgidian sphere?" I asked.

"Precisely," she said.

"Well, that explains why I'm the first one out here."

"True. But you're not the first Earthling to meet one of us."

Wait a minute… I'm not the first one? Was she serious? Whether she was or not, I still had to find out.

"So, all of those abduction stories over the years, were they all just made up?" I asked.

"Most of them," she said. "But not all of them."

"Holy shit!"

It was true. When people said they were being abducted by aliens, they weren't kidding.

"Not all of them were abductions," she added. "Some of them were an actual meeting."

"A meeting? What do you mean, a meeting?" I curiously asked.

"You know a lot of those science fiction movies that were made over the years?"

"Yeah? What about em'?"

"Well, a lot of those were made based on a chance encounter with another alien species."

After hearing that last comment, I simply couldn't believe my ears. Many of my favorite movies and TV shows were based loosely on fact and weren't made up at all? After hearing that, I just had to know which ones.

"Which ones?" I asked.

"I couldn't tell you," she said. "No names were ever given."

Damn. It would've been nice to know which movies and TV shows were real and which ones weren't.

"But, that's it," she said. "We've been a lot more careful as of late concerning your planet. Well, other than the sphere."

"Yeah, about that…" I said. "How did that get on Earth, anyway? And, who's this employer of yours that hired you to get it?"

Both valid questions, if you ask me. When I asked them, though, she didn't seem to want to answer them. Well, the employer part, anyway. When it came to the sphere, however…

"I honestly don't know how the sphere got to your planet," she said. "The only ones who can tell us that are the Morgidians."

"Great! Let's go find them and ask!" I enthusiastically joked.

She apparently didn't think that was funny and just gave me a dirty look.

"As for my employer, well, I'll tell you that when the time is right," she said. "But, for now, that's all *you* need to know."

Great. First, she takes me off of my home planet, and then she lies to me. Wonderful. However, she does eventually tell me who her employer is. And after she did, I was just absolutely stunned. But, we'll get to that during a different…

Wait, you want me to tell you now? I can't do that.

Look, if I tell you now, the story will be ruined. After all, you are here to listen to the whole thing, right? Of course, you are. You don't have a choice. But don't worry, all of your questions will be answered as the story goes on. I promise.

Rob J. LaBelle

Chapter 5

One thing was definitely for sure… after sleeping only a couple of hours from the time I left Earth until we stopped on Jipduk, I was pretty fuckin' tired. Yes, I may have gotten to see a lot of cool things, meet some pretty cool aliens, and almost get shot out of the sky, but I desperately needed some sleep.

We both sat there and ate our meals for the next hour or so. For the most part, it was pretty quiet, mainly for the fact that while I was eating, I was busy trying to dissect all of the information that had just been presented to me. But, no matter how hard I tried, I had to believe everything that Sartia said. I mean, other than who her employer was, she's been honest with me from the start.

After we left the restaurant, she booked us a room on the 450th floor of the building that we were currently in. The entire hotel itself spanned the top 50 floors of that building and had about 100 rooms per floor. Luckily, we got a room on the first floor.

Except for the fact that the hotel rooms were always 100 percent clean, they were really no different than the hotels on Earth. Yeah, right.

The hotels on Jipduk were about three times the size, the minibars and food didn't cost extra when you used them, and it was a bit homier. We got a room so that we could both get cleaned up and rest if need be. It had been a long trip so far, and we weren't even close to Morgide yet. We still had a long way to go.

When we got into the room, I didn't waste any time and immediately hit the bed, which had the same cloud-like mattress the bunks had in the sleeping quarters on the ship. However, after I laid down, I didn't remember a goddamn thing as I instantly passed out.

I didn't dream while I was on the ship, but this time, I did. Some of my dreams had to do with the Morgidians catching up to us and blowing our ship to smithereens, killing us both. Some of my other dreams had to do with most of the alien species I had seen while walking around downstairs.

I dreamt that they all knew who I was and kept chasing after me. Of course, I couldn't run anywhere because my legs felt like they were made of cement, allowing the aliens to catch me and kill me.

And then there was Sartia. I'm not even gonna get into the dreams I had about her because you would probably only get bored. And, frankly, they were a bit graphic. Not graphic in the bloody sense, but graphic in the pornography sense. Wait, why am I even telling you this?

Anyway, I was out for a good while, that is until something woke me up. But it definitely wasn't anything terrible… yet.

I slowly opened my eyes to feel really refreshed and relaxed, kind of like you do after you sleep for about ten hours straight. When we got to that planet, it was just before sundown. I was now looking out the windows to see the sunrise.

Holy shit. Did I really sleep that long? I thought we only had a couple of hours until we left? And why was Sartia curled up behind me in the spoon position? That's right, we must've slept through the whole night. She probably just said screw it and decided to get some shut-eye herself. Yes, there was only one bed in the room, but I would gladly have taken the floor so that she could get it. At that point, I was so tired, I could've slept on cement and still gotten plenty of rest.

We were both lying on our right sides, and I couldn't help but notice that her left arm was hanging over me. I wanted to get up without disturbing her, so I gently (and quietly) tried to get myself out of bed. When I moved, however, she took her arm and grabbed hold of me tightly. That's when I got a good feel for just how strong she actually was.

When I saw her overpower that vampire and lift him up to throw him onto the reactor, I was so scared and didn't really think anything of it until now. She gripped me with such force that I almost couldn't breathe. Luckily, though, I managed to take her arm and lift it up so I could roll over and see if she was awake yet. Instead of spooning, we were now facing each other. Why we were spooning in the first place was way beyond my understanding. But I really didn't seem to mind.

Also, I don't know what it was, but she looked like a sleeping angel. And, I know I told you that I already thought she was hot, but there was just something so peaceful about watching her sleep. It was so beautiful and so relaxing. I'm getting all mushy, I know. Just try not to throw up. Okay?

Anyway, as I was lying there, now seeing how even more beautiful she looked, I couldn't help but think of the kiss she gave me on the ship. I know that it was only a friendship thing, but I felt something when she did that. Now, I don't know if she did or not, but I definitely did.

I just stared at her face and lips, thinking to myself how great it would be if I could just kiss her and have her kiss me back. But what happened next, well, I'll just tell ya.

For the first time in my life, I just said fuck it and decided to go for it. My mouth was now ready. So, I slowly leaned in and pressed my lips up against hers. They were so soft. When I touched them, I instantly went weak in the knees and could feel my whole body go limp. It was a magical moment for me. That is, until…

"What the hell are you doing?" she asked before opening her eyes.

That's it. I was busted. The magical moment was now gone and reduced to a single memory.

I mean, what do I say to that? I can't directly come out and tell her, *Well, I just wanted to know what it would feel like to have my lips pressed up against yours.* No. That would make me sound desperate.

But, as usual, I couldn't think of an answer to give her and just fumbled over my words. Again. "Well, you were sleeping and, uh… I just thought that… see, here's the thing…"

I was a mess. In that one single moment, I instantly reverted back to being 'myself' before I manned up about two seconds before the kiss. I was now speechless. But what she said next totally caught me off guard, and frankly, I didn't care.

"Why did you stop?" she asked.

Why did I stop? I didn't wanna seem like a pervert, that's why. But now, I didn't know how to take that.

Asking me why I stopped could now mean one of two things: either she was messing with me because she knows I've been caught, or she liked it and wanted me to keep going.

"I don't know," I said. "I just thought-"

But before I could even finish my sentence, she leaned in and starting kissing me back.

At that point, I've now officially kissed four women in my life: three humans and an alien. Jesus, when I say it like that, it sounds weird. But it's true. And compared to the other three women that I've kissed, Sartia ranks far higher. So much so that the kiss made the other three women seem like amateur hour.

I was in heaven. My lips have never felt anything like that before. She must've been into it as well because as we were kissing, she put her left hand on the right side of my face to caress and touch it. I immediately did the same with my right hand on the left side of her face. Other than her lips, *that* was the first time I actually felt her skin. Her's felt just like an average person's skin, only softer and smoother.

I don't know. I think it must've been her alien DNA that was helping her out with that one. The 20 or so seconds that we kissed was one of the best 20 or so seconds of my life. That is until we heard a knock on the door.

"Dammit," I muttered.

"Who is it?" she loudly asked.

"We are here with your wake-up call as requested," I heard a female voice say from the other side of the door.

"Hold on a second," Sartia said.

But before she got up out of bed, she looked me right in the eyes, caressed my face one more time, smiled at me, and then left the bed. My hormones and adrenaline were now in full overload. But, I knew that if we were to miraculously take it beyond kissing, it would be under different circumstances. Or, so I had hoped.

She then went over to open the door, and when she did, a female Dukian hostess came walking in with a tray of food and some drinks. She put it down on the table before exiting the room, and Sartia closing the door behind her.

"Room service?" I confusingly asked.

"It's all part of the stay here," she said. "It's all included."

I quickly sat up in the bed and immediately asked her something that was on my mind since the moment I opened my eyes.

"I thought we only had a couple of hours until the ship was ready?" I asked.

"We did," she replied. "But I figured that we could use the rest."

"I like how you think."

I then got up off of the bed and went over to the tray. When I glanced down at it, I noticed something on there that looked all too familiar. Something I haven't had in, how long has it been, two days now? Yeah. It looked just like a coffee carafe.

"Is that what I think it is?" I asked, pointing to the carafe.

"Coffee," she replied. "But on this planet, it's called Dukian caf. In other parts of the sector, it's simply known as cafaln.[6] Only, out here, it'll give you a slightly bigger boost of energy."

"A bigger boost? How? What's in it?"

"It's probably best that you don't know."

---

[6] (Pronounced *Calf-uln*)

"I'll take your word for it."

I picked up the carafe and immediately started pouring myself a cup. Of course, the cups themselves were metal with a heatproof handle to keep your fingers from burning while holding them.

After I finished pouring the coffee, I put the carafe back down before glancing over at the cream and sugar. Or, at least, what I thought was cream and sugar.

"What is that?" I asked, pointing to the milky, tan substance.

"That's milk," she replied.

Now, of course, any milk that I've ever seen has been white, except in *Star Wars.* I'm just glad it wasn't blue.

"Do I even wanna know what animal that comes from?" I asked.

"Just put it in your coffee," she said. "The sugar too. You won't be disappointed."

What did I have to lose? If the aliens could drink it, why couldn't I? Besides, she hasn't steered me wrong yet.

So, I poured in my usual amount of milk and what was equal to four teaspoons of sugar. Yeah, I know. You're probably thinking, *Jesus, Sam. Why not have a little coffee with your sugar?* Well, I like it sweet. What can I say?

I stirred it up and paused for a moment before taking a sip. When I did, the rush of flavor and caffeine hit my tongue hard. Kind of like a car crashing into a brick wall. However, I have to say it was pretty damn good.

I then took my cup and went over to the chair near the window to sit down and enjoy my coffee for a few minutes while I looked out over the awe-inspiring skyline.

"I'm gonna go take a quick shower," Sartia said. "Will you be okay?"

"I'll be fine," I replied.

And with that, she went right into the bathroom and closed the door behind her.

While she was in there, I continued to stare out of the window and sip my coffee. I then thought about my trip so far and how insane it all actually was. All I knew was that I was looking forward to seeing what else that galaxy had to offer. Also, what the hell was I gonna tell everyone when I got back home? Even with all the photos that I've taken and the ones yet to come, there wasn't a chance in hell that anyone would believe me. Oh well.

It took Sartia just a little over an hour to shower and be done. The first thing that came to my mind was, *Typical female.* Even the alien women take forever in the bathroom.

By that point, I had managed to down like three cups of coffee. See, I always like to drink it first thing in the morning, only because there's nothing like sitting down with a cup and just relaxing for a few minutes before you get your day started. Plus, it's been almost two days now since I've had any. Well, in the story, anyway.

When Sartia came out of the bathroom, I was still sitting in the chair, still feeling fine and wondering when this so-called 'boost of energy' would actually show up.

However, I didn't think anything of it and stood up, as I was now ready to go get cleaned up myself.

"It's all yours," she said.

"Took you long enough," I remarked.

Of course, she knew that I was joking but decided to push my buttons anyway.

"Well, if you needed to get cleaned up so badly, why didn't you just come in with me?" she asked.

Even though I knew she was kidding, my eyes were now as wide as half dollars.

"Ha-ha," I said. "Very funny."

"Who's joking?" she replied, now sporting a big, devilish grin. "Enjoy your shower."

Oh yeah. I both hated and liked her all at the same time. She knew that she could put me through the wringer, and I'd still perk back up.

Regardless, I proceeded to make my way into the bathroom. However, as I started closing the door, I just gave her a dirty look, letting her know how I felt about that.

There was really nothing different about how their bathrooms looked compared to a bathroom back home. It had a toilet, a sink, a mirror, a shower, and some shelves to hold towels, washrags, and toilet paper. The only two differences were the towels and the toilet paper. They were made and transported from the same planet that the mattresses were made. The towel felt like I was drying myself off with a cloud, and the toilet paper never hurt or left any raw skin.

Anyway, after a nice, 20-minute soak, I turned the water off, got out, and wrapped the towel around my waist. Of course, like any other man would do, I looked at myself in the mirror and wondered what she would think of me naked. I'm not a real muscular guy by any means, but I do have some definition. For the most part, I'm pretty skinny.

Since I wasn't worried about getting any nasty bugs or diseases from that place, I proceeded to use the free comb they provided and ran it through my four-inch-long hair. However, no sooner did I put the comb down, and with me still being a little on the wet side, Sartia thought it would be okay to just barge in on me.

"Hurry up and get dressed!" she said with a purpose. "We have to leave. Now!"

"Why? What's going on?" I asked.

"Just hurry!"

Now, nobody barges in on someone like that unless it's a dire emergency. So, rather than wonder what all the fuss was about, I quickly dried off, got dressed as fast as possible, and then ran straight into the other room.

"What's going on?" I asked.

"They're here," she said.

"Who's here?"

"The Morgidians. They've tracked us."

"How did they know we were here?"

"I don't know. But we have to leave right now."

Okay. I guess it was time to go. The time for rest and relaxation was over.

So, we quickly gathered all of our things and hightailed it out of the room, down the hall, and straight to the elevator.

• • •

Once we got ourselves back down to the 300th floor, we immediately got out and quickly made our way through the big crowd of aliens before reaching the landing port doors. But not before I noticed something odd.

Before we got to the doors, I stopped dead in my tracks when we passed the store where I had bought the Dukian burrower the day before. Sure enough, there she was. That same Dukian cashier was still there, now talking to three Morgidian hunters. *That's* when I knew how they found us. When she asked where I was from and I said Earth, that must've tipped her off. She must've called them to collect some kind of a reward.

Sartia then noticed I wasn't with her and came running back over to get me.

"What the hell are you doing?" she asked.

"Look," I said, pointing to the Dukian cashier. "That bitch must've tipped them off."

Sartia looked in the cashier's direction and also noticed the three Morgidian hunters standing there.

"Holy shit. You might be right," she said. "Let's get out of here before they…"

I knew what she was gonna say. Unfortunately, they managed to spot us before we actually got the hell out of there.

"Shit! Run!" she shouted.

The both of us then ran as fast as we could, dodging some but bumping into most of the aliens there. When we finally reached the door and got outside, Ronak was already waiting for us with the hover cart.

"Ronak? What are you doing here?" Sartia asked in a confused manner.

"Sam used his signaling device to call me," he said. "So, here I am."

Upon hearing his response, she quickly turned to look at me.

"I could kiss you right now," she said with a smile.

As much as I wanted to say yes, I didn't. Instead, I just smiled back before we both jumped onto the back of the hover cart.

"Step on it, Ronak!" I said.

"Step on it?" he confusingly asked. "I'm not sure I've ever heard of that-"

"Just get on the goddamn cart and drive us as fast as you can toward the ship!"

"Oh. Right."

He then put the proverbial 'pedal to the metal' and drove us toward the ship.

Once we arrived, everyone got out. Sartia didn't waste any time running up the ramp and opening the hatch.

"I take it that your stay was exquisite?" Ronak asked me.

"Loved it!" I replied. "I'd definitely stay here again. You know, this planet is-"

"Will you get your ass up here?" Sartia ordered.

By that time, she was already on the ship and slightly peeved that, well, I wasn't.

"Unless you wanna stay here and become laser dust, I suggest moving your ass, now!" she added.

Seeing as how that was my only other choice, I obviously got back on the ship. Once I was on, Sartia closed the hatch, but not before I got a chance to wave goodbye to Ronak.

We immediately went straight to the cockpit to hop in our respective seats. Our harnesses automatically buckled and adjusted themselves as we sat down. The panel then came out as Sartia quickly put her hands on the controls, prompting the engines to start right up. Then, we bolted upward toward the heavens.

• • •

It didn't take us long to break through the atmosphere and make our way into wild space. However, the trip was short-lived.

"What the fuck is that?" I asked, now staring at what looked like an armada of ships.

"Four Morgidian warships," she replied with an affronted tone.

"What do we do now?"

"Now… we fight."

Holy shit. This was it. I thought to myself.

That was definitely one of those moments where you know you're about to die. But I didn't wanna die. I wasn't ready. I still had a life ahead of me. I wanted to do all sorts of things I haven't done yet. I wanted to…

Sorry about that. Thinking about it got me a little emotional.

"You're gonna man the guns," she said.

"Umm… do you wanna run that by me again?" I replied.

"I said, you're gonna man the guns."

No sooner did she that, a similar panel to hers came forward and was now in front of me. But the one that I was now looking at was a little bit different.

Instead of two glowing half orbs, it had very simple-looking joystick controls… two cylindrical-shaped joysticks that you could wrap your hands around, each equipped with its own button on top.

The center panel almost looked like a video capture of our surrounding area. There was a little circle in the middle, which I used as my target. I could also see the four warships on the top of the screen. Once one of them was in the circle, I would fire and try to hit it. To me, it was just like playing a video game. Except this time, I didn't get any extra lives.

"You want me to use the cannons?" I asked.

"There's no better time to learn than right now," she said before explaining everything to me that I just explained to you. "You ready?"

I was now nervous and shaking so bad that my skin felt like it was gonna slide completely off my body. Of course, if it did, I would be nothing but a skinless guy, sitting there and getting blood...

Sorry. I think you get the picture.

Anyway, I swear to you, it was right then and there that I felt like I could throw up. But, I took a deep breath and swallowed all my fears.

"Let's do this," I said.

"Okay. Hang on!" she said, taking off toward the warships like a bat out of hell.

She zoomed right up and over them, trying to get away from our current location while leaving them and the planet in our space dust. But, just as expected, they immediately turned around and came after us. However, we didn't get too far, as it took them no time at all to catch up and start firing at us.

Now, the ship we were flying in only had one distinct weakness that I knew of. And because it was shaped like a capital letter *T,* I couldn't fire the cannons backward. Otherwise, I'd just wind up hitting our own engines. So, to actually fire at someone else, we had to be facing them, which would require a really good pilot. However, compared to other pilots that I've seen in films and real life, Sartia definitely wasn't a good pilot. She was a great pilot.

"It looks like it's clear for a while," Sartia said. "You ready?"

"I'm as ready as I'll ever be," I replied.

Without missing a beat, she did a complete one-eighty mid-flight and was now flying the ship backward.

"Holy shit!" I yelled.

"I'll try to angle us so you can get them in your center," she said.

I immediately focused all of my attention on the screen on my panel. As she was flying backward, I could now see the four warships directly in front of us, moving around on the screen like a game of *Asteroids.* Except those weren't asteroids, and they were moving much faster.

I saw one ship pass through the center circle on my screen and hit the buttons on my joysticks. Unfortunately, I missed. Of course, it wasn't as easy as I'm explaining it because, along with Sartia flying the ship, I could also move the cannons around as well. Combine that with the warships moving around, and it made it extremely difficult to hit something. Plus, she was now dodging their cannon fire as well.

Another ship was now coming close to the center circle, and when it passed over it, I fired. But this time, I actually hit it. I screamed out with joy as I watched the ship explode off in the distance.

"I got him!" I shouted.

"You're a natural at this," she said.

Of course, playing all of those video games over the years definitely helped with my coordination.

"What can I say, when you're good, you're good," I said, acting all cocky.

"I'll be the judge of that," she said, grinning at me.

I then refocused my attention back on the monitor to continue firing at them. As I did, a second ship came into my sights and passed through the center before I fired and missed. My adrenaline was now in overdrive, and I think that the Dukian caf was starting to take effect.

I don't know what came over me. Even though I never did any, it's almost as if I had taken a few more caffeine pills than I should have. I instantly got the shakes, and every shot that I took made my smile get bigger and bigger. My eyes were also getting wider and wider.

After that second ship came into my sights again, I fired and took it out.

"Fuck yeah!" I screamed. "Did you see that?"

I think it was at that point, she knew the caf was starting to have an unthought-of side effect on me. Besides being all kinds of jittery, she could now see it in my eyes that I was all amped up.

"Are you okay?" she asked.

"Who? Me?" I said with excitement. "I've never been better!"

Of course, I was lying. I was now on a high that I've never been on before. And I… was loving it. However, I wouldn't love it in a few hours after I came down from it, only to acquire a monster headache. But we'll get to that soon enough.

By now, my legs were shaking so hard that if I were Superman, I'd be putting holes in the floor. Every time a ship crossed paths with the center circle, I would fire and practically jump out of my chair with excitement. I then grabbed the two joysticks even tighter, and my eyes grew bigger as I was now ready to destroy the last two ships.

Now, as we were flying toward them, I swear that I could hear some more music playing throughout the ship. Again, I've heard the random music twice before and was still very curious about where it was coming from. But at that point (and being so high), I didn't care.

"Danger Zone" by Kenny Loggins was now blasting throughout the ship, and it fit perfectly. I now felt like I was actually in the movie *Top Gun,* only I wasn't flying fighter jets. I was in a spaceship… fighting aliens.

Anyway, the music was now blaring, and I was trying really hard to get the other two ships in my sights. But they weren't having any of it.

Because they were flying around, now doing their own basic maneuvers, coupled with Sartia maneuvering our own ship, it made them very hard to hit. We wound up taking a couple more shots to our shields before I was finally able to take one of them down.

Three down. One to go. But by then, I was literally starting to drool.

No, really. I had this big string of drool sliding down my chin, which I can only assume was one of the caf's side effects.

Regardless, I was now like a cat, focused on a field mouse, trying my hardest to blow the other ship to pieces. I shot and missed. He also shot at us and wound up missing. Again, Sartia was a pretty damn good pilot and definitely wouldn't let him blow us up. I still tried to get him, but he wasn't having any of it.

"Dammit!" I angrily screamed. "This guy is really starting to piss me off!"

"No offense," she said. "But, I kind of like it when you're mad."

"You do?"

"To be honest, it kinda turns me on."

Wait a minute… it turns her on? Did she really just say that? I mean, what kind of freaky alien was I traveling with, anyway?

However, I didn't have any time to think about it. The only thing I was now thinking about was taking down that last warship. And, as luck would have it, a prayer was answered in the form of an asteroid field.

"Asteroid field, dead ahead! Or, behind us," I said.

"You seriously don't want me to fly in there, do you?" she asked.

"It's our only chance. Besides, I have a plan."

"*You* have a plan?" she asked, doubting me.

I turned to look at her. "Yeah. Is that so hard to believe?"

"Alright. If you say so."

And with that, she just shrugged her shoulders before hesitantly turning the ship around and flying us straight into the asteroid field.

As we were flying into it, I thought back to all of the countless space movies that I've seen, and therefore, just had to test out a theory. So, we positioned ourselves on the backside of one of the larger rocks, hoping that the warship would immediately lose us, allowing us to disappear from its radar. And, as much as I would love to tell you that it worked, well, how about if I just tell you what happened instead?

We sat there on the rock with all of our systems disengaged while we waited patiently, hoping that the warship would fly in and try to find us. I was also hoping that the asteroids would take it out before we did. Unfortunately, that didn't happen.

We were looking out of the cockpit window, waiting, and hoping that the other ship would fly right by us without noticing we were even there. When it did, I got a really evil look on my face. My devilish grin spanned from ear to ear as I watched that helpless piece of space junk fly right by us.

Sartia knew precisely what to do and wound up disengaging from the rock while powering our ship back up. I then looked down on the screen and saw the warship directly in front of us. It was now in the exact center of my circle, and I had it dead to rights.

I grabbed my joysticks and put my thumbs on the firing buttons before giving the warship one last look through the cockpit window.

"Smile, asshole," I said with a cocky grin. "You're on candid camera."

I pushed the buttons on top of the joysticks and fired at the warship until it was nothing more than a glorious fireball. The vacuum of space immediately put it out, and the ship was now gone. Of course, I couldn't help myself and quickly let out something reminiscent of a war cry before turning my attention back to Sartia.

"Did you see that? I got all of them!" I screamed out with excitement.

"I saw that," she said. "You're a pretty good shot."

"Of course, I am!" I excitedly continued. "They never stood a chance! I've never felt so alive! The way those lasers hit them and just blew them up. Oh! You know what we should do? We should celebrate!"

She could now tell by looking at me that the caf was doing its job because I was now going into overload.

"How should we celebrate?" she asked.

Now, what happened next, I'm not proud of. But, unfortunately, it happened.

"How about this?" I asked before leaning in and planting a big one right on her lips.

She definitely wasn't expecting that and was totally caught off guard. I held my lips there for only a few more seconds before we eventually separated.

"And you know what else we could do?" I continued on. "We could…"

But I couldn't spit the rest out. I suddenly felt this wave of nauseousness and warmth come over me, and I couldn't figure out what it was. I've never felt anything like that before. Sartia could see the worry in my eyes, as she, herself, was now concerned about my well-being.

"Sam? Are you okay?" she asked.

But I still couldn't say anything. I didn't know what was happening or what I was feeling, but whatever it was, I knew it wasn't good.

I immediately turned around to try and make my way out of the cockpit. But before I could do anything else, that was it. Without warning, I quickly fell to the floor and passed out.

Rob J. LaBelle

Chapter 6

Dukian caf…

I never would've thought that in a million years, alien coffee would be my downfall. Of course, Sartia did warn me about the 'extra boost' it would give me. I just didn't realize that it would make me feel like I'd been snorting cocaine. And, as quickly as the caf overtook my system, it made me crash just as quick.

I was definitely out for some time, and when I finally opened my eyes, I noticed that I wasn't in the sleeping quarters. I saw that I was now lying down on a circular, king-sized bed in a room I've never seen before. The mattress was the same cloud-based sleeping foam that I've been on before, while the red sheets and maroon blankets were as soft as could be.

The room I was in was about one and a half times the size of the sleeping quarters. The bed itself was right in the middle of the room, with the door directly in front of it. To the right and left of the bed was a pair of two-tier shelves that ran almost the entire wall's length. Directly behind the bed was a six-foot-tall, wooden armoire, which had two doors that swung outward.

Well, let's see… I was on a bed, but not in the sleeping quarters, which could only mean one thing… I was in Sartia's room. This was the last room of the ship that I hadn't seen until now. I also never asked her about it, because frankly, it wasn't my room and none of my business.

I won't lie. From the start of my trip, I was very curious about what her room would actually look like. Well, there it was. Along with me, waking up in her bed.

After I realized where I was, I immediately sat straight up and was ready to head back out to the cockpit. But before I could leave the bed, the door to the room swooshed open, and Sartia walked right in.

"How are you feeling?" she asked.

Now, remember the headache I had mentioned to you before? Yeah. It was now there in full force.

"My head feels like it's gonna pull itself apart," I replied.

"It's one of the after-effects of the caf," she said.

As I was sitting there, holding my temples, trying to keep my head from exploding, she came right over and sat down next to me.

"I'm sorry," she said. "I would've told you about this, but I had no idea how your body would react."

"Well, now we know," I said.

She then just gave me a little pity smile, followed by a snicker.

"Don't worry about it," I said. "It's not your fault. Like you said, you had no idea."

"I know," she said. "But I told you that no harm would come to you, and now here you are, sitting on my bed with a headache."

"It's just a headache. It'll go away."

I could tell just by how she was looking at me that she definitely didn't like seeing me in pain. With the current look on her face, I also couldn't help but wonder what she was thinking about. At that point, I just wanted to dive into her mind and see how it all worked.

But while I was deep in thought, I noticed that it started to get unusually warm in there. Could it be that our attraction to each other has finally reached its breaking point? Was that the moment that we were finally going to give in to our animal instincts and have at it with each other? Yeah. In my dreams.

"Is it just me, or is it getting warm in here?" I asked.

"Nice try, egomaniac," she replied.

"No, really. I'm starting to sweat."

By now, I could feel the sweat beads start to pour out of my skin. But because her species is a little more tolerant of heat, she didn't notice it until she took one look at me and saw that I was now dripping.

"You're right. It is warm in here," she said.

She then looked like she almost had some kind of an epiphany, as she immediately got up off of the bed and started searching the room for something. As she looked under all the boxes and things on the shelves, I just thought she was losing her mind. I mean, what the hell was she looking for, anyway?

However, after a few minutes of searching, she finally found what she was looking for behind the bed.

"There you are," she said while bending down to pick something up.

I had no idea what she had found or what she was even looking for. But nothing could've prepared me for what she was holding in her arms as she stood up. Yeah, I know. You'd figure by that point, I'd be used to seeing weird shit. Well, get used to it. Because I never got used to seeing anything.

When she stood up, she was holding what looked like an orange housecat. But it also differed from a regular cat in so many ways. Its ears were about three times the size, its tail was twice as long, and its paws were also nearly double the size. Those things I could get used to. But what the cat actually did, well, that's a story in itself.

"You were looking for a cat?" I confusingly asked.

"Not just any cat," she said. "This is Rawr. He's my pet suncat."

"Your pet suncat?"

She then came back over and sat down on the bed right beside me. I just stared at the cat for a few seconds before deciding that it was weird-looking but still cute.

"That's quite the cat you've got there," I remarked.

"You don't like him?" she asked.

"No. Of course, I do. Actually, he's kind of cute."

"He's also the reason why it's so warm in here."

The moment she put her hands on his head, I understood why that particular breed of cat was called a suncat.

As she started to pet him, I swear I could see him start to glow. The more she rubbed him, the brighter he got. And the brighter he got, the more heat he would put out.

"Ah!" I said while nodding. "Suncat! Now I get it."

"He only puts off heat when someone pets him, or he rubs up against something," she said.

"Won't you get burned just by touching him?"

"That's the thing with these guys. Their fur gives off heat that you can feel. But when you touch them, you don't get burned."

After hearing her response, I was now curious and just had to find that out for myself.

"May I?" I asked, putting my hands out to grab him.

She then let go of Rawr, but I didn't even have time to grab him. For some reason, he took an instant liking to me, jumped right up into my lap, and started purring. It was one of the most amazing things I've ever seen.

Right away, I could feel the intense heat coming off of him. But my skin wasn't getting singed at all. Although I did break out into a massive sweat, that was pretty much the extent of it.

"Do you ever let him roam around the ship?" I asked.

"On occasion," she replied. "The only time he roams freely is when I return home and let him loose in the house."

"Doesn't it ever get lonely out here, traveling all by yourself?"

"Of course, it does. But that's why I bring Rawr with me. He loves to travel."

"No. I'm talking about human, err, alien companionship."

I waited for her to reply, but she never did. Instead, she just looked away. That's when I could tell that something else was bugging her. I didn't know what it was, and I didn't want to pry either, as it was definitely none of my business. Besides, if she wanted to tell me, then she would have.

"You know what?" she said, quickly changing the subject. "It just occurred to me that if you're gonna be traveling with me, we'll need some medicine."

"Medicine? For what?" I curiously asked.

"It might come in handy. You never know."

"Where the hell are we gonna get medicine out here?"

She paused for a moment to think about it before turning back to me and smiling.

"I know just the place," she replied.

Now, I won't bore you with the travel details, so I'll just skip ahead to the good part.

• • •

After a couple more hours of travel, we were now orbiting a bluish/green planet, similar to Earth. Only the one we were now high above was about half the size.

Its name was Ckrob[7] , and it was home to the Ckroblodites, a race known for its extraordinary healing abilities. The aliens themselves had all different shades of blue skin, yellow eyes, hair of all colors, and were no taller than four feet. Now, the thing that I found interesting about them was that they were all chubby.

Still having trouble painting a picture in your head? Then, picture this... picture an exercise ball with arms, legs, and a head, and that's basically what they looked like. Very weird, but a very hospitable species.

We continued orbiting the planet while we waited for them to clear us for landing. I was now sitting in the passenger's seat with my head still pounding from the after-effects of the caf. Thankfully, after only five minutes of waiting, someone from the planet's surface came through the speaker on the panel.

"Aranxian ship, ID number zero six one nine seven nine, you are now free to land in landing field ten," the somewhat high-pitched male voice said.

"Well, that was a lot quicker than the last time we waited," I remarked.

---

[7] (Pronounced *Krob*)

Sartia immediately put her hands on the controls and proceeded to guide us down through the planet's atmosphere.

After we broke through, I was surprised at how much it looked just like Earth. I could see green and blue all the way to the horizon in a 360-degree rotation. I could see oceans and lakes and fields. And, for the first time since I left home (minus the giant headache), I felt pretty good.

• • •

We eventually touched down in landing field ten, and when we did, I figured out why they called it a field instead of a port. That's precisely what it was… a big, giant field.

Those landing fields weren't like the ones on Jipduk at all. They were spread out a little further across the planet and were only about the size of one airfield. Plus, you were landing on grass instead of tarmac.

We now had to find an open spot to land because there, it was pretty much a free for all. They didn't have everything neat and organized like the last place we went to. But that didn't really seem to matter.

Sartia turned off the engines, and both of our harnesses instantly retracted. She then got up out of her seat and went over to the side door, pushing the button to open it. I also got up out of my seat before making my way over there to join her.

When I got there, the door opened, and a burst of air came rushing into the ship. I took one sniff, and let me tell you, it was probably the cleanest air that I have ever smelled in my entire life. I honestly don't know how it could've smelled any better than being out in the woods, but it did.

"Holy shit! Do you smell that?" I asked.

She then raised her nose to take a sniff. "I don't smell anything."

"Exactly. The air here is so clean."

She just smiled at me because she could now see how excited I was to be there. We then made our way down the retractable ramp until we both stepped foot onto the grass.

Now, I don't know what came over me, but instead of standing there waiting with her for someone to come and greet us, I just laid down right there in the field and closed my eyes. I wanna say that I did it because I haven't seen grass in a few days, who knows? All I knew was that it felt incredible.

After a few minutes of lying there, enjoying the sun, grass, and fresh air, a little blue male Ckroblodite came right over to greet us. He was light blue in color with short, green hair, a satchel over his left shoulder, and was wearing some kind of a fancy loincloth to cover up his parts.

"Greetings!" the little blue fella said in a somewhat high-pitched tone. "My name is Morg. What is the purpose of your visit?"

"Hello, Morg. I'm Sartia, and this is Sam," Sartia said.

I quickly stood back up to join in on the conversation. "Hello," I said.

"We're here to pick up some medical supplies and receive a bit of healing ourselves," Sartia said.

"Well then, you've come to the right place. May I be of some assistance before we get to the huts?" Morg replied.

"Do you have anything to cure a massive headache?" I asked.

Morg then proceeded to reach into his satchel before pulling something out.

"Here you are," he said, handing me the item.

Once it was in my hand, I just held this thing up and stared at it. I shit you not. It looked just like a Brussels sprout. The leaf on the outside was wrapping all of the ingredients on the inside into a nice little ball. But knowing where I've been and all the strange things that I've seen, we all really know it wasn't a Brussels sprout.

"What is it?" I curiously asked, staring at the rolled-up piece of whatever it was.

"It'll cure your headache," he said. "All you have to do is put it in your mouth, chew it up, and swallow it."

"That's it?"

"That's it."

I hesitated before taking a deep breath and stuffing that thing into my mouth. Once I started to chew it, the flavor hit my taste buds almost instantly.

Now, I would like to say that it tasted like mint, berries, or some other fruity/leafy flavor. No. It felt like I was chewing on a tiny ball of dirt. And it was absolutely disgusting.

"Please, follow me," Morg said.

He then led us away from our ship and started walking toward the hut village. I immediately turned to Sartia so I could express my displeasure.

"That fucking little weeble wobble gave me a ball of dirt," I angrily (and quietly) said.

"I know their medicines aren't the greatest tasting," she replied. "But they are the best in the sector."

"Thanks for the heads up."

She just shrugged her shoulders and said, "Sorry," before taking off and catching up with him while I followed closely behind.

· · ·

It was a short, five-minute walk through the airfield to the village. Once we reached the gates and were now in the clear, I looked in amazement at how closely it resembled a hobbit's.

The huts were all covered in moss and made entirely of stone. The windows were glass, and the doors were wood. Some of the huts were constructed into cliffs or hills, while others were built as stand-alone structures in the middle of a field. After a few seconds of staring, I suddenly felt like I was getting prepped to take a journey to Middle Earth.

We walked down a dirt path until we reached Morg's hut. Once we arrived, I noticed that his was built into a little cliff. While Morg was able to open his door and simply walk right in, Sartia and I both had to duck to get ourselves in there.

The front door led right into their living room. However, I was totally unprepared for what the inside of the hut actually looked like. Instead of seeing the inside of a hobbit house, like you would see in pictures or movies, it looked just like a regular house.

The rooms were square in shape. The walls were painted to match the carpets, and some of the floors were made of wood. The only thing that looked different was the furniture, which was all made from trees and branches to give it that 'cabin in the woods' type of feel.

"Please, have a seat on the couch," Morg said. "I'll be right back."

Sartia and I both sat down on the couch while he went into the other room.

While we were sitting there, I just continued to look around at everything. However, as I did, I suddenly noticed something different about the whole situation that I didn't notice before. My headache was now completely gone, and I felt like a million bucks.

"My headache's already gone," I said.

"Told ya they were the best," she replied.

We sat there for a few more minutes, waiting for Morg to come back, when all of a sudden…

"Welcome, dear guests!" a somewhat high-pitched female voice said behind us. "Would anyone care for a drink?"

We both turned around to see a female Ckroblodite come walking into the room. Except for the fact that she had long, blue hair and was wearing almost like a cavewoman type of outfit to cover up her parts, she looked just like Morg.

She came around to the front of the couch and put the tray of drinks down on the table. And when I saw what was on it, I immediately started to drool.

"Oh my god. Is that water?" I asked.

"Some of the freshest," she said.

Without thinking twice, I quickly grabbed one of the wooden cups and chugged down the whole thing in less than two seconds. Once the cup was empty, I just leaned back on the couch as I enjoyed the spring-like taste.

"Would you care for some more?" she asked me.

"Yes, please," I replied, quickly holding my cup out.

She poured me another cup, and I quickly downed that one, again, in two seconds flat. I've never drunk water so clean and so fresh before. I mean, I've had plenty of bottled spring water, but nothing like that.

"I take it he's a big fan of water?" she asked Sartia.

"Something like that," Sartia replied.

As soon as Sartia finished speaking, Morg came back into the room holding a strange tacklebox-looking thing made entirely of wood.

"I see you've met my wife?" he said.

"Dear me. Where are my manners?" Morg's wife said. "Allow me to introduce myself. My name is Cran."

Cran? I thought to myself. *What the hell kind of name is Cran? She doesn't look like a cranberry.* Although she definitely had the shape of one.

"Nice to meet you, Cran," Sartia said. "I'm Sartia, and this is Sam."

"Hello," I said.

"Well, now that Morg is back, I'll just leave you to it," Cran said before exiting the living room.

Morg then placed the tacklebox-looking thing on the table next to the water tray and opened it up. When he did, it was filled to the brim with all kinds of different medical supplies. The only items I could make out were some gauze and some band-aid-type-looking things. Other than that, I had no fucking clue.

"So," he said, sitting down on the grass-covered chair across from us. "I hope these supplies will be sufficient enough for your travels?"

Immediately following his question, Sartia started rummaging through the box. While she was browsing, I couldn't help but think to myself, *Was he talking about the whole thing? Was she really gonna purchase that whole box of supplies?* Of course, it only took her less than ten seconds to give him an answer.

"Thank you," she said. "This will do nicely."

"I'm glad it pleases you," Morg said.

She then closed up the box and paid him, using a small thumbprint scanner, just like the one she used back at the Jipduk gift shop. I just looked at her and then at him, waiting for one of them to say something to the other. But they didn't. I mean, was that it? Were we done already?

"So, is that it? Are we done?" I asked.

"I believe we are," Sartia said.

"Damn! That was way too quick."

"We need to get going."

"Can't we stay and check this place out a little more?"

"I know you said that you only came for some supplies," Morg interjected. "But before you both go, would you care to take a relaxing dip in our hot springs?"

Hot springs? My eyes instantly shot open, and the thought of relaxing in a hot spring suddenly sounded pretty damn good.

"I would love to!" I said with a smile.

"Sam," Sartia started to say.

"What? There's no timetable on returning the sphere, is there?"

"Not that I know of."

"Then why can't we just enjoy ourselves every chance we get?"

I stared at her intently, waiting for her to give me some bullshit excuse about getting back to it before some bounty hunters track us down and kill us. But instead, she didn't say anything. I think that's when she knew that rushing to get the sphere back to the Morgidians wasn't as important as she thought.

"You know, you're right," she said. "They didn't give me any specific time to get that back to them. And so what if we're being hunted every step of the way. Let's go enjoy ourselves."

"Now you're talkin'," I said, grinning from ear to ear.

"Oh, good. Please, follow me," Morg said before getting out of his chair.

After both of us followed suit, he led us out of his house and down the path, going a little further into the village.

• • •

On the way to the hot spring, we passed many different types of shops, stores, and theaters. Not movie theaters, mind you, but theaters for conducting plays.

As far as I could tell, they weren't a very technological species. But what little technology they did have, they used it on things like radar and machines to make specific medicines and fabrics that they couldn't make by hand.

After a short, ten-minute walk, we arrived at the hot spring, located in the center of a ring of cliffs. A single hut, which was also used as the entrance, was built directly in the middle, connecting the whole circle. It was very well hidden, and I didn't understand why. That is until we went inside.

We walked through the hut to get a good look at the spring. And once we were in, I couldn't help but be amazed at what I was now looking at.

It looked like an oasis. The steam was coming up through the pond-sized pool while lots of trees surrounded it and the neighboring cliffs. There were all kinds of different alien species just sitting in there, relaxing and enjoying themselves.

However, as much as I was taken in by that place, I couldn't help but notice one thing about everyone there. The so-called *reason* why it was so well hidden.

"Holy fucking shit," I muttered to myself.

"I hope that nudity won't be an issue for you?" Morg asked.

Yup. That was it. Every single alien in there was completely naked. I mean, I definitely wanted to enjoy myself, but not like that. Sartia could now see the expression on my face and knew exactly what I was thinking.

"What's the matter, Sam? You're not afraid of a little nudity, are you?" she sarcastically asked.

Who? Me? Afraid of nudity? Come on. I mean, seriously. What kind of a question is that, anyway?

Only five people have ever seen me naked in my whole life: my parents, the two women that I've slept with, and of course, my doctor. Now, I've never gotten naked for anyone that I didn't know, let alone a whole group of strangers. Of course, I was afraid. I already felt a little uncomfortable getting naked in front of one person, let alone a whole group.

Regardless, I definitely couldn't chicken out now, or Sartia might think less of me. If this whole situation were a pickle, it definitely wouldn't be kosher.

See what I did there? Kosher? Yeah, never mind.

Anyway, I just looked back at Sartia and decided to play it off real cool like.

"Who, me? Of course, I'm not afraid of nudity," I nonchalantly replied.

She just eyeballed me from top to bottom before smiling at me and raising both eyebrows.

"Good," she said. "This should be fun then."

Fuck me. Now what? After my previous comment, there was no way I could back out now. So, there was only one thing left for me to do… I had to man up and just go with it.

"Is it possible to go in wearing only my underwear?" I asked Morg.

Yeah. Don't judge me. To hell with manning up. I'll save that for another time.

"It's not a crime. Feel free," Morg replied.

Thank god! I thought.

Yes, I knew that many of the aliens in there may look at me weird for not going in naked, but frankly, I was never gonna see them again after this. And, at that point, I could give two shits.

"After you find a chair and get undressed," Morg continued. "Leave your clothes there and go have fun. If you need anything, just ask the person working in the hut. They'll know how to get in touch with me."

"Thanks, Morg," I said.

And with that, he gave me a little head nod and a smile before leaving the hot spring.

After he was gone, I just stood there and took a deep breath before heading over to one of the chairs. We grabbed one of the empty ones closest to the spring so I could just strip down and hop in without anyone really noticing me. I quickly took all my clothes off, minus my underwear, of course, and slipped right into the spring. It felt just as warm as a hot tub and was just as relaxing.

Now, the thing is, I'm still a guy. I always wondered from the moment that I met her what Sartia would like naked. Does the rug really match the drapes? I mean, come on. Who wouldn't want to see a hot alien in the nude? But, I shit you not, I don't think I could've fully prepared myself for how she actually did look.

Yeah, right. You really thought I would look? Of course not. She let me know when she was getting undressed, and I simply turned around. If I were gonna see her naked, it would be under better circumstances. If you know what I mean?

When she finally got in, she got right next to me on my left and was now fully submerged up to her shoulders so that I couldn't see anything. That's when I turned to look at her.

"Now, *this* is how you relax," I said.

"It definitely is nice," she replied.

Now, it would've been nice to sit there in the peace and quiet while enjoying the warm, relaxing spring, but she had the audacity to ask me a question. Not just any question, mind you. This was a question that I personally think was solely responsible for turning the tide on this whole trip. She only asked it because I think she was actually quite impressed at how gentlemanly I was.

"I've gotta say that most, if not all guys, would've taken the opportunity to see a naked woman," she began. "But not you. You're different. Why?"

And there it was.

In my opinion, that was definitely a question to end all questions. I mean, I could've just told her that my parents had raised me to be a responsible adult and a gentleman when I needed to be. Or I could've just made up some random bullshit. However, I decided to take neither route. Instead, I just gave her the truth.

"You really wanna know why?" I asked.

"Yeah, I do," she replied.

"Well, the reason why I didn't look at you is because I respect you. If I were to see you naked, I'd rather it be under different circumstances."

"You mean, if we were gonna have sex, right?"

"Well... yeah."

She didn't immediately give me a reply but instead just stared at me for a moment with one eyebrow now raised, almost as if she was trying to determine where this whole conversation was now heading.

"Are you saying that you wanna have sex with me?" she asked.

Holy shit. What do I say now? Do I say yes? Do I say no? I mean, of course, I wanted to. I've wanted to ever since the first time she kissed me in the cockpit of the ship.

So, I tried to give her a straight answer without making myself seem too desperate.

"It's definitely not out of the realm of possibilities," I said. "I mean, I like you, and I definitely would. But only if you wanted to?"

And there you have it. I basically said yes, while leaving the ball in her court. However, me going into the spring wearing nothing but my underwear wasn't actually all that embarrassing compared to what happened next.

After hearing my answer, she leaned in, got really close to me, and whispered into my ear.

"Wanna know a secret?" she said. "I've wanted to have sex with you ever since we first kissed."

And *that's* when it happened.

Sartia took her right hand, put it on my left leg, and slowly started sliding it upward. Inside, I was going nuts. And I now knew how she felt about me. The problem was, it got me just a little too excited, and I definitely wasn't ready for that. So, just like the Flash, I bolted out of the hot spring like lightning.

Standing at the chair to collect all of my clothes, I suddenly felt many holes being burned into my head. When I glanced around, I noticed everyone was now staring at me. They must've heard my ruckus and turned to look at where the noise was coming from. However, no sooner did I look up at everyone, I could hear a collective laugh come out of their mouths. I didn't think much of it and just figured it was because I was in my underwear.

After I got a good look at everyone else, I turned my attention back to Sartia. When I did, I could see that she was now looking at me as well. But she wasn't laughing. As a matter of fact, she wasn't even looking me in the eyes. But by that point, I had enough of everyone laughing at me and decided to call them all out on it.

"What? You pricks never seen someone in their underwear before?" I asked aloud.

"That's not what they're laughing at, Sam," Sartia said.

"Well then, what the fuck are they laughing at?" I asked in a more slightly agitated tone.

And that's when I noticed Sartia looking down toward my underwear with her eyes open as wide as they could possibly go.

"Wow!" she mumbled to herself.

But I still heard what she said. That, coupled with the fact that she was now looking down at my crotch, I looked down to see that I had just suffered the most embarrassing moment in my entire life.

Yup. You guessed it.

Apparently, her touch on my leg got me so excited that I was now pitching a tent. And that doesn't mean you can laugh about it either. Trust me, that wasn't fun.

Anyway, now utterly embarrassed, I quickly covered myself with my clothes to try and hide my shame.

"Shit," I muttered.

But that was it.

Ignoring Sartia's calls, I immediately hightailed it out of the spring while running as fast as I could to get away from there.

Rob J. LaBelle

Chapter 7

Whether we want to admit it or not, we've all had some pretty embarrassing things that have happened to us at one point or another in our lives. Some have happened by sheer accident, and some have happened because other people made them happen.

Like I said, I was always the loner, while Darius would be the one to have my back. But most of the time, he was off doing his own thing and wasn't around to help me out. This was one of those times where the embarrassment fell 100 percent on my own shoulders.

For me, it all started back when I was in fifth grade. All the kids in my class would have to read some sentences off a chart from their seats. When it was my turn, however, I couldn't do it. I had to get up out of my chair every single time and go up to the chart to read them. That's when I knew I needed glasses.

Sixth grade is when I actually got my first pair. That's when all the name-calling and put-downs started. You see, kids back then weren't very forgiving when it came to that sort of thing. Wearing glasses didn't seem as widely accepted as it is now. Nowadays, no one really bats an eye if you have to wear them because they're so common.

But all the name-calling, bullying, and everything else that happened to me, really made my self-esteem go way down. That is until I met Darius. He looked past all of that and saw beyond my four eyes that deep down, I was a pretty nice guy. He became my best friend during the last half of that year and has been ever since.

As you could probably already tell, I don't have any glasses on right now because I decided to get vision correction surgery a few years back. *That* was a lifesaver. Although I didn't need corrective lenses anymore, my self-esteem was still in the shitter, and it took me a long time to even get to where I am today.

Again, we all have a few setbacks from time to time, and the thing that happened to me at the hot spring, well, that was a pretty big one.

• • •

Okay. So, I ran out of the hot spring. But I didn't exactly run back to the ship either. If I did, I knew that Sartia would eventually find me there. And there's no way in hell I could face her after what had just happened. I was way too embarrassed.

Instead, I ran beyond the village and straight into the surrounding forest. I figured that being alone by myself in nature was probably what I needed. No one around to laugh at me or anyone to look at. Just me and the woods.

Of course, I was now all by myself, alone on an alien planet, in the middle of nowhere. I mean, come on. A forest is a forest no matter where you go, right? Wrong.

After what I've recently been through, I should've known better than to go traipsing around in an alien forest all by myself with no one to guide me. But, going against my better judgment, I did it anyway.

Now, I already had a feeling that before going in there, that forest would be a lot different than the ones back on Earth. I'd probably see many different creatures, bugs, plants, trees, and all sorts of other things a forest would have. However, shortly after entering, I came across something I wouldn't ever have thought to have existed. I know. The whole story seems ridiculous. But, come on, are you really that surprised?

Also, just in case you were wondering, I stopped and got dressed long before this point. And no, I wasn't still pitching a tent. So get your mind out of the gutter.

Now, where was I? Oh yeah…

I went into the forest and came across a little stream. I just sat down on a log to enjoy the sound of the moving water when I thought I heard someone cry out for help. With me not being from that planet and knowing that the cry for help could literally be anyone or anything, I just decided to brush it off and continue sitting there. After all, I wasn't really in the mood to talk with anyone at the moment.

And, yes. I understand that you're probably thinking of many bad names to call me because I didn't go and help, but just chill out. We'll get there.

I found a flat stone on the ground, which looked just like any other regular stone, and bent down to pick it up. I then positioned it in my right hand and pulled my arm back so I could try to skip it across the water. And just as I was about to hurl it, that's when I heard the cry for help again. But this time, it seemed much louder. I definitely couldn't ignore it now. So, I quickly threw the rock into the water and started to make my way in the direction of the voice.

As I continued walking toward it, I noticed the ecosystem in that forest was all over the place. I saw pine trees, oak trees, ferns, and a few other trees and plants that I couldn't identify. However, mixed in with all of that, I saw palm trees and cacti. I had stopped walking at one point merely to stare at them, only because those two things are something I definitely didn't expect to find in a forest. Regardless, I just shrugged my shoulders and moved on.

I had to have been walking for a good ten minutes in one direction before I stopped. I did so because I hadn't heard anything in a while and thought that my ears might have been playing tricks on me. Either that, or it was the forest playing tricks on me.

And because I hadn't heard anything in a while, I decided to call out. "Hello?"

Nothing.

At that point, I couldn't decide if I should go deeper into the forest or turn around and head back toward the village. While I was standing there debating, however, I heard the cry for help again.

"Help me!" a voice said.

It was still faint, but I knew I was getting close. So, instead of walking toward it, I started running toward it.

I ran for what seemed like two minutes before stopping and calling out again. "Where are you?"

"Help me! I'm trapped!" the voice said.

I knew I was now getting close because I heard the faint voice even clearer this time. That's also when I was able to decipher that it was a female voice. However, it didn't sound like a typical female voice. It almost sounded like a high-pitched squeaky voice. But that didn't concern me. I was now solely focused on helping out whoever it was that was asking for help.

"Keep talking to me!" I yelled out.

I only said that so I could hear whoever it was while I was running and be going in the right direction at the same time. However, it didn't take much longer (maybe another five minutes) before I finally found *what* was calling out for help.

When I arrived at the location that the voice was coming from, there was 'something' caught in a cage. The cage itself was just big enough to hold a parakeet. But anything that small couldn't possibly be asking for help, could it?

I didn't make a move toward it. I just stood there and stared because I had no idea what the hell I was looking at. Whatever it was, it was tiny, hovering in the center of the cage and glowing a bright, yellow color.

"Please, you have to get me out of here," the squeaky, glowing figure said.

"I'm sorry, but what the hell are you?" I curiously asked.

"What does that have to do with anything?"

"I've just never seen anything like you before."

"There's no time to converse. You have to get me out of here!"

"First, tell me what you are, and if you're going to hurt me or not?"

"Ugh!" the little creature groaned. "You've never seen a harmless little fairy before?"

Holy shit. I couldn't believe it. She was an actual fairy. I always thought they were just made-up, mythical creatures, but they really do exist. Upon hearing that, I just wanted to clap my hands and say, "I do believe in fairies," because now, I had definitely seen it all.

"*You're* a fairy?" I asked her, still in disbelief.

"Yes, I'm a fairy," she replied. "And you have to get me out of here before he comes back."

Before he comes back? Who the hell was she talking about?

"Before who comes back?" I asked.

Of course, no sooner did I ask that I saw exactly *who* she was talking about.

This 'thing,' whatever the fuck it was, well, it looked like a giant, two-legged snake. It was definitely humanoid (maybe a mutant), but it had a greenish, brownish, scaly type of skin, a pair of green snake eyes, a snake's tongue, and was wearing some sort of metallic battle armor that covered its whole body, except for its head. It walked on two legs, had two arms, two hands, and two feet. It was a real-life walking, talking snake man.

I guess I was wrong. I guess I hadn't seen it all.

"Who are you?" the snake-like figure asked me.

"I was about to ask you the same thing," I replied.

"My name is Slith. I'm a bounty hunter from the planet Rumvak."

"A bounty hunter?"

"What do you want?"

"I heard the little fairy's cries for help and thought I would come to offer some assistance," I replied.

"Help her out?" he curiously asked before pausing. "You mean you want to steal my bounty?"

"Trust me, I have no intention of stealing your bounty."

"Who are you? I've never seen your species before."

Now, I knew that every bounty hunter and Morgidian in the sector were out looking for me, and that thing was *definitely* no Morgidian. Plus, from what I could tell, he was all by himself.

So, do I tell him who I really am? Or do I lie and make something up on the spot? I mean, he was only one bounty hunter. If he didn't recognize me by now, what are the odds he'll even know who I am?

"My name is Sam," I proceeded to tell him. "And I'm from the planet Earth."

"Sam from Earth?" he asked me, now sporting a curious look.

"The one and only."

I could then see the look on his face change, almost as if he had just figured out a really tough riddle.

"You're the one with the sphere," he said.

Oh shit. He did know who I was. Well, that really backfired.

"Fuck," I muttered.

"I guess it's my lucky day," he said. "I can now collect two bounties in one shot."

Up until that point, I've only come face to face with the Morgidians. Slith was the first bounty hunter I encountered, and I can assure you, he definitely wouldn't be the last.

I wasn't sure what I should do. I mean, there I was, out in the middle of the woods with only my wits and a snake-like creature looking to kill me. Well, at least, not yet.

"Where's the sphere?" he asked.

"It's not here," I answered. "And besides, I wouldn't tell you where it is anyway."

"Hmm… I see we've come to an impasse then."

"What do you mean?"

"Well, I now have to take you alive. Because if you're dead, I'll never find the sphere, and I won't get paid."

"Lucky me," I said.

"Now, tell me where the sphere is!" he demanded.

"Over my dead body."

Over my dead body? Why would I even say that? Why would I want to provoke an intergalactic bounty hunter into trying to kill me in the first place? I mean, was I crazy? Probably. But I don't know who's crazier... me for telling you this story, or you for sticking around and listening to it? Yeah. Who's crazy now?

Sorry. I tend to get carried away sometimes.

Anyway, Slith pulled out his sidearm, which was black in color, and looked like a shotgun. But that was definitely no shotgun. It was the same length, with a regular-sized pistol barrel, and was about twice as thick. It also had two settings on it, which allowed you to switch back and forth between a bullet type of ammo and electrical pulse rounds. That thing was awesome. But I had nothing.

After having heard my last ridiculous comment, he just laughed at me before making his own remark.

"I thought you might say that," he said with a smile.

And with that, I immediately turned around and started hauling ass away from him. As I did, he began firing the electrical pulse rounds at me. I can only assume that he was trying to knock me out so he could question me later. Of course, he wound up missing as I continued to zig-zag through the trees.

After a few seconds of running, I was finally able to get away from him and hide behind a gigantic redwood tree, hoping that he wouldn't see me. Yes, redwoods were there as well.

I hid behind the tree for what seemed like forever while I tried to come up with some kind of a plan. However, in between my nerves being shot and I, myself, being shot at and hunted, my mind was blank. I couldn't think of anything. So, I took a couple of deep breaths and started simple.

I cautiously peeked out from behind the tree to see if I could find out where he was. Sure enough, the second my head popped itself out, he fired at me and hit the tree.

Oh shit. He's still coming. I thought to myself.

"I see you, Sam," Slith said, still walking toward me. "And I will get you."

He was right. The longer I stayed there, the better chance he had of capturing me. And I simply couldn't let that happen.

So, it was either run left or run right. Which way did I wanna go? At that point, it didn't really matter. Both ways gave me the same chance of getting captured. And if I did stay there, I would get caught for sure. I then took a couple more deep breaths before finally taking off toward my right.

The second I left the tree, he fired shot, after shot, after shot at me. Luckily, there was enough tree cover around to protect me because they all missed.

"You can't run forever!" he shouted.

I certainly did try, though. I don't know how long I ran or how far I went, but I finally stopped to hide in a ditch, covered by some fallen trees. I now had a little bit of time to think about what I was gonna do and how I would do it. Unfortunately, I still had no idea.

I did know one thing, though. I couldn't leave that fairy out there to be taken by the bounty hunter. If I left her there to die, there's no way in hell I would've been able to live with myself.

So, I just sat there, thinking about everything I learned while I was in the boy scouts, hoping that one of those skills would be useful. After all, 95 percent of the stuff they teach you requires you to be out in nature. Also, with my father being an ex-military sergeant, I learned a few 'extra' things that the boy scouts technically aren't allowed to show you.

However, no matter where you start, no matter what you do, every basic skill begins with a knife. And I didn't have one. I didn't even have a gun. I left my burrower on the...

"My burrower!" I said out loud. "Of course!"

I immediately reached down toward my right pants pocket, only to feel the handle of the burrower sticking out. So, I quickly grabbed it and pulled it out of my pocket.

But how much damage could the burrower actually do? I haven't even fired it or had time to try it out yet. Regardless, there was now only one way that I could find out. I had to go out there and face him.

My plan was simple… I only wanted to fire at his legs and disable him. I didn't wanna kill him because I've never killed anything before, except maybe a few bugs and spiders. But he was different. He was a person… sort of.

I slowly peeked my head out of the ditch and looked around, scanning every inch of that forest in a 180-degree rotation. And, after a few minutes of searching, I finally spotted him.

Slith was slowly walking toward me, looking around, while trying to find me. I quickly looked at my gun to make sure all of the safeties were off and that it was ready to go. I then peeked back through the downed trees and aimed my burrower directly at his leg. I had him dead in my sights. All I had to do now was pull the trigger.

Again, all I had to do now was pull the trigger.

Of course, I couldn't do it. I was the biggest chicken shit in the world. I mean, seriously, what made me think I could actually shoot a gun at someone? But, no matter how scared I was, I had to. It was now a life or death situation. It was either gonna be him or me.

So, to calm some of my nerves, I took another deep breath before re-aiming my gun. And once I had him dead to rights again, I didn't hesitate. This time, I pulled the trigger.

The gun made a similar sound that a .45 would make after it was fired. Only, it wasn't as loud. My first ever shot, and I missed. And because of it, he saw me and now knew exactly where I was hiding.

"There you are," Slith said with a smile. "I hope you're still watching?"

Directly following his question, *that's* when the unthinkable happened.

As he stood there, I could literally see him camouflage himself before disappearing into the surrounding area. It wasn't any type of light refraction or cloaking device, but more along the lines of what a chameleon would do to blend in. Within seconds, he was completely invisible. Now what? How was I supposed to fight something that I couldn't see?

Great. I thought. *I'm fighting the fucking predator.*

Well, he wasn't quite like the predator, just a little less scary and almost as dangerous. I mean, if I couldn't fight something I couldn't see, I only had one option left. I had to run. And I had to do it without getting hit. Again, my plan was simple…

First, I head back to the birdcage and grab the fairy. Then, I run back to Sartia as fast as I can. That way, we could just get on the ship and get the hell off the planet. Piece of cake, right? You would think.

I sat there for just a few seconds more before taking a deep breath and hauling my ass out of the ditch. Sure enough, the second I made it out of there, it was like open season on Sam. Electrical pulse rounds were hitting the trees beside me and behind me. A few of them hit the ground in front of me, and one zinged right by my face, hitting the tree in front of me. That was a little too close.

I eventually made my way back to the fairy, who was still trapped in the cage. Since I knew she wasn't gonna hurt me, I didn't hesitate to let her out this time.

"You came back!" she excitedly said. "I didn't think you would."

"I couldn't just leave you here," I said.

"Quick, get me out, and you'll be rewarded."

My eyes quickly narrowed out of curiosity. "Rewarded? How?"

"I'll tell you after. Just open the cage and set me free."

Not wanting to waste another minute, I quickly looked over the cage's architecture and saw that it had a keyhole, which I didn't have a key for. I then tried grabbing the bars to pull them apart with my hands. No luck. I mean, it looked just like any other birdcage, except for one small thing.

"How can I get you out?" I asked. "I don't have a key, and I can't seem to bend the bars."

"Are your species known for having a lot of strength?" she asked.

"Yes and no."

"Then, you must be on the no side. Because anyone else would be able to bend these bars just enough so I could fly out."

"Thanks for the vote of confidence."

The fairy then did something to me that I never thought was even possible. I know, not possible seems to be the running theme for this story.

"Okay. This one's a freebie," the fairy said. "But it'll only last for a few seconds."

"What will?" I asked.

She then took out a tiny magic wand and waved it around before pointing it at me. The only thing I saw come out of it was a little tiny spark.

"There," she said. "Now, bend the bars."

"Are you insane?" I asked. "I can't just-"

"Bend the bars!" she said again in a slightly louder tone.

She was now so adamant that I could do it. However, I thought she was nuts but still had to prove her wrong. So, I immediately grabbed the bars and tried to bend them.

"Holy shit!" I said, shocked.

I shit you not. Whatever she did to me must have given me a short burst of superhuman strength because I pulled those bars apart like they were toothpicks. And once the hole was big enough, she flew right out.

"How did I do that?" I said, staring at my hands in amazement.

"I'm a fairy," she said. "I grant wishes."

"Are you serious?"

"Of course. Why would I-"

But before she even got a chance to finish what she was saying, an electrical pulse shot her down to the ground, leaving her lying there unconscious. I quickly turned to my left, only to see that Slith was no longer camouflaged and was now standing there with his gun pointed directly at me.

"You raise that gun toward me, and you'll be hit with something other than my electrical pulse," he said. "Put your gun down on the ground, and then put your hands over your head."

What choice did I have? I definitely didn't stand a chance against him. So, I merely did as he requested. I laid my gun down on the ground and then put my hands over my head.

"So, you're Sam Watson of Earth?" he said.

"That's what it says on my birth certificate," I replied.

"Do you realize the size of the bounty that's been put on your head?"

"Why don't you enlighten me?"

"Let's put it this way, the Morgidians want that sphere so badly, they're offering a hundred million barcs to anyone who returns it."

"A hundred million barcs?" I asked, my eyes now wide from shock. "Holy shit!"

"They also said that it doesn't matter if you're dead or alive," he explained. "Just as long as they get the sphere back. However, they prefer you dead, so you can't cause any more trouble."

"Again, lucky me."

"That's why you've put me in a tough spot," he continued. "You see, I'm ready to kill you, but I can't do that until you give me the sphere. Now then, I'll ask you again. Where is it?"

"Kiss my human ass!" I replied.

"Funny you should say that. Because by the time I'm done with you, you'll be kissing your own ass."

Now, at that point, I knew that Slith was gonna tie me up and take me and the fairy back to his ship. However, I thought that if I stalled him long enough, Sartia, or someone else, would eventually find and rescue me before he did. Of course, *that* didn't exactly go as planned either. But the outcome, well, let's just say even I was surprised.

"You just wait," I said. "Sartia will find me. And when she does, she'll kill you."

"Ah! The Arnaxian *bitch* that you travel with," he said while nodding. "She doesn't scare me either."

"Hey! She is *not* a bitch."

Of course, with me wording it the way I did, he was easily able to figure something out.

"Oh, I get it," he said with a smile. "You're infatuated with her, aren't you?"

"Hell no. Well, maybe. Just a little," I replied.

"Do you even know who you're traveling with?"

"What do you mean by that?"

He then looked at me like I had two heads or something before getting a look of solid clarity.

"She hasn't told you yet, has she?" he asked.

I was now very curious as to what the hell he was talking about. Of course, with him being a bounty hunter, he'd probably say anything at that point, just to rile me up and give him a reason to shoot me.

"Told me what?" I curiously asked.

"Who her employer is," he replied.

As I've said, up until now, Sartia's only mentioned that someone hired her to come and find me so she could return the sphere. And, of course, as you already know, that's kind of a touchy subject. However, she hasn't said who yet and promised to tell me when the time was right. But, Slith wouldn't just bring that up for no reason, would he?

"She might have mentioned that someone had hired her," I said.

"But she didn't tell you who?" he asked.

"No."

"This sure has taken a turn," he said, stroking the bottom of his chin with his left thumb and pointer finger. "Every bounty hunter in the sector knows who hired her. That's why we're all hunting you."

I was no fool. I could easily see where this was going.

"You wanna collect the paycheck too, don't you?" I asked.

"You're smarter than you look," he said.

"Which means you only need the sphere."

"That's why my employer prefers you dead. They could care less about the both of you. The only thing that matters to them is the sphere."

Something now didn't add up. Why would someone hire Sartia to find me, and at the same time, make a request to keep me alive so she could bring me home in one piece? Yet, all the bounty hunters wanna collect the same thing and don't care if she lives or dies? I think there was definitely something else going on that even she didn't know about. And I now felt that it was my duty to find out.

"Enough beating around the bush! Who hired her? Who's her employer?" I demanded.

"This should be fun," Slith said. "The person who hired her is her f-"

But that was all he said. Before he even got a chance to finish his sentence, I heard a muffled gunshot go off, followed by him looking up at his forehead, only to now see a little saw blade sticking out of it. I saw it too, but before he could react and pull it off him, there it went.

It cut right into his head, twisting and turning, going deeper and deeper. He just screamed out in agony, and at the same time, dropped his gun to the ground. A stream of green blood was now pouring out of his forehead, dripping down the center of his face. He just kept on screaming until finally, he stopped, looked at me, and fell forward, hitting the ground like a rock. Someone had to have shot him with my gun. But who? I thought it was Sartia coming to save the day. But when I turned around to see who it was, man was I in for a surprise.

"What the fuck?" I blurted out.

The little, tiny fairy that I had freed from the cage wasn't so little anymore. She was now just a little shorter than me, standing there, holding my gun.

"He had it coming," she said.

With her being so big, I could now see what she really looked like. And she was beautiful.

Her wings were nothing like I expected, though. They were very colorful and looked just like butterfly wings. She had mocha-colored skin, long rainbow-colored hair, bright green eyes, and her outfit was a green dress, very similar to what a Disney princess would wear. Also, her somewhat squeaky voice was now gone, and she sounded just like an ordinary woman.

I then tried to say something to her. But, with me being me, I just fumbled all over the place.

"How did you… but you were… how?" I asked.

"First of all," she said. "Allow me to introduce myself. My name is Fayre, and I come from the planet Faeory."[8]

"But you were small. Now… you're huge!"

"Fairies come in all different shapes and sizes and can also change their own size at will. I chose this size because I thought you would be more comfortable with it."

"Wait a minute," I said, realizing what she just told me. "Fairies? Did you just say fairies? As in, more than one?"

"My planet is home to the fairies," she replied.

---

[8] (Pronounced *Fay-or-ee*)

"Holy shit!"

"Now, about your reward."

"Yeah, about that. When you said I would get a reward for saving you, what exactly did you mean by that?" I curiously asked.

"First of all, who are you?"

"My apologies. My name is Sam."

I then hesitated a little bit before telling her where I was from. But since we were both pretty much in the same predicament, I didn't think it would be all that big of a deal.

"And, I'm from the planet Earth," I added.

"Oh! So, *you're* the Earthling?" she asked.

"You're not gonna kill me or anything, are you?"

She just laughed. "Of course not. I'm no bounty hunter."

"Phew!" I said with a sigh. "That's a relief."

"So, Sam of Earth. Let me tell you how this works. Fairies grant wishes, but only to those who help or do good deeds. And now that you've freed me, you are granted one wish and one wish only."

Immediately after she said that, a lot of things started racing through my mind.

See, we've all dreamt of different things that we would wish for in life: money, power, the ability to fly, and immortality, just to name a few. Of course, my list goes on and on. But to only get one? Well, that's tough. However, I did have a question regarding my wish.

"Even though I only get one wish," I said. "Are there any kinds of limitations on what I can wish for?"

"Just one. You cannot wish for more wishes," Fayre replied.

"That's it?"

"That's it."

"So, you're telling me that I can kill someone, bring someone back from the dead, or even make someone fall in love with me?"

"Correct. Whatever your heart desires, it's yours."

Now *that* was something worth thinking about. There were so many things I've always dreamed of doing or seeing, or even people that I wished were still alive. I definitely wasn't gonna kill anyone, so that was already off the table. But what should I do? Do I become rich and famous? Do I become the strongest person in the world? I had no idea.

"How long is my wish good for?" I asked.

"You may use it whenever you'd like," she said. "Whether it'd be today, tomorrow, or a week from now, it doesn't matter."

"Can I think about it?"

"Take as much time as you'd like."

"Thank you," I responded with a polite nod. "Are you going back to the village?"

"I am."

"Would you like some company?"

"You read my mind," she replied with a smile.

But before we left, I just looked at the dead bounty hunter, now lying there on the ground. As I did, I couldn't help but think, *How many more would I encounter? And, are they all like this one?*

However, I didn't wanna waste a whole lot of time just standing there thinking about it. So, I picked up the bounty hunter's gun and accompanied Fayre through the woods, straight back to the village.

Rob J. LaBelle

Chapter 8

After facing off against a bounty hunter, almost getting killed, and taking a nice, leisurely stroll through the forest, Fayre and I finally made it back to the village.

When we arrived, I decided that the safest place for me to go would be back to Morg's house. I figured we could wait inside until Sartia came back from the hot spring. Plus, Fayre could also get some much-needed rest before she heads back home.

We came walking down the path, and I could now see Morg's house off in the distance. I could also see Sartia waiting outside the door. The closer we got, however, the more I could see that she looked upset.

I don't wanna say that she was crying because I could be wrong, but she definitely didn't look good. She was worried. And she definitely let me know exactly how she was feeling.

Fayre and I were about to enter the short path that led to Morg's house when Sartia spotted us and came running over as fast as she could. I was kinda surprised when she immediately grabbed me and wrapped her arms around me, embracing me with a tight hug. I honestly thought that she was gonna get mad at me or hit me or something.

"Where the hell were you?" she asked. "I was worried something might have happened to you and that I would never see you again."

"You were worried about me?" I curiously asked.

"Of course, I was."

The brief moment of jubilation was cut short not long after she came to her senses and slapped me across my left arm.

"If you *ever* do that again, I'll kill you myself," she said.

Okay. So, she wound up hitting me after all.

"I'm sorry," I said.

She then smiled at me and embraced me with another short hug before letting go. It also didn't take her long to notice who I was with.

"Who's she?" she asked.

I swear to you, at that moment, I could almost sense a hint of jealousy in her voice.

"Oh, sorry," I said. "This is Fayre. She's a fairy."

"I know she's a fairy. Where did you meet her?"

"He rescued me from a Vaknoid," Fayre said.

"Apparently, he was a bounty hunter," I added.

"You rescued her from a bounty hunter? Are you out of your mind? You could've been killed!" Sartia angrily pointed out.

No. She wasn't upset at all.

"I couldn't just leave her there," I said. "Besides, I was granted a wish."

"A wish?" Sartia asked.

"Yeah. Apparently, I get one for-"

"I know how you get one. What I meant was, have you used it yet?"

"Not yet. I'm gonna think about it for a while. Since I only get one, I want it to be perfect."

"You know," Fayre said. "You should give him a lot more credit. He's a brave man."

"Who? Him?" Sartia asked in disbelief, now pointing to me.

"He stood up to the Vaknoid to try and save me."

Of course, with Fayre coming to my defense, I was now smiling from ear to ear while my ego had inflated ten-fold.

"Oh, really?" Sartia said. "And you were able to take him down?"

"Well…" I paused. "I wasn't the one who took him down, per se, but I did help."

She then turned to look at Fayre. "He really helped?"

"He kept the hunter at bay long enough for me to kill him," Fayre said.

"Well then, I guess you proved yourself, didn't you?" Sartia remarked.

"I also took his gun," I added, showing her the weapon.

"Why would you do that?"

"I don't know. I just thought it might come in handy. Either that, or we could sell it for a profit."

"Good thinking."

"Well then, I guess I should get going. It's a long trip back to Faeory," Fayre said before turning toward me. "You were very brave out there, and I can never repay you for saving my life. However, the wish is the best I can do. When you think of something that you really want, come to Faeory and find me. I will then grant to you whatever it is that your heart desires."

She then leaned in and gave me a hug, followed by a kiss on the cheek. As we were hugging, I swear to you, she smelled just like strawberries.

"You're very welcome," I humbly replied. "And thank you. I'll come find you when I'm ready."

"Thanks for taking care of him," Sartia said.

"Anytime," Fayre replied. "He's a good one. Make sure he stays alive."

"You can count on that," Sartia replied before turning to me and smiling.

And with that, Fayre left us and headed back toward the airfield, leaving Sartia and I standing there alone, just staring at each other.

I was feeling good about everything and now had an elated look on my face. She, on the other hand, was still mad that I took off by myself. But, our time on Ckrob was done, as it was now our turn to go.

• • •

We blasted off from the surface, and I just stared out of the cockpit window as the blue and green planet got smaller and smaller. I thought to myself how great it was to enjoy something so far away from Earth but still have it feel like I was home.

We were probably about ten minutes into our flight path away from the planet before Sartia put the ship on autopilot and turned to face me. I could tell, just by the look on her face, that we were about to have a long, overdue chat.

"Look," she began. "I'm really sorry about what happened at the hot spring. I don't think I helped that situation at all, and I know I'm partially to blame for you running out of there like that."

"That was the most embarrassing thing that's ever happened to me," I said. "What did you expect me to do? Look down at my pants and start laughing with everyone else?"

"I didn't realize you felt that way about me."

"You couldn't tell? I mean, how did you not realize that? I thought it was blatantly obvious."

"Well, I mean, I knew that you liked me," she said. "I just didn't know how much."

"Well, now you know."

Then, it went silent as we both sat there quietly, now feeling awkward about the whole situation and not really knowing where we should go from there.

As we were sitting there, though, I thought I could hear some more music coming from within the ship. As it got louder, I then realized it was the theme from *Jeopardy!*. I just bobbed my head back and forth for a few seconds, knowing that it fit the mood perfectly. However, I quickly shook it off after realizing that this definitely wasn't the time for that.

"Seriously?" I asked out loud. "Just turn that shit off!"

Then, the music stopped. I still didn't know where it was coming from, but that didn't matter.

I then remembered something that the bounty hunter told me when we were all alone in the woods. He knew about Sartia's employer, and I also knew that she would tell me about them when the time was right. But why not now? Might as well get it all out in the open.

"So, when I was alone in the woods with Slith," I began. "He started to tell me something that didn't make a whole lot of sense.

"Apparently, he and every other bounty hunter in the sector know who your employer is. But that's not the weird part. He told me that they were also after the hundred million barcs that was being offered for the sphere's return and that they didn't care if we lived or died. Would you care to explain?"

As soon as I finished, she immediately looked over at me. And, let me just say, I have never seen a face filled with more distrust than what hers now looked like. I think I might have touched a nerve with that one. I honestly wasn't sure.

"You still don't trust me, do you?" she asked in a calm yet, disapproving sort of tone.

"Of course, I do," I replied. "But why won't you tell me? What's the big deal?"

But she still didn't say anything. All I knew was that she was hired to find me and the sphere and to return both of us home safely. I just think that if I knew the whole story, I might be able to help her out a little more.

"Look, if we're gonna be traveling together," I said. "I think you owe it to me to tell me the whole story. I haven't hidden anything from you, and after the recent hot spring incident, I definitely have nothing left to hide now. I just wanna know what the fuck is going on."

I also may have gotten just a tad upset.

"And if you won't tell me," I continued. "Then I'll just ride the rest of this trip in the sleeping quarters. Because, frankly, I don't wanna die, or get blown up, or get hunted by intergalactic bounty hunters. I just wanna go home!"

Okay. Maybe I was a little harsh? Maybe I could've worded things a little differently? Maybe I should've just left it alone? Honestly, though, I wasn't gonna ride the rest of the trip in the sleeping quarters, and I definitely didn't wanna go home. However, a little reverse psychology never hurt anyone because, apparently, it worked.

"Do you remember when I told you that the women on our planet were usually forced into a marriage?" she reminded me.

After hearing that, I was now very curious as to where this conversation was suddenly headed.

"Yeah," I replied.

"And, do you remember how I told you that I wasn't promised to anyone?"

"Again… yeah."

"Well… I lied. It's my fiancé."

"Come again?" I asked, making sure I heard her correctly.

"My employer is my fiancé."

Okay. Hold on. Timeout. Flag on the play. Foul. Hooking and all that other shit. Did she just tell me that her employer was her fiancé? Why didn't she just tell me that from the start? That's a pretty big piece of information to withhold from someone.

"Tell me you're joking?" I asked.

"I wish I was," she replied.

"Then why didn't you tell me earlier? If I had known, I wouldn't have tried so hard not to make myself look like an ass in front of you."

"I just didn't think it was relevant at the time. Regardless, it's not what you think."

"Oh yeah?" I then leaned back in my chair, folded my arms, and was now ready to hear her ridiculous excuse. "Then what is it?"

"The only reason why I took this mission was because my fiancé and I struck a deal," she began to explain. "He knew I didn't want to be married to him. So, I proposed that if I brought the sphere back to him safely, then he would call off the wedding, and I would be free to go back home."

After she finally told me what the deal was, I just sat there dumbfounded for a moment, not really understanding what she just said while trying to make heads or tails out of this whole thing.

"However, you're right," she continued. "I should've told you this earlier. I just thought it would've been better if you didn't know."

Come on, this is me we're talking about here. I've never been the type of person to ever hold a grudge in my life. Grudge isn't even a word in my vocabulary.

You see, anytime I've ever been mad at someone or knew that someone had lied to me, yeah, I was pissed off about it. But I never stopped talking to someone or hated someone for it. And I always gave them the benefit of the doubt. I mean, we are only human, well, in this case, humanoid, after all, right?

Besides, the only people I've ever stopped talking to were my ex-girlfriends. But we're not talking about them, so let's just drop it. Okay?

"Eh, don't worry about it," I said. "I completely understand."

"You do?" she asked. "You're not mad?"

"Nah. To be honest, I probably would've done the same thing."

"Thank you for understanding."

We just sat there in more awkward silence for a moment before I continued on with the conversation.

"So, your fiancé… he's a Morgidian?" I asked.

"Soon to be my ex-fiancé, but, yeah," she replied.

"Now, how does that work if you two are in an arranged marriage and someone doesn't wanna marry the other?"

"Well, as it turns out, he doesn't wanna be in an arranged marriage either."

"He doesn't?"

"No. You see," she proceeded to explain. "He was already in love with someone else, but his father didn't approve of her. So, instead, he set him up with me."

"I still don't understand how he can set you free if it's already been arranged?" I asked, still confused.

"Morgidian law states that the women on that planet don't make any money. Only the men do," she replied.

"They're really living in the dark ages, aren't they? But I still don't see how finding the sphere will get you out of the marriage?"

"Well," she continued. "The law states that if any woman set to wed a man is to make any money before, or during a marriage, then that marriage is to become null and void."

"That sounds like a pretty good deal if you ask me."

"Not really. Once the marriage becomes null and void, the woman is to be executed immediately."

Wait a minute, what did she just say? Is she telling me that this trip is a one-way ticket to the promised land? No way.

"Hold on a minute," I said. "So, once you return the sphere, they're gonna kill you?"

"No," she said. "You see, Harok, my fiancé, is going to fix it so that I can leave unharmed."

"Do you really think he'll hold up his end of the deal? And besides, what about me? After hearing that, do you honestly think they're just gonna let me fly all the way back to Earth alive?"

"If Harok holds up his end of the deal, then, yes."

And there it was. The truth was finally out there. And I'm not talking about the end of *The X-Files* either.

After we return the sphere, we were both gonna be able to just walk away and be free, all based on a promise from a man that I've never even met. Yup, that's it then. I was doomed.

"This is why I'm asking you to trust me," she said. "Because I don't wanna see you get hurt either."

"I'm gonna trust you from this point forward," I said.

"Thank you."

As we sat there in awkward silence yet again, one thing still lingered in my mind. And, I probably shouldn't have asked it because it was none of my business, but I did anyway.

"So, if your fiancé was in love with another woman while he was promised to you, how did that work with, well, you know?" I asked.

"You mean sex?" she responded.

"Yeah. You guys didn't..."

"That custom is old-fashioned, and we don't consummate the marriage until after the ceremony. It's against the law to do it beforehand and is punishable by death." She then paused. "But, to answer your question, no. We didn't."

"Thank god," I accidentally blurted out.

As soon as I said that, I immediately looked over at her with wide eyes and my right hand covering my mouth. Apparently, my mouth decided that it wanted to be just a little quicker than my brain.

However, that moment *officially* took over the hot spring incident as being the most embarrassing moment in my life. Well, not really. But it was a very close second.

She didn't say anything either. Instead, she just sat there with an intrigued look on her face, almost as if she was trying to figure out precisely what I meant by saying that. However, after only a few more seconds of contemplation...

"Follow me," she said.

She then got up out of her chair, and I followed suit, wondering where she was now taking me. Why were we leaving the cockpit? What does she have planned?

After a short walk down the corridor, we stopped at her quarters. She pushed the button to the left of her door, and after it swooshed open, we went right inside. I immediately thought to myself, *Why are we in here?* But, of course, I didn't have an answer.

"Have a seat," she said.

After briefly looking around the room, I found that the only place to sit down was on the bed. So, that's where I sat. But she didn't. Instead, she just looked at me.

"Don't move," she said.

She then went behind the bed and over to her armoire so she could open it up. When she did, she took out something that resembled one of those cardboard file boxes you would typically see at a law firm or something. Once she had it, she closed the armoire doors and then came back to stand in front of me.

"I'll be right back," she said.

And with that, she simply smiled at me and left the room as I watched the door close behind her.

I just sat there for what seemed like forever. I had no idea where Sartia went or when she would even return. I only knew that she would eventually come back.

While I waited, I glanced around her room and tried to look at all of the stuff she had on her shelves. Most of the items looked like trinkets and other keepsakes, while a few of the others looked like, well, I don't know what they were. I never bothered to find out either. I also saw Rawr lying down in his little, fluffy cat bed in the corner. *Where was she going? What was she doing?* As those two thoughts ran through my head, I just sat there as clueless as can be.

Now, I'm very hesitant about telling you this next part because it was kind of a personal moment for me. And it's definitely one of those things that should only take place in the privacy of your own home. So, yeah. I think I'm gonna skip it. Anyway…

What's that? You wanna know what happened? Okay. But don't say I didn't warn you.

So, there I was, still sitting on her bed, waiting for her to come back, wondering what the hell she's doing. I must've been waiting for at least 15 minutes before the door to her room finally swooshed open. I looked around and waited for her to come back in, but she didn't. Well, not yet, anyway. And after staring out into the corridor for the next few seconds, that's when it happened.

I heard the sound of a motorcycle, followed by an infamous rock beat, which I recognized immediately. "Girls, Girls, Girls" by Mötley Crüe was now playing throughout the ship.

The song progressed past the opening beat and went into the first riff before the floor in front of me opened up. A silver pole rose from it and stretched all the way to the ceiling. At that point, I couldn't help but wonder why that song would be playing, followed by a rising silver pole. Who the hell would just have a random pole sitting in their ship waiting to be used? I mean, the only time I would ever put *those* two things together would be in a...

I was immediately stopped mid-thought by the song's first two words, followed by Sartia coming back into the room. However, when she did, I took one look at her, and my eyes fell out of their sockets, while my jaw broke as it hit the floor. She was no longer wearing her alien clothing, but instead, she was now wearing a full, black leather get-up. She had on a leather hat, a leather bra, a leather thong, knee-high leather boots, and to top it off, she was carrying a whip.

Holy fucking shit! I thought to myself. *Was this really happening?*

I had to close my eyes and shake my head, just to make sure I wasn't dreaming. When I opened them, there she was, swinging around the pole, just like a stripper would.

Now, let's get one thing straight. Yes, I am a guy, and yes, I do like women. However, I've been to strip clubs before, and after a while, they just got old and never did anything for me anymore. I've always preferred my women to be naked in front of me and me alone. I just think it's more special that way. Plus, I think it amps up the intimacy a little bit. But don't mistake my words because I was absolutely *loving* what she was doing.

Still, there she was, swinging around the pole with the song still blaring throughout the ship, while I just sat there on the bed, watching her, trying not to get too overexcited. I was just totally enamored at the way she moved and how she did it. She definitely moved around that pole like a stripper, but she did it with a little more grace. If that really makes any sense?

Anyway, after a few more seconds of her swinging around the pole, she then made her way over to me. Once she was directly in front of me, she took her left leg and put it up on the bed next to me while her right leg was still planted on the floor. She took the whip and put it around the back of my neck while holding on to each end of it with both hands. She pulled me in, and out, and in, and out, as she thrusted, moved, and grinded away. I won't lie. I was enjoying it. But why she was doing it, I didn't have a clue. That is until she went just a little bit further.

She removed the whip from around my neck and threw it behind her. She then took her right hand, placed it against my chest, and pushed me backward onto the bed before crawling up there and traversing me while still on her hands and knees.

She made her way up to my face and looked at me. As I looked back at her, I could see something in her eyes. It was a look that I hadn't seen yet during this trip and definitely a look that I've seen in other women before. I knew what was about to happen, and before I even got a chance to react, that's when she leaned down and started kissing me. Her soft lips touched mine, and I could instantly feel myself sink into the cloud-like mattress we were lying on.

As we were kissing, she slowly started to lower herself down on top of me. Once her body was pressed fully against mine, I could immediately feel how warm it was. I couldn't help myself and wrapped my arms around her to hold her as close to me as possible.

At that exact moment, the song that was blaring throughout the ship had stopped and was no sooner replaced by a different song, one that fit the current mood a little better.

"Girls, Girls, Girls" was gone, and "Faithfully" by Journey was now playing instead. As soon as I heard the change, I stopped kissing her to look around the room, as I was still curious about the mystery music and where it was coming from. But she didn't care. She took her right hand, put it on the left side of my face, and directed my lips toward hers once again. However, after a few seconds of action, I stopped. Not necessarily because I wanted to, but because something inside of me told me to.

After hearing her story about how anyone having sex before marriage is punishable by death, that really started to make me think about what that meant for me and my current position. Literally.

"Hold on a second," I said, immediately putting a stop to the passion.

"What's wrong?" she asked.

"Well, since we're about to do what I *think* we're about to do, how will this affect me personally? Cause', frankly, I don't wanna die."

"What the hell are you talking about?"

"I can't stop thinking about what you said," I started to explain. "You know, the whole death before marriage part? If someone finds out what we're about to do, does that mean I'll get executed as well?"

"Look, Sam, you have nothing to worry about. As far as I'm concerned, this…" she said, motioning to the both of us with her left pointer finger. "Never happened."

I took a second to think about that before shrugging. "I can live with that."

"But, if by some chance they do happen to find out what we did, then we're both dead."

"Wonderful," I responded with an eye roll.

"And that's why we have to get the sphere back first. Once Harok has it, that's it. I'll be free from that arrangement, and then it won't matter what we did."

It's true. I definitely didn't wanna die over something as stupid and ridiculous as adultery. Although it would be an excellent way to go.

But, she was right. If her fiancé holds up his end of the bargain after we return the sphere, it won't matter what we did. However, with the Morgidians and bounty hunters currently hunting us, there was a strong possibility that this would be my one and only shot with her.

So, with that being said, what would you have done? Probably the same thing I did.

"You're right. Fuck it," I said, pulling her lips back down toward mine and continuing on.

The kissing soon became hot and heavy, and, well, you can pretty much figure out what happened next on your own. And no, I don't care how much you beg me. I'm not giving you any details. That's personal. Besides, this ain't no erotic thriller.

Although I could write one about the stuff we did on this trip. But that would be an additional book and a half. Plus, I would need an entirely different audience, and this definitely… wait a minute, what the hell am I saying? Instead, I'll just skip ahead to the part *after* we were finished.

Sometime later, we were now both lying in her bed, cuddling with each other underneath the blankets. I was still thinking about what had just happened and couldn't stop thinking about it. I mean, of all the people in the world, well, humans anyway, I kept thinking to myself that I was the first human in history to ever have sex with an alien from outer space. I did wind up asking her about it later, and of course, I was right. However, now that we've done the deed, I was still curious about her situation and what that now means for her and her arrangement.

"So, what happens now?" I asked.

"What do you mean?" she replied.

"I mean, now that we've slept together, and other than my possible death, how does that affect the current situation with your fiancé?"

"It doesn't. Harok's free to see whoever he wants."

"But what about me?"

"What about you?"

Apparently, she's not listening to a damn thing that I'm saying.

"What's gonna happen to me? I mean, once the mission's over, then what?" I asked.

"I'll have no choice but to bring you home," she replied.

"Why can't I stay out here with you?"

"I don't know if you remember me saying this, but no one is allowed off of Earth unless it's absolutely necessary. I wish you could stay out here with me, but you can't. I'm sorry."

Yeah. Unfortunately, I do remember her telling me about that near the beginning of the trip. I really hated that that was a law out in this sector because now, I kinda wanted to stay.

I didn't wanna go back home to Earth and live my old life. Would I miss my friends and my family and my job? Of course, I would. But to be out here amongst the stars was a once-in-a-lifetime opportunity. I didn't wanna just give it all up on account of a rule, or law, or whatever the reason was. Besides, I was really starting to like Sartia. I mean, *really* starting to like her.

And that's where my dilemma officially began. Not because we just had sex, either. (Although, that was pretty fuckin' good.) No. I really liked her personality. She was very kind and generous, and I could tell that she had almost the same sense of humor. Even though we were from two different galaxies, we actually had quite a bit in common.

I was now thinking about telling her how I felt and everything that I pretty much just told you, but I was afraid that if my feelings came to the surface, she'd shoot me down. But, you have to take chances in life, and this was one of those times I definitely had to try.

"Look, I know I haven't been out here that long, and we've only known each other for a few days," I began. "But I like you. A lot! And, call me crazy, but I don't wanna go back home. I wanna stay out here with you. I wanna continue visiting other worlds and seeing the stars with you."

"Sam," she said, using a sincere tone. "I-"

And that's when the alert started beeping up in the cockpit. It wasn't the attack kind of alert. It was more of an approaching planet type of alert.

"I'm sorry," she said. "But this'll have to wait."

She then got up out of bed, got dressed, and immediately made her way to the cockpit.

"Dammit," I whispered.

I was now ever so curious as to what she was gonna say. I mean, I would eventually find out, just not then. Besides, since we were now coming up on a new planet, I had to get up and get myself dressed as well. Also, this next planet, well, I can't even put into words how awesome it was. Or ridiculous. It doesn't matter.

The one thing I do know, however, is that between every place I visited and everything that happened to me throughout this whole trip, this one planet and everything on it was definitely, without a doubt, the highlight of my trip.

Chapter 9

Since we're now approaching a different part of the story, I think I should share one last piece of info about myself that I haven't told you yet. Another reason why I was ridiculed and picked on when I was younger (and this is a big one) was because of my music choice. As if the glasses weren't enough, my different taste in music really set it over the top.

I was never really into anything that came out beyond the mid-'90s. To me, when grunge was introduced, that was pretty much the end of music as we knew it. Now, I'm sorry if I've offended you and your love of grunge or any of the other shitty music that came out following that, but let's face facts here. It just plain old sucked. Well, minus a few current bands that I listen to.

Don't get me wrong, I was definitely into all kinds of rock, hip-hop, and pop music. But nothing sounded even remotely close to the decade of decadence. That's right. My favorite type of music came out in the 1980s.

Again, I was always different when it came to liking the same things that other people liked, and my music was a big one. That's another reason why I wasn't dancing at Alice's party. The type of music they were playing was definitely not my thing. Also, I don't dance. I mean, I can slow dance, but when it comes to shakin' my booty, I'm as white as they come.

Anyway, I loved every aspect of the 1980s: the music, the games, and the clothing. It was all different, and to me, it seemed like people had the most fun during that decade. I mean, come on. Look at the world now. How can you argue with that?

Okay, enough of my digression. Let's just get back to the story.

As soon as I got dressed, and after thinking about how the planetary alert couldn't have happened at a more shitty time, I made my way back up to the cockpit to see what the deal was.

"What's going on?" I asked.

"We're approaching Planaties,"[9] she said.

"Planaties? What the fuck kind of a name is Planaties?"

"I wouldn't be so harsh. When we get down there, you may never wanna leave."

The planet we were approaching had one of the best themes and civilizations I've ever seen. It was a theme that I never thought would ever exist again in my lifetime or all the way out there, for that matter.

---

[9] (Pronounced *Plan-eighties*)

Let's put it this way… once we landed and I was able to take a look around, I knew that if I were to ever move out there, that place would be my new home.

As we were now orbiting the blue and green planet, I thought to myself, *Thank god! More grass and water.*

We were waiting for them to clear us for landing, and at the same time, I couldn't help but wonder what exactly was down there. Why would Sartia tell me that I may never wanna leave? What was so special about it? Well, I would soon find out.

"Arnaxian ship, ID number zero six one nine seven nine," I heard a male voice say through the speaker in the panel. "You are now free to land in docking bay Dragon."

Now, there were two things that I noticed while I was listening to him clear us. One, being the name of the docking bay. Dragon? That was an unusual name for a landing port. The second thing I noticed was actually the first thing that caught my attention.

While he was clearing us, I swear to Christ that I could hear music playing in the background over his voice. It was hard to make out, but it sounded a lot like "Master of Puppets" by Metallica. But that's impossible. There's no way that music from Earth could ever make its way out here. Could it?

"Did I just hear-"

"Hold on!" she shouted, interrupting me and taking control of the ship.

As she flew us through the planet's atmosphere and down to the surface, I noticed something about that planet that I didn't notice about any of the other planets we visited. Of course, that was technically only the fourth one I'd been to and the third one I'd be stepping foot on. But the closer we got, the more déjà vu I began to have.

· · ·

We eventually made it down to docking bay Dragon, and before going in, we hovered there for a few minutes until the hangar bay doors were opened.

The docking bay itself was about the size of two football stadiums. The whole thing was silver in color, and it kind of reminded me of a domed playing field with one of those retractable roofs to let in sunlight when need be.

After the doors opened, we slowly began to descend until we touched down on the cement-type floor. Once Sartia turned off the engines, our harnesses retracted, and then it was on to the usual protocol. We got up out of our seats and went over to the side door, where she then pushed the button to open it up. Once it was open, we went down the retractable ramp and waited for our emissary to arrive.

The inside of the hangar looked exactly like one of those airplane hangars that you would see on an airfield. Except, instead of being filled with planes, that one was filled with spaceships.

While we stood there and waited, I couldn't help but wonder why Sartia would say I might never wanna leave this place because I hadn't really seen anything yet that would make me wanna stay. Of course, we were only still in the hangar bay. But when our emissary came up to greet us, I took one look at her, and *that* was my first clue.

Our female emissary had parakeet green colored skin. (Yes, parakeet green is a color. Look it up.) She also had long, black hair that was teased to high hell, lime green colored eyes, big hoop earrings, and underneath her black outfit, which was very reminiscent of what a stewardess would wear, I could see some of her tattoos.

"Holy shit!" I immediately blurted out.

"Welcome to Planaties!" the emissary said. "My name is Sheila. What's the purpose of your visit here?"

Whoa! Hold on. Timeout. Did she just say her name was Sheila?

"Hi, Sheila," Sartia said. "We're here strictly for pleasure. But while we do enjoy ourselves a bit, why don't ya give this thing a once over for me?"

"You got it!" Sheila excitedly replied.

Now, doesn't that seem a little weird to everyone? I mean, how in the hell was I eons away from Earth yet, I run into an alien who goes by the name of Sheila?

"Excuse me," I said to her. "But, um, Sheila? You said your name was Sheila?"

"That's me. Why? Do I know you?" she asked.

"Highly doubtful."

She shrugged. "Okay, then. Please, follow me."

Sheila then led us away from the ship and through the hangar bay toward the exit.

Since the hangar itself wasn't very big, it took us no time at all to get through the security checkpoint, which looked exactly like one of those security checkpoints you would go through at an airport.

Once we left the building and made it outside, we stopped and were now standing on a sidewalk. As a matter of fact, I took one look around, only to realize that we were now standing in the middle of a fucking airport, just like you would see on Earth. The cars themselves also looked just like the cars back home, except for two slight differences.

First, they all looked like they were older cars ripped straight from the 1980s. Second, they were all hovering. At that point, I thought I was losing my mind. Either that, or someone had drugged me, and this was all just a very lucid dream. However, just to make sure, I closed my eyes and shook my head before reopening them. Yeah. No such luck.

There were valets, aliens of all kinds, taxi cabs, shuttle buses, and everything else you would find while driving aimlessly around an airport looking for a parking spot.

After seeing all that, only one question was now racing through my head. *How the hell does this look exactly like an airport on Earth? Especially way out here.*

While trying to figure everything out, I heard Sheila whistle, and when she did, a hover cab came right over and was now parked directly in front of us. It was yellow in color and looked just like a cab you would see in New York City. I mean, seriously. How was this even happening?

"Here's your cab," Sheila said.

"Thank you," Sartia replied.

Sheila then handed us both a little black box, which looked just like an old-fashioned beeper.

"Take these," she said. "If you need anything at all, feel free to give me a buzz."

Give her a buzz? Really?

"Will do," Sartia said before getting in the back seat of the cab.

But I hesitated before getting in.

I don't know. I think it was the shock of seeing it all go down, but knowing damn well that I wasn't even close to home. Not by a long shot.

So, without saying anything, I got in the back seat of the cab and closed the door. When I did, the chubby, green-skinned male cab driver, with a messed up shave and spiky hair, hoarsely asked us where we wanted to go.

"Where are we off to?" he asked.

"Take us to the nearest pizza joint," Sartia said.

"You got it."

And just like that, the greased stained, tank top wearing cab driver hauled ass out of the airport and headed straight for the neighboring city.

• • •

On the way to, where ever it was that we were going, I just hung myself out of the window like a dog going for a car ride. That planet had buildings, cars, outlet stores, movie theaters, electronics, bowling alleys, and everything else Earth would have to offer. But how? How the hell did all of that stuff get way out there? *That* was the déjà vu I was having, and I couldn't wait for Sartia to explain everything to me.

After about another 15 minutes in the cab, we finally arrived at our destination… Tony's Pizza and Subs.

Yeah, I know. But we'll get to that soon enough.

We both got out of the cab, but not before Sartia paid our fare. Once we were settled, the cab driver immediately took off.

So, there we were, standing on the sidewalk in the middle of a city, just like you would see on Earth, with all kinds of aliens walking around and doing their everyday thing.

The main species on that planet were the Planatians.[10] They all had different shades of green skin, different hair colors, different eye colors, and about 80 percent of the population had tattoos. I just stood there in absolute shock. I mean, could it be? Is it possible that a whole planet's evolution and civilization was based on a decade that ended many years ago on Earth? I just couldn't wait to find out.

---

[10] (Pronounced *Plan-at-ee-ans*)

"Before we go in," I said. "What is this place exactly? And more importantly, where the hell are we?"

"Let's go inside, and I'll tell ya," she replied.

So, without further ado, we walked right through the front doors and straight into Tony's Pizza and Subs.

• • •

When we got in there, my eyes bugged out, and my jaw hit the floor before I was able to collect myself and sport the biggest Cheshire grin that anyone could ever have.

Sartia then turned to me and smiled. "Sam, welcome to Planaties. Also known around the sector as Planet Eighties."

The pizza joint itself was about the size of a bowling alley, with the front half being where everyone ate their food and the back half being an oversized arcade. There was also a jukebox in the far right corner blasting "Funky Cold Medina" by Tone Loc.

The pizza part of that place looked just like any old pizza place. The only difference was the style of clothes that everyone was wearing. To me, it was almost as if someone had ripped a photograph straight out of a book dedicated to the 1980s and placed it directly in front of my face.

The back half was filled with all kinds of '80s style stand-up arcade games. When I looked at all of the kids playing them and how they were dressed, it was almost like

I was watching those arcade scenes from *Wargames, The Karate Kid,* or even *Terminator 2.*

Okay. I know *Terminator 2* wasn't an '80s movie, but I liked the reference.

Anyway, they had all kinds of games in there, ranging from *Asteroids* and *Centipede* all the way up to *Pac-Man* and *Zaxxon.* They even had those old-fashioned cocktail arcade tables for people to sit down at and play while they ate.

"Oh my fucking god!" I said out loud. "Call me Eddie Money because I just got two tickets to paradise!"

"Told ya you might never wanna leave," she said.

"How is this even possible?"

"Why don't we order a pizza, and I'll tell you?"

"Yeah. Let's do that," I said, still looking around in shock.

We then went left and made our way over to the counter to check out the menu. The green-skinned teenager working back there had a blonde mullet for hair and definitely sounded like a surfer dude.

"Welcome to Tony's," he said. "Like, what'll it be?"

I perused the menu a bit before turning to Sartia and asking what she likes.

"Have you ever even had pizza before?" I asked.

"This'll be my first time," she said. "Just get what you want, and I'll try it."

"Okay. Well, in that case…" I said before turning back to the kid behind the counter. "We'll have a large pizza with pepperoni, mushrooms, and garlic."

"Nice choice," he said. "Anything else?"

"Oh, and uh, two large sodas."

"Done. That'll be twelve barcs."

"Twelve barcs?" I asked out loud. "That's it?"

"Not so loud, dude. People are trying to enjoy their pies."

Even though the term is still somewhat used today, that was the first time in a long time I've ever heard someone refer to a pizza as a pie.

Also, just by how he talked and moved, the kid behind the counter sort of reminded me of Sean Penn's character, Jeff Spicoli, from the movie *Fast Times at Ridgemont High.* I'm just glad it wasn't him, though, because that would've been really weird.

Sartia then paid for the pizza, and we both sat down in a booth while we waited for it.

"How is everything so cheap?" I asked.

"When you're on a planet that lives in the eighties, you get eighties prices," she replied.

"This is insane. I mean, how is all of this even possible?"

"I had a feeling you'd ask that," she said.

She then proceeded to tell me the history of not only that planet but some more history about her own planet as well.

"Remember how I told you that people on Earth have come in contact with some of us before?" she began. "Well, I'm not the first Arnaxian to visit Earth.

"You see, pretty much ninety percent of all the aliens that have been to Earth were Aranxian. Because we have the ability to shapeshift, we can make ourselves look like a human, and no one would ever know. That's what happened with Omra Surcy. Or, as he was known on your planet, Bill.

"Omra landed on Earth in the year nineteen eighty," she continued. "So he could live there for ten years and study your planet's customs. It was all purely a scientific research mission. And after his ten years were up, he returned home with tons and tons of information regarding Earth's lifestyle, music, movies, electronics, food, politics, and pretty much everything else that the decade had to offer.

"He had so much of it stored in a memory box that he couldn't wait to start building and sharing it with our own species. The problem was, it was way too much to do on our own planet. So, he was granted leave to find a suitable planet and species to share it with. That's when he landed here.

"Apparently, the Planatians loved his ideas so much that they gave him full power to do whatever he wanted. So, he started to build up the planet and eventually turn it into what you see today."

After hearing her story, I honestly couldn't tell if she was yankin' my crank or not. I mean, was she for real? Did all of that really happen? After looking around at everything in that place, I had no choice but to believe her.

"Let me get this straight," I said. "An Aranxian took information off of Earth and built all of this in under three decades? What were these people doing before he arrived here?"

"They were kind of in a state of flux," she replied. "I mean, they had cities and vehicles and everything else. It's just that the planet itself was only a couple hundred years old at the time, and they didn't really know which direction their society was headed."

Just then, the pizza guy behind the counter came over to us and placed our pizza and sodas down on the table.

"One large pie and two large sodas," he said. "Enjoy."

After he took off, we were now left with this really good-looking pizza, sitting on our table, just staring us in the face.

"Well, that story seems like complete nonsense to me," I said. "However, looking around at this place, it's kind of hard for me not to believe it."

And with that, I grabbed a piece of pizza off of the tray before taking one long whiff of it. It smelled just like the pizza back on Earth, and man, was I drooling.

Could it be? I mean, aside from the decade it's based on, is it possible that this planet had everything I missed about being so far away from home? There was only one way to find out.

So, with every inch of excitement that I had, I opened my mouth really wide and took my first ever bite of alien pizza. And holy shit, was it good. The pepperoni, mushrooms, and garlic all hit my taste buds at once. I just couldn't believe it. I was so far away from home yet, somehow, I felt like I *was* home.

Sartia didn't eat any of her pizza right away, but instead, she just stared at me with a smile on her face while I wolfed down my first couple of slices.

We spent the next three hours in that joint, eating pizza, drinking soda, listening to awesome '80s tunes, and playing the arcade games. Of course, the first one I played just happened to be my favorite arcade game of all time… *Double Dragon.*

Up until now, I've had almost every iteration of the original arcade game that you could possibly think of… sort of.

I owned the original three games for Nintendo, *Battletoads/Double Dragon,* and *Super Double Dragon* for Super Nintendo, plus the app for your mobile device. And finally, the classics of the first two arcade games I bought for my PlayStation Four. Nah. I wasn't a fanboy or anything. Also, it's the only game I've ever played that I beat with just a single quarter.

Anyway, after I had finished playing almost every video game in there, and after showing Sartia how fun playing video games actually was, we left Tony's Pizza and Subs behind as we got into a cab and headed even further into the city.

• • •

A few miles in, we stopped at a local nightclub called Whiskey Shots, and when we did, I couldn't believe how long the line was outside to get in. The only time I had ever seen lines that long to get into any nightclub was if a washed-up band was playing while trying to make some kind of triumphant comeback. However, I didn't care. Seeing that was just awesome.

It was definitely one of the more popular nightclubs in town because we stood in line for what seemed like forever. But, in all reality, it was only about an hour.

We made it past the bouncer at the door who, I shit you not, because the species on that planet was green, looked just like the Incredible Hulk, minus the hair. That guy was huge and stood about six feet, five inches tall. He had massive muscles, long, light green hair pulled back in a ponytail, green eyes, and a chiseled chin.

As soon as we passed him and finally made it into the club, the first tune that I heard, again, I recognized immediately. I looked down on the dance floor to see everyone dancing while "Obsession" by Animotion was blasting over the club's sound system.

"Holy shit! Check out this fuckin' place!" I shouted over the noise.

I was just floored at how awesome it all was. Because that place had so many neon lights in it, almost everybody in there was wearing sunglasses. The disco ball over the middle of the dance floor shined down on all the dancers, while each square they danced on lit up so that when people moved on them, they changed colors.

The bar was off the right of the club, while a lounge area with chairs, circular tables, and booths was off to the left. In the front of the club was a stage with band equipment set up on it. It was comprised of two guitars, a bass guitar, a microphone stand, and of course, my personal favorite, a drum set. It literally looked like I had just stepped through a portal and traveled back in time.

Jean jackets, ripped jeans, shiny shirts, baggy pants, tattoos, gold chains, 1980s style sneakers, big hair, and almost everything else you could think of about that period made up the dress code of nearly everyone in there. I was in my element. I knew that I could go in there, walk around, and enjoy myself without getting ridiculed by my friends and other people. And, seeing as how I was the only human in there, well, that made it even better.

"Wanna get a drink?" Sartia asked.

"Sounds good," I replied.

We immediately went to our right and headed straight for the bar. The female bartender working back there had blue eyes and teased red hair that almost touched the ceiling. Her outfit was comprised of a pair of Daisy Duke shorts and a top that looked very reminiscent of a denim bra.

"What are ya drinking?" she asked us.

But because I didn't know what they had to offer, I just looked over at Sartia and shrugged my shoulders, knowing that she would be able to order something good for me. She just gave me a little devious smile before turning back to the bartender.

"Two of the same mixed drinks, please," she said. "Something fruity."

"You got it," the bartender replied before turning around and getting our drinks in order.

While we waited, I turned around to face the dance floor and do a little 'people' watching. No sooner did I turn around, the previous song had ended, and Wang Chung's "Everybody Have Fun Tonight" came on immediately after it.

It only took a couple more seconds before the bartender came back to give us our drinks. When I grabbed mine, I looked at the blue liquid inside the glass and wondered what the hell it could possibly be. Out of the corner of my eye, I could now see Sartia grinning and snickering to herself as I just stared at this thing, wondering if it was gonna kill me or not.

"Will you just taste the damn thing?" she ordered.

She was right. I had to let loose a little and stop being so paranoid. So, I took a deep breath, followed by a small sip.

"Holy shit!" I said. "This is really good!"

"Have I steered you wrong yet?" she asked.

I didn't give her a verbal response, but instead, I just shook my head while I continued to suck down my drink. To me, it kind of tasted like a Blue Hawaii. But who was I to argue about something that tasted so good?

With our drinks in hand, we went up to the railing and stood there, so we could watch over everybody and have a good time in the process.

Also, just in case you were wondering, the dance floor itself was lower than where we were currently standing. About five or six stairs led down to it in three different places: the bar area, the front entrance area, and the lounge area. That place was amazing, and it was everything you could've hoped for if you enjoyed that sort of thing. But absolutely nothing could've prepared me for what happened next.

In the blink of an eye, the music stopped, and the lights went down. Darkness immediately overtook the place while the crowd erupted in loud applause and cheer. And I, myself, was now curious as to what was going on.

Now, I've been to plenty of clubs in my life, and I'm smart enough to know that when the music stops and the lights go down, the hired band for the evening usually comes out on stage. But who was it? Did this planet have their own version of '80s bands that frequently played the clubs? Yes and no.

When the lights came back on, the band was now on stage, ready to play, and the crowd got even louder as the lead singer stood there with his arms stretched out, a microphone sitting in his right hand, and his head tilted toward the sky. I immediately had to do a double-take because I could've sworn that I'd seen those guys before. Well, not in concert, but I've definitely seen them in photos.

With his long, black curly hair and black top hat, the guitar player started playing his guitar. The opening riff was now blasting through the speakers, and I instantly recognized it as the opening riff to "Sweet Child O' Mine" by Guns N' Roses. Hearing that and looking back at those guys on the stage, that's when I put two and two together. The band not only sounded like the band back on Earth, but they also looked like them too.

Since 90 percent of all the music and movies on that planet had come from Earth, the actual actors and musicians only existed on TV and the radio. However, that place literally took it to the next level. Basically, they were a glorified tribute band. If the members of Guns N' Roses had cloned themselves and dyed their skin green, that's exactly what you would get.

At the same time, I was now ecstatic and shocked at how awesome those guys were. It was like I was actually watching them live in concert... sort of.

They also had the lights, the fire, the girls, and the whole shebang that an '80s rock show would have. A whole planet that dedicated itself to Earth's 1980s? Oh yeah. I was home. And I never wanted to leave. I mean, we still had to return the sphere to the Morgidians. But for now, I was home.

• • •

After the band finished their night, Sartia and I left the club and decided to hail a cab. This was when the night took an unusual turn because I don't remember much of anything after I got in the back seat. I think I may have had one too many blue drinks. Who knows?

Now, the weird thing is, I was drinking all night long and hadn't felt a damn thing. It was probably the alien alcohol that did it to me. It was almost like when the drinks stopped entering my system; that's when the alcohol took effect. It was pretty weird, but then again, I wasn't on Earth.

The rest of my night there was pretty much a blur, and I only know how it went on account of what Sartia told me. She claims that once we got in the cab and the alcohol started to take effect, I completely lost it. And by 'completely lost it,' she meant that I found everything funny, laugh for no particular reason, act like the Joker kind of lost it. And because of my condition, she thought it'd be best if we got a hotel room for the night. So, we did.

When we got to the hotel, and because of her superior strength, she carried me from the cab all the way up to our room. She also had a little help from the elevator as well.

Anyway, after we got in the door, she threw me onto the bed because I was already out. Or, at least, that's what she told me. The last thing I remembered before waking up the next morning was getting into the cab. But, that was it. I was done.

• • •

When I finally woke up the following morning, I had the biggest headache ever. Sartia must've known that would've happened because when I opened my eyes and sat up in the bed, she was already standing next to me, waiting there, holding a glass of water in one hand and some type of alien Advil in the other. To top it off, she had the biggest smile on her face.

"Good morning, sunshine!" she said, just a little too perky.

"What the fuck happened?" I asked with a groan.

"Here," she said, handing me the water and medicine. "Take this."

I immediately took it from her and downed it as quickly as possible before putting the glass down on the table beside the bed.

"You passed out," she added.

"I did?" I asked.

"You did. And you were hysterical."

"Oh man," I groaned while closing my eyes and holding my head. "I didn't do anything too embarrassing, did I?"

"Nothing I couldn't handle," she replied. "What's the last thing you remember?"

"Well, I remember getting into the cab with you, and now I'm here."

"So, you don't remember throwing up down in the lobby or us having sex like animals?"

"Wait, what?"

She laughed. "I'm only kidding," she said. "We didn't have sex like animals."

"Damn," I replied, disappointed that it didn't happen.

"But you did throw up in the lobby."

"Damn! Look, I'm sorry about that. I didn't mean for that to happen."

"Don't worry about it. We didn't know that would happen to you."

"Well, we do now."

Then, it was quiet. I just sat that there for the next few moments, thinking about everything she just told me while realizing how much of a possible asshole I was.

"Damn!" I said again out loud.

"Look," she said, taking a seat on the bed next to me. "Like I said, don't worry about it. We've all done some stupid shit that we're not proud of in our lives."

"Yeah, well, this is a first for me."

"You mean to tell me you've never been drunk before?" she asked, now looking at me as if I had two heads or something.

"Not to the point of passing out. I mean, with you around, I'm trying my hardest not to make an ass of myself. Or, did you not catch that during our previous discussion on the ship?"

"No, I did. But I still wanna know why?"

Man, was this woman thick. If she couldn't figure it out by now, then I couldn't help her. Regardless, even though she already knew I liked her, I didn't want her to know how much I *actually* liked her.

I don't know. For some reason, me telling myself that in my head made me seem like a desperate fool or something. But by that point, there was really no other way to explain it. Honestly... I think I was in love with her.

But that possibly couldn't be the case, could it? I mean, I've only known this woman for a few days now. Was it love at first sight? Did our auras match? Were our souls intertwined with each other from the moment we met? Or was it just destiny? It didn't really matter what it was.

So, once again, I beat around the bush and only told her what I wanted her to hear.

"Yeah," I said. "I just didn't wanna make a fool of myself. That's all."

Of course, I could now see it written all over her face. She knew that my answer was the biggest load of bullshit she's ever heard. But, for some strange reason, she decided not to press the issue.

"I don't blame ya," she said.

You know, it was weird. As we were sitting there in that room, I took a look around and thought that it was so odd to see a hotel room that looked exactly like a hotel room back home. Yet, there I was, five million light-years away, and it felt like I never left.

"Besides," she continued. "You don't have to worry about what happened last night."

She then put her left hand on my right cheek, turned my now sad-looking face toward hers, smiled, and kissed me.

Again, her lips were so soft and sweet that I wanted to stay there and kiss her forever. But I couldn't help but wonder why she would wanna kiss me, as I haven't even had time to brush my teeth yet? Plus, I threw up. Gross.

After a couple of seconds, she let go of me.

"I still like you and think you're cute," she added before smiling again.

And, that was that.

She got up off of the bed and went straight into the bathroom, closing the door behind her.

Chapter 10

Headaches, hangovers, alien coffee, alien alcohol, nudist hot springs, heated cats, and sex. What a story this was all gonna be when I got back home. Yeah, right. Like I said before, no one would ever believe me. They'd just think I was nuts. And that's only the beginning. Because we're now about halfway through this story and still have plenty to go.

Look, there's no need to cry about it. The story's not that bad. Besides, I can guarantee you more action, more shooting, and more aliens from this moment on. Well, to a point. But you're stuck listening to me no matter what. So too bad.

I'll save you the boring part of us leaving the hotel, getting in the cab, going into the hangar, getting on the ship, and me crying because I didn't wanna leave in the first place. So I'll just skip straight ahead to when we were back up in space, headed toward our next destination.

The ship was on autopilot, Sartia was up in the cockpit looking over some star charts, and I was in the bathroom, puking my guts out. It must've been the combination of me being queasy and being up in space all at the same time. Who knows? But, at least my headache was gone.

After ten minutes of puking up blue liquid and ten minutes of dry heaving, I washed my hands and my face and then brushed my teeth before returning back up to the cockpit. Once I finally slumped down in the chair, Sartia looked over at me, and when she did, I could tell by the look on her face that she was trying as hard as she could not to laugh.

"You don't happen to have a breath mint, do you?" I sheepishly asked.

"Sorry, I'm fresh out," she replied. "I used the last of them when I drank myself to death on a different planet."

If she wasn't laughing before, she was definitely laughing now.

"Ha-ha. Very funny," I said.

I just glared at her intently for the next few seconds until she finally stopped laughing.

"Are you done?" I asked.

"I'm sorry," she said. "You're right. It's not funny."

"Thank you."

"It's fucking hilarious."

And there she went again, having an even bigger laugh at my expense. I'll tell ya, there was no quit in her.

You know, it's funny. If it were one of my friends, and that happened to them, I'd be doing the exact same thing she was doing to me. And you know what? I didn't even hate her for it. As a matter of fact, it made me like her even more. We really were like two peas in a pod.

"Okay. I'm not mad," I said. "Just get it *all* out now while you can."

Apparently, that made her laugh even harder. Of course, it was one of those moments where you realize that you've made a complete ass of yourself before thinking about one of your friends doing the exact same thing. With that in mind, I eventually broke down and started laughing with her.

Oh, admit it. You would've laughed too.

But, after a good, solid minute of laughing, we both stopped to catch our breath.

"You really are something, Sam Watson," she said.

"I am?" I asked. "You really think so?"

"Of course. It's just too bad I gotta bring you home when this is all done."

It was at that moment, I could sense the sadness in her voice.

"Yeah, about that. Why can't you come with me?" I asked.

"Where? Back to Earth?" she replied.

"Yeah. You're a shapeshifter. You could just make yourself look like an Earthling and live a normal life with me."

"I don't think you fully understand how that works. I can't just turn into a random person. I can only turn into someone I've seen."

"Oh, that's right. I forgot about that. So, if someone sees you as a human and then sees whoever you're turned into somewhere else, they'll start to ask questions."

"Correct."

Well, I guess that idea went totally out the window.

"What about my wish?" I asked.

"What about it?" she replied.

"Other than extra wishes, I can use my wish for anything I want."

Of course, she's no fool and immediately realized what I was getting at.

"No, Sam. Don't use your wish on me," she said. "I want you to use your wish for something that you want."

"What if I wanted you?"

When I asked her that, she didn't answer me back. Instead, she just looked at me, wide-eyed. I think she was both shocked and surprised by the fact that I wanted to use my wish to keep us together. However, that brief moment didn't last much longer.

"No," she said while shaking her head and coming to her senses. "Do not use your wish on me. Do you understand?"

"Why not?" I asked. "What's the harm in-"

"No! And that's my final answer!"

She then got up out of her chair and stormed off down the corridor. I was now sitting there, wondering why she objected to me using my wish on her. I mean, if that's what

I really wanted, who's to stop me? Besides, it's my wish, and I'll use it for whatever I damn well please.

Anyway, I sat in my chair for a good couple of hours by myself, just staring out the window and daydreaming before the planetary alert started going off. I knew we were approaching another planet, but I wasn't prepared for Sartia not to come back up front and take control. I was now left wondering where she had gone to and if she was okay. But, we were coming up on the planet fast, and I didn't have time to go back and get her. So, it was now my job to be the captain.

I looked down the corridor again to see if she would be coming up front anytime soon. I was hoping that I'd see her walking toward me, ranting and raving about where we were going next. However, when she didn't appear, I quickly jumped into her chair and pushed the button to take the ship off of autopilot. Because the planet was approaching fast, and because I had watched her do it so many times before, I dropped us out of light speed and put my hands on the glowing half orbs so I could pilot that thing myself.

Since I didn't know if the alert was our next stop or not, I figured we could land there anyway and take in some sights. Also, I was hoping that whatever funk she was in, being on a new planet would help her break out of it.

Steering the ship wasn't as hard as I initially thought it would be. It was actually surprisingly simple. While my hands were on the controls, I could guide them to the left, and the ship would go left. If I guided them to the right, the ship would go right. It was basically the same principle for up and down as well. If I moved the controls forward, we would go down. If I pulled the controls toward me, then we would go up. And that's pretty much all I knew how to do. Sartia knew how to do all the fancy stuff, but I still had no clue where the hell she was.

I slowly piloted the ship toward the planet until it was in view. The closer I got to it, the quicker I realized that it wasn't even a planet at all. As a matter of fact, it was a big, giant meteor, and everything it had was built directly inside of it. I had never seen anything like it before. Except for in movies and on TV, of course.

Once we got close enough, I put the ship into orbit and started transmitting our ID codes to the station's controllers. Either that or I sent them a threatening message. Regardless, I would soon find out.

I must've sat there for a good ten minutes, sweating, wondering if I sent them the right information or not, waiting for their response, until finally, they sent one.

"Arnaxian ship, ID number zero six one nine seven nine, you are now free to dock at docking station three," I heard a robotic voice say through the panel.

Apparently, I did send them the correct information. Great. I can now dock at docking station three. But there was just one small, little problem. Where the hell was docking station three? How does Sartia do this and still be able to remember everything? I panicked for but a hot second before remembering that they transmit the docking station's flight path right into the ship's computer, which was then shown to me on the monitor. Oops.

Okay. This was it. Time to see how much I had actually learned from Sartia by watching her fly that thing. Could I do it? Maybe. Will I do it? *That's* the big question.

After looking at the monitor to see where docking station three was, I took the controls and turned left to start my docking run. Slowly but surely, I piloted the ship around to the back of the meteor, where docking station three was located. That place was completely different than the previous three planets I'd been to.

Instead of landing in a field or in a hangar, I had to hold the ship steady so that a big, giant, long, metal square-shaped tube could attach itself to the side of our hull. After it was connected, it would pressurize and get filled with oxygen, allowing me to walk through it and into the station. So, now that you know what I'm up against, back to docking.

After a few minutes, I successfully located docking station three and slowly guided the ship in sideways until the red light on my monitor beeped, letting me know that I was now close enough. I then switched over to hover mode and watched as the tube came straight out from the station before clamping itself to the side of the hull.

Success! I did it. My first successful docking run. Only one question now lingered in my mind, and that was, *Where in the hell was I?*

Now that the ship was docked, my harness retracted, and I got up out of the seat to make my way toward the side door. I briefly stopped at Sartia's room and raised my fist to knock on her door. But, for whatever reason, though, I didn't. Something must've made her mad during our last conversation, but what? I didn't have a clue. However, I was smart enough to know that when a woman wants her space, you give it to her. So, for this stop, I was on my own.

Knowing what lurks out there in wild space, I definitely needed to protect myself. So, I went back to the sleeping quarters to grab my burrower and the gun I took from Slith. Once I was packing, I made my way over to the side door and pushed the button to open it up.

I stepped off the ship and carefully walked a hundred or so feet through the tube until I got to another door. I pushed the button on the right side and watched as it swooshed open. Then, after taking a quick deep breath, I went inside.

• • •

I noticed that I was now standing in some kind of a control room, measuring about 30 feet by 30 feet. Computer equipment lined the entire room, except for three places: the door that I walked through, the door to get out into the hallway, and the window next to the door that allowed you to get into said hallway. No windows were looking out, as everything was done by cameras placed on the outside of the meteor.

Also in the room were two AI-driven robotic controllers who helped land all of the ships, and the emissary, who was waiting for me just inside. That guy was awesome, and I had never seen anyone like him before.

He was about my height, had dark brown skin, white hair, pulled to the middle of his back in a ponytail, bright, white eyes, and he had on a white robe that was tied around the waist with a rope type looking thing. He also had on white sandals to match.

You know, it was funny. The second that I saw him, he almost reminded me of what God would look like. Well, if there really was one. I was never really religious, anyway.

"Greetings," the emissary said with a deep voice. "Welcome to Metoria. My name is Brith. What is the purpose of your visit?"

Well, now that I knew where I was, I just had to figure out who *he* was and what went on there.

"Nice to meet you, Brith," I said. "My name is Sam, and I'm here to have a little bit of fun."

"Well then, you definitely came to the right place. Metoria has everything and more that a trade hub should have."

"A trade hub? What's that?" I curiously asked.

"Hmm... you're not from around here, are you?"

That was a colossal understatement. I shook my head.

"Metoria is a trade hub that specializes in everything," he continued. "When one wants to buy and sell goods, they come here. That's what its main purpose is. However, we do also have other forms of entertainment as well."

"What kind of entertainment?" I asked.

"If you can think of it, then we have it. To an extent."

"To an extent?"

"We're not full scale. Mostly private owned. We have many forms of gambling, all types of food, different kinds of theaters, and even a hotel."

"Ah! I get it," I said while nodding. "Kind of like a mom-and-pop type of place?"

As soon as I said that, he looked at me, almost as if I had two heads.

"Mom and pop?" he asked.

"Never mind," I said.

Now, usually, when we went places, Sartia would purchase everything for me. But how in the hell was I supposed to have any fun if she was absent and I didn't have any money?

"I have a question," I started to ask. "Normally, my captain handles all of the transactions when we go places, but she's a little under the weather and can't make it out this time. If I wanted to buy something, how exactly would I do that?"

"It's quite simple," he said before pulling out one of those little thumbprint scanners that I've seen a few times before. "Place your thumb here."

I put my thumb on the scanner, and after a few seconds, it beeped.

"You're all set," he said. "Your thumbprint is now linked to your ship's ID number. When you want to purchase something, simply scan your thumb, and if the credit associated with the captain of that ship is good, it's all yours."

"That's it?" I asked.

"That's it."

Holy shit. I now had free-roam of the whole station and could purchase anything I wanted. Well, as long as Sartia had the funds to do so. But I couldn't just go on a shopping spree and spend her money on myself, could I? Of course, I could. I just wouldn't go crazy, that's all.

"Thanks for all your help, Brith," I said.

"It was my pleasure," he replied.

I was still curious about him, though. I've never seen his species before and wanted to know a little bit about him and what his kind did. Man, was I in for a surprise.

"So, uh, Brith… I've never met your species before," I began. "Where are you from, and do you specialize in anything?"

"We do. I am a Lith, and my species comes from the planet Hedlit," he replied. "We specialize in making pillows, mattresses, towels, and cleansing paper."

"Holy shit! So you're the ones that make the clouds I've been sleeping on?"

"That is correct," he replied, nodding once.

"Can I take your picture?"

"I don't see why not."

Definitely not wanting to miss this opportunity, I quickly pulled out my phone, turned the camera on, and snapped a photo of us together.

"Thanks!" I said.

"You're welcome," he replied. "Enjoy your time here on Metoria."

"Oh, I plan on it."

He then pulled out a little disc, just about the size of a quarter, and handed it to me. It was also the very same type of disc that Ronak gave me back on Jipduk.

"If you need anything at all," he said. "Don't hesitate to call me."

"You got it," I replied.

Brith then went over and pushed the button to the left side of the hallway door. After it swooshed open, I smiled and nodded at him while he did the same in return. I then stepped out into the hallway before hearing the control room door close behind me.

• • •

So, there I was, all by myself, inside of a trade hub, built into a floating rock. I was now wondering what the hell I was gonna do or where I was even gonna go.

The whole place kind of had that underground bunker, space station kind of feel. You know, where the walls were made of cement, rock, or brick, and the lights lined the middle of the ceiling in a single row. However, I did know two things…

First, I wanted to walk around and look at everything before attempting to do anything. Second, I didn't have a clue as to how I was even gonna get there.

I first looked down to my right, only to see the hallway wrap around and continue on. I then looked down to my left and noticed what I had hoped would be an elevator. So, I made my way down there first.

When I got down there, sure enough, it was an elevator. But as I looked around for any type of buttons to push, I couldn't find any. I just stood there for a few seconds, thinking about how I would get on that thing. And not before long, the answer revealed itself to me.

Once those doors opened, I looked inside and saw a few aliens just standing there, staring at me. I thought about getting in. But before I even got the chance to do so, the doors closed, and the elevator was gone. What the hell? Did I miss it? Did it take off because they were sick of waiting for me? Well, let me tell you…

The elevator system in that place was a button-less one. It would automatically stop at every floor, regardless of who needed to get on or off. The sensors in the doors also worked pretty much the same way. If you stood in between them, they would stay open and wouldn't crush you. If not, they would close. Apparently, I was a little too slow to get on.

When the elevator came back down, the doors opened again. And this time, I got right on. Thankfully, I was all by myself for a couple of floors. That way, I could get used to how the whole thing worked. And man, did it move.

I swear, they must've had some kind of gravity-inducing system in there because at the rate that it went between floors, I should've been either a pancake on the floor or stuck to the ceiling like a piece of gum.

I waited and took a couple of rides up and down the whole thing. That way, I could look out of the floors and see what was there. Plus, it also gave me a little bit of time to converse with the patrons that got on and off as well.

• • •

I finally stepped off the elevator and onto the tenth floor. I only picked that one because that's where most of the aliens were getting off. I just figured that I'd follow the pack. And when I saw what was up there, I was glad that I did.

I stepped off into a giant room that took up the entire floor of the meteor. The middle portion of it was one big, giant gambling ring, while the outside sported other places like restaurants and shops.

Now, remember when I mentioned earlier in this story that I would touch upon some of the things I saw at Jipduk but didn't really get a chance to do? Well, you're about to get a firsthand account of what all of that was really like. See? Told ya the story would be getting good.

As I walked through the middle of the gambling portion of the floor, I noticed that many of the games there were very similar to the games on Earth. They had stuff like poker, roulette, slot machines, and even craps. They also had a few other games that they didn't have back home either. *Those* games, however, were a little more on the barbaric side but still fun to watch.

One of those games that I came across (when translated) was a game called Victory. The premise was pretty simple. You would take one sidearm, which contained about 20 shots, and the contestant would put themselves in an enclosed, 12 by 12, bulletproof glass cage so that the people on the outside could see in and not get hurt. There, the contestant would face off against 15 bloodthirsty creatures that were about the size of rats. They were called roks.

The roks had dark fur, razor-sharp top, and bottom teeth, a pair of snake-like eyes, a tail, no ears, and they all ran about three times as fast as an average rat. Each one of them was knocked out beforehand so that a different colored band could be placed on each of their ankles. They would then be woken up soon after.

Everybody placed their bets on a different color, including the contestant that was inside the glass enclosure. When the bell sounded, the starved roks were released, and then all hell broke loose.

Even though the contestant had more bullets than there were roks, the rodents' size and speed gave them a considerable advantage. It was tough to hit them, and you had to be spot on. Basically, whoever bet on the last color (or contestant) left standing in the enclosure, would win the prize. Again, it was pretty brutal but surprisingly enjoyable to watch. My whole thought about that was if you were stupid enough to even attempt it, you got what was coming to you.

Another game they had (after it was translated) was a game called Mystery Cups. Now, that one was a lot less bloody than Victory, but the consequences were just as severe.

For that game, there were six cups lined up in a row on top of a table. Each one of them was numbered one through six, and each one of them was filled with a mystery liquid. Yeah, you can pretty much tell where this one is going.

Anyway, the only ones who participated in this game were the ones with iron stomachs. Most of the players who played had already built up an immunity to some of the liquid. However, one cup out of the six contained a highly toxic poison. Of course, if you got that cup, there was a zero percent chance of survival, and it was game over.

Mystery Cups had two ways to place your bets: you could either bet on which cup the player would drink, or you could bet on whether the player lived or died. However, if you were lucky enough to win both of the bets, you won big time.

The player would then choose a cup to drink out of. Again, if you had an immunity to them, five out of the six cups would just make you incredibly ill. If not, well, there was definitely more than one way to die in that game.

The last death-defying game that they had was a game called What's in the Box?. That one was still pretty brutal, but in my opinion, it was a lot more fun to watch than the others. It was also a lot harder to win at, as well.

They had a six-foot by six-foot wall, filled with metal boxes, each containing a hole in the middle, kind of like the Dukian torture cubes I saw back on Jipduk. All the holes were covered with a cloth so that the player couldn't see inside them.

Now, I'm pretty sure you could imagine what was in there. They had almost everything in those boxes, ranging from things that could bite you, things that could remove a finger or a hand, things that could inject poison into you and kill you, all the way up to things that weren't even dangerous at all.

On the betting table was a picture of every single cube and what was inside them. The trick was that the boxes on the wall were arranged in no particular order. So you had no idea where any of them were placed. You would then place your bet on whatever box you thought the player would stick their hand into. You could also bet on whether or not the player lived or died. Again, if you were lucky enough to bet on both, you won big.

I was never a big gambler, though. Every time I would go to a casino with my friends, I'd bring about 20 bucks with me to play in one of the dollar slot machines. I refused to play at any of the tables because the one time that I did, it wasn't a pleasant experience. *That* was at one of the blackjack tables.

I was on the far left and just happened to be the very first one to grab a card when you were asked to hit or stay. I knew the rules well and was smart enough to know that if you had at least 17 or higher, it was a good bet to stay. After all, you only needed to beat the dealer, not the other players. However, when I played, I liked to get as close to 21 as possible, even if that meant taking a risk and pissing off the other players because I stole their cards.

So, the first and *only* time that I ever played was also my last. Apparently, pissing people off so I could win was pretty frowned upon. And from that point on, I just stuck to the slot machines.

I decided to try my luck with What's in the Box?. So, I went up to the table and looked at all of the boxes I could possibly bet on. I only wanted to play one game, you know, just to try it out. When I was ready, I looked around for the table master, and when I found him, I was shocked as to who it was. He was an Arnaxian. Up until now, the only Arnaxian I had seen was Sartia.

He stood about six feet tall, and instead of the violet-colored eyes that Sartia had, his were maroon. His purple hair was about five inches long and combed neatly into place. He also wore a black, silk-like shirt with buttons running down its middle, silvery, silk-like pants, and black, flat-footed shoes.

"Place your bets!" he said, using a clichéd game announcer's voice.

"How much is it?" I asked.

"There's a ten thousand barc anti."

"Fuck me! Ten thousand barcs? You've gotta be kidding me!"

Upon hearing my remark, the table master immediately came over to me, leaned in close, and spoke quietly.

"Look, are you gonna bet or not?" he asked, using his normal voice. "We got other people here waiting to play. And, frankly, I don't think you wanna upset them."

I then looked down at the line of aliens, who were all now staring at me, waiting for me to play while looking none too happy. That's when I realized that he was right. I was holding up the game. And I definitely wasn't ready to get shot by a group of gambling-hungry fiends just yet.

"No, no. I'll bet," I told him before placing my thumb on the scanner.

When I did, the scanner beeped, and I was now good to go.

Holy shit. I thought to myself. *Did I really just bet ten thousand of Sartia's barcs on a game?* Well, the only thing I could do now was just pray that I won.

I placed my bet on a box that had a snake inside of it. The snake itself came from the jungles of Rumvak and was highly poisonous. I just hoped that if the player picked that box, they would be immune to the venom. I would soon find out.

"All bets have been placed!" the table master shouted. "Player, please step up to the wall!"

As soon as he said that, an alien that I've never seen before came right up and stood in front of the wall.

He was about five and a half feet tall, had teal-colored skin, green, spiky hair, and aqua-colored eyes. He was also wearing something very reminiscent of a black tuxedo, complete with a bowtie. The thing that really set him apart from most of the aliens I've seen so far was that his particular species had necks almost twice as long as ours. Frankly, it made them look a little weird, but I was pretty much used to it by now.

"Player, are you ready?" the table master asked.

Without saying a word, the teal-colored guy just nervously nodded his head yes. Then, the table master stepped aside, and the game was now on.

The patrons looking on were now cheering and yelling to this guy, trying to get him to pick a particular box. They were also messing with his mind, yelling things like, "You have to die so I can win!" And, "Watch out for the death box!" Personally, that's the part I didn't like about it, but it was all legal.

He just stared at the wall for what seemed like forever. However, there was only a one-minute time limit to do it. If you didn't pick a box by the end of the minute, you lost all of your money.

It didn't take him as long as I thought it would to pick a box, though. After only about 15 seconds, he reached his hand into the third box from the left and the fifth one from the bottom. But, nothing happened right away, and that's when the crowd got silent.

They all stood there in anticipation, hoping that something would bite him or poison him. However, when nothing happened, he pulled his hand out, and the inside of the box was then revealed to be nothing but a pile of grass.

Every patron there was now pissed off because no one picked the grass, and everyone had bet that the man would die. However, only one person bet that the man would live, and that person was me. Yes, I did pick the box with the snake in it, but I also said that I hoped he had an immunity to the venom.

"We have a winner!" the table master shouted before coming over to me.

And, of course, because I was the same person that everyone wanted to shoot just a few minutes ago, all the gamblers were now staring at me, almost like I just stole all the money out of their bank accounts. But I didn't care. I won, and it felt great.

After everyone had gotten a final, good look at me, they all just left the table and went on their merry way.

"Did I really just win?" I asked the table master.

"Congratulations!" he said, using his own voice once again. "Your ten thousand, plus an additional twenty thousand, have been added back into your account."

"Holy shit! Thirty thousand? Thanks!"

"You got a name?" he asked.

"Uh, Sam," I replied.

"Again, congratulations, Sam! Not a lot of people actually bet on the player living."

"I guess it's my lucky night."

He then reached down under the table and pulled out what looked like a business card before handing it over to me.

"What's this?" I asked.

"For being so lucky," he said. "This is a ticket for a free massage."

"Really?"

"You've earned it."

"Wow! Again, thank you!"

And with that, I took the ticket before making my way off of the gambling floor.

• • •

I couldn't believe it. That was the first time in my whole life I had won that big on anything. And it felt great. So much so, in fact, that I was now riding a high. Not a drug high, but more like an adrenaline high.

I immediately rode that high straight to the nearest massage parlor so I could use my ticket. There were a few of them up there, and they all looked pretty much the same. However, I could use my ticket at any one of them. But which one do I choose? It took me a while, but I scoped all of them out before finally making my decision.

I eventually made my way toward one of them in particular, but not because it was the best, the cheapest, or the most expensive. No. I made my way over to the one that had a female Planatian working at it. I don't know why, but I've always had a thing for women with tattoos, and since she was from the best planet to ever grace the stars, I wanted her to do it.

She stood about five feet, eight inches tall, and had long, blue hair, down to the middle of her back, yellow eyes, was slim and covered from head to toe in tattoos. She was also wearing a silver strapless dress that stopped just above her knees.

I went through the doors and walked right up to her, politely smiling in the process. As she returned the gesture, her smile and perfect pearly whites instantly lit up the room.

"May I help you?" she asked.

I then showed her the ticket that I had gotten from the table master.

"I have this ticket for a free massage," I said. "Can I use it here?"

"Of course you can. What kind of massage would you like to get?"

Now, usually, when you get a voucher for a free anything on Earth, there's always some kind of limitation on what you can get with it or where you have to use it. But not there. That ticket was good for anything I wanted.

"I can use this for anything?" I asked.

"Whatever you desire," she replied.

She had such a beautiful voice, as well. And, not to be derogatory or anything, but she had the perfect voice to work as one of those old-fashioned phone sex operators.

"What kinds of services do you offer?" I asked.

"Well, we have the basic service," she continued. "Which is just a shoulder massage. We also offer the full experience, in which we massage the whole body using various oils. And, finally, we have what we like to call 'the secret service.'"

Go figure. They also had a secret service. But I bet theirs was a lot better than ours.

"What's the secret service?" I asked.

"It's the same as the full body massage," she replied. "The only difference is that we throw in a manicure and a pedicure. However, for a little extra, we could-"

"No, no. The full experience is fine."

"In that case, please, follow me."

I then gave her my ticket and followed her over to the first room on the right.

Inside, the room looked just like a standard massage room that you would find anywhere else. Apparently, it's the same no matter what galaxy you visit.

Directly in front of us, in the middle of the room, was the massage table. A stand with all of the various massage oils on it stood against the back wall. Candles also protruded out from the walls to light up the whole room.

"Strip down and hop up on the table," she said.

"Strip down?" I curiously asked.

"Yes. Normally when you strip down, you get naked."

Fuck me. I completely forgot about the whole nudity thing out there.

"Is it okay if I leave my underwear on?" I asked.

"You're not from this sector, are you?" she asked, now giving me an odd look.

"No, I'm not."

"Well then, would it help if I left the room?"

"Yes, please."

And with that, she happily obliged and left the room, closing the door behind her.

Shit. What do I do now? When she comes back in, do I tell her that I wanna switch to the shoulder massage? Or do I just get naked and hop up on the table so that a beautiful woman can rub oil all over my naked body? Hey, I was no fool. It had to happen at some point or another, right?

Besides, I was still unsure about Sartia and me. I mean, it's not like we were a couple or anything. And she did kind of blow me off before we landed there. So, who knows what's up with her?

I put my weapons down on the chair before stripping down to my birthday suit. I then tossed my clothes on top of the guns before hopping up on the table. I was now lying face down on a cloud, with my bare ass facing the ceiling. I'll tell ya, those Lith *definitely* knew what they were doing.

A few minutes later, the masseuse came back into the room and closed the door behind her. She immediately went over to the table and began pouring some of the oils into her hands. After a quick rub, she made her way over to my right side, placed her hands on my back, and started the massage.

Her fingers were magnificent. Of course, I had nothing to compare them to because that was the first massage I had ever gotten. But it… felt… great.

"How does that feel?" she asked.

"So good," I replied.

I was loving it. And I've seen enough movies and TV shows to know that if I just closed my eyes and relaxed, I would feel even better. So, I took a deep breath, closed my eyes, and let her work her magic.

She started up at my neck before slowly working her way down to my shoulders, my back, my legs, and then finally, my back again.

After my hour was up, I felt good. Hell, I felt great. I was so relaxed that I didn't even think I could walk out of there. However, she wasn't quite done yet. Now, if you thought the thing that happened to me back at the hot spring was bad, well, just keep listening.

"Since you're not from this sector," she said. "I think you deserve a freebie."

"A freebie?" I asked. "Nah. I think one massage is enough for-"

Holy… fucking… shit. She was now rubbing my butt. I didn't think they did that sort of thing there. But then again, I was all the way out in the middle of wild space with a bunch of nudist-loving aliens.

As she was massaging my butt with her left hand, she reached under the table with her right, opened up some sort of secret panel, and before I even knew what was happening, she started massaging something else. That must've been the secret service she had mentioned before. And, for me, that's where I drew the line. I was definitely not having any of that.

"Whoa!" I shouted, jumping off of the table.

"Is something wrong?" she curiously asked.

"I definitely did not sign up for that!"

She then looked down toward my crotch with her eyes now opened wide.

"You could've fooled me," she said with a smirk.

I also looked down and saw what I was sporting before quickly covering myself with a towel.

I always told myself that if I ever became a movie star, I would never do any love scenes or kissing scenes because I was always so easily turned on. (Case in point.)

However, I quickly tried to think of an excuse for why that happened but just wound up fumbling all over myself. Again.

"Look… this isn't the… I'm not… this would've never…" I started to say.

But before I could find the right words to say and finish what I was getting at, I heard another voice ring out.

"I have to agree with the masseuse," the mystery voice said.

When I turned and looked over at the doorway to see who it was, the now stupid yet, innocent-looking smile on my face said it all.

With her leaning up against the door frame and her arms folded, the intense look that I was now getting gave a whole new meaning to the term 'if looks could kill.' Sartia did not look happy at all.

Chapter 11

So… *that* embarrassing moment made the event at the hot spring look like a walk in the park. To Sartia, however, I totally looked guilty. There was no way in hell I could ever explain to her what was happening. I mean, I could always try to come up with some lame-ass, bullshit excuse, but she probably already knew about what kinds of things they did at those massage parlors.

Besides, she doesn't know any of the stuff that I just told you. Come to think of it, other than my name, where I'm from, and what decade I like, she doesn't know a damn thing about me.

Okay. She does know a few things, but not everything.

"Hey, Sartia," I cautiously said before trying to plead my innocence. "Look, this is definitely not what it looks like."

"Then what the fuck am I looking at?" she asked.

The masseuse could obviously read into this whole thing and decided to make herself scarce.

"I think I'll just wait outside," she said before leaving and closing the door behind her.

I turned to Sartia. "Look, I had no idea that this place was one of *those* kinds of massage parlors," I replied.

"Oh, really? Then why'd you get naked?" she asked.

I immediately opened my mouth to give her an answer but then stopped. At that point, to her, I looked guilty. And anyone would've definitely thought the same thing after barging in on me like that. It doesn't matter what I could've said because there was no way in hell I was winning that one.

However, after seeing her standing there, a thought had just occurred to me, *Why was she there, anyway?* I thought she was mad at me for some reason.

"Wait a minute," I said, quickly changing the subject. "Why are you here? I thought you were on the ship?"

"Don't try to change the subject," she said.

"I thought you were mad at me?"

"I'm not mad at you."

"Then why are you here?"

"Because someone thought it would be a good idea to spend *my money*," she replied, her hands now on her hips. "I got a notification on the ship's computer informing me that someone was gambling."

"Hey, I just wanted to have a little fun," I replied. "Besides, I thought I deserved it after docking the ship all by myself because *someone* wouldn't come out to help me."

"I would've come out."

I just gave her a look of disbelief.

"Eventually," she added. "Besides, you still didn't answer my question about what you're doing here."

After hearing that whole conversation take place, I knew she wasn't there just to bitch about the money I spent or me now sporting a towel rack.

"What's it to you, anyway?" I asked. "Are you jealous?"

"I am *not* jealous," she defensively replied.

"That's what it sounds like to me. We're not even together. Why should you care?"

I could tell that she wanted to say something but was now too afraid to do so. I called her out on it, and she knew I was right. I mean, it's not like we were a couple or anything. Besides, anyone in that same situation would assume that the other person would be free to do whatever the hell they wanted. But, apparently, she didn't see it that way. And *that's* when it happened.

Without saying a word, she reached her right hand behind her, locked the door, and then ran over to me. She picked me up and threw me onto the massage table before jumping up there and straddling me.

So, to recap, I was now five, six, or was it seven days into my trip? I don't know. By that point, I lost count.

Anyway, there we were, so many days into our trip, with the both of us now lying naked up on the massage table after a rousing sex session, and I still haven't figured her out. I mean, what was her issue? I think that she liked me, but she hadn't exactly come out and told me yet. Plus, all the sex on top of everything else didn't help either. However, I did have a theory.

Because I was a TV and movie buff, I've seen enough romcoms and love stories to know when a woman has issues. Damaged, if you will. I know that men are the same way, but they're just portrayed very differently. Trust me, she was damaged. And, no offense, but I'm pretty sure you know what I'm talking about. Let me explain...

First, she's nice to you. Then, she's all mean to you. Then, she's all nice to you again and then mean to you. In the middle of everything, sex gets thrown in there, and then your whole brain is out of whack because you don't know what the fuck is going on. But I digress.

That was my theory. She was troubled. And I never did get around to finding out why or how. But by the time the mission was over with, I didn't really need to.

"I see you took advantage of the situation," I said while trying to catch my breath.

"I'm sorry," she said. "I shouldn't have jumped down your throat."

"Don't worry about it. It's okay."

"No, it's not. You were right. When I came in here and saw what I saw, I got a little jealous. I shouldn't have, but I did."

"What are you trying to say?" I curiously asked, now looking her right in the eyes.

"All I'm saying is that if anyone's gonna give you a happy ending massage, it's gonna be me."

Wait, what was that? Was she trying to tell me that she wanted to be exclusive? Was she finally changing her mind about this whole situation? I was so confused about everything.

"Are you saying that you wanna be-" I started to say.

But before I could finish my own sentence, we heard some commotion coming from outside the door.

"What the fuck is that?" I asked.

Of course, neither one of us wasted any time getting up off of the table to put our clothes back on. And once we were dressed, Sartia quickly unlocked the door and cautiously opened it up just a bit to take a peek outside.

"Holy shit," she muttered to herself before closing and re-locking the door.

"What is it?" I asked.

"Morgidians."

"Morgidians?"

"Three of them, to be exact."

I then shouted the one word that I thought could sum up our current situation. "Fuck!"

"You might wanna delay saying that," she said.

"Oh shit. Why?"

"Because there are also three bounty hunters with them."

"Fuck!" I shouted even louder. "Now, what do we do?"

I looked around the room and realized that the only way out was through the door. No windows and no other doors were coming in or going out of that room. I mean, come on, let's face it. We couldn't go anywhere because we were inside of a fucking rock floating in outer space.

Trapped, with nowhere to go. This was it. We were both in the same place at the same time, and from what I already knew, they would only need one of us to tell them where the sphere was. The other one, well, you could pretty much kiss their ass goodbye.

Both of us tried really hard to think of something, anything, to get us out of there. Even if we stayed and fought; between the six of them and the station's security forces, I highly doubt we would've survived. Plus, the only weapons we had were my two guns and Sartia's sidearm. And we definitely didn't wanna start a shootout in the middle of a casino because we were afraid of hitting innocent people. I know the hunters wouldn't have cared, but I would.

And that's when shit got really weird. (As if this whole story wasn't already.)

Sartia came up with a plan that I definitely didn't like. But it would buy us some time to get away and avoid getting captured. Well, one of us, anyway.

"I have a plan," she said. "But you may not like it."

"No. I don't like it when people say stuff like *that*," I remarked. "What do you mean, I may not like it?"

Then, without consulting me first, or even letting me know what she was gonna do, there she went.

Her skin started forming and moving like jelly, just like I saw it do when she shape-shifted from the vampire back into her regular form aboard her ship. And as the end of the minute got closer, the shape started to become more evident. I now simply couldn't believe what I was seeing. I had to close my eyes and shake my head just to try and remove the image of what I would soon be looking at. But by the time it was all over, I was now looking into a literal mirror.

"What do you think?" she asked.

"Holy shit! You're me!" I said.

She had shape-shifted herself to look just like me. I won't lie. It was pretty fuckin' weird to be looking at myself, even though I knew it wasn't me. I think it was at that moment I finally understood how identical twins felt around each other. And there's no way I would pass up an opportunity like this. So, I walked right up to her to get a closer look.

"It looks so real," I said while touching and poking her skin.

I was absolutely mesmerized at how much she looked just like me.

"It's supposed to look real," she said, now using my voice.

"You even sound like me, too."

"That's usually how it works."

After a few more seconds of staring at my rugged good looks and being in awe (yeah, right), I quickly came to my senses.

"Wait a minute… how is looking like me gonna help?" I asked.

"This is the part I mentioned that you wouldn't like," she said. "I'm gonna be a decoy while you get back to the ship and fly out of here."

"Like hell, I am! We're in this together."

"Look, Sam. I haven't been fair to you at all. I've done nothing but keep stuff from you, and now I'm gonna make it right."

"How's that? By getting yourself killed?"

With her hands on her hips, she lowered her head and shook it before pausing to let out a huff of air. And after a short moment, she looked back up at me.

"You were right," she said.

"I was? About what?" I asked.

"You're innocent in all of this and should never have been put in this situation, to begin with."

"I never said that."

"Maybe. But I think it's true." She paused. "I want you to go back to the ship, use the star charts to plot a course to Morgide, return the sphere, and then go to the fairies so you can use your wish. I want you to wish yourself home and get the hell out of here."

"But I-"

And before I could say anything else, she used her hands to grab both sides of my face and pull me in for a kiss. When we broke, she looked me right in the eyes before smiling and unlocking the door. Then, in the blink of an eye, she was gone, and I was now standing there all alone.

Maybe she was right. Maybe I was out there when I shouldn't have been. I mean, I should just listen to her and take this opportunity to get the hell out of there and finish the mission, so I could go home. But up until that point, she's done everything for me and helped me out, minus the recent space dock.

I was now at an impasse with myself. Part of me was saying, *Get out there and finish this thing.* While a different part of me said, *Don't just stand there like a stooge, go and rescue her.* Regardless of my current dilemma, only one thing kept racing through my mind that I just couldn't shake. *Did I really just kiss myself?* Even up until this very moment, I still haven't been able to forget that. Not only was it weird, but it was just downright creepy.

Anyway, I opened the door just a tiny bit to peek out through the crack and see what was happening. Sure enough, there I was, err, there *she* was, surrendering to the Morgidians and the bounty hunters.

I recognized one of the bounty hunters as being a Vaknoid like Slith. He was wearing the same armor and carrying the same weapon as well. The other two were different from the Vaknoid but were both the same species, which I recognized almost instantly. They both looked like that long-necked, teal-skinned guy that I recently bet on while playing What's in the Box?.

Their armor looked very reminiscent of something that someone would wear while scuba diving and covered their whole bodies, minus their heads. It was basically a glorified, skin-tight, bulletproof wetsuit. One was wearing a blue one, while the other was wearing a purple one. Both of them were also carrying small fire sidearms.

Oh yeah! I almost forgot. Even though I didn't get a chance to visit, I found out that those long-necked freaks are from a planet known as Drapin,[11] which is home to the Drapinians. They're an aquatic species with teal-colored skin, blue, green, or aqua-colored hair, aqua-colored eyes, and live on a planet made up of 90 percent water. So, that's that.

Now, where was I? Oh yeah.

I watched as Sartia went over to them with her arms raised. She voluntarily gave herself up before one of the Morgidians punched her in the face, while the other two quickly put restraints on her wrists. That was it. There was no struggle and no resistance. She had given herself up so that I could get away.

Now, you would think that since she sacrificed her freedom, I would immediately run back to the ship and fly my ass out of there.

You would think.

But there was no way in hell I was finishing this thing alone. And besides, whether I wanted to admit it or not, and

---

[11] (Pronounced *Dray-pin*)

whether it seemed right or not, I don't think that I liked her anymore. As a matter of fact, I think I was in love with her.

You don't even have to say a word, as I already know what you're thinking. Yes, it is possible for someone to fall in love with someone else that quickly. The only way you could understand that is by believing in love at first sight. If you don't, then this whole thing makes no sense.

But, it was true. Other than being in love with her, I couldn't figure out for the life of me why I wouldn't wanna get on that ship and fly away. I had to save her. And if I couldn't, then I was certainly gonna die trying. Well, hopefully, without the dying part.

I quickly gathered my guns and then tried to form a rescue plan of my own. It went something like this…

I would follow them until we were in a sparsely populated hallway and then show myself. Once they saw me, and since Sartia already looked like me, I planned on messing with their heads a bit. If they got confused enough, I was hoping that there would be plenty of time to shoot our way out of there, get on the ship, and go. But does anything really ever work out as planned? Of course not.

After they disappeared from the casino floor, I opened the door and made my way out to the massage parlor's main entrance. But before I left, the masseuse stopped me for a very brief moment.

"Was that your wife?" she asked.

"No," I replied. "But *you* were fantastic."

"Well then, maybe the next time you come back, we can finish-"

"Sorry. But I gotta go."

And with that, I quickly left the massage parlor to follow them through the casino.

• • •

When I initially went up there, I took the elevator across the casino floor and straight ahead from the massage parlor entrance. They took the elevator that was located on the left of the casino floor. I waited until they got in and then quickly made my way over there. The only problem was the way that the elevator worked.

If you recall, they moved really fast, had no buttons, and automatically stopped at every floor. I was just hoping that once the elevator stopped and the doors opened, I would see them walking away on the floor they got off at. Of course, I wasn't so lucky. So, instead, I got off on the docking bay ring, hoping that I would be able to find out where their ship was docked. After all, how else would they get there?

I sprinted down the hallway, looking through every window I went by, hoping to catch a glimpse of them getting ready to depart. It wasn't until I hit docking station 20, the very last one on the floor, that I finally saw them in there chatting with one of the emissaries.

I quickly hid out of view for a few seconds to catch my breath before going in there. Once I was full of hot air (no pun intended), I armed myself with Slith's gun, opened the door, and went right in.

"What's up, fellas?" I said.

The moment I opened my mouth, they all turned around to face me. Utter confusion rested on their faces, as they were probably trying to figure out who the hell I was and why there were now two of me.

"What are you doing here?" Sartia asked. "I thought I told you to leave?"

"Shut up, Sam!" I responded.

When I told her to shut up, the hunters started looking back and forth at us, trying to figure out who was the real Sam and who wasn't. Even the robotic controllers and the female Lith emissary were trying to figure out who was who. Perfect. That's exactly what I wanted to happen.

"What's going on here?" the Morgidian in the middle asked. "Who are you?"

"I'm Sam of Earth," I replied.

"Very funny," the Morgidian on the left said before pointing to Sartia. "*This* is Sam."

"Are you sure you have the right Sam?" I asked.

"Of course, we do," the third Morgidian said.

"But how do you know?" I asked again, hoping to keep them guessing.

"Because we know that the Earthlings are weak," the first Morgidian said. "And when he gave himself up so easily, we knew we had the right one."

"Impressive," I said. "Most impressive."

"What the hell are you doing?" Sartia asked.

"That means if this is the human," the second Morgidian said. "Then *you* must be the Arnaxian."

"Are you absolutely sure this time?" I asked them, now smiling from ear to ear.

Now, I don't know if it was my superb acting skills or simply my boyish charm, but it must've worked. Because now, they were all looking at each other like the both of us were out of our minds. However, as I mentioned before, nothing ever goes as planned.

"No matter. We only need one of you to tell us where the sphere is," the first Morgidian said before pointing his gun at me. "Which means you die!"

Oh shit. It appears that my plan has backfired.

Oh, come on. Who are we kidding? That was never really a solid plan anyway. I was just hell-bent on getting Sartia back and wasn't thinking straight. But now, I was really screwed. There was no way in hell I could ever take on six killing machines by myself. I mean, before the other day, I never even fired a gun. How was I supposed to get out of this mess?

Having my life quickly flash before my eyes, I immediately put my brain into overload and tried to think of any situation or scenario that would possibly work for something like this. After a few seconds of hard thinking, only one thing came to my mind in the form of a distraction. But how? It was just me in there. How could I possibly distract all six of them at once without giving anything away? Well, we were out in space, after all.

"Instead of dying, wouldn't I make a better prisoner?" I asked.

"No," the first Morgidian said. "You die."

The other five also pointed their guns at me and were now ready to blow my head off.

But before they got a chance to fire, I looked right at Sartia and gave her a wink, followed by a smile, before implementing my somewhat brilliant backup plan.

I opened my eyes as wide as they could go and started to act all panicky before pointing behind them toward the back wall.

"Holy shit!" I yelled. "It's gonna crash into us!"

Because there were no windows, if something was gonna crash into us, one of the robotic controllers would've said something, and it definitely wouldn't have come from me. But, as stupid as that plan sounded, they actually all turned around to look, just like the morons they were.

Once they turned around, I immediately slid my burrower over to Sartia. The others were distracted just long enough for her to break free from them.

With her hands still chained in front of her, she quickly bent down to pick up the burrower. But instead of getting back up, she just laid there, so she wouldn't get hit when I opened fire on them. Once I did, I unloaded my gun with everything I had before they started firing back.

Since there was no place to hide in there, I had to think fast. So, I quickly ran over and grabbed one of the robotic controllers to stand it up in front of me and use it as a shield.

The robotic controllers were no bigger than I was. They were standard, walking, talking machines with a limited A.I. Their only purpose was to guide the ships in and help them take off. So I didn't feel too bad when the one that I was using took all of the hits for me. Unfortunately, they were only big enough to hide my chest and my head. With their arms and legs constantly moving, it would've been a miracle if I didn't get hit.

In the distraction of all the firing, Sartia saw what I did and decided to make the exact same move. She immediately got up, grabbed the other robotic controller, and hid behind him. The bounty hunters, on the other hand, weren't so lucky.

I managed to hit and kill one of them, while Sartia managed to hit and kill the other. The third one was killed when one of the Morgidians saw what we did and decided that the bounty hunters were no longer needed. Well, no longer needed alive, anyway.

All three of the Morgidians now had the dead bounty hunters propped upright and were also using them as shields. During the scrum, the Lith emissary just kind of ducked down into one of the corners and curled herself into a ball while putting her hands over her head. But Sartia and I just kept on firing.

After a few minutes of exchanging gunfire, the Morgidians suddenly stopped. I looked over at Sartia, and she looked back at me as we were now wondering what the hell they were doing. But not before long, that's when I heard an all too familiar sound.

If you recall, when I first saw the Morgidians back at my apartment, they managed to blow two of my doors and my couch to dust. But before they did, that was the first time I had heard the sound I'm referring to. That was the sound of their guns charging up, getting ready to disintegrate everything in the room... including us.

I had to think fast and wound up doing the only thing I could think of at the moment. Like a moron, I tightened my grip on the robot I was holding and charged right toward them.

As I bolted forward, guiding the robot, keeping it in front of me so that I wouldn't get hit, I wound up unloading the last of my bullets. When I got over to them, I threw the robot toward them and knocked two of them over. I then took the opportunity to switch over to the EPRs (electrical pulse rounds) and knock them both out. But I just couldn't seem to hit the third one. He was now facing me with one of the dead bounty hunters staring me right in the face. Thankfully, though, they weren't that bright.

The whole time I was going all kamikaze on their asses, they were so focused on me that they completely forgot about Sartia, who was still standing off to the side.

With the dead bounty hunter still staring me in the face, the Morgidian reached his arm out from around the side of him and pointed his gun at me. I was now dead meat. My body was about to be blown into a pile of Sam dust. At least, he thought so.

I just smiled. "Hey, asshole," I said before pointing to Sartia.

Oh yeah. He definitely forgot that she was standing there. Because after I pointed in her direction, his eyes grew huge before turning to see exactly where I was pointing to. But for him, it was already too late.

He couldn't even make a move before Sartia unloaded a few shots from the burrower directly into his face. He immediately dropped the dead bounty hunter to try and remove the blades. But by the time the hunter hit the floor, it was bye-bye, birdie.

The two shots, one in his left cheek and one in his forehead, started twisting and burrowing deep into his head. The farther in they went, the more the Morgidian screamed out in pain, and the more red blood dripped out of the holes. It only took a couple of seconds to work their magic because once both of the burrower shots hit the brain, he stopped screaming and moving and fell flat on the floor, just like a tree getting chopped down. Once he was down, the only thing I could do was breathe a massive sigh of relief. But, unfortunately, that wasn't the worst part of this whole thing.

Sartia then dropped her bot, and I quickly ran over to her to make sure she was still in one piece. However, when I got over there, I noticed something was off about the way she was looking at me. And I didn't like it.

"Are you okay? Are you hit?" I asked.

She groaned. "Sam…" before collapsing onto the floor.

Luckily, I caught her mid-fall and helped lay her down gently onto the floor so that she wouldn't injure herself any further. I then knelt down beside her to see exactly what was wrong.

"What happened?" I asked.

Unfortunately, I had to wait a little bit so that her body could transform itself back into its original form. Once she looked like herself again, she then took her right hand and uncovered the bullet wound on her right side, allowing a river of purple blood to come charging out.

"Holy shit!" I said. "We gotta get you to a doctor!"

"There's no time, Sam. I won't make it," she said.

"No. No! There's gotta be something we can do?"

"I'm sorry, but it's over for me."

She then started to cough up some blood as well.

"No!" I yelled. "I'm not gonna let you die! You can't!"

"Listen to me, Sam," she said, placing her right hand on the left side of my face. "You have to take my body back to Arnaxia. They'll know what to do with me."

"You can't go," I said again, my eyes now welling up. "I…"

I couldn't believe it. I actually started to cry. I mean, it wasn't a full-blown cry, but I began to cry, nonetheless.

You see, back on Earth, when one of my relatives passed, I always handled it pretty well. I know everyone always says that you should be sad and mourn someone when they die. But I didn't think that way. If it was their time to go, and they lived a good life, I was always happy I got to know them and would think back to all the good times we had together. I also never cried because I knew that death was always a part of life. It happened, and unfortunately, there was nothing anyone could do about it. But with Sartia, it was different.

She was young and did everything she could for me ever since I got out there. She never lied to me (to a point) and was always kind to me. I understood why I was crying and knew right away that her life was being cut short. But that wasn't it either.

"I…" I started to say.

"What is it, Sam?" she asked.

After all that time, wrestling with my feelings in my head, trying to decipher if what I felt was true or not, and seeing her lying there on the brink of death, I didn't care anymore.

"I love you. You can't leave me," I finally said.

Man, did that feel great to say.

The moment I said it, though, I could see a few tears fall from the corners of her eyes and drip down the sides of her face.

"Sam," she started to say, her lower lip now quivering. "I…"

But before she could finish her sentence and tell me whatever it was that she was gonna tell me, she died right there in my arms.

"Sartia?" I quietly called out to her, the tears now pouring out of me like a running faucet.

When she didn't answer me, I shook her a little bit, hoping she would wake up. After a second or two, I then realized that she wouldn't be waking up at all.

That beautiful woman, who showed me different things, introduced me to a world I didn't even think existed, was with me every step of the way, and with whom I spent the last few days with was now gone. I was now all alone, out in the middle of nowhere, with no one left to guide me.

Rob J. LaBelle

Chapter 12

None of my friends have ever been taken by the reaper, and the last of my grandparents died about ten years ago. So even though I didn't know her for that long, losing Sartia was one of the most significant losses I've had in recent memory. And it hurt.

The Lith emissary in the control room had eventually called the proper authorities, which resulted in the two Morgidians that I had stunned being taken into custody. The bounty hunter and Morgidian bodies were then cleared out before a few members of the trade hub's medical personnel helped get Sartia's body back aboard her ship.

Once she was on board, they encapsulated her in a skin-tight, transparent membrane to keep her body fresh for the ride. It kind of reminded me of one of those plastic storage bags that you would put food or clothes in before taking a vacuum and sucking all the air out of it. But this had a little something extra to it. The membrane itself kept whatever was wrapped in it cold and basically eliminated the need to put it on ice or store it in a freezer.

They put her body on one of the beds in the sleeping quarters, per my request. I definitely didn't want them to put her in her room because with Rawr being in there, I didn't know if his superheat would be able to nullify the effects of the membrane or not. I didn't wanna chance it either.

I was now sitting in the captain's chair, heading out toward my next destination. Apparently, after the most recent events, I now had one more stop to make before delivering the sphere to the Morgidians. I now had the unpleasant honor of going to Arnaxia to deliver Sartia to her own people.

Once I was in the clear and away from the trade hub, I took a quick look at the star charts, plotted a course to Arnaxia, and jumped to light speed. The only thing I could do now was put the ship on autopilot and enjoy a somber ride there.

• • •

Wild space. Alone. With no one to talk to. That's where I stood. Just me, the ship, the stars, and the planets. Well, I also had Rawr, but he's a cat, and I could only stand to be around him for so long before I lost all of my bodily fluids through my sweat glands.

Since I knew that in previous situations like these, the ship, computer, or whatever, would play some type of music to fit the mood I was currently in. However, nothing was playing. Come to think of it, I hadn't heard any kind of music come from within the ship for a while now. So, just to make sure I wasn't making this whole music thing up in my head, I decided to see if it would play something for me.

"Okay, ship," I said out loud. "What do ya got for a lonely, depressed man who just lost someone he loves?"

I listened for the next few seconds or so to see what would happen. But nothing did. No music. No noise. No nothing. All I could do was lower my head in sadness because, at that point, even the ship wasn't listening to me.

Also, I still hadn't figured out where the mystery music was coming from. Whether it was the ship itself, or some unknown type of spectral plane that I couldn't see, was still yet to be determined.

Anyway, not really wanting to stay in the cockpit all by myself, I decided to get up and take a walk back to the sleeping quarters. That had to have been one of the slowest most, depressing walks I've ever made. I wanted to go in and look at Sartia's body. Since I was bringing her home, I wanted to spend as much time with her as possible before her people took care of her. Once they took her off of the ship, I knew that I would never see her again.

Usually, it only takes a few seconds, but after the long couple of minutes that it took me to get back there, I just stood there, hovering over her body, staring at it like it was a piece of art.

But there was now a small part of me that felt guilty. I felt guilty because if I had just listened to her and took off like she wanted me to, none of this would've happened, and she would probably still be alive. She knew that the

Morgidians needed her to tell them where the sphere was because if they had killed her, they would be right back to square one. Regardless, after a few more moments of looking, my eyes started to well up again. And as I was standing there crying, that's when it happened.

I could now hear a song start to play over the ship's speaker. It was low at first and then got louder over the next few seconds. Once it was loud enough, I could make out exactly which song it was. "Don't Dream It's Over" by Crowded House was now blaring throughout the ship. Definitely fitting for the current situation and mood.

I couldn't even begin to tell you how long I just stood there and stared at her angelic presence. Even dead, she looked beautiful. But even I couldn't look at her anymore. I just had to get out of there. Because the longer I stared at her, the sadder I got.

So, I left the sleeping quarters and made my way down to her room. I guess, for the time being, it would be my room. Come to think of it, until I landed on Arnaxia, that was my ship as well. And Rawr was my cat.

Once I made it into her room, I immediately went over to the bed and crawled on top of it, instantly burying my face in her pillows. I took in a long, savory deep breath so I could smell her essence in the pillowcases. After a few minutes of wallowing in her fragrant odor, I rolled over and just stared up at the ceiling.

As I lay there, I thought about the first moment I saw her when she showed up on that riverbank. I thought about how kind she was to me and how she never put me down for being, well, me. I then thought about the hot spring incident, and of course, what moment that led up to.

Even though I hadn't known her for that long, she made me smile and laugh. Judge me all you want because I don't care what you think. I was in love with her. And I missed her.

I took out my phone and powered it on to look at some of the photos from my trip so far. Since I didn't have a charging cable out there, I had to turn it off after every use to save the battery. It was kind of a pain in the ass, but it worked. However, after a few minutes of looking, I decided that my heart just wasn't in it. So, I turned it off and quickly fell asleep.

While I slept, I had some of the worst dreams I've ever had. And they were so vivid too. I dreamt that the Morgidians had finally caught up to me and captured me. They tortured me for hours on end, asking me where the sphere was. Every time I wouldn't tell them something, they would take a piece of me… literally.

The first time they asked me where the sphere was, and I wouldn't tell them, they grabbed hold of my right arm and ripped it clean off my body. Then, it was my left arm, followed by both of my legs. The worst part was after my last limb got pulled off, everything instantly grew back, and we started all over again. It was awful. And I couldn't help but toss and turn the whole time. That is until I was woken up by the planetary alarm.

I opened my eyes and sat right up in the bed, just like one does when they're suddenly awoken from a deep sleep. I then looked around the room to make sure that I was still on the ship and still alive. After I looked myself over to make sure that all of my parts were still there, I finally realized what the hell was happening before getting out of bed and heading toward the cockpit.

Now moving like a zombie, I turned off the planetary alarm and looked down at the screen. Arnaxia was approaching fast. So I decided to take the ship out of light speed and guide it the rest of the way on my own. It didn't take long, though, because, after a few minutes of flying, the blue and green planet was directly ahead.

The time had come. I was finally gonna be able to see Sartia's homeworld and where she comes from. Unfortunately, it wasn't under the circumstances I had hoped.

Also, in case you were wondering, all Arnaxians had amethyst-colored skin, purple hair, either violet or maroon-colored eyes, and they could shapeshift. But, you already knew that last part.

Anyway, because I was already in an Arnaxian ship, that was, by far, the quickest time I ever had to wait in orbit. They immediately granted me landing rights ahead of everyone else waiting up there. I could only imagine how pissed off they all were. But I didn't care. Because I had some urgent business to take care of.

After I broke through the planet's atmosphere, I started making my way down toward landing pad eight. While on route, I looked out of the cockpit window to get a bird's-eye view of her homeworld. They had oceans, beaches, forests, and cities. Everything that Earth would have, with the exception of one small detail.

They did have forests and cities, but all of the houses and buildings were built right onto the beaches. The sand went in for miles and miles on end. Personally, I thought their cities were kind of ass-backward. However, it kind of reminded me of what Manhattan looks like. Except, instead of Central Park being a ten-block park in the middle of the city, they had four or five-mile wide forests in the middle of theirs. It was kind of strange but very aesthetically pleasing.

I finally made my way down to landing pad eight, which on that planet, all the landing pads were on top of one of the skyscrapers. If you were afraid of heights, then you were definitely screwed. Thankfully, though, I wasn't.

Once I touched down and shut down the ship, my harness retracted, and I got up to make my way over to the side hatch. But instead of pushing the button to open it, I just stood there, hesitating for a moment, wondering in my mind what exactly they would say to me or if they would accuse me of murdering one of their own.

But that was ridiculous. Because from what Sartia told me, someone on that planet would know of her mission and who I was. However, I still had to tread carefully because, to them, I was now the visitor from another world.

• • •

I pushed the button to open up the side door, and after it did, a burst of air came rolling into the ship like one of those industrial-sized fans blowing through a wind tunnel. I then walked down the retractable ramp until my feet were firmly planted on the rooftop of the building. The building itself was probably a little shorter than the Empire State Building, and its roof was perfectly flat.

I stood there for a few seconds and waited until three Arnaxian emissaries came walking up to me. All three of them were females, and all three of them were packing small fire sidearms.

The one in the middle had maroon-colored eyes, while the other two had violet-colored ones. They also weren't wearing the same type of clothing that Sartia was wearing. Instead of the skin-tight armor that she had on, all three of them were wearing white, button-down shirts, which were tucked neatly into their black, khaki-type pants. They were also wearing black, high-heeled shoes. When they saw me and realized that I wasn't Sartia coming off the ship, all three of them immediately drew their guns and pointed them at me.

Okay, so maybe they weren't emissaries.

"Who are you?" the woman in the middle asked.

But before I answered, I raised my hands to let them know I wasn't a threat.

"My name is Sam," I calmly said. "Sartia picked me up from Earth, so we could return the sphere back to the Morgidians."

"Where is she?"

"She's in the sleeping quarters." I then lowered my head in sadness and took a deep breath before looking back up at her and continuing on. "But, she's dead. I'm sorry."

"What?" the woman asked, almost not believing my story. "Don't move!"

She then signaled to the other two women, who quickly ran past me, up the ramp, and into the ship. I just waited there with my hands now folded on the top of my head while she continued to point her gun at me.

After a few minutes of searching around the ship, the two women came back out, one of them confirming my story.

"He's right," one of the women said. "She's dead and wrapped in a cold membrane."

"Let's get her off the ship and over to medical right away," the lead woman responded.

The two women obeyed her orders and went back onto the ship to grab her. While they were gone, two more different people, another woman, and finally, a man dressed the same way as the other four women (minus the high heels), came over to me with their guns drawn.

"Give me your hands!" the lead woman demanded. "If you try anything funny, these two will shoot you on the spot."

Since I was only there for diplomatic reasons, I guess you could call it, I didn't protest or say anything and quickly put my hands directly in front of me. She then pulled out a pair of restraints that I've never seen before. They were made of some type of steel and were round in shape. Once she slapped them on me, they automatically locked themselves and adjusted to fit my wrists perfectly. The only person that could essentially escape from those was Superman.

You know, now that I think about it, with everything else that I've seen and learned, I wonder if Krypton really exists? Nah. That would just be plain old stupid.

Anyway, she and the other two 'security guards' (I guess you would call them) escorted me across the rooftop and over to a steel door. After walking through it, we went down a few flights of stairs before getting into an elevator. We rocketed to the bottom at three times the speed of a standard elevator before reaching the ground floor. Once the doors opened, we exited and walked through the building's lobby, which looked just like any other lobby, before stepping through the front doors and out onto the sidewalk.

Other than the technology they had and the clothes that everyone wore, that planet drew a very similar resemblance to Planaties. It looked very Earth-like, and it didn't dawn on me until after standing there for a few minutes that the reason everything looks so similar is because the people on that planet have been visiting Earth for tens of thousands of years.

A few seconds later, a hover limo drove right up to us and stopped. I immediately thought to myself, *Now why would a limo be picking us up? And where exactly could it be taking me?*

Usually, when you're walking around in handcuffs or whatnot, you don't typically get picked up by limos. It's more like you get picked up by a bus or a car, both coming from some type of correctional facility or jail.

The lead woman opened the door to the back of the limo and got in. I then followed suit while the other two came in directly after me. After we were all comfortable, they closed the door, and the limo took off.

"Where are you taking me?" I asked. "And who are you?"

"Shut up and don't say a word!" she barked. "You'll find out soon enough."

Great. Fantastic. I'm all by myself, already getting yelled at, and I have no idea where they're taking me or what the hell's going on. For all I knew, they were going to kill me, or possibly, something else.

As we continued driving through the city, my mind suddenly started to wander. The Arnaxians have their own cities, technology, ships, and weapons. And judging by what I've seen, and from what Sartia's already told me, they looked pretty advanced. So, what's stopping them from destroying the Morgidians and getting rid of this so-called 'treaty' they have? Other than the fact that they outnumber the Arnaxians ten to one, what makes the Morgidians all-powerful, anyway?

Of course, after thinking about that second one, I realized I had just answered my own question.

• • •

We were out of the city and were now driving straight into the forest. At that point, I thought they might be taking me to some remote outpost in the middle of nowhere to torture me for answers. Of course, that would've been just a little more interesting than where we actually went. Sorry.

Deep in the forest, a big, five-acre plot was cut out to house a giant complex, which sat right smack dab in the middle. A 20-foot wall surrounded the whole thing, as well as a force field. No ships, missiles, or laser cannons, were ever getting close to what was in there.

We drove right up to the gate, and after a few minutes of chatting with the female guard standing outside, the gate opened, and the force field came down, just long enough for us to go in. The gate's two massive steel doors swung inward, and once we were inside, they closed behind us as the force field went back up.

The building behind those walls, however, was definitely not what I was expecting. I thought it would be some kind of fortified concrete building that you would see in most movies with an outpost in the middle of the jungle. Well, not necessarily the fortified concrete ones, but others like the remote village in *Romancing the Stone,* the insurgent camp in *Predator,* or even the POW camp in *Rambo: First Blood, Part Two.*

Nope. It was none of those. In fact, it was just a house… a very nice house at that.

It looked like a three-story mansion made entirely out of glass. And although it wasn't really built that way, the vast, open view windows surrounding the place gave it that impression.

Along with the handful of guards on the outside of the gate, there was also a nice compliment on the inside as well. I mean, who were they taking me to meet anyway, the ruler of the whole entire planet?

The car pulled up to the front of the house before the driver stopped. The doors opened, and we all piled out. As I stood outside of the car, I just looked around in amazement at the surrounding forest and the purple hue of the force field that rose high above the entire complex. But the astounding view was short-lived, as I was immediately hurried into the house.

• • •

Now, I can't tell you much about what the house looked like because I didn't get to see the whole thing. But what I can tell you is that the house itself kind of reminded me of Tony Montana's mansion from *Scarface*. Only, it had no fountain, looked less 1980s, and was more modern.

The foyer itself had a giant, brown carpet that covered a good portion of the floor. On said carpet, basically where Tony's fountain would've been, sat two black, leather-type couches and two black, leather-type love seats that all formed a circle around a glass coffee table. On either side of the foyer were a set of stairs that went up to the second floor. We immediately took the set that was located on the right.

The second floor's half-moon-shaped walkway was lined with doors that went god knows where and had a railing that went all the way around it, spanning from stairwell to stairwell. I was brought toward the door directly in the middle of the two sets of stairs.

Once we arrived, only two of us entered the room: the first woman I met when I landed on the roof, and of course, myself. The other two stayed outside in the hallway to keep watch.

Inside the room sat a desk, smack dab in the middle of it, with a black, leather-type chair behind it and two in front. There was a juice bar off to the right and an elevator off to the left. The back of the room had a vast, wide view window that overlooked the entire back portion of the complex. Whoever this person was, well, they had more money than I could ever dream of.

"Take a seat," the woman said.

I immediately sat down in the chair on the left while she stood behind me to watch over me like a hawk.

I must've sat there for a good five minutes before I heard the elevator doors open. When they did, a tall, maybe six-foot woman walked out of there and sat down in the chair behind the desk.

She had long hair, pulled up into a bun, and had maroon eyes instead of violet. She was wearing a red sequin dress that went all the way down to her ankles. The dress also complimented her red, high-heeled shoes. I didn't know who that woman was, but she looked very much like a movie star. However, the person that I was about to meet was *definitely* no movie star.

"Sam Watson… the Earthling," she said with a smirk.

"You know who I am?" I asked.

"Of course. Sartia transmitted your info back to us shortly after you left Earth."

The woman behind the desk then lowered her head in sadness and shook it before looking back up at me.

"Poor Sartia," she said.

"Speaking of which, why did she want me to bring her back here, anyway?" I asked.

"Don't you worry about that. We'll take good care of her."

"Good. So, now that you know who I am, and forgive me if I'm overstepping my bounds here, but who the hell are you?"

The woman behind the desk immediately looked up at the other woman standing behind me.

"Merka, please take the restraints off of him," she asked.

"Are you sure?" Merka replied.

"He's no threat to us."

"Thank you," I politely said.

Merka then came around to my front side and took the restraints off of my wrists.

"That'll be all," the woman behind the desk said.

And with that, Merka quickly left the room, closing the door on her way out.

"Now, allow me to introduce myself," the woman behind the desk continued. "My name is Del Surcy. And I'm the ruler of this planet."

"Holy shit!" I said, shocked. "Your last name is Surcy? As in Omra Surcy, the dude who created planet eighties?"

"I see Sartia has already mentioned him to you?"

"Mentioned him? Hell, we already visited the place."

"And what did you think?"

"Let's put it this way… if I were to ever move out to this sector, I'm calling that place home."

"Good to know," she said while slowly nodding her head. "So, how's your trip been so far?"

"Well, let's see…" I began to tell her. "I visited some pretty cool worlds, saw some vampires, which I always thought were a myth, got semi-naked in a hot spring, rescued a fairy, which in turn granted me a future wish, gambled, had a naked massage, and have also been shot at and almost killed multiple times. My reviews are kinda mixed at this point."

"I see. And what did you think of Sartia?"

Okay. I was now talking to the ruler of the planet. How in the hell was I supposed to answer that one? I mean, do I answer her honestly and tell her that I fell in love with her? Or do I just make up some random bullshit, so she doesn't question me any further?

"You couldn't have sent a nicer person to come and help me out," I merely responded.

Yeah. I took neither route. I didn't lie, but I didn't tell her anything else either.

"If I may ask, how did she die?" Del asked.

"Well, we were on Metoria, and she got captured by three bounty hunters and three Morgidians so I could escape in the ship," I proceeded to tell her. "Of course, I couldn't just leave her there, so I decided to go and help. We got into a huge firefight, and it wasn't until afterward that she collapsed due to a gunshot wound."

"You went back for her?"

"Of course. Why wouldn't I? She's done so much for me already. Besides, it's not like I could just let her get captured. Why do you ask?"

"I don't know," she curiously responded. "Most people in your predicament would've just run home."

"I had no choice," I said. "It was either, go home and have her possible death hang over my conscience, or die trying to save her."

It wasn't until I said that I could now see the intrigued look on Del's face, almost as if I said something I shouldn't have. Either that, or she had figured out by the tone of my voice or something that I was in love with Sartia.

"That's it?" she asked, her eyes now narrowed while giving me the most intense stare.

But I didn't break, though.

"Is there something else?" I nonchalantly responded.

"I guess not."

Then, on sheer impulse, I let out a big sigh of relief. Of course, to no one's surprise, Del immediately caught wind of that.

"Is there something else you're not telling me?" she asked.

"No, no. That's it," I replied before quickly changing the subject. "So, uh, what happens now?"

"Well, now that Sartia's body is back home, you'll stay on the planet while someone takes the sphere back to the Morgidians. Once that's done, you're free to leave."

"Do I have to go back to Earth?"

"You definitely can't stay out here. It's the law. I'm sorry."

There was an immediate bout of silence that followed as I just sat there with my head hung low, thinking about Sartia and all that she's done for me.

I don't know. Maybe I was depressed because deep down in my gut, I didn't want my trip to end. I wanted to keep exploring. But, you know what they say, all good things must come to an end.

"In the meantime," Del continued. "Because of your great service to the planet and all that you've done, we'll put you up in a hotel, free of charge, of course, and anything else that you wanna do is on us."

Wait a minute… did I just hear that right? The *government* is going to pay for anything I wanna do while I stay here?

"Are you shitting me?" I asked. "I can do anything I want, and it's all on the planet's dime?"

"Just until we return the sphere," she replied. "Again, once the sphere is back on Morgide, you're free to go. In the meantime, go see my driver out front, and he'll bring you to the hotel."

"Thank you!"

"You're quite welcome. Oh, and uh, here, take this," she said, handing me a little business card with her personal contact info on it. "If you need anything, don't hesitate to ask."

"Thanks again."

With her business card in hand, I stood up out of the chair, opened the door, and made my way out of her office.

Once I was in the hallway, I just stared at the business card for a moment before making my way down the stairs and out the front door. I then jumped into the back of the same limo that I arrived in, closed the door, and made myself comfortable. The driver wasted no time and immediately took off away from the complex.

• • •

About 30 minutes later, we arrived at the hotel, where, after a long elevator ride, I eventually made it up to my room. It took me so long to get up there because I stayed in room 5500 on the 55th floor. Those hotels were fucking huge. The one that I was in was 75 stories tall.

Now, when the government said that everything was on their dime, they weren't kidding. The room I was staying in, which also looked like a hotel room on Earth, was one of those fancy, presidential-type suites that only the rich and movie stars could afford.

When I walked through the door, I immediately entered the living room, which was about the size of a studio apartment. Off of that was a bedroom with a king-sized bed and its very own master bathroom. Also off of the living room was another smaller bathroom and full-sized kitchen. And just past the kitchen was a dining room, which seated eight.

As I stood there and looked around, I thought to myself, *This was it. This was the moment when I finally felt like I had achieved rockstar status!* With that big ass room and a foreign city to explore, I could do anything I wanted for free. The problem was figuring out where to start. And, again, I now had to do it alone.

After a few minutes of looking around and thinking that I was King Shit, I had a good idea of what I wanted to do first. So, I kicked off my shoes and stripped down to my birthday suit. (Trust me, it's not what you think.) I then crawled into the Lith made bed and immediately fell fast asleep.

And don't make fun of me because I sleep naked. I'll just say this... if you've never slept naked at some point in your life, then you don't know what you're missing. What's that old saying? Oh yeah. 'Don't knock it until you've tried it.'

Rob J. LaBelle

Chapter 13

With everything now behind me and being on an alien planet where I know I can trust everyone, I slept for a good ten hours straight before finally opening my eyes. I haven't felt that refreshed since before I left Earth. The problem was, that was the first time I've woken up on that trip all by myself. Yeah, I took little naps here and there, but when it came down to sleeping for more than six hours at a time, Sartia and I were usually in the same bed. Not this time, though.

After I awoke, I just laid there and wallowed in sadness for a few minutes before I finally decided to get out of bed. I immediately went into the bathroom to grab a long, hot shower before finishing and coming back out.

After I was all done with the bathroom, getting dressed, and all that other jazz, I decided to take advantage of whatever the government was gonna pay for and make a whole day out of it. I didn't exactly know how long I had until they delivered the sphere back to Morgide, and I definitely wasn't gonna waste the opportunity either. So, I quickly gathered all of my stuff and went downstairs to hail a cab.

When I got outside, I immediately noticed the very same limo and driver that carted me around the day before was already waiting for me. But because of all the hustle and bustle that was going on, I never really got a good look at him until now.

The driver was a male whose hair was neatly combed and parted on one side. He was a big guy, probably around six foot five, had violet-colored eyes, and was wearing a tuxedo. His suit consisted of a white, button-down shirt with black, shiny buttons, a pair of black silk pants, and black dress shoes. Along with his patented chiseled chin type of look, he was also carrying a small fire sidearm.

Now, if you're also curious as to why that was only the second male I've encountered during my visit there, just think back to when Sartia told me that 80 percent of the Arnaxian population is female.

"Mr. Watson," he addressed me in a low, resonant tone. "I'm sorry that we didn't get to formally introduce ourselves yesterday, but my name is Krite, and I'll be your escort for the duration of your stay."

"It's nice to meet you, Krite," I said.

"So, where are we off to this morning?"

Where are we off to, indeed? I thought to myself.

Since everything was on the government's dime, and since I've been going for a whole week or so in the same clothes that I left Earth in, I decided to do a little bit of shopping. However, I just needed to make sure I could.

"Can I ask you something?" I asked.

"Sure," he replied.

"Are there any limitations on what I can get?"

"No, sir. You can get anything you'd like. Why? Did you already have something in mind?"

"I could definitely use a new wardrobe. Any recommendations?"

He had to think about it for a few seconds before giving me an answer.

"I know just the place," he said.

He then opened up the limo's back door, and I got inside before he closed it behind me. After walking around to the driver's side of the car, he hopped in and drove us toward our first destination.

• • •

Arnaxia didn't have the same look as Earth or even Planaties, for that matter, but it had a very familiar one. You could take one look around at all of the purple aliens, the clothes, the transportation, and everything else, and you instantly get that Earth vibe. But it definitely wasn't Earth. It was almost like you were visiting a parallel Earth. An alternate dimension, if you will.

Even though Sartia didn't get a chance to tell me yet, I found out later on that because the Arnaxians have been visiting Earth without us knowing about it, and the reason why certain planets looked similar to home was because the Arnaxians have been trading tech ideas with us for years.

Although they didn't physically build anything for us, they basically just gave us the means to do so while pointing us in the right direction. Hence the reason why everything looked so similar.

Anyway, after a 20-minute ride, we finally arrived at our destination. Krite came around and opened up the door to let me out. As soon as my feet were firmly planted on the sidewalk, I looked up to read the name of the store.

"Purple People Casual?" I remarked.

"It's one of the top-rated clothing stores on the planet," he said.

"This should be interesting."

We then walked through the front door and into the store. As I took a quick look around, my mouth gaped, and I was in awe of how huge that place actually was. It was three floors of sneakers, socks, jeans, underwear, t-shirts, button-down shirts, and anything else you would dress in for everyday attire. Casual was in the name, and that pretty much said it all. This place was right up my alley. I mean, I definitely had no interest in buying a suit and looking all fancy. Besides, who was I gonna impress now that Sartia was gone?

The bottom floor housed all of the footwear, which included socks, shoes, and sandals. The second floor housed all of the jeans, shorts, and underwear, while the third floor housed all of the t-shirts, long-sleeved shirts, button-down shirts, and jackets. I was now extremely curious to see exactly what they had in there, and because of the sheer size of the place, I knew it might take me a while.

I took the elevator up to the second floor to start with pants, just like I always do. They had khaki-ish type pants, silk type pants, and jeans that felt like denim. But the closer I looked, I soon realized that they definitely weren't made of denim. Regardless, I decided to skip the other two and go straight for the jeans, of course.

Their jeans were pretty dull. They didn't have any of the ripped or stonewashed variety, but just your basic blue, light blue, black, and other various colors of those three. I picked out two light blue pairs, one pair of regular blue, and one black pair. While I was there, I also grabbed some fresh underwear, which was long overdue. After I had everything that I needed for my bottom section, I made my way up to the third floor to pick out some shirts.

I took one look at the shirts and thought, *How dull.* None of the t-shirts had the V-neck style because all of them had a round neck. A lot of them sported the standard colors like white, red, blue, black, etc. Some of them had pictures on them, but of course, I didn't recognize any of the photos. So, I picked out a few t-shirts of my favorite color, red. While I was there, I also grabbed a couple of long-sleeved shirts: one red and one black.

Finally, I made my way down to the sneaker department. First, I grabbed a few pairs of socks because that was the easy part. However, the next part is where it gets pretty interesting. I shit you not, most of the shoes looked like a mix between the old Air Jordans, Converse, and the futuristic, auto lace shoes from *Back to the Future, Part II.* They came in all sorts of colors as well, even hot pink and bright yellow. However, I only stuck with one red pair and one black pair.

Come on. Does my color choice *really* surprise you?

Anyway, after I had all the clothes I wanted, we brought them down and over to the first-floor register, where a teenage girl was waiting for us.

She had long hair dyed a light blue, and it was pulled back into a ponytail. She also had maroon-colored eyes and a piercing in her left nostril.

"That's a lot of clothes," she said, using a typical valley girl, don't care teen attitude.

"Yeah, well, I'm a little rank, and I need some new ones," I replied.

She then proceeded to start ringing them up for me.

"I've never seen your species before," she said. "Where are you from?"

I then turned to Krite and looked at him to see if it would be okay to tell her the truth. He nodded his head.

"I'm from Earth," I replied.

"I've never heard of it," she said.

Upon hearing her response, I just gave her a funny look. I mean, you'd figure that on a planet like that, *everyone* would've heard of Earth.

"You've never heard of Earth?" I asked.

"No," she replied. "Why? Should I have?"

"How about Omra Surcy? Ever hear of him?"

"Again, no."

"Don't they teach you anything in school?"

"What's a school?" she curiously asked.

I don't believe it. A planet that doesn't send their kids to school?

"You know, school?" I proceeded to tell her. "A place where you learn about history and math and all that other stuff?"

"Oh!" she said, now nodding and smiling, finally realizing what the hell I was talking about. "Yeah, we got that here. But it's not called a school. It's called the tube."

"What's the tube?" I curiously asked.

"You know, it's a big, square, electronic box that broadcasts signals into it, and you watch it?" she replied.

"You mean, a TV?"

"What's a TV?"

Unbelievable! I thought to myself. *This place has television, but they call it the tube. Interesting. I wonder where else I've heard that expression?*

By the way, that last thought was a joke. And, yes, I did have a TV in my hotel room, but I didn't have any time to turn it on, nor would I for the duration of my stay. But don't worry. You'll understand why soon enough.

Anyway, I was broken away from my own thoughts by the cashier, but because I was thinking so hard about the tube and the lack of schools, I didn't hear a damn word she said. That's okay, though. Krite took care of the bill, and then we made our way out of the clothing store. After I piled into the limo with all of my stuff in tow, he rang in from the front seat.

"Where to next?" he asked.

I had to think about that one for a bit because Arnaxia was a relatively decent-sized planet. And because of that, there were probably a million places I could've visited while I was there. I just had to figure out what I was feeling at the moment.

Should I go and grab a bite to eat? Nah. I wasn't really all that hungry. Maybe I could go and check out some of the modern-day cinemas they have. Nah. I wasn't in the mood for a movie either. Oh, I know! A strip club! Definitely not.

After a few more minutes of racking my brain, a smile, now spanning from ear to ear, made its way to my face as I finally figured out where I wanted to go.

"Do you guys have any good coffee shops?" I inquired.

"What kind do you like?" he asked.

"All kinds."

"Then I know just the place."

• • •

About ten minutes later, we pulled up to a coffee shop on one of the main street corners and a little side street. The place must've been pretty well-known because the aliens (err, people) were going in and out of there like a colony of army ants.

I got out of the limo and just stood there so I could watch everyone for a few minutes. The service must've also been quick because people weren't even spending more than two minutes inside that place.

As I was standing there watching, I looked up at the sign to read the shop's name.

"Caf and a Half. How appropriate," I commented before turning toward Krite. "I haven't had a cup of coffee since Sartia and I left Jipduk. That was the first and only time this trip I've had some. It really gave me a high that I couldn't possibly understand."

"Say no more," he said. "When we recovered the ship's logs, your *coffee incident* happened to be in there. Therefore, I came prepared."

He then reached into his right front coat pocket and pulled out a little plastic case about the size of an egg. He opened it up and poured the contents of it into the palm of his left hand. It was a small, green pill, just about the size of standard ibuprofen.

"What the hell is that?" I asked.

"This will nullify the effects of your high after you drink the coffee," he replied. "Once you finish drinking, take this, and it'll feel like you never drank it at all."

"Do you happen to have any more of those?"

"In the car. And they're all yours."

Krite was awesome. The whole time he was carting me around the city, he never once complained.

"Shall we?" he asked, extending his left arm toward the shop door.

I didn't waste any time and practically ran into the shop like a dog chasing after a tennis ball. When I got in there, I took one look around and was just amazed at how massive the place actually was. To get a mental picture, think of any standard, solitary coffee shop, and then multiply that by six.

The whole middle of the shop was just an open floor, while a row of tables and chairs ran down the entire left and right sides. The electronic menu spanned across the whole top of the front wall behind the counter and went on for ages. They must've had every flavor of coffee ever made, and you could get it any way that you wanted: iced, hot, frappé, smoothie, small, medium, large, extra-large. The list just went on and on.

Again, I just stood off to the side, perusing the menu, trying to decide what the hell I wanted to get. I also did some people-watching as well. I studied what everyone else was getting and what the most popular form of coffee was. Of course, I also had Krite to translate the stuff I couldn't figure out myself.

Because I was on my own for a little bit, and because I had to read the star charts and other various pieces of equipment on the ship, I successfully deciphered and learned a little bit of the Arnaxian language. However, I was, by far, no expert. But from what I could tell, the most popular drink in that shop was an extra-large, chocolate-based, hot coffee. Which also happened to be right up my alley, because man, did I love chocolate.

In fact, I loved it so much, I used to get ribbed by everyone for saying that I would gladly choose chocolate over sex any day. I always told everyone that when it came to chocolate, I was worse than a woman. But I don't care. I love it.

For instance, every flavor of ice cream, coffee creamer, cake, and piece of candy I would buy was chocolate-based. And don't even get me started on how plain vanilla is. That's beside the point and would be an additional two-page argument.

Anyway, I finally got in line and waited until it was my turn to order. When I got up to the front counter, I could then see why everything was moving so quickly.

About ten screens were located on top of the front counter, allowing the patrons to place their own orders. After they selected what they wanted, they paid for their order by thumbprint. The baristas behind the counter would then make the order and hand it off to the customer. They were in and out without the hassle.

After receiving my extra-large, chocolate-based, hot coffee, we left the coffee shop and went back out to the limo. We both entered our respective seats, and once we were inside, Krite handed me the pill. I know he said to take it when I was done, but I couldn't help it. I wound up swallowing it with my first sip of coffee. Once the liquid entered my mouth, the flavor hit my taste buds almost instantly, and I was in heaven.

"Holy shit!" I said. "This stuff is awesome!"

"I'm glad you like it," he said.

We both sat there in silence for the next few minutes while I continued to sip my delicious coffee.

"Where to next?" Krite asked.

That was definitely a good question, as I had no idea what to do. All I knew was that I had my coffee, and life was now great. Mainly since I was now able to drink the stuff and not get high off of it.

"Would it be alright if we just drove around for a bit?" I asked.

"You got it," he replied.

He wound up driving me around for a good two hours while I sipped my coffee and enjoyed some of the sights out the window. It was the perfect thing to do, too, because it gave me enough time to snap some photos of what seemed like everything before I had to shut my phone off and save the battery.

However, after about two and a half hours, it hit me. I finally figured out what I wanted to do. It's also something I'd hoped to do since the moment I got there. Though, I was hoping I wouldn't have to do it alone. But, with my current situation, that was no longer an option.

"Hey, Krite?" I asked.

"Yes, sir," he replied.

"By the way, you really don't have to call me sir."

"Well then, what would you like me to call you?"

"Just call me Sam."

"Okay, Sam. What is it?" he asked.

"Is it possible to visit Sartia's house?"

As soon as I asked that question, he wasted no time immediately pulling the car over and putting it in park before turning around to stare at me with a somewhat disturbed look on his face. Of course, I was now curious about what the hell was going on and why he was now looking at me like that.

"What?" I asked. "Was it something I said?"

But he still didn't answer me. Instead, he just got out of the car and closed the door behind him.

Because I had asked him a question relating to Sartia, his actions immediately after that should've been my first clue that something was up. At the time, however, I had no idea what it was. But don't worry, though. You'll find out what it is soon enough.

He must've stood outside for a good ten minutes before climbing back into the car. However, he still didn't say anything. At that point, my curiosity had officially gone through the roof, and I just had to find out what was up.

"Is everything okay?" I asked.

"Are you absolutely sure you wanna visit her house?" he replied.

The way he asked me that question almost sounded as if he was urging on the side of caution.

After asking a question and getting a return question like that as a response, it can only mean one of two things: either there's something at her house that nobody wants me to see, or there's something I won't like. Regardless of what it was, I didn't care. I was hoping that I would eventually get to see where she lived, and I definitely wasn't gonna pass up the opportunity to do so.

"I do," I replied.

"Okay. But I hope for both of our sakes that no one sees us," Krite said.

I hope for both of our sakes that no one sees us? What the hell does he mean by that? That was the second thing that alerted me somebody was hiding something. But who? And why? Was it the government? Was it Sartia herself? Of course not. She was dead. It couldn't be her. However, my curiosity was now through the roof, and I just had to keep going.

Now, because of her profession, I pictured her living in an apartment high in one of the buildings, or maybe living in one of those basement joints with a panic room that was full of various weapons and armor. Nope. I was way wrong on both counts. Well, this time, anyway.

· · ·

We pulled up to the front of a two-story house on the outskirts of the city and parked. It was tan in color and looked just like one of those houses you'd see on a farm. It was all by itself with no one around it for a good 500 yards in every direction and was located on the beach in the middle of nowhere. The sand, not to mention a couple handfuls of palm, pine, and oak trees, made up the surrounding landscape. The forest was far behind it, while the ocean was directly in front of it.

I didn't even wait for Krite to open my door, as I was practically standing outside of the car before it even stopped. I just stood there, staring at her house, wondering what it would be like if she were there to show it to me. But she wasn't. So, I took a deep breath before stepping up onto the wrap-around porch.

Even though the houses and buildings looked normal, they still used advanced technology for granting access anywhere. The windows were made of an unbreakable, see-through material, very similar to bulletproof glass. To enter the house, you needed to use your thumbprint on the scanner, which was located on the steel door where the key lock would usually be.

Because she was gone, only the government now had access to her house. I just assumed it was because she had recently died and that they had to wait until the investigation was closed. Man, was I wrong.

Krite came over and pressed his thumb firmly on the scanner. When he did, there was a beep, followed by the door opening up all on its own. The anticipation was killing me while I waited to get inside. Once the door was all the way open, I crossed the threshold directly into her…

"What the fuck?" I blurted out.

Confusion isn't even the word I would use to describe what I was feeling or what I was now looking at.

I thought I would be crossing the threshold into her living room. But when I stepped foot in the house, there was no living room. The whole first floor looked like it had been gutted and replaced with a bunch of scientific equipment I'd never seen before.

Tubes, funnels, beakers, computers, wires, cables, and a bunch of other stuff filled the house. From the outside, it looked just like a typical, two-story house. But, apparently, that was all just an illusion.

"This isn't her house, is it?" I curiously asked.

"No. But I thought it would be best if you knew the truth," Krite said. "After all, you did bring her back to us."

My eyes immediately narrowed in confusion. "The truth about what? What is this place?"

"Follow me."

As usual, I was right. Something was definitely up. But what?

Krite led me straight ahead, through this first room, and into the next room. Once we got in there, the room itself looked like one of those basement scientific research facilities that you would only see in a horror or science fiction movie.

The whole inside of the room was made from solid steel and had no windows looking out. On the left wall was one table, which had only a towel, and a pile of neatly folded clothes on top of it. On the right wall was another table, which had a single digital clock on it. All the tubes and cables that I saw in the previous room led straight into the back of this room.

On the back wall sat a steel tube-looking thing, which all the cables ran directly into. It was about six feet long with a small window toward the top of it, which allowed you to peek inside.

"What the fuck is this place?" I asked, still not believing what I was seeing.

"This is a lab," Krite replied. "One of many labs on this planet."

"A lab? What kind of a lab? Are you guys doing some kind of weird, mad scientist shit in here?"

I then waited for Krite to give me an answer, but he didn't. When I turned to look at him, I noticed him staring at the lone clock sitting on the table along the room's right side. When I looked over at it, I noticed something about it that I didn't notice when I first entered the room. I saw that it was counting down. Of course, all of the numbers were in Arnaxian. But with the small amount of experience I had flying the ship and reading its coordinates, translating them was no problem.

I watched as the last five seconds ticked away: five… four… three… two… one.

Once that timer struck zero, I heard a loud hissing noise and immediately looked in the direction that it was coming from. It was coming from the steel tube along the back wall.

"What's going on, Krite?" I nervously asked.

"Just watch," he quietly replied.

The hissing coming out of the steel tube was followed by some smoke coming out of its cracks. The top half then started to rise up, and the more that it opened, the more smoke came out of it. A massive fan turned on, sucking the smoke right out and up through a huge pipe in the ceiling. After a few quick seconds, the steel tube was all the way open, and the smoke was completely gone.

But I just couldn't bring myself to go over there and see what was inside. Instead (and not a word about this to anyone), I kind of hid half of my body behind Krite to safely peek out at whatever was about to happen.

Oh, give me a break. Like you wouldn't have been scared either.

Anyway, I saw an amethyst-colored hand come out of that thing and grab the side. It was very creepy, almost like I was now watching some kind of twisted *Frankenstein* film.

Once the hand grabbed hold of the side, a body started to rise out of the tube. Whoever it was, they were completely naked. And, for obvious reasons, I could easily tell that it was a female. I couldn't see who it was, though, because she was covered in some kind of an opaque membrane, different from the one I saw cocooning Sartia.

Once she was sitting upright, she then took her hands and started to tear the membrane away from her body. That's when my eyes grew big. And because of who I was now looking at, I was no longer hiding behind Krite. Instead, I was standing directly in front of him, still not believing what I was actually seeing.

The membrane-less figure then turned to look at me, while confusion hit my face and my jaw hit the floor, just like a cartoon character.

It took me all but two seconds, as I immediately recognized *who* was coming out of that tube and *who* exactly I was now looking at. Of course, after seeing who it was, I tried my hardest to say something. Anything, for that matter.

But, no matter how hard I tried, only one single, solitary word managed to eventually leave my lips.

"Sartia?"

Rob J. LaBelle

Chapter 14

Okay. So, Sartia was dead, and then she was alive. Either that or my mind was playing tricks on me. Seeing her standing there now made me curious, confused, happy, and scared shitless, all at the same time. If that was even possible?

But, there I stood, practically wanting to piss myself from being so nervous. Regardless of anything I was currently feeling, it wasn't until after that very moment that for the rest of my trip, nothing shocked me anymore, and I just accepted everything as it was.

"You're alive?" I asked. "How?"

"Look, I know that I owe you an explanation," she said.

"Damn right, you owe me an explanation!" I said, slightly peeved. "I thought you were dead and that I was never gonna see you again!"

She turned to look at Krite. "Krite, can you give us a minute?" she asked.

Krite simply nodded before making his way out of the house.

She then turned back toward me. "Can you at least help me out of here?"

Immediately, I went over to the tube, grabbed her hand, and helped her step down onto the floor. I then took a few steps back while I watched her tear the rest of the membrane from her body. It fell onto the floor and now looked like a big, nasty, disgusting pile of skin. Once all the membrane was off of her, she grabbed the towel from underneath the pile of clothes, wiped herself off, and then used those very same clothes to get dressed. Sartia was now wearing a newer version of the outfit that she had on when she died.

"Much better," she said, happily looking over her new attire.

She then looked up at me. And when she did, I didn't know what I expected to happen next, other than her giving me an explanation, of course. Instead, she just smiled and ran over to me as we embraced each other with a hug. I held her so tight that I never wanted to let her go. She had died in my arms, and I remembered how bad I felt about it afterward. And I never wanted to feel that way again.

After what seemed like the longest hug in the history of hugs, she took her right hand, placed it on the left side of my face, looked deep into my eyes, and smiled. But what happened next, well, *that* was officially the last thing on the trip that took me by surprise.

"Oh, Sam. I love you, too," she said before planting one on my lips.

I couldn't believe it. She actually remembered the last thing I said to her.

If you recall, I had wound up spilling my guts to her right before she died and told her that I loved her. It was obviously an impulse thing because, at the moment, I thought I would never see her again. However, I meant it. And, apparently, so did she.

After she kissed me, we hugged once more before we stood apart from each other.

"I'm so sorry," she said.

"How in the holy hell are you standing here right now?" I asked.

"Did I forget to mention that my species can also clone themselves?"

Nah. She didn't forget to mention that. I managed to figure that one out all on my own.

"Yes!" I said. "That would've been, need to know information! When I thought that you had died, I cried my eyes out. I finally told you how I felt, and then you were gone. I thought I was never gonna see you again. But here you stand."

"You're right. Just like the whole shape-shifting thing, I should've told you sooner," she said.

"Yeah, you should've."

We then just stood there in awkward silence. She was silent because she knew that I was mad at her for not telling me. And because of it, she probably now felt guilty about the whole thing and didn't wanna say anything else.

I, on the other hand, was now standing there in silence for two reasons. The first being that I was still a little upset over her not telling me she could be cloned. The second was not knowing what was gonna happen now that she was alive again.

"So, uh," I began. "This body of yours... when you say clone, do you mean an actual clone? As in, your old body is now gone, and this is a fresh one grown from your DNA?"

"Correct," she replied.

"But how do you remember everything?"

"When a new clone is created, the consciousness from the old body is transferred into the new one."

"Oh. Well, that makes sense," I simply responded.

Again, at that point, nothing surprised me anymore.

"And," she began. "With this being a new body and all, everything you see is brand new."

"What do you mean, everything I see is brand new?" I cluelessly asked.

"Think about it," she said, staring at me intently with both eyebrows now raised.

It took me a second, but my eyes grew wide after I finally figured out what she was getting at.

"Oh!" I said.

"Which means..." she started to say before walking up to me.

Starting from my mid-section, she took her hands and slowly moved them from my stomach all the way up to my shoulders.

"You're coming back to my apartment with me, right now," she said, a colossal gleam now in her eyes.

Of course, it didn't take a genius to figure out where *that* whole thing was going. And even though I still had plenty of questions, I quickly decided to put those on the back burner. So, we wasted no time as we left the house and jumped into the back of the limo.

Thankfully, though, their limos also have privacy windows, which were both soundproof, and you couldn't see through them. Needless to say, we couldn't wait until we got back to her apartment. And I'm not even gonna tell you what the back of the limo looked like afterward, either.

• • •

When we finally arrived back at her apartment, we were already exhausted. If you know what I mean?

She lived on the 80th floor of one of the skyscrapers, which was located smack dab in the middle of the city. But the thing that really caught my attention was the fact that she needed to do a fingerprint and a retinal scan just to unlock her door.

Now, why would someone have so much security just to get into an apartment? Well, she did mention that she was a bounty hunter. She had also mentioned who she was going to marry, which made perfect sense after I thought about it. Regardless, I was still curious. Once we were inside, however, I finally understood why.

We entered her two-bedroom, one-bathroom apartment directly into her living room. It looked just like a typical apartment that you would see on Earth, including the furniture and the paintings.

To the left of the living room were the two bedrooms. The rightmost bedroom was the master bedroom, with the bathroom being accessible from both there and the living room. To the living room's right was a kitchen/dining area, and the whole apartment itself was about the size of two two-bedroom apartments built into one. It was actually surprisingly big.

I was now very impressed because, apparently, bounty hunting was a lucrative job and paid very well. And I'm sure that, along the way, you would probably make a few enemies in the process. Hence all of the security. But what I wasn't prepared for was what she had in that second bedroom.

The steel door leading into it would be my first indicator that something dangerous or top secret was in there. Also, the fact that she had to do another fingerprint and retinal scan to get in kind of gave it away. Once the door opened and we walked inside, however, I couldn't believe my eyes.

Just like the clone room, the walls were also made of solid steel. Three of the walls were lined with all kinds of guns and explosives, while the back of the room had a table with a computer on it and six different LED-type monitors secured to the wall above it. So, apparently, I was right about the basement-type apartment with a panic room. Only hers wasn't in the basement.

"Holy shit!" I said. "What the hell kind of bounty hunter are you, anyway?"

"An excellent one," she said. "But you have to be prepared for whatever job you decide to take."

I continued to peruse the weapons along the three walls. She had all kinds of alien grenades, bombs, rifles, knives, and even swords. Of course, I just couldn't help myself and wound up pulling out my phone to snap a few photos.

I then went to the back of the wall that housed the computer. The computer itself looked just like the one on her ship, and the monitors looked like they were showing video feeds of different places around the apartment, including the roof.

"Is that your ship?" I curiously asked, pointing to the top middle monitor.

"It is," she replied.

"Is that on this roof?"

"Of course."

"Are you telling me that your ship has been on the roof of your building this whole entire time?"

"Yeah. Why?"

I didn't say anything to her at the time, but as we walked through the lobby downstairs to come up, there was a part of me that thought, *This lobby looks really familiar.* I didn't really think anything of it because after I initially landed and came through here the first time, I was basically in and out in under five minutes.

Anyway, there it was. I landed her ship on the top of her building and didn't even know about it. I didn't really talk to her about it and just wound up adding it to the ever-growing list of things her people never told me.

"So, is your whole species a race of compulsive liars?" I asked. "Or are only a few of you?"

"What do you mean?" she replied.

"Where do I start? Let's see…" I began. "Oh yeah! First, you kept from me the fact that you were a shapeshifter. And now, after recent events, the fact that you can also be cloned. Your government also kept from me that very same fact while leading me to believe that you were truly dead. Then, out of the blue, they take me to see you, and somehow, you're alive.

"So now, I have to wait for them to return the sphere to the Morgidians. Because after they do, I'm no longer allowed in this sector and must return to Earth."

Whew! That felt good to get off my chest.

After I finished my tirade, I expected her to instantly jump down my throat in defense of her own people. But that wasn't the case. Instead, she now had a curious look on her face, almost as if something I said didn't make sense.

"Hold on a second," she said. "You said that the *government* is bringing the sphere back to the Morgidians?"

"Yeah. Why?" I replied.

"This was supposed to be my mission."

"But you died. They didn't have a choice."

"Really, Sam?" she asked, almost as if I was totally clueless.

"What?" I asked with a shrug. "Am I missing something?"

"Think about it. My whole race knows that we can be cloned. Once I was done processing, I should've been back to delivering the sphere myself. Not them."

"Then, why would they wanna take your bounty?"

"That's just it. Bounty hunters do all the dirty work, while the government just sits back on their asses and does nothing."

After she explained everything to me, something was now starting to not add up.

I then remembered something that happened back when I faced off against Slith. Something he told me that didn't make a lot of sense at the time, but now does. This also happens to be an essential conversation that Sartia and I never finished.

"Do you remember when we left Ckrob?" I asked.

"Yeah," she replied.

"Well, you told me that your fiancé wanted you to bring the sphere back to him and that I was to be unharmed. However, Slith told me that whoever sent out the bounty to them wanted us dead. To me, that makes no sense whatsoever."

She thought about that for a second before giving me a reply.

"You're right. That doesn't make sense," she said.

Now, with me being me, and because of our current conversation, my brain was suddenly working overtime as I started putting all of the variables into place while trying to make sense out of everything that was happening.

"I do have a thought," I said. "But you may not like it."

"What is it?" she asked.

"I think there's a second employer out there somewhere. I think that someone is undermining your fiancé and going behind his back without either of you even knowing about it. I also think your government is involved somehow."

"Are you talking about some kind of government conspiracy?"

"Not quite," I continued. "Because the Morgidians and the Arnaxians have the treaty, I think that your government has no choice but to be involved. Now, whether it's good or bad, I don't know. But because I was left in the dark and because both the Morgidians and the bounty hunters want us dead, I'm leaning toward bad."

"But why would my people allow you to see me if they wanted you gone?"

"I don't think they did."

Her eyes quickly narrowed. "What do you mean?"

"Right before Krite took me to see you, he was acting kinda weird. Almost as if he knew that what he was about to do was wrong. Plus, he never mentioned anything about the government."

Then, there was silence, as we both just continued to stand there with our brains in overload, trying to make heads or tails out of this whole situation.

Now, we could've easily just waited there until the sphere was returned, and I was sent home. But being on that trip had seemed to wake me up somehow. It made me come out of my shell and man up to take on specific challenges that I never thought would be possible. Let me explain…

If I was still on Earth, there's no way in hell that I could've ever been that brave. I would've just went on living my everyday, monotonous life as a future video game store manager. Although the money would've been pretty good. And with it, I probably could've gotten a lot more dates as well. But, again, I digress.

As I was saying, I owe a lot to Sartia. I've been with other women before, but no one has made me want to be a better person than she did. When I was around her, she brought out the best in me, and I can't explain why.

So, having said that, and her knowing my real personality, what came out of my mouth next, totally caught her by surprise.

"I say we find out," I said.

And, just as I expected, the look on her face was priceless. Of course, I couldn't help myself and quickly pulled out my phone to snap a photo.

"Are you out of your fucking mind?" she asked. "You wanna fly off after my people and go to Morgide, just to see what's up?"

I shrugged. "Why not? Instead of you helping me, I now have a chance to help you. Besides, if they get the sphere back to Morgide before you do, the deal with your fiancé is off, and we're both dead. Personally, if I have no choice but to return to Earth, I'd rather do it amongst the living."

Instead of giving me an immediate response, she just stared at me intently for what seemed like the longest few seconds of my life. By that point, I think I understood her enough to know exactly what she was gonna say. However, nothing could've prepared me for what she actually did say.

"Let's go to the bedroom," she said, grabbing my left hand with her right.

She then dragged me out of her panic room and straight into her bedroom.

Again, I'm not gonna tell you what happened in there. Instead, I'm just gonna skip the next hour or so and let you use your own imagination.

• • •

After getting the hard part out of the way (pun intended), we both showered, got dressed, and then made our way back into the panic room. I know it wasn't really a panic room. I just liked to call it that because it was easy to remember.

I was also now wearing some of the new clothes I had purchased earlier that morning. I threw on some new underwear, socks, one of my red t-shirts, and a pair of blue jeans. Even though I had bought some new sneakers, I just couldn't bring myself to wear them. I loved my Converse way too much.

We were now both just standing there, thinking, while I continued to stare at all of the weapons on the wall. As I was looking around, I recognized a few of them I'd seen before. One of them being the Dukian burrower. I also saw the same Vaknoid pulse rifle that Slith had. And some of the small arms guns were the same ones used by the bounty hunters on Metoria.

I also saw a Morgidian death ray, as I liked to call them. It was the same rifle the Morgidians used, and it was also the very same one that they disintegrated my apartment with. After I was done looking over the weapons, I eventually turned my attention to the monitors.

The first thing I looked at was the ship sitting on top of the roof, and I couldn't help but think that her apartment was right under my nose this entire time. I then started thinking about my experience so far and why everyone kept lying to me. But, that was quickly put on the backburner when I noticed some movement coming from the monitor that allowed us to view the building's front door.

"Fuck me," I whispered.

Without saying a word, she turned to look at me before looking at the very same monitor I was now staring at.

"Oh shit," she said.

Apparently, my theory about government conspiracies and wanting to kill us was right. We could now see about 20 or so Arnaxian military members, in full riot gear, storming the building with their guns drawn.

"Well, I guess that answers that," I said.

"We need to get out of here," she said.

"How much time do we have before they get up here?"

"I'd say around five minutes or so."

"Five minutes?" I remarked, my eyes now wide. "That doesn't really give us a lot of time. What do we do?"

"We gather whatever weapons we can carry, and we run."

"Run? Run where?"

"You're cute," she said, briefly placing her right hand on the left side of my cheek. "But could you please try and keep up? We have to intercept the ship that has the sphere and get it back."

"Oh, right. And, thanks. I'll follow your lead."

Five minutes? Yeah. Five minutes isn't even long enough to go to the bathroom, let alone gather a handful of weapons, stuff them into a duffel bag, and get our asses to the roof.

Anyway, we were now busy prepping, and for the first time, even though we weren't on the ship, I could hear some music playing. Up until that point, I had only heard music while I was on the ship. However, I didn't care. And I didn't even have time to ask. But, in my mind, it was the perfect moment for a song.

"Invincible" by Pat Benatar started playing, and suddenly, I felt like I was in one of those movies where a music montage is overdubbed into a scene showing people loading their weapons and getting ready to head into battle. Sorry, I can't think of any movie references off the top of my head. But it seemed to help, though, because I was now energized and gathering weapons like there was no tomorrow.

After the quickest weapons collection in history, we had two minutes left to spare. So, we both threw the bags over our shoulders, left the panic room, and quickly went out the front door. Once we were in the hallway, our two minutes quickly turned into five seconds, as we could now see the Arnaxian military running toward us.

"Stop!" one of the military members ordered.

"This way!" Sartia said, taking off in the opposite direction.

The moment we ran, and wouldn't you know it, they started firing at us. Luckily, we managed to get through the door and into the stairwell without getting hit. Once it fully closed, the music we heard coming from within the apartment was playing no more.

• • •

When I first landed on the rooftop the day before, I said that the building was a little shorter than the Empire State Building. Yeah. Two floors. Two fucking floors shorter. Do you know how hard it was to run up eight flights of stairs with a full armament of weapons strapped to your back? Let's put it this way…

By the time we reached the top, I literally felt like I was gonna die. And seeing those scenes in different movies where people are carrying backpacks full of weapons and running around like it's no big deal? Yeah. Nothing but a big load of shit. The sack that I had draped over my back was fucking heavy. It literally felt like I was carrying cement bricks.

Sorry. That's enough of my bitching. I'll just get back to the story.

Once we were on the roof, we went through the door and started running for the ship. When we were only a few feet away from it, the side hatch opened, and the ramp came down. It was almost as if the ship knew that it was Sartia coming toward it. Don't ask me how, because I never got the chance to ask her either.

We darted up the ramp and immediately dropped the heavy bags of weapons down in the corridor. She headed straight for the cockpit, but I just stayed put and was now bent over, huffing and puffing, trying to catch my breath.

"Thank god. We made it," I said, still gasping for air.

"Will you get your ass up here?" she ordered me from the captain's chair.

So, I stood up and hit the button next to the side hatch to close it. I then immediately went up to the cockpit and sat in the passenger's seat. The second that I did, my harness buckled itself, and the engines were primed.

But before we took off, though, the military members came bursting through the rooftop door and started firing at us, yet again.

"They're shooting at us!" I said.

"Don't worry. They can't get through the shields," she reassured me.

The glowing half orbs then came out, and Sartia quickly placed her hands on them.

"Hang on!" she said before lifting off and sending us skyward.

We shot straight up like a missile. And, again, it took us less than two seconds to break through the planet's atmosphere and reach wild space. The problem was, it took us less than two seconds to leave the surface, only to now be surrounded by a fleet of Arnaxian ships. Well, it sure looked like a fleet, anyway.

"Son of a bitch!" I said, annoyed. "Don't they ever give up?"

"Nope. And they probably won't until we're dead," she replied.

"What do we do now?"

But before she could answer me, we heard a female voice being broadcast through the ship's speaker on the panel.

"Arnaxian ship, ID number zero six one nine seven nine, drop your shields and prepare to be boarded," the voice said.

I turned to Sartia with a panicked look on my face.

"You're not really gonna drop your shields, are you?" I asked.

"Of course not," she replied.

"Then what do we do?"

At that point, in my mind, we now only had two options: we could either stay, fight, and probably get blown to bits, or we could try to outrun them and still get blown to bits.

Knowing what our options were and what we were now up against, I thought back to how much trouble we had against the four Morgidian warships. I couldn't even begin to imagine how we'd fare against ten Arnaxian ships.

"Arnaxian ship, ID number zero six one nine seven nine, this is your last warning. Either drop your shields and prepare to be boarded, or you will be destroyed!" the female voice said again.

"They really know how to sugar coat it, don't they?" I remarked.

Without saying a word, Sartia then pressed a button on the panel. Of course, at that very same moment, I just happened to be looking over at her and saw exactly which button she pressed.

"Light speed? Tell me you're not serious?" I asked.

"Do you have a better plan?" she replied.

"But we'll be jumping blind."

"Either we jump blind, or we stay, fight, and die. Your choice."

"Shit," I muttered.

She was right. We didn't have any other choice but to jump to light speed from our current location.

Usually, when people jump to light speed, they are already in a known travel route, and therefore, don't have to worry about running into an asteroid field or a planet. But, with a few ships and a couple of moons currently surrounding us, that was gonna be pretty dangerous.

"Okay," I said. "Light speed it is."

"I was hoping you'd say that," she said. "Hold on!"

Immediately, she pushed the button to jump to light speed, and we now had about two seconds before the ship took off. So, she put her hands on the controls while I just closed my eyes. I silently prayed that we didn't hit something and blow up shortly after takeoff.

But once the ship jumped, and after leaving everything in our space dust, it was smooth sailing. I then opened my eyes and was now looking ahead to reaching that ship and getting the sphere back.

Rob J. LaBelle

Chapter 15

Well, here we are. We finally made it. The last official leg of this story. There are only a few chapters left to go, and I know that by now, you probably think I'm nuts. Or crazy. Or just plain old insane. Or, you could even be thinking about when this whole ridiculous story is gonna end just so you can get the hell out of here. But don't worry, we're almost done. So, just do what I do… sit back, relax, and enjoy the craziness.

Okay. Let's continue, shall we?

Anyway, there we were, now on our way to intercept the Arnaxian ship that was carrying the sphere. We were flying through wild space and had put our ship on autopilot, so we could sort out our weapons and figure out who would use which one. The whole lot was spread out in the galley, taking up the entire island and table.

"Is Rawr gonna be okay by himself at your place?" I asked.

"He'll be fine," Sartia said. "Someone will stop by and take care of him."

"So, uh, how come you never told me that you could be cloned?"

"I was going to, but then I died. Remember?"

"*That's* what you were gonna tell me?"

She laughed. "Of course not. First, I was gonna tell you that I love you, and then I was gonna tell you about my cloning abilities."

"Oh. Good."

"That's why I told you to bring my body back to Arnaxia."

"I now understand why," I replied while nodding.

"You know, I'm surprised you didn't connect the dots once you saw me come out of the tube?"

"Well, I'm sorry. But I was a little busy trying to figure out how in the hell *you* were still alive."

"I really am sorry."

"Don't worry about it. I'm just happy to have you back," I said with a smile.

She also smiled before we continued sorting through the weapons.

For the next few minutes, we organized everything on that counter and table to exact precision. However, by the time we had finished, another tantalizing thought was now burning a hole in my brain.

"So, how many times can one be cloned?" I asked.

"That's an excellent question," she replied. "Until someone is married, they can be cloned as many times as they'd like."

"And, afterward?"

"That's it. The cloning process stops."

"That's kind of a weird rule," I remarked.

"It's not a rule. It's the law."

"Are there any laws regarding yours, or any other species, marrying an Earthling?"

Holy shit. I can't believe that just slipped out of my mouth. What the hell was I thinking? Did I really just ask that? Well, it was too late to take it back now.

However, I think she could immediately tell how embarrassed I was after asking that question because once my face turned a bright red, she cracked a little smile.

"No," she said. "There are no laws regarding that subject matter."

"Yet, we aren't allowed in this sector unless it's an emergency?" I remarked. "They should really change that."

"What does it matter? Yes, there are no laws saying we can't marry an Earthling, but there are also no laws stating that we have to stay in the sector either."

"Good to know."

Now that I knew the basics about cloning laws and how many times someone could be cloned, another exciting thought had entered my mind. And, remembering what she told me of the treaty, this next thought was a pretty big one.

"Hold on a second," I said. "How many other species in this sector know about your cloning abilities?"

"I had a feeling you'd ask that. No one, other than the Arnaxians, is allowed to know about it," she replied. "As far as I know, you're the only other non-Arnaxian that knows."

"Well, what about the treaty?"

"What about it?"

"I mean, if you were to marry one of the Morgidians, wouldn't they know about it?"

"Oh, that," she said before nodding. "Well, like I told you before, once we're married, we're not allowed to be cloned anymore."

"Then, what happens if you're promised to one of them, and you die beforehand?" I asked.

"Our bodies are then shipped back to Arnaxia so we can be cloned. Once we're walking around again, we either live in solitude on the planet, or we move away."

"That's a really shitty way to live. I mean, what if-"

Unfortunately, we never got a chance to finish that conversation because we were swiftly interrupted by the ship's alarm system. And it definitely wasn't the planetary alert either.

"What the hell's that?" I asked.

"We're approaching a ship," she said.

"The other Arnaxian ship?"

"I don't know. Let's go find out."

We both immediately dropped what we were doing and made our way up to the cockpit. After we sat down, she took the ship out of light speed. We both then looked out of the cockpit window, only for us to now see two ships heading straight for us. But the closer we got, we noticed that they weren't actually flying toward us. Instead, we noticed that they were floating toward us. Both ships were dead in the water. One of them was still intact, but the other one, well, let's just say that I felt really sorry for the crew.

Once we got close enough, we started hitting the debris field of the ship that was blown to smithereens. Pieces of its hull, seats, bodies, and other miscellaneous things were now banging up against the side of our ship.

"What the hell happened?" I asked.

"I don't know," she said. "But it looks like they were in some sort of a battle."

Sartia then turned on the scanner to do some preliminary scans of the outlying area.

"Well, I don't see any other ships around," she said. "And these two are definitely Arnaxian. Most likely, the ones bringing the sphere back to Morgide."

"Who would wanna blow them up?" I asked.

"Pretty much anyone looking to make a profit by returning the sphere."

"Damn. Well, is the sphere floating around or still aboard the other ship?"

"It's definitely not floating around, but we can't check the other ship from here either."

As soon as she said that, I now feared the worst and just hoped she wouldn't say what I *thought* she was gonna say.

"What do you mean we can't check it from here?" I curiously asked. "Are you saying that we have to get aboard the other ship?"

"That's exactly what I'm saying," she replied.

Yup. She said it. And after hearing it, all I could do was just slump down in my chair and sigh.

But perhaps there was a way I could still get out of it.

"Wait a minute," I said. "If whoever was looking for the sphere had left, don't you think they would've taken it with them?"

"Probably. But we have to be thorough," she replied.

"I was afraid you'd say that."

Well, so much for the idea of not going aboard the other ship.

"Let's go put on our spacesuits," she said before getting up and making her way down the corridor.

I then got up out of my chair and followed her down to the sleeping quarters. We stopped right outside the door but didn't go in. Instead, she bent down and pulled up one of the floor panels, revealing a hidden compartment underneath that occupied six spacesuits. They definitely didn't look like any spacesuits I've ever seen. Well, except for in the movies, of course.

The six suits were black in color and had a round, fishbowl-style glass helmet that fit over your head. At first glance, they looked a little weird. But after I wound up putting one on, I knew it would be able to get the job done.

"Here," she said, throwing one of the suits at me. "Put this on."

As I held this thing in my arms, I just stared at it for a bit. And after looking it over, I realized that it had many different parts to it. But because I was unsure how to put it on, I just decided to follow her lead and put mine on the same way she did.

First, we started with the boots. The boots looked more like a pair of boots that a superhero would wear. But the look basically fooled me, as they were actually quite comfortable.

Second, we put on the pants, followed by the chest piece. The pants themselves had a weird belt-type looking thing around the waist, with round metal hooks attached in four spots: the left side, the right side, the front, and the back. The chest piece already had the sleeves and gloves attached, making it reasonably easy to just slip right on. It also had three metal tubes attached to the back of it that held our oxygen.

Lastly, we put on the helmet. Once the glass dome was over our heads, we then had to activate the whole suit by pushing a button on the control panel located on the left wrist. Once the button was pushed, the entire suit magnetically sealed itself shut at the ankles, waist, and head. Once the activation process was complete, you would then hear a hiss come from the suit, letting you know that everything was now sealed and airtight.

After the whole suit was on and breathable, something happened that I wasn't entirely prepared for. The suit immediately started to shrink and conform to fit my body shape. I then found out the reason it did that was to allow for effortless body movement while walking around in zero gravity.

Other than the suit activation button, the panel on the wrist also had many different functions. When it was activated, it would tell you the atmosphere outside of the suit, how much oxygen you had remaining, and if there were any cracks or flaws within the suit itself.

So, there it was. A skintight, easy to move in spacesuit that, unfortunately, if you were a man, didn't hide much of anything. It was also a good thing I was wearing clothes underneath there because, like I said, those suits left nothing to the imagination. If you catch my drift?

After both of our spacesuits were on and our wrist monitors were green across the board, Sartia pulled out two tethers from within the floor panel and attached them to our backside hooks.

"Are you ready?" she asked.

"As ready as I'll ever be," I replied.

"Good. And if anything happens to your suit, come back here immediately. Once you're inside, close the hatch, pressurize the cabin, and then take off your suit. That whole process should take no more than thirty seconds."

"Close, pressurize, strip. Got it."

Of course, I told her that I got it. But in all reality, I didn't have shit.

Now that I knew I was about to take my first-ever spacewalk, my heart was beating so fast that I felt like it was gonna punch a hole right through my chest. I also started to sweat, which caused my suit to become a bit moist on the inside and made my helmet begin to fog up.

"Activate the magnets on your boots and hold on to something," she instructed.

I quickly hit the button on my wrist pad, and when I did, my boots instantly grabbed hold of the floor beneath me. I then grabbed onto the tether, looked at her, and nodded.

Wasting no time, she pushed the button on the side door to open it up, and as soon as it did, a powerful suction that felt just like an overpowered vacuum cleaner started pulling me toward it. Thankfully, that only lasted a couple of seconds. And once the atmosphere was completely sucked out of the ship, we were ready to go.

Sartia went first as she lept from the ship and hurled herself into space. About halfway across, she activated the jets on her suit and guided herself over to the side hatch of the incapacitated ship. Once she was safely over, I then took my own leap of faith.

I will say this, though, floating through space without a care in the world is an utterly indescribable experience. I could tell you that as I was floating out there, staring at the stars, feeling like I could fly, and not worrying about a single thing, was the best feeling in the world. But it wouldn't make much of a difference unless you actually got to experience it for yourself.

Anyway, I was now hurtling through empty space, and once I got halfway there, I activated my own jets and guided myself toward the dead ship.

"Took you long enough," she said.

"Well, excuse me, Miss 'I've already done all this stuff before,'" I sarcastically replied.

"Okay. I'll give ya that one," she replied with a smirk.

With the way she said that I could tell she was already thinking of a way to get back at me.

She then turned her attention back toward the ship and, using the wrist pad on her suit, logged in a few commands, which she used to override the dead ship's current systems, opening up the door in the process. After it opened, we floated right inside.

• • •

You could tell it was an Arnaxian ship because inside and out, it looked just like Sartia's ship. The only difference was that the one we were now in was about double the size. Once we were safely inside, I cautiously followed her toward the cockpit.

As we started to navigate the empty, dark, spooky corridor, I suddenly felt like I was in some kind of a space horror film like *Alien* or *Pandorum*.

After we made it to the cockpit, Sartia navigated the control panel to try and get the ship up and running. Unfortunately, someone had already decided to turn it into Swiss cheese. There were blaster marks strewn across the entire thing, as it was now completely inoperable.

"What the hell?" I remarked. "Why would someone wanna disable the ship? And where's all the crew?"

"Two excellent questions," she said. "Let's go."

We then left the cockpit and started to make our way down the corridor. One by one, we checked out each room of the ship while also looking for the sphere in the process. First up was the captain's quarters.

As we stood outside the door, Sartia punched in a few commands on her wrist pad to override it. Once she got it open, we went inside to have a look around.

"Empty," she said.

After exiting the captain's quarters, we immediately made our way down to the bathroom. I already knew it was highly unlikely that anyone would be in there. Although, I've seen one too many movies where someone gets shot with an arrow or gun or even gets mutilated by a suicidal maniac while sitting on the shitter. But, my hopes were high, and my gut was telling me that it was empty. And when Sartia got that door open, we took a look inside.

"Empty," she said.

Thank god! I thought to myself.

We then made our way down to the sleeping quarters, where, thankfully, the door was already open. And, thankfully, no one was inside.

"Well, that was quick and painless," I said.

"Come on," she said before heading further down the corridor.

Next up was the galley.

We entered the oversized kitchen to, once again, see that no one was in there. I, for one, was glad it was empty.

However, at that point, all the rooms on the ship have now been checked, except for one… the engine room.

So, we turned right out of the galley and were now standing at the back door. Sartia then punched a few more commands into her wrist pad to try and open the door. But, for some strange reason, the override codes seemed to be giving her an issue.

"Dammit!" she said.

"What's wrong?" I asked.

"Someone locked this one up pretty good."

"Oh shit. That's never a good sign."

Now, as you probably already know, when someone locks a door up tight and doesn't want you to get in, there's always an excellent chance they're hiding something inside. Whether or not it was good or bad was still yet to be determined. But, from my experience in watching various horror and science fiction films, it was usually bad.

"Just give me a few more moments, and… got it!" she said, successfully inputting the proper codes.

No sooner did those words leave her lips, the door to the engine room swooshed open. We were instantly greeted by a purple swarm of floating blood crystals. They hit my helmet like shards of glass hitting the floor in slow motion.

"Tell me that's not what I think it is?" I cautiously asked.

"Blood," she replied.

Both of us took a deep breath before going through the door. Once we stepped foot into the engine room, we took one look around as our jaws hit the bottoms of the insides of our helmets.

A few of the bodies were melted to the back of the fusion reactors, while others just floated around aimlessly. However, the one thing they all had in common was that each one was riddled with bullet holes. Or laser holes. Or whatever they were shot with.

The entire complement of 15 crew members, including the captain, was dead. And don't even ask me about the crew from the other ship because they were nowhere to be found.

"Who would do something like this?" I asked.

"I'm guessing it's someone who so badly wanted to get their hands on that sphere," she replied.

"That's just barbaric."

"Come on. The sphere's not here. Let's get off this graveyard and head back to the ship."

"That's the best idea I've heard in a while."

The crew was dead, the sphere was gone, and we were none the wiser for going over there in the first place. So, we quickly made our way back to the side hatch, where we then hurled ourselves out into space and back toward her ship.

• • •

Again, she went first and was able to make it back safely. I then followed suit and jumped back over there myself.

Unfortunately, what happened next, I don't wish on anyone, not even my mortal enemy. Well, maybe my mortal enemy.

I mean, if they wanted to kill me, I suppose it would be better if it was them and not me. Sorry, just rambling thoughts.

Anyway, I was about halfway over there and was just about to activate my jets when out of nowhere, a slew of laser shots rang out from behind me, hitting the ship.

"Sam!" Sartia screamed out.

But I couldn't do anything. When the laser shots hit the ship, the tether got jostled and pulled me around into a spin. In all of the confusion, I panicked and activated my jets, hoping that once they turned on, I'd be able to straighten myself out and navigate myself back to the ship. That didn't quite happen.

"Hold on, Sam!" I could hear her scream at me. "I'm gonna try and pull you in!"

As far as I could tell, she was able to grab onto the tether with her hands and start to pull. But because I was still spiraling out of control, it was difficult for her to get a good grip. After a few seconds of trying, and just when she was finally able to start pulling me in, a couple more shots were fired, hitting the ship while knocking her down in the process. I, again, was spinning around and had a hard time seeing what was going on.

But after a few more minutes of spinning and turning, I was finally able to get myself under control and now had a good view of her ship, along with whatever it was that was firing at us. It was a Morgidian warship. I've seen plenty of them on that trip already and recognized it almost immediately. But that didn't matter. The only thing that currently mattered was me getting my ass back onto the ship so that we could get the hell out of there.

I looked down at Sartia from my view high above the ship while the tether continued to hold me in place.

"Hang on! I'm coming!" I shouted.

I activated my jets once again and was now on my way. That is until a rogue shot broke the tether and sent me hurtling over the ship and into wild space, missing everything entirely. Unfortunately, at my current rate and speed, my jets had pretty much the same effect as a water hose, and I knew that I wasn't gonna make it back.

"Sartia!" I screamed out, hoping she would hear me.

"Hold on, Sam!" I heard her say. "I'm coming to get you!"

As I was floating farther and farther away, the ship's view just kept getting smaller and smaller. I could still see it, but by that point, I was so far out that it looked just like a matchbox car. But that's when I saw something that gave me just a little bit of hope. That's when I saw the ship start to move.

Apparently, Sartia was now back to piloting her ship while engaging the Morgidian warship in a game of cat and mouse. Shots fired from her ship hit the warship before the warship retaliated and fired back, hitting her twice. She swirled, and turned, and dove, and rose up, trying to avoid the warship's onslaught. But from where I was, I wasn't able to get a good look at everything. I just hoped that I was still close enough for her to hear me.

"Sartia, can you hear me?" I asked.

However, the only noise I could now hear coming from the speaker in my helmet was a small crackle, followed by silence. I was too far away. She couldn't hear me, and I couldn't hear her. I felt so helpless floating out there, and the only thing I could do now was watch the ensuing battle in hopes that she would come out alive.

Because her ship was powered down when we were doing our spacewalk, it was already pretty vulnerable. So when the Morgidian ship fired upon it, it got severely damaged. Even though she was able to fly it around, it was already weakened by the previous shots. And, unfortunately, after a few more minutes of battle, the unthinkable happened.

I saw the Morgidian warship take one more swoop toward hers. And when it fired upon her, that was it. The ship was instantly lit up like a star gone supernova.

"Sartia!" I screamed, hoping that she somehow survived and was still able to hear me.

The explosion quickly dissipated into nothing, and I just couldn't believe it. For the second time in as many days, Sartia was gone. And there was no coming back from it this time. With that kind of an explosion, there's no way in hell anything could've survived. The only things left floating around out there was space debris and the other dead ship.

As for myself, I was now drifting into oblivion, with only 15 percent of my oxygen remaining. I was gonna die out there in the middle of space, leaving my body to just float around for all of eternity. Or, at least, until I entered a planet's atmosphere. In which case, I would just burn up and disintegrate into nothing.

I'll tell ya, though, being out in space where you can hear absolutely nothing anywhere was pretty creepy in itself. Yet, floating around in the serenity of silence was very calming and soothing.

So, I just waited out there, floating around, breathing nice and shallow to conserve whatever oxygen I had left. I just looked around at all of the stars and thought how lucky I was to have been able to visit some of them. But, my time had come to an end. There was no way in hell I would be coming out of that one alive.

Oh, come on. I'm sitting here talking to you. Of course, I came out of it alive. Just not the way I had hoped.

As I was floating there, I looked down at my wrist and saw that I only had two percent of my oxygen remaining. Definitely no time to panic. Yeah, right. That was the *perfect* time to panic. Primarily because, once I looked up from my wrist, I could see a ship way off in the distance now coming toward me. I knew that it couldn't be Sartia because, well, she was dead. So, if it wasn't her, then who was it? Who could it be? I would soon find out.

• • •

As the ship got closer and closer, a shape started to appear. Once it was in full view, I could then tell that it was, above all other possible ships, a Morgidian warship. Most likely, the same one that destroyed Sartia's ship. That was also the first time I got the chance to see one up close and personal. That thing was massive and was about double the size of Sartia's. And as I just floated there, now feeling insignificantly small, I finally understood why it took a lot of reasonable skill and piloting to beat them.

Once it got close enough, I noticed that it wasn't the front of the ship I was looking at, but the back. Before I realized what was happening, the back hatch started to come down, and I could now see into the ship's hangar bay. But it was empty. There was nothing in there except a few Morgidians and an unknown figure that I couldn't make out, all wearing similar spacesuits to the one I had on.

One of the Morgidians then pulled out some type of a gun before firing it at me. After, whatever he shot struck me, I suddenly realized what it was. It was a tether.

I now had a big choice to make. Either I could grab the tether and have them pull me into the ship so they could question me, torture me, and then kill me later, or I refuse and stay out there to die of oxygen deprivation.

So, with my options now literally dangling in front of me, I did what anyone else would do. Well, at least me, because I wasn't ready to die just yet.

I grabbed the tether and hooked it to the front of my belt. As soon as it was secure, I signaled to them, and they started to pull me in. The closer to the ship I got, the more I began to sweat. Now, if you thought that my heart was pounding and I was sweating bullets before, well, that was merely a false statement on me.

After a quick 30-second pull, I was finally inside the cargo bay, which could easily fit one of Sartia's ships. The hatch was then closed, and the pressure was reinitialized, along with the oxygen levels. One of the Morgidian beasts undid my tether, and I watched as they both walked away.

They didn't leave the hangar bay, though. They merely went and stood up against either side of the hangar bay doors. Once they were set, the person standing in front of me, whom I couldn't see before and still didn't know who it was, spoke out.

"It's alright. You can take your helmet off now," the female voice said.

Wait a minute, I said to myself. *I recognize that voice. I've heard it before. But where?*

I immediately stood up, undid my helmet, and took it off. The female, whose back I was now staring at, also did the same. When her helmet came off, I could then see a big ball of purple hair just fall down to the middle of her back.

An Arnaxian? I thought. *What was she doing aboard a Morgidian ship? And why?*

But whose voice did I recognize that I couldn't quite put a finger on? Before I even got a chance to think about all of the female Arnaxians I'd met so far, she turned around and spoke to me, face to face.

"Hello, Mr. Watson," she said. "It's so nice to see you again."

Utter shock had now taken over, and the look on my face said it all, as I just couldn't believe *who* was now standing there directly in front of me.

Chapter 16

"Del Surcy?" I said, confusion now written all over my face.

I honestly had no idea what the hell I was gonna do with myself now. Sartia was dead for a second time, and there was absolutely no chance she would come back from that. I know because I saw the ship explode.

As luck *wouldn't* have it, I get rescued by the Morgidians and taken aboard their ship, only to find out that the ruler of Arnaxia is somehow in league with them.

From what Sartia told me about the history between Morgide and Arnaxia, and just as a quick recap, they signed a treaty of sorts to have any unspoken for Arnaxian woman marry a Morgidian in order to keep the peace. I had no idea if Del was already married or not, but she had to be aboard that ship for a reason.

So, what was it? Was she promised to marry some red-skinned beast herself? Or was she merely working with them somehow? I think it was about time she gave me some answers.

"What the hell are you doing here?" I asked Del.

"That's the kind of thanks I get for saving your life?" she snidely replied.

365

"Saving my life?" I said, annoyed before throwing my helmet onto the floor. "You blew up one of your own ships and murdered sixteen crew members!"

"*Fifteen* crew members."

"If you include Sartia, it was sixteen."

"I'm really sorry about that. She was an outstanding pilot and one of my best hunters."

Like I said, until this little adventure had started, I probably would've never done or said what I was about to do and say.

"You purple-haired bitch!" I angrily shouted before running at her like a bull charging a piece of red cloth.

Of course, my heroic moment was cut short because she and the other two Morgidians all pulled out their guns and were now pointing them at me. Once that happened, I stopped dead in my tracks.

"I really thought you were smarter than that," she said.

I could then see her start to glare at me intently. Her intense stare slowly turned into a smirking smile, followed by a nodding head, almost as if she had just figured out a really tough riddle.

"Now I see it," she said.

"See what?" I asked.

"You liked her, didn't you?"

"I'm not telling you a damn thing."

"You can't hide it from me now. It's written all over your face. As a matter of fact," she said before pausing. "I think you were in love with her."

Although I now hated her for what had just happened, I had to admit, she was good. I don't know how she knew, but she did.

"No, I'm not," I replied.

"If it makes you feel any better to deny it, then that's your problem," she said.

"Whatever. You owe me some answers."

"Oh, I'll tell you everything you wanna know. But before I do, let me show you around the ship."

"I'm not taking your shitty tour until you talk."

"Look around you, Sam," she said, motioning to our current surroundings. "I can either kill you now, or I can kill you later. The choice is yours. But I implore you to take the tour. After all, it's a long trip back to Morgide from here."

Unfortunately, she was right. I was now on a ship surrounded by the enemy. What choice did I have? However, I still needed to know what the hell was going on, and I definitely wasn't gonna let my own death get in the way of that... yet.

"Fine! I'll take the stupid tour," I said, just like a little kid who doesn't get their own way.

"Good," she replied. "But before we do, why don't you take that spacesuit off? Then, we'll go."

As she stood there, pointing her gun at me, I took off every piece of my spacesuit and just left it right there in the hangar bay. I didn't care. And, frankly, I didn't like that thing anyway.

I then walked ahead of Del and made my way toward the two Morgidians standing on either side of the hangar bay doors. Once I got over there, I watched as the doors pulled apart, just like a set of doors that you would see at a supermarket. The Morgidians went through first, then me, and then Del. Once we were all through, the doors closed, and the tour was officially underway.

• • •

The ship itself was two stories high. We were currently standing in the bottom corridor, which housed all of the sleeping quarters, two bathrooms, and the engine room. The ship's second floor had a couple more bathrooms, a galley, a conference room, and the cockpit. I was actually pretty impressed at how well it was all set up.

It had a total of six engines, compared to the four on Sartia's ship. They also had four guns, two of them located underneath each front part of the ship's wings, and could rotate and fire in a 360-degree rotation. I would say that gave them a little bit of an edge.

The corridors were completely square in shape, as opposed to the half-round corridors on the Arnaxian models. Plus, the lighting was better too.

"I gotta say, this ship is pretty impressive," I said while looking around and trying to make small talk.

"Just another reason why we have the treaty with them," she said.

"Let me ask you something… are you afraid of the Morgidians?"

"Us? Afraid? Of course not."

"Then why do you still go along with this treaty? Why not back out?"

"And start a war? I don't think so."

I could tell just by the tone of her voice that she was definitely afraid.

"That's it, isn't it? You're afraid," I said.

"We are *not* afraid," she defensively replied. "If it weren't for the fact that they outnumber us ten to one, we'd break this treaty in an instant."

"Uh-huh. That's what they all say," I remarked, not believing a damn word she just said.

By that time, we were now at the end of the hallway, ready to take the elevator up to the ship's second floor. One of the giant, red bastards pushed the button to call it, and once it came down, we all got on.

After we rode up and got off on the top floor, we all started walking straight down the hall in front of us.

"So, why am I here, exactly?" I asked.

"Because you survived," she replied.

"That's it?"

"What else is there? You see, we planned on you dying in that explosion. But, since you're here, and seeing as how you're not gonna be living much longer anyway, I thought we might as well tell you what's going on."

"Gee. Thanks," I snidely responded.

When we finally made it down to the end of the hallway, we turned left and walked into the conference room. The room itself was about the size of a one-bedroom apartment and had about 30 chairs set up in a circle, encompassing a massive, round glass table.

All three of the walls to the left, to the right, and straight ahead, each had a built-in screen, which, when used in conjunction with the screens built into the glass table, were used as mirrors, pretty much the same way you would project a laptop onto a TV. At that point, I didn't know if I was gonna be briefed on something or give some kind of a report.

"Nice room you got here," I said, admiring its setup.

"Take a seat," she ordered.

Of course, they made me sit down in the chair closest to the screen on the back wall. It also happened to be the farthest chair from the door. I could only assume they did that, just in case I tried to make a run for it. Even if I did, I'd be long dead before I got there.

Once I was seated, Del took the seat to my right while the same two Morgidian guards stood watch over us from within the room on either side of the door.

"So… you betrayed your own people," I said before turning to her and shaking my head in disgust. "If he were alive, what would Omra think of you doing all of this?"

"Well, he's not alive," she replied. "And he never had any political say about what happened on our planet."

"Political say? I'm not talking about politics. Politics can suck a fat one for all I care. I'm talking about his good name and what he did."

"Look, I may be one of his relatives, but we are two completely different people."

"And, I get that. But, why kill your own?"

"It's for the good of the planet and this stupid treaty," she replied.

For the good of the planet and the treaty? I was now more confused than before. I mean, why would she say that? Did she have some devious plan of her own to thwart the Morgidian rule? And, where was this conversation suddenly going, anyway?

"I think it's about time you gave me some answers," I told her.

Now, I had no idea how she would respond or what she was even gonna say. But I did know one thing... she gave me an answer that I desperately needed to know. However, it definitely wasn't an answer that I was entirely prepared for.

"Again, you're gonna die anyway, so what the hell," she began. "When you found that sphere on Earth, it activated the homing beacon, and as you already know, Sartia was sent out to retrieve it. If she had brought the sphere back first, her arrangement with her fiancé would be nullified, and the treaty would stay put. But I just simply couldn't let that happen.

"So, I wound up striking my own deal with the Morgidian ruler. If I were to find the sphere and bring it back to him first, then we would rule this sector as equals, and the treaty would no longer be valid."

"So, *that's* why every bounty hunter and Morgidian were hunting us," I remarked. "They had to bring the sphere back to you."

"Correct. And when I deliver it, any unspoken for woman won't have to worry about marrying someone they don't love. I'd consider that a victory."

"And you believed him?"

"I had no choice."

And there it was. I quietly just sat there in disbelief, saying nothing, while staring at her like she had a screw loose. I mean, was she being serious? Did she really do all of this simply as a power play? Oh yeah. She was definitely insane.

But there were still a few more things I needed to know before they killed me. And more importantly, I desperately needed to confirm a theory.

"Okay. So you're a gullible bitch. We get that," I began. "But if I was supposed to be killed, why would you allow me to visit Sartia in the mad scientist house?"

"I didn't," she replied.

"You didn't?" I asked, trying to sound as surprised as possible.

"Of course not. Krite was always fond of her and would continuously bend over backward for her. They were the best of friends. And that just makes what I did to him even harder."

My brows furrowed. "What did you do?"

"After someone spotted him dropping you two off at Sartia's apartment, they immediately alerted me." She disappointingly shook her head. "Poor Krite. He never even saw it coming."

"Never saw it coming? You killed an innocent man!" I angrily pointed out. "Not only that, you sent a squad of dick bags to come and kill us!"

"Those dick bags were some of my best," she said, pointing an angry finger at me. "And with the two of you out of the way, my conscience would be clear."

And there you have it. In my mind, I was right. This whole thing was merely part of one big government conspiracy.

"Well, I guess that's that," I said, leaning back in my chair and folding my arms. "So, what happens now? Are you gonna kill me and send my body off into the cold depths of space?"

"On the contrary," she replied. "I'm taking you to Morgide to meet their ruler. Once there, and as the last act of our agreement, he'll publicly execute you while the whole sector watches."

"The whole sector, huh? I didn't realize I was so popular?"

"Trust me, you're not."

Let's do another recap, shall we?

I was pulled away from Earth, shot at, lied to, embarrassed (twice), had some fun, went on a spacewalk, and to top it all off, I was now gonna be executed for something I didn't even do. Great. This trip was turning into a real nightmare.

"But until then," she continued. "You will be our guest. You can walk around the ship freely, talk to whoever you'd like, and look at anything you wish. Within reason, of course."

"I'm so touched by your generosity," I snidely responded.

And with that, she got up out of the chair and made her way toward the door. But when she got there, she did something odd that I wouldn't find out until later, exactly why she did it.

She turned back toward me, looked me up and down, and gave me a flirtatious little smirk before leaving the room. After she was out, the two Morgidian guards followed suit. I was now left sitting there, wondering why she would give me such a look in the first place. I mean, did I think she was hot? Hell yeah. Did I have any interest in her whatsoever? Hell no.

I just continued to sit in that empty room all by myself for god knows how long, thinking about everything that had happened up until that point. Sartia has now died twice, and this time, she wasn't coming back. I was now gonna die out there all alone. And since I was gonna die anyway, I made the most of what little time I had left. Once I figured out what I was gonna do, I got up out of the chair and left the room.

The first thing I did was go across the corridor to the bathroom. After all of the nervous space flying and thinking I was gonna die, I really had to pee.

Now, here's something that you may or may not want to hear, but honestly, before I got taken aboard the ship, I was just gonna hold it until I couldn't breathe anymore. That way, when I did die, and if my body decided to let itself go, it wouldn't have mattered. I'd already be dead. I know, TMI. Sorry.

Anyway, once I finished in the john, I turned left and made my way to the room directly next to it. That room was the galley. I figured that if I was gonna die soon, I didn't wanna die with an empty stomach. So, I walked in through the doorway, only to be greeted by a seven-foot, brutish-looking Morgidian chef. I swear that the man could bench press a bulldozer. However, if it wasn't for the apron he was wearing, I think I would've been just a little more afraid.

He quickly walked over to the stove, turned his head around to face me, and spoke. Of course, just like the first Morgidians I had encountered back at my apartment, I couldn't understand a damn word he was saying.

"You need to turn on your intergalactic translator," I told him.

Okay. So, you're probably wondering why the Morgidians were the only ones that needed translators. Well, to be honest, I had no fucking clue.

By that point, I knew that the Arnaxians, along with 90 percent of the other species out in that sector, could understand each other's languages. But for some strange reason, only the Morgidians couldn't speak English. It was the weirdest thing.

However, I eventually found out that, because of the law regarding Earthlings never being allowed to leave Earth, the Morgidians just never learned the language. They thought that they never had to. And now that I think about it, I guess I just answered everyone's question. Maybe I did have a fucking clue?

He wound up trying a couple more different language settings before finally coming across mine.

"A human?" he remarked, a confused look on his face.

"The last time I checked," I replied.

His confused look slowly turned into a dirty look, and after seeing it, I don't know if I should've trusted him to cook my food or not. But, I was starving, and I needed to eat.

"Look, I got no beef with you guys," I said. "I'm just here looking to enjoy my last meal and flight before I die."

"They're gonna execute you on Morgide?" he asked.

"That's the plan."

"Well, in that case, what'll it be?"

Upon finishing his question, his evil look of hatred was instantly replaced by a cocky smile. Apparently, the thought of me dying made him happy.

Now, knowing exactly what some of the species ate out there, I couldn't even begin to imagine what the Morgidians ate. However, since I've seen it work in the movies about a thousand times over, I decided to try something a little different, hoping to quickly get on his good side and possibly gain an ally in the process.

"What would you eat?" I asked.

He just let out a massive gut laugh before answering me.

"You wouldn't wanna know what I would eat," he replied.

"Why? You don't think I can handle it?"

"Ha! I know you couldn't handle it."

Of course, in retaliation, I let out one of those sneaky little laughs before giving him my reply.

"Try me," I said, now glaring at him.

He glared back at me for the next few seconds, trying to size me up while seeing if I was actually ready for his challenge. It was almost like we were now two boxers at a press conference, staring each other down before the big match.

"Take a seat," he said before grumbling at me and turning around to face the stove.

With his back turned, and because he couldn't see my face, I was now sporting a huge shit-eating grin. *I'll show his ugly red ass who's boss,* I thought. I then took a seat at the table against the wall and waited nervously, wondering what he could possibly cook for me.

Ten minutes went by. Then 20. And then 30. I wondered if he was leading me on and wasn't even going to cook me anything at all. For all I knew, because he was so excited at the prospect of getting an opportunity to witness my execution, he was going to let me starve. But just as that thought had crossed my mind, he came over to me with a bowl in his hand and set it down on the table directly in front of me.

"There you are, Earthling. Try that on for size," he said in a low, cocky voice.

I took one look at the bowl, bent down to smell it, and practically threw up in my mouth. It definitely wasn't the best smelling stuff, but it wasn't too horrible either. As a matter of fact, it wasn't the smell at all that got me. The thing that got me was whatever was still moving in the bottom of the bowl.

I just stared at it for a few seconds before determining that it looked like a couple of baby snakes swimming around in mud. The brown, thick, chalky liquid was still bubbling in certain spots. Of course, I tried to delay the inevitable by creating small talk.

"What is it?" I asked.

"We call it Grefarian stew," he replied.

"May I ask why you call it that?"

"It's a good mix of certain roots, spices, and liquids. But the main ingredient that you see swimming around in there is what gives it its name. Those are Grefar worms."

"What the hell's a Grefar worm?" I curiously asked.

"Come on, Earthling. Quit stalling! What are you waiting for?"

He just stood there and watched me intently, immediately calling my bluff, hoping that I would chicken out so he could laugh at me and make fun of me a little more. But I'd show him who got the last laugh.

So, I grabbed my fork and stabbed one of the slimy bastards to take it out of my bowl. The moment I speared it, the creature made a high-pitched squealing noise, almost the same sound that a small pig or some kind of weird alien bat would make. When it was out of the bowl, however, that's when I got a really good look at it.

I swear to god, it looked like someone had crossbred a worm and a snake. If you can picture a worm's body with a baby snake's length and head, that's exactly what you got.

The six-inch creature was now squirming and squealing on the end of my fork. I wanted so badly to throw up and toss whatever cookies I had left in my stomach. But I didn't. I couldn't. There's no way in hell I was gonna let that red bastard beat me.

I looked back up at him, noticing that he was now smiling and laughing at me, before looking back down at the Grefar worm. This was it. Time to put up or shut up.

Time to become a man. Well, as much of a man as I could ever be.

As the chef continued to stand over me and laugh, I took one big, deep breath before shoving that Grefar worm into my mouth. The second that it was in there, I wasted no time and started to chew. Immediately, I could feel the tiny bones crunch in between my teeth, as its insides just sloshed around in my mouth. I literally wanted to hurl. In my head, I was screaming so loud at how gross it actually was. But on the outside, I held my ground as I continued to chew and chomp on this thing that tasted like dirt. Once it was all finished and sitting down at the bottom of my stomach, I took a brief second to collect myself before going for worm number two.

The moment I stabbed it with my fork, it was the exact same thing all over again. Somehow, though, I was able to tune out all of the squealing before shoving that sucker right into my mouth. But this time, however, as I was chewing it, I thought that I might be able to cheat a little bit.

So, I quickly grabbed the bowl, put it up to my lips, and started slurping down the contents, hoping to wash everything down in one gulp.

I don't know what worm shit tastes like, but if you grabbed all of the end trails that came out of a worm's ass and mixed it in with mud, that's pretty much what the liquid was. And because it was so gross and nasty, that had to have been the quickest meal I have ever eaten in my life.

Within five minutes, both worms and mud were down. And I was done.

Once I finished, I wiped my mouth before looking back up at the chef, who was now looking down at me with a slightly more surprised look on his face. I honestly don't think he expected me to take one bite, let alone finish the whole thing. Hell, I didn't even expect to finish it. But I did. And I was proud.

"Hmm… I guess I was wrong about you, Earthling," he said.

"Glad I could prove you wrong, Morgidian," I replied.

"You have a lot more guts than most people. And aside from that, you also now have my respect."

"Thanks, chef."

"Call me, Remlok."

"Thanks, Remlok. You can call me Sam."

I then stood up out of my chair and extended my right hand toward him as a show of good faith. He didn't immediately understand what kind of gesture I was making. But after a few seconds, he put his hand out so I could grab it. And once I shook it, I think he finally understood.

"Nice knowing you, Sam," he said. "It's just too bad they gotta kill ya when we get back."

"Yeah. Too bad," I replied.

"I'll be seein' ya."

And with that, he let go of my hand, grabbed the empty bowl off the table, and went back over toward the sink.

Now, going back to that whole 'gaining an ally' thing, I was hoping that after I had gotten on Remlok's good side, he would come to my aid at some point later on in this story. Unfortunately, I never saw him again.

However, I did learn one crucial thing… I learned that the Morgidians weren't as mean and unforgiving as the Arnaxians thought. It also led me to believe that there was a little more going on with this whole treaty business than the Arnaxians realized. But we'll get to that a little bit later.

With Remlok's back turned away again, and because I didn't wanna show him any signs of weakness, I immediately ran out of the galley so I could use the bathroom. Once I was inside, I bent over the toilet, and it was like Niagara Falls pouring out of my mouth. I was actually surprised I didn't fill that thing to the brim.

Anyway, after I had completely emptied the contents of my stomach, I left the bathroom. And because I was now so exhausted from puking, I decided to head to the lower level and find an empty bunk. Once I found one that didn't have anybody's stuff on it, I quickly hopped on, laid down, and within two seconds, I was off to Neverland.

Chapter 17

I couldn't even begin to tell you how long I was out for. But while I slept on the Morgidian ship, I had one *very* vivid dream.

I dreamt that I was in New York City, hunting down giant Grefar worms and killing them before they destroyed all of humanity. I kept trying to tell everyone it was my fault and that I brought them back with me from my travels in outer space. However, no one would believe me or really seemed to care.

I was in an SUV, driving after one worm, while I had it dead to rights through the sight of my gun. The roads were a little bumpy from all the decaying worms and human remains, but I tried really hard to keep on him.

Darius was driving, and I had the upper half of my body hanging out of the window, getting ready to fire. I took one more look through the sight, and just as I was about to pull the trigger, there was an earthquake. Or, at least, that's what I thought it was.

I opened my eyes, only to realize that I was still lying down in one of the bunks on the Morgidian ship. When I looked up, I saw Del standing over me and shaking me while trying to wake me up.

"Sam," she said. "Let's go. We're here."

Still a little discombobulated, I quickly sat up in the bed.

"What?" I asked her, my eyes still squinted. "Where are we? What's going on?"

"We've reached Morgide."

"Oh, good. I can go and die now."

With the thought of my death still looming in my mind, I slowly stood up and immediately followed her out of the room.

We took the elevator back up to the top floor, and once we got off, we headed straight for the cockpit. Let me tell you, their cockpits looked way different than the ones on the Arnaxian models.

Because the Morgidian ships used four laser cannons instead of two, they had to use two crew members, one on each side, positioned directly behind the pilot and co-pilot to fire them. Also, unlike the Arnaxian ships having just one piloting panel, the Morgidian ships had two: one in front of both the pilot and the co-pilot. To be perfectly honest, I don't know whether it was the Dukian caf making me high or what. But after being inside one of those things, I honestly don't know how the hell we were able to destroy four of them by ourselves.

"Nice cockpit," I said, admiring its impressiveness.

"Morgide, straight ahead," the Morgidian pilot said.

After all the talk about returning the sphere, getting shot at, meeting aliens, getting high, avoiding capture, and having the adventure of a lifetime, I was finally gonna get an up-close and personal look at what Morgide had to offer. Whether I survived or not, that was inevitably the last stop on my tour.

As Morgide came in to view through the cockpit window, I looked out and could now see the massive red planet. However, only about 75 percent of its surface was actually red. The other 25 percent of it sported blue and green spots. Its two moons also looked dangerously close together.

"Figures that Morgide would be red," I remarked.

"Why do you say it like that?" Del asked.

"Well, with their red skin, I just pictured them living on a red planet."

"Not all of it is red."

"Yeah. What's up with that, anyway?"

I was now very curious to know why the planet looked like an oddly colored soccer ball.

"It wasn't always this red," she began. "When the planet was discovered thousands of years ago, it was quite the opposite of what you're looking at now. It was actually ninety percent green and blue and only ten percent red.

"Over the years, the two moons gradually crept closer together. As they did, it started wreaking havoc on the planet's surface. The lush blue and green landscape started giving way, as more and more volcanos started popping up."

"Shit. I had no idea," I said.

"Pretty soon," she continued. "The moons will collide and break apart, sending hundreds of thousands of meteor rocks crashing to the planet below. Once that happens, Morgide will be no more, and the planet will become uninhabitable."

"How long until that happens?"

"I'd say that the planet has about another five hundred years left."

My eyes immediately shot open from shock. "Five hundred years? In scientific standards, that's not long at all."

"No, it's not."

We then both went silent as we continued to stare out of the cockpit window.

However, as I was standing there, I couldn't help but think about everything she said and what I already knew of the treaty. But the more I thought about it, the more I realized that there might be an even bigger power play going on behind the scenes. Something that even Del hasn't anticipated yet.

It occurred to me that the treaty wasn't put into place to keep the Morgidians from destroying the Arnaxians. I think it was put into place because they already knew they were living on a dying planet, and therefore, needed to keep their species alive elsewhere when the time came. The treaty wasn't about domination. It was about survival.

Now, the big question was, did the Arnaxians know about it? I don't know. Of course, there was a high probability that I could be reading too much into it and be insanely wrong about the whole thing. Then again, I could've been right.

But because I loved Sartia so much, and regardless of how much I now hated Del, I had to at least let her know what I was thinking. For the sake of Arnaxia, of course.

"Can I talk to you in private?" I asked.

"Not right now. We're landing," Del responded.

"It's really urgent."

"Ugh," she groaned while rolling her eyes. "Okay. Let's go."

We then made our way out of the cockpit, went down to the end of the hall, and turned left into the conference room, where Del immediately pulled her gun and pointed it at me.

"Now, what is it?" she asked. "And if you try anything, I'll shoot you where you stand."

I quickly backed up a few feet and put my hands over my head, just to show her I meant no harm.

"I promise," I said. "No funny business."

"Okay. Now, what is it that you needed so desperately to speak with me in private?" she asked.

"When you were telling me the history of Morgide, a thought had popped into my head. Don't you find it strange that a treaty was brokered between your people and a species living on a dying planet?"

"No. They'll destroy us."

"Do you know that to be a fact?"

"What the hell are you talking about?" she angrily asked. "You better not be wasting my time."

"I'm not. Just hear me out," I calmly said.

It took her a moment to decide whether or not she actually wanted to hear what I had to say. And it wasn't until long that she finally nodded at me.

"Fine. Go ahead," she said.

"Thank you. Now, I thought that the Morgidians were very evil and wanted to destroy me from the moment I met them," I began. "But it wasn't until we got on this ship, and I went toe to toe with Remlok, the chef who made me a bowl of Grefarian stew, that I thought otherwise."

"Disgusting," she said, now sporting a look, almost as if she just sucked on a lemon. "Tell me you didn't eat that slop?"

"Oh, I did. And Remlok was very impressed. But, the thing is, after I gobbled it down, he seemed to have a little bit of respect for me, and I wasn't afraid of him anymore."

"Where are you going with all of this?"

"Sorry. All I'm saying is that I don't think they're so bad. And, personally, I don't think they signed that treaty with you as a show of dominance. I think they signed it so they could preserve their own species on a different planet."

After I finished my rousing speech, Del didn't say a word. Instead, she just looked at me like I had two heads or something.

"Do you know how incredibly stupid that sounds?" she remarked.

"It may sound stupid, but I think it's the truth," I said.

"If their species is doomed, where else could they *possibly* go to save their own…"

It was almost as if a light bulb had suddenly gone off inside of her head.

"Are you telling me that they're going to move in on Arnaxia?" she asked.

"Possibly," I replied.

She then thought about it again for a few more seconds before coming to the realization that my moment of trying to save my own ass might, in fact, just be a rouse.

"All this coming from a dead man," she said. "Do you take me for a fool?"

"Maybe a dumbass," I responded. "But definitely no fool."

Now, the last thing anyone would wanna do is piss off a person that holds any kind of power. Or, in this case, a gun.

But at the time, and seeing as how I was already on death row, that was probably the wrong thing to say. And, as you can already tell, I obviously didn't care. However, she definitely made sure I did.

"Get in here!" she shouted out to one of the guards.

Within a second, one of the brutish, seven-foot-tall Morgidian guards came walking into the room.

"Stay in here with him until we land," she told him. "And make sure he understands the penalty for lying."

The Morgidian simply turned to her and nodded as she left the room, closing the conference room door on her way out. With Del gone, he slowly turned his head back toward me while sporting a devilish grin that spanned from ear to ear.

I have never been in a fight in my entire life. Remember, I was always the one on the receiving end of a beat down, while Darius was the one who defended me. Hell, I didn't even know the first thing about fighting. Well, other than what I've seen in movies and on YouTube. But, I guess I was about to find out.

Not really knowing what to do, I simply balled up my hands into fists and raised them up in a fighting position, just like a boxer would. The Morgidian saw that I was now ready and then rubbed his hands together, cracking his knuckles in the process, before walking toward me. I just danced around like a fool before realizing that it wasn't gonna help me any. But he just kept on moving closer and closer to me.

With all of my fears now coming out and my adrenaline stuck in overdrive, I took my right hand, brought it back as far as it would go, and then lunged forward, hitting him in the face as hard as I possibly could. That was the first time in my life that I ever punched someone. When my fist struck the side of his face, I knocked his head to the side and made him stumble a bit. Once he was able to regain his balance, he turned his head toward mine and ran his right index finger across his lips to check for any signs of blood. He pulled his fingers away and noticed that he had a tiny red spot on them, stemming from the small cut he now had on his lower lip. After licking his wound and swallowing his non-life-threatening injury, he just smiled once again before continuing his way toward me.

Now, I could've run around the table to try and avoid him until I was blue in the face. But that would've made absolutely no sense, primarily because of his size. If I ran, he could've easily thrown the chairs or the table to the side and blocked me in. So, instead of running, I decided to take everything he had like a man.

Unfortunately, that was the last thing I remembered until I woke up sometime later down on the planet's surface. Needless to say, he handed me my ass, gift-wrapped and ready to go.

• • •

From the time that Sartia's ship got blown to pieces, up until I woke up on Morgide, it had been a good 11 hours. Taking a nap and getting knocked unconscious will definitely make the time fly by.

When I finally opened my eyes, I sat up and noticed that I was in some sort of a stone hut. It was very crudely built, and I don't think that it was used to house visitors.

The bars on the windows and the doorway kind of gave that one away.

The hut basically had all of the necessities that a typical jail cell would have: a bed, a toilet, and a window. The bed was definitely not brought in from Lith because when I woke up, it felt like I had slept on a pile of straw. Also, I was sweating profusely. It would make sense that being on a planet full of volcanos and lava would do that to you.

Once I realized where I was, I looked toward the door and noticed a bowl of food sitting on the floor. So, I immediately got up off the bed to check it out. Thankfully, the stuff in the bowl wasn't Grafarian stew and looked a little more appetizing.

I took the bowl, which was filled with some type of gravy and a piece of bread, and brought it back to my bed, where I then proceeded to wolf it down like a hungry tiger. I honestly don't know what I ate, but it wasn't too bad, and it didn't wanna make me hurl either. Once I finished, I put the bowl down and went over to the doorway to take a peek outside.

The landscape on Morgide literally looked like a volcano apocalypse. The dark red sky loomed over all the black rock and red lava that filled the ground as far as the eye could see. Houses, huts, buildings, and skyscrapers were built all around it and almost looked like perfectly placed pieces on a chessboard. In between everything else was the grass and the water.

Each green and blue section almost kind of reminded me of a mirage. A big lake sat in the middle and was surrounded by greenery on every single side. Each one also supported plants, trees, and creatures of all kinds. Well, whatever was left of them.

From what I could tell, though, it was true. The planet was dying. And my theory was becoming more plausible by the minute. How an entire civilization could possibly survive in those kinds of conditions was beyond me.

But I had more important things to worry about. My death was now looming, and as I was standing in that hut, staring out over the volcanic wasteland, it became painfully clear that I wasn't getting off of that planet alive. Not unless I came up with a plan. A really good plan.

However, I didn't have very long to think because the moment I had this realization, I could hear footsteps coming toward the hut. So, I backed away from the door and waited to see who it was. Within a few moments, two Morgidian guards, including Del Surcy, appeared outside.

"Well, it's good to see you upright," Del said.

"I don't go down so easily," I replied.

"That's not what I heard."

I just sneered at her. "Very funny. What do you want, anyway?"

"The Morgidian ruler requests a meeting with you."

"Does he now?"

"He?" she asked with one eyebrow now raised. "What makes you assume the ruler's a man?"

"Wild guess."

She then had one of the Morgidian guards unlock the door to the hut. But the guards never came in. Instead, Del came in by herself with her gun drawn and pointed directly at my face.

"I'm not gonna have to use this, am I?" she asked, almost annoyed.

"Where would I go?" I replied. "I'm on a planet surrounded by lava."

After hearing my comment, she took a moment to think about that before holstering her weapon. Then, she turned to the two guards.

"Lock the door and leave us," she ordered.

Without hesitation or question, the guards shut the door, locked it, and stepped away from the hut. And even though I could still see them through the window, they were now way out of range from hearing our conversation.

"Good," Del said with a smile. "Now that they're out of the way, we can talk freely."

"What the hell are you doing?" I curiously asked.

But she didn't reply to me right away. Instead, she just stood there, looking me up and down with an inquisitive look on her face.

"I'm very curious," she said.

"Curious about what?" I asked.

"If what Sartia said about you is true or not."

That little comment prompted an immediate red flag to go off in my head.

"What did she say about me?" I asked. "And when did she have time to talk to you?"

"She didn't," she said. "I obtained everything she said about you from her ship's logs."

Then, in an unusual fashion, Del slowly started inching her way toward me.

"Okay? I'm a little confused," I said. "What are you getting at?"

"I'm very curious to know how good of a kisser you really are," she replied.

"Wait, she put in her log that I'm a good kisser?"

Immediately after I said that, Del's voice almost instantly changed from being curious to now being borderline seductive.

"That's not all she put in there," she said.

She then continued inching her way even closer to me. Of course, by that point, I didn't trust her as far as I could throw her. So I, myself, slowly started to back up.

"What, what, what are you talking about?" I stuttered.

"I wanna know what *she* felt," she said.

"What... *she* felt?"

"Apparently, according to her," she said, still inching even closer to me. "You're very good at sexual pleasure."

"Who? Me? No. She... she must've recorded that by mistake."

But, that was it. I had backed up as far as I could possibly go and was now pressed right up against the back wall. Unfortunately, by the time I realized that I was out of room, Del was already right up in my face.

"Well," she said, now slowly rubbing her hands all over my chest. "I'd like to find out."

And, without warning, she leaned in up against me, as our 'parts' were now touching. She also took her right hand and started caressing the left side of my face. At that point, I couldn't speak, and I had no idea what to say either.

They say that when a woman seduces a man and depending on the type of woman, it's almost impossible for the man to resist. Well, from what I've seen in real life and movies, anyway. I mean, after all, we are only men.

Along with caressing my face, she had her left hand on my right hip, trying to pull herself in even closer to me.

"Are, are, are you…" I said, still stuttering like a fool. "Are you trying to seduce me?"

"Seduce you?" she said. "Of course not. I'm *way* past seduction."

And that's when the unthinkable happened.

She took her lips and placed them on mine, planting a gentle, soft, sensual kiss on me. I tried to pull away, but already with my literal back against the wall, I couldn't. So, I just went with it. And you know what the weird part was? I actually liked it. I couldn't understand how, but I was *really* into it. So, at that point, I just said fuck it and kissed her back.

That went on for a few more seconds until I finally came to my senses and threw her backward, watching her land on the makeshift bed. However, when I did that, she looked up at me with an even hungrier look on her face.

"Oh!" she said. "I didn't realize you liked the rough stuff?"

"What? No," I responded, now trying to forget that the recent kiss ever happened.

"I want you to take me, right here, right now."

"Are you out of your fucking mind?"

"I'd rather we just be fucking."

Now, I couldn't figure out what happened, but something hit me the moment she said that. Something suddenly popped into my mind that I completely forgot about.

If you recall, I had mentioned to you that when we were aboard the Morgidian ship, and she left me in that conference room the first time, as she was leaving, she gave me an odd look that I couldn't make heads or tails out of. Until now.

"Look!" I sternly told her. "If you hadn't tried to kill me, I'd be all over you."

She then leaned back on the bed. "I'm right here," she said. "All you have to do is-"

"What kind of sick, twisted game are you playing, anyway?"

"I don't know what you mean?"

I pointed at her. "Don't bullshit me!"

Oh yeah. She was busted, and she knew it. By that point, she knew the jig was up and that she would finally have to come clean.

"Fine!" she said, standing up off of the bed. "Do you really wanna know why I'm doing this? I'll tell you. I promised to marry the Morgidian ruler so our species could act as one. But I don't wanna marry that fool. As a matter of fact, once I hand over the sphere, I'm gonna kill him. I want Arnaxia and all of its people to rule the galaxy by themselves."

"Is that all?" I asked, knowing full well and good that there was more.

"No. As a matter of fact, I want *you* to rule it with me."

No sooner did that come out of her mouth, my eyes lit up, and I just couldn't believe it. She wanted me to rule the galaxy by her side? That was, by far, one of the highest offers I have ever received. And it definitely felt like one of those *Star Wars* moments.

"Why me?" I curiously asked.

"Because you're the only Earthling out here," she said. "Do you know how powerful and famous I'd be for marrying someone like you? Plus, you are pretty cute."

"So, this is all just one big power play?"

"Well," she said, slowly putting her arms over my shoulders. "Not all of it."

She then gave me another soft, quick kiss on the lips, and I was definitely in a real pickle now. However, instead of death, I now had a different option.

I could agree to her terms and, hopefully, get out of this alive, or I could still be executed. Again, did I find her highly attractive? What man in their right mind wouldn't? But I didn't wanna marry her just for power, and money, and fame. However, the thought of it did sound pretty good. Regardless, I now had a big decision to make, and I knew that I didn't have a lot of time to make it.

"When am I scheduled for execution?" I asked.

"In about thirty minutes," she replied.

Okay. So, I literally had *no* time to think about it.

Now, if you were in my position and had the exact same offer put on the table, what would you do? Would you choose death? No. I don't think you would. And neither did I.

However, during my rousing conversation with Del, I finally came up with a plan. One that I felt would finally be able to blow the lid off this whole thing and one that would allow me to get away unscathed. Well, no more than I already was.

"Okay," I said. "If I was to say yes, what would I need to do?"

"Well, first…" she said before leaning in close to my ear.

As she whispered what she wanted me to do, my eyes grew wide, and I just couldn't believe it. One of the things she said I wasn't particularly fond of doing. But if this whole thing was to pan out, I had to forget everything I recently learned and take one for the team.

Okay, yes. I did sleep with her right then and there. And don't even think about judging me by my actions.

Look, I'm not proud of what I did, and even though Del was 15 years my senior, I only did it to avoid being executed. Plus, and I'm definitely not afraid to admit this, it was pretty fuckin' good. But she didn't even come close to Sartia. So, let's just drop it and not give me any more shit about it. Okay?

Anyway, after everything was said and done, we got dressed and then left the hut to begin our journey. And, when I say begin our journey, I meant leave the hut and walk up a long and winding path behind it that went straight up to a stone castle sitting high atop the hill.

• • •

During our walk, I finally got a good look at the surrounding landscape. But the more of Morgide I saw, the more confused I became. I honestly couldn't tell if I was now gonna be marching toward Mordor, Snake Mountain, or the building on Mustafar where Anakin slaughtered all of the separatists.

The castle on the hill was massive and had six tall towers that connected 25-foot gray stone walls at even points to form a hexagon. Instead of the moat being filled with water, it was filled with lava that carved its way through the rocks below. And once we finally got to the entrance, the tall, 20-foot steel doors opened inward, allowing us to walk inside.

Once we were through, we entered the courtyard, or what I only assumed was the courtyard. I took one look around and could swear that I was now in some type of medieval-style film. It was filled with armed guards, civilians, blacksmiths, and everything else you would find in a castle's courtyard. It was basically where all of the lower class hung out. The only difference between that castle and those I saw in films was that everything was technology-based instead of manual labor-based.

There were also three huge buildings inside: one to the left, one to the right, and one straight ahead, all standing as high as the walls. The six towers themselves, however, easily stood at least 50 feet tall.

"Holy shit!" I said, amazed by what I was now looking at. "I never thought I'd ever see anything like this!"

"Impressive, isn't it?" Del asked.

"It definitely is. But this is nothing compared to what you have on Arnaxia."

She then leaned in and whispered in my ear. "And that's why we'll destroy them."

At that point, I started to think that whatever I said to her on the ship was finally starting to hit her. Either that or it was because she was ultimately hell-bent on ruling the galaxy. Who knows?

We started to make our way through all of the Morgidians going about their business in the courtyard before reaching the building directly in front of us and going inside. Through those doors, I expected to see all the glitz and glam of the royalty living there. I expected to see chandeliers, fancy rugs, tapestries, servants, gold, and everything else associated with a king or a queen.

Not so much.

When we walked through the front doors, the inside was dark and dank, while torches hung from the walls to light up the whole first floor. From what I could tell, it looked like we had entered into some kind of dining area, or at least, that's what I thought it was. I never bothered to ask either.

We walked around all of the tables and chairs to head straight for the elevator in the back. Yeah. On top of all that *fancy royalty,* they had an elevator. Go figure.

The four of us got inside and rode the elevator up to the fifth floor. Once the doors opened and we all got off, we were now standing in what looked to be a mix between a throne room and a computer room. On the left and right-hand sides, tables were set up along both walls. They had Morgidian computer specialists, strategists, and other miscellaneous brainiacs working, typing, and keeping watch over all planetary functions. The touchpads that were built into the tables mirrored themselves on the LED screens that lined the walls. Pretty much the exact same way they did in the conference room aboard the ship.

Straight ahead of us was literally a golden throne. Its back faced me, while its front faced out through a giant square opening in the wall overlooking the courtyard. To keep from plummeting to your death, a metal safety railing went all the way across. The outside of the room was made of stone, while the inside was made from some form of steel, probably to keep it from getting blown to bits. Also, in royal cliché fashion, there was literally a red carpet that extended from the elevator entrance all the way up to the throne itself.

We started walking down the carpet, which ran about 100 feet from the elevator to the throne. Once we stopped just shy of it, I got to see a fascinating twist. No, seriously. The throne twisted right around so that the front of it was now facing us. Sitting atop of it had to be the Morgidian ruler. Because, well, who else would it be?

He was about the same height as the rest of the Morgidians and had a lot more muscle. His long, black hair with bands holding it in place about every five or six inches went all the way down to his ass. The typical red skin, red eyes, elf-like ears, and squid-like tentacles made up the red monstrosity.

But he wasn't wearing the same type of armor as the rest of them. As a matter of fact, he wasn't wearing any armor at all. He was dressed in a black, button-down, long-sleeved shirt, along with a pair of black silk pants and black flat-footed dress shoes. The whole situation blew my mind and was totally weird. But hey, so was this entire trip.

He also had a nose ring that came out of one nostril and went into the other. Three warlike, native tribal-type earrings sat in each ear. And to top it off, a fucking crown was perched on top of his head. Upon seeing him, I immediately turned to Del and whispered in her ear.

"That's who you're gonna marry?" I asked.

"Yeah," she whispered back.

"You could do so much better."

"Tell me about it."

"My wife to be!" the Morgidian ruler said.

He then stood up off the throne and came over to her, embracing her with a hug, followed by a kiss.

"My dearest fiancé," she said.

My dearest fiancé? I thought to myself. *Who the hell talks like that?*

After their kiss, he turned his gaze in my general direction.

"And you must be the Earthling I've heard so much about?" he asked with a deep, cool, calm, and collected voice. "I do apologize for your accommodations, but it's all we had on such short notice."

Before I replied, I just looked at him in a confused manner. I mean, how could that guy, who seemed like he had a decent head on his shoulders, possibly be the one who would want to destroy another race for breaking a treaty? He'd only said a few words to me by that point, but in my mind, he didn't seem too bad.

"That's okay," I told him. "My experience in the hut…" I then turned to Del and grinned before looking back at him. "Wasn't too bad."

"Allow me to introduce myself. My name is Marok Trok," he said. "And I am the ruler of this planet."

"Really? I would never have guessed," I sarcastically responded.

"*Hahaha.* I like you. You're funny."

"In that case, maybe we could possibly hold off on killing me?"

Upon hearing my question, his tone quickly changed to a more serious one.

"You're not that funny," he replied.

I shrugged. "It was worth a shot."

One of the Morgidians that escorted us up there then stepped forward to deliver something to Marok. I couldn't see what it was right away, but when he moved to the side, I could see that Marok was now holding the Morgidian sphere in the palm of his hands. He was now looking down at it, smiling from ear to ear, almost like a kid in a candy store.

"Finally," he said in a low, devilish tone before raising the sphere to the sky and shouting. "The ceremony can now begin!"

"Umm, before you start the *entertainment* portion of your evening," I said, completely interrupting his joyous moment. "Can I ask you something?"

He immediately looked back at me, none too pleased yet, willing to let me speak.

"What is it?" he asked me.

"I just wanna say that I'm happy for you. You know, getting your metal ball back and all. But seeing as how I'll be dead soon anyway, I just gotta know one thing… what the hell is that?"

His eyes narrowed upon hearing my question. "What?"

"I mean, I flew all the way out here and almost got killed, many times, I might add, just to bring that thing back to you. What the hell is it? Why is it so important?"

As he looked down at me, he didn't do so with an angry or mad face, but almost a sad one. When I asked about the sphere, it's almost as if it hurt him to explain to me what it was.

"You wanna know why this is so important?" he asked, almost confused by my curiosity.

"Yes, I do," I replied.

"Then, I'll tell you. You see, this little sphere has been in my family for generations," he proceeded to tell me. "When I was a little boy, I used to play with this all the time. My father before me played with it when he was a little boy, and my grandfather before him, and so on.

"If this were lost to me, I wouldn't be able to pass it down to my son, and he wouldn't be able to pass it down to his son. That's why it's important to me. And that's why I needed to retrieve it."

Wow. That whole time. The whole entire trip that I spent running for my life, getting high, getting shot at, killing bounty hunters, flying ships, walking in space, and now facing my imminent demise, for what? A family heirloom? No. It was a *fucking* children's toy.

"That's it?" I asked him, believing there was more to it.

"What else is there?" he replied.

I was now furious. "What else is there? I came all the way out here and avoided getting killed just so I could bring you a fucking children's toy? You're out of your goddamn mind! Do you know that?"

"Actually," Del interjected. "*I* brought you the sphere."

"Stay out of this bitch!" I yelled at her before turning my attention back to Marok. "Do you really wanna marry this woman? We were doing just fine until she stepped in and stole our thunder. She killed her own people just to bring that back to you."

"That's why I love her," Marok replied.

"You…"

But I had to stop myself right there and cool down before any other bad things accidentally slipped out of my mouth.

"You seem like a reasonable man," I calmly continued. "Would you mind if we spoke in private?"

I could then see him look over at Del and the other two guards before looking back at me and nodding his head.

"Follow me," he said.

Perfect. Now that I had his attention, I could quietly speak with him while I enacted phase two of my plan.

I followed him behind his throne and over to the railing that overlooked the courtyard. We were also now far enough away from Del and the guards so that they couldn't hear what we were saying.

"Look… I know that you're gonna execute me soon, but I just gotta know something," I said.

"What would you like to know?" he asked.

"What's the deal?"

He looked at me with a confused expression on his face.

"What's the deal?" he asked.

"Yeah. What's the deal with you and your species?" I replied.

"What do you mean?"

"Come on. I'm no fool. I know what the long con is here. That treaty you signed all those years ago… that wasn't about destroying the Arnaxians. It was about having a place to live after this planet goes supernova."

Before responding, Marok just stood there, now glaring at me intently, not saying a word. I could see it in his eyes, though. He knew that I was right. Little did I know, however, that was only part of his plan.

"That's an interesting theory," he said. "But, you're wrong."

Whoa! I was wrong? How could I be wrong? I was so sure that I had it all figured out.

"Well, partly wrong," he continued. "You see, once this planet ceases to exist, we will already be involved with the Arnaxians on their homeworld. By then, we wouldn't just be living there. We'd be ruling the planet with them as our servants. The treaty will become no more, and then their species will become extinct. Minus the women, of course. We kind of need them to breed."

And there it was. Apparently, I wasn't wrong after all. I was right. And because I was right, a cocky smile quickly hit my face before I took a few steps back and pointed at him.

"I knew it!" I shouted, knowing that my theory was spot on.

However, I think I may have shouted just a little too loud because after I did, both of us could now see Del staring in our general direction, almost as if she overheard what I just said.

"You dirty son of a-" I started to say.

But, that was it. It was lights out for me again as Marok punched me in the face, knocking me out cold before I could say anything else.

It now appeared as if both sides were conspiring against each other, and I was the only one who knew about it. With my execution now looming, there was only one thing left for me to do. One *final act,* if you will, left for me to carry out.

Rob J. LaBelle

Chapter 18

Well, here we are. We've now reached the climax of our story, and there's only a couple of chapters left. So, just sit back, relax, and enjoy the ride. Because from here on out, it's gonna get pretty bumpy.

See what I did there with… the ride, and… bumpy? Yeah, never mind.

Anyway, the time had finally come. It was officially time for me to pay the piper. Visit the Sandman. Melvin Death! That's right, I said it. The time for my execution had arrived, and honestly, I still didn't understand why I had to die. I mean, who was I gonna tell? You? Them? No. Telling *them* is why I'm here telling *you* this whole thing in the first place.

Still, because Marok had knocked me out, they had to delay the execution for another couple of hours. I bet by then, they would be finally glad to see me go.

When I awoke, I slowly opened my eyes to see that I was now back in the middle of the courtyard, standing on top of a steel platform. The platform itself looked just like the one you would see someone standing on right before they got hung. Kind of like the gallows. Except that this was just a platform, and there were no gallows or rope to be found.

I was looking straight ahead and could now see roughly thousands of Morgidians standing there, ready to watch me die. My hands were tied together in front of me. And while I was out, they had put a gag over my mouth to keep me from speaking. I personally think it was because of what I knew and what I could do with that kind of information. However, even though I couldn't speak, it didn't matter because I was still gonna die. But, apparently, I wasn't gonna die alone.

Looking to my left, I noticed that there was someone else standing next to me. But I never, in a million years, ever expected to see another Morgidian. I didn't know what, but he must've done something pretty treacherous in order to get executed by his own kind.

He was about the usual seven feet tall and was wearing almost the same exact outfit as Marok. He had on a white, button-down, long-sleeve shirt, black silk pants, and black flat-footed shoes. He also had short, dark, spiky hair, no nose ring, and instead of the three that Marok had, he only had one tribal type earring in his right ear. But who was he? And why was he up there with me?

I then turned around to see Marok, Del, and four Morgidian guards standing behind us. The guards had their weapons pointed directly at our backs, while Marok himself was now stepping forward, ready to start a big speech.

"Today is a special day for us!" he began, his voice blaring over the courtyard speakers for all to hear. "You see, when we lost the sphere…"

As he continued his speech, the Morgidian next to me leaned in and started chatting with me. It was quiet enough so no one else could hear us, but it was just loud enough for me to hear him.

"You must be Sam," he said, using a low, deep voice.

Since I still couldn't speak, I just nodded my head yes.

"I'm sorry I got you into this," he said. "My name's Harok, by the way."

Holy shit. I couldn't believe it. That was Sartia's fiancé. Well, now soon to be ex-fiancé. I then tried saying something to him but forgot that I still had the gag in my mouth.

"They incarcerated me after they found out I sent Sartia after the sphere," he continued. "I was really hoping you guys would get here first so that none of this would happen."

How about that? Even though I doubted her, she was right about him all along. He was actually telling the truth about letting us go after we gave him the sphere. I mean, after seeing him standing up there alongside me, why wouldn't he be telling the truth? Nothing we could do about it now.

"I also heard what happened to her," he said. "I'm sorry. Even though I wasn't in love with her, she was very nice and didn't deserve to die the way that she did."

I don't know what it was, but at that very moment, I kinda started to like him. I mean, he seemed like a pretty decent dude. It's just too bad we were about to die. Or were we?

"I wish I could get us out of this, but they won't listen to me. Do you have any ideas?" Harok asked.

We were surrounded by thousands of Morgidians, all armed to the teeth with weapons. Also, we were on a planet surrounded by lava with no way out. And he has the audacity to ask me if I have any ideas? If he only knew what I had in mind.

So, merely as a courtesy gesture, the only thing I could do was look at him and give him a wink. But by that point, Marok had finished his rousing speech and was now looking back at us for any last words that we might have had.

"So," Marok said. "Harok, my one, and only son. Do you have anything to say for yourself before we carry out your sentence?"

Harok slowly looked out over the crowd to see all of their now intrigued faces staring up at him, ready to hear what he had to say.

"I just want everyone to know..." he started.

And that was my cue.

While Harok delivered his plea of innocence, I stuck my tied-up hands into my front right jeans pocket and pulled out my cell phone. It was finally time for me to execute the last phase of my plan.

"I'm sorry that I shamed all of you," he finished up. "I never meant for any of this to happen. But just know that I could've been your greatest leader."

"Well, that was very touching," Marok said.

After he was finished with Harok, he then walked over to me.

"Now, Sam of Earth. Do you have any last words before we carry out *your* sentence?" he asked.

Because I still couldn't say a word, I knew he was doing all of this just to make himself look good in front of everyone. It was almost as if he was actually trying to be funny.

"Nothing to say?" he asked with a smile.

The crowd followed that up by letting out the collective sound of laughter. Well, little did they know, I would show them who got the last laugh.

"Well then," Marok continued. "If you have nothing left to say, then let's get-"

Along with Del and Harok, the crowd was now looking at him funny and were all wondering why he stopped talking. Marok could now hear a strange sound coming from the platform. And the quieter that everyone got, the louder the sound became.

"What is that?" he asked, curiously looking around, trying to find whatever it was he was now hearing.

Okay. So, I haven't told you the whole thing yet, and I bet that by now, you're very curious as to what my plan actually was. Well, your wait is finally over.

Little did Marok and Del know that when I was alone with the both of them, I turned on the voice recording feature installed on my cell phone. When Del initially came into the hut to chat with me, I knew it had to be something good. I mean, why else would she tell the guards to leave? Obviously, it was because she wanted to tell me something that she didn't want them to hear. That's when I first thought of my plan.

Phase one was to get all of her devious plans recorded on my phone. Phase two was to, hopefully, get Marok to confirm my theory and get all of his plans recorded on my phone as well. Phase three, the final phase of my plan, was to happen so that when we were all alone, I could play it back for both of them. After they heard it, my thinking was that they would practically start a war with each other. Once they were distracted enough, I would then make a break for it and try to escape.

I know. It wasn't the best of plans, but it was all I could think of at the time.

Anyway, Marok was now walking around the platform, furious that he couldn't find out where the noise was coming from. So, to help him out, I decided to turn up the volume. When I did, Del's voice was now blaring over the speakers for him and everyone else to hear.

"I'm very curious to know how good of a kisser you really are," Del's recording said.

"Wait, she put in her log that I'm a good kisser?" my recording asked.

Marok definitely understood that and immediately turned to Del for answers.

"I *never* said that," Del quickly said defensively. "I would never in my life-"

However, she was immediately interrupted by a part of our conversation that came up shortly after.

"I wanna know what *she* felt," Del's recording continued.

"What... *she* felt?" my recording asked.

"Apparently, according to her, you're very good at sexual pleasure."

After hearing that last bit, Marok was now starting to get a little on the furious side. I'll tell ya... if he wasn't red already, he definitely would've been by that point. Of course, Del still tried to plead her case.

"I never said those things," she said. "Those recordings were made up. He manipulated my voice somehow."

"That sure sounds like you," Marok said.

Now, instead of letting the rest of the conversation play out, I decided to skip ahead to the good parts.

"Fine!" her voice recording continued. "Do you really wanna know why I'm doing this? I'll tell you. I promised to marry the Morgidian ruler so our species could act as one. But I don't wanna marry that fool. As a matter of fact, once I hand over the sphere, I'm gonna kill him. I want Arnaxia and all of its people to rule the galaxy by themselves."

"You Arnaxian bitch!" Marok shouted.

I swear to god, at that very moment, I could see smoke start to billow out of his ears. The rest of the crowd couldn't believe it either.

So, with Del exposed and phase one complete, it was now time to enact phase two of my little plan. But before I did, I decided to play something a little extra for everyone. Something that I skipped over earlier when I was talking about it with you.

"Oh, Sam," Del's recording continued. "Sartia was right about you."

That little bit came up, followed by a few more sexual moans and groans from Del. At that point, I was now laughing to myself and was thoroughly enjoying every minute of it. Even if I wasn't gonna make it out of there alive, I wasn't going down without having a little fun first.

"You'll die with them!" Marok ordered before backhanding her across the face. "Get her over there!"

His guards immediately tied up her wrists and then brought her over to stand on the other side of Harok. We were now like three peas in a pod, just waiting to be cooked. However, I was now ready to enact phase two, which meant that it was time for me to cue up a different voice file.

"Del Surcy," Marok said. "Ruler of the planet Arnaxia. For crimes to conspire against all of Morgide, I hereby sentence you to die immediately. So, without further ado, let the-"

But before he could finish his sentence, Marok was once again silenced, along with everyone in the crowd, as they were all now listening to *his* voice come out of the recorder.

"Well, partly wrong," his voice recording started. "You see, once this planet ceases to exist, we will already be involved with the Arnaxians on their homeworld. By then, we wouldn't just be living there. We'd be ruling the planet with them as our servants. The treaty will become no more, and then their species will become extinct. Minus the women, of course. We kind of need them to breed."

The look on Marok's face was priceless. And although I didn't have any time, I really wish I could've snapped a photo of him. He couldn't have looked any more guilty even if he tried. Not only that, something else unexpected happened as well. When I looked out over the crowd, I could tell, just by the looks on their faces, that almost all of them knew nothing of his plan. It was almost as if the Morgidian council had kept that under wraps for generations.

"You son of a bitch!" Del shouted. "That was your plan all along? You were just gonna move in and destroy us all?"

"We have no other choice," Marok said.

"Is that true, father?" Harok asked him. "You were going to destroy an entire civilization?"

"This is a dying planet. By showing no mercy and acting the way we did, the treaty was the only way to do this without causing a war."

And there you have it.

Apparently, with me accepting this mission and going out there, I did something that no one else could do. I uncovered a plot that had been kept secret for thousands of years. Everything I had initially thought to be true was. And, to tell you the truth, I was actually kinda proud of myself. Also, by that point, I was finally able to chew my way through my gag and speak.

"And, I'm guessing that by now," I started to say. "You no longer outnumber everyone ten to one, do you?"

Yup. Me and my big mouth.

"You," Marok said in a low devilish tone. "You did this."

He then followed that up by coming over and backhanding me across the left side of my face. Oh yeah. That one really hurt.

After I finished spitting a big wad of blood out of my mouth and onto the ground, the front gates to the castle opened pretty quickly and closed just the same, followed by one of the Morgidians running toward the platform.

"Marok! They're coming!" the messenger screamed.

"Who's coming?" Marok asked. "And why didn't you contact me from your post?"

"I tried, but all communications were knocked out," the running Morgidian said, now hunched over, trying to catch his breath.

"Knocked out?" Marok asked, with one eyebrow raised. "How'd they get knocked out?"

But before the messenger could even give him an answer, a loud, rumbling sound, very reminiscent of thunder, came roaring over the crowd. I looked up to the sky and (to mine and everyone else's surprise) saw the most impressive armada of ships I had ever seen. Come to think of it, it was the *only* armada of ships I had ever seen.

Arnaxians, Dukians, Ckroblodites, Planatians, and a whole slew of other ships that I didn't recognize, were now hovering about 500 feet above the castle. I had no idea why they were there, but I was definitely glad they were. And seeing all of those ships hovering up there, I knew that they weren't there just to say hello either. No fleet of ships would jam a planet's communications just to show up and say hi. Something big was about to go down, and I was about to get the surprise of my life. Again.

"They destroyed our communications arrays," the messenger said.

"Then you've failed me," Marok responded before grabbing the messenger's neck and snapping it like a twig.

I had to watch that poor guy's lifeless body tumble to the platform like a jelly roll.

You know, I might have been wrong about Marok. Instead of him being the reasonable man I thought he was, he was just a big dick.

"Get all of our ships in the air!" Marok yelled. "I want them destroyed!"

As soon as the Morgidians started to break away and head toward their warships, all hell broke loose as the fleet above began firing on the crowd below.

"So much for the treaty," I blurted out.

It was utter madness, as every Morgidian in there was now running for their lives while trying to get to safety or get out of the castle so they could reach their warships.

"We've got to get out of here, or those ships will blow us to bits," Harok said.

"Ya think?" I sarcastically replied. "Where do we go?"

"Our only safe bet is to head back into the castle."

"Are you insane? Those ships will blow the stone from its foundation."

"Not if we can make it back to the throne room. That whole building's protected by a shield."

Of course, he was right. But I was still focused on other matters.

"What about your father?" I asked.

"We'll deal with him later," he replied. "Now, come on!"

What choice did I have? That man standing next to me was now my only ally.

Regardless, I only had two options: I could stay out on the platform and risk getting vaporized, or I could follow him into the castle and risk the wrath of Marok. Hey, I was no fool. I wanted to live just a little bit longer.

So, I quickly stuffed my phone back into my pocket and followed Harok down the platform stairs so we could then make our way through the crowd. Del, Marok, and his band of merry men had already split. Luckily, everyone else was too busy running for their own lives to notice a couple of runaway captives. And, after a few more pushes and shoves, we finally made it safely into the main building.

While we were now safely inside, the battle outside had become a little more fierce. I could now hear what sounded like mortar shells being shot off. Either that, or it was the sound of fighters crashing into the ground and blowing up upon impact. And I definitely wasn't gonna go look either.

Luckily for us, Harok was able to get his hands on a Morgidian war blade, which looked very similar to a scimitar. The difference was that on the outside of the curve where the blade sits, it looked more like a saw instead of a smooth edge. The handguard was square, and the handle was wrapped in a red cloth. He was then able to get himself free before cutting me loose.

"Thanks," I said.

"Don't mention it," he replied.

"So, what happens now?"

"I have to get to the throne room and stop my father."

"Stop him? From what? The whole planet's surrounded. He's as good as dead."

"Not if he activates the electron pulse."

Wait a minute… what did he just say? The electron pulse? What the hell's that? And how come I didn't know about it?

"Could you say it in a way that I'd understand what the hell you're talking about?" I asked.

"If he activates the electron pulse," Harok began. "It will send out a shockwave that will emanate just beyond our planet's atmosphere. Any ships that the wave touches will shut down and come crashing to the planet's surface, killing tens of thousands of people."

"Sartia never mentioned one of those."

"She never knew about it. And, unfortunately, I never got the chance to tell her either."

"Oh shit," I muttered.

"You stay here while I go and stop him."

That was his plan? He wanted me to stay put in a castle swarming with Morgidians while he goes to the throne room and leaves me there all alone? Hell no.

"No way. I'm coming with you," I said.

"You won't stand a chance up there," he said.

"Neither will you. Plus, after what she did for me, I owe it to Sartia to try and keep you alive."

I owe it to her to keep him alive? What the hell was I talking about? I was now either out of my mind or having one of those 'be the hero' type of moments. Whatever it was, I clearly wasn't thinking straight.

"Are you sure about this?" he asked.

"No," I replied. "But let's do it before I change my mind."

"You're braver than I thought."

"I'm glad one of us thinks so."

And with that, we wasted no time getting on the elevator to began our ascent toward the throne room.

• • •

On the way up, a million scenarios ran through my head about what would happen to us when we got off. One of them being that a slew of Morgidians would already be waiting for us, and once those doors opened, they would simply kill us.

Another scenario was that once we got off, and this was a pretty big longshot, by some miracle, the throne room would already be destroyed, and a group of allies would be there waiting for us. Not so much.

Instead, a scenario happened that I would've never in a million years ever dreamt of happening after what I just witnessed on that platform.

Once we arrived on the fifth floor, the elevator doors opened, and we stepped out to not only a group of people pointing their guns at us but Del standing side by side with Marok.

"You gotta be fucking kidding me!" I blurted out. "Even after she betrayed your trust and fucked my brains out, you still let her stand beside you? I thought sex before marriage was a means to death?"

"Maybe with the old laws, it was," Marok said. "But we are ushering in a new age and a new set of laws."

"Yeah? What's that? Adultery?"

He just glared at me and apparently wasn't amused by my comment.

"If I didn't want you to see this, I'd kill you," he said.

"I'm touched," I replied.

"You are about to witness the first-ever planetary protector. This weapon will make the entire galaxy fear us and bow beneath our feet."

"You weren't, by any chance, born with a small dick, were you?"

"You should be one to talk," Del interjected.

"Hey, I didn't hear you complaining," I said. "Besides, I could always play the recording again if you'd-"

"Enough!" Marok screamed.

"Now what?" I asked Harok.

"I'm sorry, but I never got that far into my plan," he said.

"So, your whole plan was to just come charging up here, attitudes a-blazin'?"

"Pretty much."

"Bring them over here!" Marok ordered the guards.

Four of his guards came over to us with their guns drawn, pointed us in the direction of where Marok was standing, and then led us over to his position in front of the open wall behind the throne.

As we all looked out over the courtyard, we could see that the aliens from the ships were now on the ground. Blaster bolts and laser fire were hitting the building in almost every spot. But thanks to its shields, nothing was getting in, and we were safe.

"Father, listen to me. What you're doing is wrong," Harok said. "I know that we've never seen eye to eye, but you have to stop this at once."

"Oh, Harok," Marok began. "You're just like your mother. She never once believed in anything I did. I also think she wound up putting all of her bullshit into your head. And that's the reason why I had to kill her, so I could mold you into what I hoped you would become. Unfortunately, it now looks like I'll have to do the same thing with you."

Oh shit. That was a huge twist, even for me.

The look of utter shock and hatred had now taken over Harok's face. "You killed my mother?" he asked.

"I'm sorry, but the bitch had to be silenced," Marok replied.

"I'll fucking kill you!"

In the blink of an eye, Harok bowled over two of the guards, and before anyone else had time to react, he tackled his father to the ground. I tried to run in and help but was quickly reminded that I still had weapons pointed at me. So, I couldn't do anything else but stand there and watch as they wrestled with each other on the ground for a few seconds before getting back up.

"No one intervenes!" Marok ordered. "I'll handle this myself."

Soon, they were in a shoulder lock, with their foreheads tightly pressed together as they just stood there, snarling and growling at one another. The only other time I've ever seen that was when two dogs went at it. In a way, it was almost comical to watch.

"You think you can run this planet better than I can?" Marok asked.

"You're not even fit to run yourself," Harok replied.

"We'll see about that."

Marok then let go of Harok and immediately moved to the side as he watched his son go crashing into the wall. Harok quickly turned around and went charging back toward his father, grabbing him around the waist and tackling him to the ground once again.

I gotta tell you, though, watching those two go at it was literally like watching a street fight. Harok threw a punch and connected with Marok's jaw. Marok then threw a couple of his own punches and connected with Harok's gut before nailing his jaw. Back and forth they went for the next five or so minutes until both of them were utterly bloodied and bruised. Unfortunately, Marok wound up getting the best of his son.

After Harok threw a punch and missed, Marok grabbed his arm and put him in an armbar of some sort. Harok tried to resist, but Marok's power was just too much for him. And within seconds, he snapped his arm at the elbow. Harok let out a monster scream (no pun intended) before falling to his knees.

"Now… you'll get what… you deserve," Marok said while huffing, puffing, and spitting out wads of blood.

He then signaled to Del, prompting her to throw him her firearm. Marok caught the gun and immediately aimed it directly at Harok's forehead.

"Go ahead and kill me," Harok said. "It won't change the fact that you'll still lose."

Marok just laughed. "Do you really think I'll lose this war?" he asked. "When I launch that weapon, not only will I have won, but I'll be a *god* as well."

"Wow!" I said out loud, quickly interrupting their little father/son moment.

"You got something to add?" Marok asked me.

"As a matter of fact, I do. I hate to break it to you, but I've seen this scenario play out a thousand times before, and every single time it happened, the bad guys lost."

"Oh, really? Well, did the bad guys ever do this?"

Without any type of warning, Marok pulled the trigger on his gun, shooting his own son in the head, and killing him almost instantly. Blood flew out the back of Harok's head, almost like a big zit had just been popped. Kind of a gross reference, I know. But I'm sorry. It works.

Anyway, I was now in complete shock, as I did not expect that to happen at all.

"Harok!" I yelled.

And because his son was no more, Marok came right over to me, with his gun now pointed directly at my forehead.

"Oh shit," I said, my eyes looking upward toward the bottom of the gun.

And that's when embarrassing moment number *three* of the trip happened.

As I was standing there with his gun pointed at me, and for the first time ever contemplating my own mortality, I somehow lost all control of my bodily functions and wound up pissing myself.

Now, I know what you're thinking. You're thinking, *Well, why didn't you piss yourself against the bounty hunter, or when you were fighting on Metoria?* Those two times were different. Those two times, I wasn't this close up to the barrel of a laser gun. When that hole is staring you right in the face, it's a whole different ball game, I can tell you that much.

Marok immediately let out a massive gut laugh as he looked down at my now pee-soaked pants.

"It looks to me like you've got a little problem," he remarked.

"What does it matter?" I asked. "In a few minutes, I'll be dead anyway."

"I was gonna wait, but I think I'll just kill you now."

"Well, you're forgetting about one thing," I calmly said before yelling out the next part. "What the hell is that?"

I pointed behind him, hoping to do my best Marty McFly impression. And, sure enough, it worked.

Knowing that the Morgidian guard on the ship didn't even bat an eye at me punching him, I knew for a fact that punching Marok in the face would pretty much have the same effect. However, if he was gonna kill me anyway, I had to at least get one last shot in before he did.

So, I balled up my right hand into a fist, and when he looked back at me, I struck him with everything I had. When my fist connected, his head jilted backward for a split second before turning it back toward me. Del couldn't believe what I did either, as her eyes were now practically popping out of their sockets.

Marok then took his left hand and put his fingertips on his lower lip to check for blood. When he pulled his hand away, I could see a little cut on his lower lip, as well as some blood on the tip of his index and middle finger.

After he finished looking at his fingertips, he then looked back at me with the most satanic look that anyone could possibly give another person.

"Now, you die," he said in an even lower yet, eviler voice. If that was even possible.

So, that was it. I was officially done. That whole thing was for naught, as I was about to be executed in an alien throne room 500 million or, whatever, light-years from

Earth. The only thing I could do now was close my eyes and prepare to meet my maker. If there really was one.

But, as luck would have it, an explosion rocked the whole castle, causing it to quake. Not even a second later, I heard a voice come from the elevator behind me.

"Keep Sam alive, but kill everyone else!" the voice shouted.

My eyes quickly shot open, and my ears instantly perked up, as I know I've heard that voice before. But I didn't have any time to look because laser and gunfire immediately erupted, followed by everyone in the room, including myself, taking cover.

I quickly jumped to my right, taking cover underneath the table against the wall, while pulling in one of the empty chairs to block me in. I know. Not very smart. And, of course, being the fool that I am, I peeked out for a split second to take a look at who the mystery person was. Again, I thought my eyes were deceiving me. I had to close them quickly and shake my head, thinking that it was merely my imagination playing tricks on me. But, after I opened them to look again, there she was.

"Sartia?" I asked aloud.

But that really couldn't be her, could it? That was impossible. She died when her ship exploded. I know because I witnessed the whole thing take place.

As my mind continued doubting my eyes, she came running over to take cover with me under the table.

"Sam!" she said with excitement before grabbing my face and planting one on my lips.

"Holy shit! I thought you were dead?" I asked.

"I thought I was too. Thankfully, though, I was able to throw the ship on autopilot and jettison myself before it blew. I then hid underneath the belly of the other ship and waited for them to leave. When they did, I got it fixed up and flew to the nearest friendly planet."

But before I could even say anything else, a few laser shots hit the wall just above us.

"Here," she said, handing me a familiar weapon.

"My burrower!" I excitedly said while taking it from her hands. "How did you get this?"

"I grabbed it right before I jumped ship."

I just looked at her smiled. "I love you."

"I know. But we'll have time for this later. You stay here and keep yourself covered."

"Wait? Where are you going?" I asked as she started to leave our current position. "Don't leave me again."

"I'll be back," she said before planting another quick one on my lips. "Trust me."

She then smiled and quickly stormed out from underneath the table to help her fellow comrades.

· · ·

Over the years, I've watched tons of science fiction and war films, but I've never seen a battle take place quite like that one.

Lasers, makeshift bullets, burrowers, cannons, and everything else, was now being fired within that throne room. And within five minutes, the whole place looked like a piece of Swiss cheese. I could also now see Del and Marok sitting behind the throne, taking cover. They would both appear out for only a second to fire their weapons before retreating back behind the safety of the gold monstrosity.

As for the rest of the Morgidian personnel who were working the control panels, well, they didn't make it. However, the remaining Morgidian guards were also now behind the throne, ducking and standing to fire at the remaining allied forces. Unfortunately, the only cover that the allied forces now had was the dead bodies strewn across the floor.

After a few more minutes of fighting, only a few from each side were left standing, including Sartia, Del, and Marok. I could also see that every time Marok looked out from behind the throne to fire, he would eyeball the control panel where the electron pulse activation button was. And judging by his actions, I knew what he was planning to do, but I just couldn't figure out when he was actually going to do it. Of course, no sooner did I think that, my own question got answered.

The remaining Morgidian guards got up from behind the chair and unloaded everything they had on the remaining forces. The fire was so heavy that the allies couldn't do anything but take cover, stick their arms up, and fire blind. Once they were all completely distracted, that's when Marok made his move. He got up from behind the throne and made a break for the control panel.

Since I was the only one paying attention to what was actually happening, and with no one else available to stop him, I did probably the bravest or stupidest thing that I have ever done in my entire life. I quickly pushed the chair hard into the middle of the room, got out from underneath the table, and ran over to try and stop him. I ran as fast as I could, hoping to tackle him to the ground. But, with my human height and weight, yeah, right.

Instead, he saw me coming, stuck his arm out, and grabbed me by the throat, hoisting me three feet off of the ground, causing me to drop my burrower in the process. When that happened, everyone in the room stopped firing at one another and quickly turned their attention toward us.

"Marok!" Sartia screamed, now pointing her gun at him.

"You make one move, and I'll snap his neck like a twig," he said, pointing his own gun back at her.

Holding onto his left arm with my right, I used my left hand and quickly signaled for her to lower her gun.

"I got this," I said, barely able to speak.

"Now, here's what's gonna happen," Marok said to me. "You're going to push that button for me. Cause' if you don't, I'll kill you. You're choice."

With his left hand wrapped firmly around my throat, it was pretty tricky for me to speak to him.

"I guess... I don't really... have a choice then... do I?" I said.

"What'll it be, Earthling?" he asked.

With no burrower and no strength to speak of, I did the only logical thing I could think of. I did something that I told myself I would never, ever do to another man, only because I knew how much it hurt. But when your opponent has ten times your strength and is also a foot taller than you, you have no other choice.

"Go... to hell," I managed to squeak out.

I then took my right foot, brought it back as far as it would go, and swung it at his crotch like a wrecking ball. Once my foot connected with his jewels, he let out a high-pitched squeal and immediately let go of my neck, dropping me onto the floor. Once I was free, Sartia wasted no time pulling the trigger on her gun. The laser shot went clean through, making a hole big enough in his head that you could peek through. Marok's body then fell backward, hitting the floor like a ton of bricks.

Thankfully, once he fell, the rest of the Morgidian troops dropped their guns and surrendered right there on the spot. With Marok now dead, there was only one other person left to deal with.

With the rest of the Morgidian troops having surrendered to the allied forces, Del realized that she was now outmatched and outgunned. So, she slowly walked out from behind the throne with her arms raised and her hands empty, ready to give herself up.

Now, the problem with that whole situation was that, since Sartia was currently alive and, well, the thought of Del and I and what we did really made me wanna throw up. I couldn't have her spilling the beans to Sartia either. Hell, like I said before, I couldn't trust her as far as I could throw her. Which meant I now ultimately had three options...

First, if she decided to talk and mention what happened, I could accept my fate and take it like a man. Second, I could hope for luck and pray that she didn't say anything at all. Or third, and this is the one I was hoping I could avoid, I could just kill her. But seeing as how I wasn't the cold-blooded killer type, option number three was already off the table.

"I can't believe you're alive!" Del said to Sartia. "I thought you died in that explosion?"

"I escaped just before *you* destroyed my ship," Sartia said.

"Well, I'm just glad you made it."

"Are you? Or are you just stalling?"

"Don't listen to her," I added. "Whatever she's gonna tell you is a bald-faced lie."

"You're just mad because I didn't hold up my end of the bargain," Del said to me.

And there it was. The proverbial 'shit' was about to not only hit the fan… but blow it the fuck up.

"What bargain?" Sartia curiously asked me.

"Uh, nothing. She's lying," I quickly replied.

However, Sartia wasn't buying it. She could tell just by the look on my face that I was definitely hiding something.

"Sam," she said. "What's going on?"

"Yeah, Sam. What *is* going on?" Del sarcastically asked, now sporting a devious smile.

The way that question was asked told me that this was Del's last hurrah before she was either imprisoned or executed for her crimes. Her final goal was to completely destroy me and make the rest of my trip out there a living hell. Well, more than it was already shaping up to be.

But, if this was to be the last leg of my trip and I would get banned from the sector the second it was all over with, and of course, never see Sartia again, then what did I have to lose?

So, I just decided to suck it up and be a man. I'd rather she hear it from me rather than from Del.

"Look, Sartia, I'm so sorry," I began. "But when it happened, I thought you were dead and that it was the only way to escape my execution."

I then lowered my head in sadness and disgust over the fact that I was about to actually go through with it.

"What is it, Sam? You can tell me," she said.

I took a deep breath before lifting my head to look at her.

"Del made me an offer that if I was to marry her," I explained. "Then she would put off my execution so she and I could rule the galaxy together. At the time, it was basically a means to an end until I figured out how to get out of it. So, I said yes."

"That's it?" she asked, now glaring at me intently.

"It is. Again, I'm so sorry."

"Why would I hate you for trying to get out of dying? You did what you had to do."

After hearing her response, I was now a little on the confused side.

"So, you're not mad at me?" I asked.

"Of course not," she replied. "I mean, it's not like you slept with her or anything, right?"

"I would never dream of it."

That's the part I was really hoping to avoid. I mean, of course, I was lying. And, of course, no sooner did I say that, Del quickly tried to blow up my lie.

"You lying son of a-" she started to say.

However, her thought was quickly interrupted by a small saw blade now sitting smack dab in the middle of her forehead. She looked over at me and could see that I was smiling with my burrower pointed directly at her head.

Okay, let's be real here. Did you really think that I was gonna tell Sartia the whole truth? You're out of your mind.

But before Del could take the saw blade out, there it went, twisting and turning, burrowing deep into her skull, as she just screamed out in agony. As it went deeper and deeper, more purple blood just kept oozing out of her head, dripping down each side of her face. However, it didn't take long before the blade hit her brain, and she just stopped screaming altogether. The lifeless look on her face just stood there for a split second before her body fell forward, smashing into the steel floor. Del was now dead, and my fate could live on to fight another day.

After she fell, I just stood there for a moment, thinking about how badly I was manipulated and used by her. I also felt dirty. I felt dirty, not only because I slept with her, but because I had to lie to Sartia.

I completely surprised myself, though. I honestly didn't think I had it in me. I mean, yeah, when I was fighting for my life back at the trade hub, I had to. But I've never actually killed anyone in cold blood like that before. After I did, though, I finally understood what they meant by the phrase 'killing in the name of love.'

They say that you'd kill for the ones you love, and I guess they were right. I loved Sartia and didn't want to hurt her in any way. So, I did it, not only to protect her but to spare her the thought of hating me and killing me herself.

If I did tell her the truth, though, would she have hated me? Or would she have forgiven me? History dictates that she most definitely would've hated me. But I loved her. And no matter how bad I felt afterward, it was all worth the pain.

"I can't believe you did that?" Sartia said with a surprised look on her face.

"Well, she tried to kill us and me. Twice!" I said. "Plus, plotting against her own people? She got what she deserved."

"But now we have no record of her ever admitting to it."

"Of course, we do," I said before pulling out my phone and showing it to her. "I got it all right here."

"You recorded her? How the hell did you manage that?"

"I'll tell you later. But, for now, let's just get off of this hell hole and go home. Well, your home."

I then smiled at her, and she smiled back before running over to me and embracing me with one of the biggest hugs I have ever gotten.

Rob J. LaBelle

Chapter 19

After all of the shit that went down on Morgide, we wasted no time, and within the hour, we were in the fixed-up Arnaxian ship, already on our way back to Arnaxia.

So, that was it. The Morgidian sphere was returned to the Morgidians, the war was over, the two perpetrators were dealt with, and my trip was finally at an end. Almost.

If it weren't for the fact that I almost got killed, committed heinous sex acts, and basically went against everything that I've ever stood for, the trip would've been pretty fun.

I got to hang out on Arnaxia for the next couple of weeks until their government and the Morgidian government got everything straightened out. I provided evidence regarding both crimes by submitting the recordings on my phone, but not before erasing certain parts.

Both planets were acquitted of ever taking place in or even knowing about the acts that transpired between Marok and Del. Their interim successors also came to an agreement about what will happen in the future between them.

443

As a show of good faith between the two species, the treaty was eliminated. But a new law was put into effect and pretty much mirrored the original treaty, minus the part about killing anyone or being used as a hostile takeover.

Even though they had plenty of time (roughly 500 years), a new planet was also chosen so that the remaining Morgidians could start their move. Of course, they wound up naming their new home Morgide II. How original.

As for me, both the Arnaxian and Morgidian governments pooled together some funds, compensating me for my troubles. Since I still had to leave the sector after the hearings were finished, I wound up giving all of my money to Sartia. However, the law regarding the Earthlings never being allowed out there, unfortunately, stayed put. Of course, I was still in love with her and had no idea how I would be able to say goodbye, knowing that I would never see her again.

But, even after all that, I still had one thing left to do. There was still one small piece of unfinished business I had to care of. Yes, you guessed it. I had a wish that needed granting.

So, that's where we stand. I was now on Sartia's new ship, which looked very much like the old one, on my way to Faeory so I could get my wish granted before I headed home. The problem was, I still had no idea what I was gonna wish for. But, just so we're all clear, let's go over the rules for wishing again, shall we?

Fayre told me that I could have anything I wanted, except for wishing for more wishes. I didn't need to have Sartia fall in love with me because she already was. I definitely wasn't gonna waste my wish on killing someone because, well, there was no one left to kill. So that just left me.

Did I wanna be rich? Of course. Who doesn't? Did I wanna be famous? Not really. Although getting recognized everywhere I went might be kinda fun. It could also get a little annoying as well. I got it. I could give myself some kind of a superpower like the ability to fly or be invisible or have super strength. But that still wouldn't get me what I wanted. I knew what I wanted, and that was to be with Sartia. But how could I?

If you recall, earlier on in this story, I told Sartia that I was thinking about using my wish on her so we could be together. If you also recall, that didn't exactly go over so well. However, I definitely had to think of something because after my wish, I was going home, and there was absolutely nothing I could do about it. Or was there?

Anyway, Sartia and I were currently in her sleeping quarters, lying in her bed after, I kid you not, two full days of adulterated fun. If you know what I mean? After all, we were never gonna see each other again and had to get it all out of our systems, literally and figuratively, before I went home.

As we were lying there, "Heat of the Moment" by Asia played over the ship's speakers.

"I just wish we could lay like this forever," I said.

"So do I," she said. "But we both know that's not possible."

"Speaking of which, who made up that law, anyway?"

"The Dromede Coalition."

"What the hell is that?"

"The Dromede Coalition is the formation of all the planets' leaders," she began to explain. "The leader or ruler of every planet in the sector gets together at least once a year to discuss our laws and any other business that needs handling."

"They all hate Earthlings that much, huh?" I asked.

"It's not that they hate them. It's just that they know how humans react to things that aren't, well, human."

"They aren't wrong on that one."

"Except for you, of course."

"Well, hopefully, one day, before the both of us are old and wrinkly, they'll change that so we can be together," I said before pausing to brainstorm an idea. "Or better yet, maybe you can try and convince them?"

"They won't listen to me," she responded.

"You never know unless you try."

"That might be a little hard, seeing as how you were the reason this whole thing started in the first place."

Wait a minute… *I* started this whole thing? The Coalition thought that this was all *my* fault? I hated them already.

"Wait, they think this was all *my* fault?" I asked. "How?"

"They think that since you initially found the sphere, you, in turn, had no choice but to come with me," she replied.

"I thought you said you were coming to get it anyway?"

"I was. I could've found the sphere and taken it back myself. But since you found it first, I had no choice but to bring you with me."

I huffed. "What a bunch of shit. Do you think it was my fault?"

"Of course not. As a matter of fact, if it weren't for you, we would've never uncovered what Del and Marok were really up to."

"Maybe you should try telling the Coalition that."

"When I get back, you can bet your ass that I will," she said before looking me in the eyes and caressing the left side of my face. "I love you, Sam. And I don't know how long I'll be able to live without you. But until then, you have a wish to make. Any idea on what you're gonna wish for?"

"I have a few ideas rolling around in my head," I replied.

"Would you care to tell me?"

"It's a surprise."

"I *love* surprises," she said before leaning in and kissing me.

But just as we were about to have some more 'fun', the planetary alert started going off.

"Dammit!" I yelled out.

"We're here," she said, getting up out of bed.

We both got dressed and immediately made our way up to the cockpit. She then turned off the alarm, and we could now see Faeory off in the distance. Once we got close enough to put ourselves into orbit, I was finally able to get a look at it.

It was a blue and green colored planet, with an even amount of land and water covering its surface. I could also see a good mix of large and small continents. Also, and this is the part which I was the most curious about, I swear that I could see a little bit of what looked like fairy dust emanating from the planet and circling its atmosphere. It was almost like watching a blue and green ball covered in sparkle dust, rotating in slow motion.

"Is that fairy dust?" I curiously asked.

"Good observation," she said.

Just then, our ship's ID had been recognized as a female voice came out of the panel's speaker.

"Arnaxian ship, ID zero zero one nine three three, you are now free to land on landing platform six," the voice said.

And with that, Sartia put her hands on the glowing half orbs and guided us down through the planet's atmosphere.

• • •

Once we were down below the clouds, I could see the lush green forests and crystal clear oceans stretch on as far as the eye could see. From what I could tell, there were very few buildings on the surface, and it wasn't until we landed that I could then see why. But I'll get to that shortly.

There on Faeory, they had regular-sized airfields, which could accommodate about a hundred ships apiece. They definitely weren't as big as the other places that we've been to, and there wasn't a lot of traffic down there either.

When we touched down on landing pad six, Sartia turned the ship off. Once our harnesses retracted, we got up and immediately made our way down to the side hatch. She pushed the button, and after the door swung open, a big gust of wind came charging into the ship. I took one whiff of the clean, fresh air and knew that my visit there would be similar to the one on Ckrob.

After the ramp touched down, we walked down it until our feet were planted firmly on the tarmac-like surface. And, for the very first time on that trip, it was nice to know that we could travel somewhere and visit other places without bounty hunters or Morgidians hunting us every step of the way.

While we waited patiently for our emissary, I looked around and couldn't help but notice how tranquil the place was. It felt very peaceful, almost zen-like being there. After waiting no more than five minutes, our emissary, whom I recognized immediately, came over to greet us.

"Sam! It's so good to see you!" Fayre excitedly said.

"It's nice to see you again, Fayre," I replied.

We then embraced each other with a hug.

"It's good to see you too, Sartia," Fayre said, embracing her with a hug as well.

"You too, Fayre," Sartia replied.

"Well, I see that you've been busy these past couple of weeks," Fayre said to me.

"Busy doesn't even begin to describe it," I replied.

"You managed to start a war and uncover a secret plot by two different species."

"I didn't start the war. It was…" I defensively replied before calming myself. "You know what? It doesn't matter. It happened, and now it's over."

"Fair enough. You must be here for your wish then. Have you figured out what you wanted to wish for?"

"You know what?" I started to say. I then looked over at Sartia and smiled before turning my attention back to Fayre. "I think I have."

"Good. But our leader has requested an audience with you," Fayre said.

"Really? Your leader wants to meet me?"

"Yes. It's customary for our leader to meet anyone who saves the life of a fairy before a wish is granted."

"Wow!" Sartia said. "Look at you, Mister Bigshot."

Okay, I'll admit. After she said that, I blushed a little bit, and my ego inflated just a tad.

"Nah," I said, looking both embarrassed and humbled.

"So, are you ready to go?" Fayre asked.

"I'm ready," I replied.

As I looked around, I couldn't help but notice that unlike our previous destinations (except for Ckrob, of course), there wasn't any transportation for us to take in to, wherever the hell it was we were going.

"Umm… where's our hovercar?" I curiously asked.

Fayre let out a little giggle. "We don't use hovercars here."

"You don't?"

Instead of giving me a response, Fayre did something that I never would've expected. She pulled out her magic wand and waved it around a few times before reciting some kind of magic spell. Once she finished the incantation, she then pointed it at us and doused us with her magic. Before I even knew what was going on, we had disappeared from the airfield before reappearing in her village.

For me, the trip was instantaneous. The only way I could describe it was that I was standing in the airfield, I blinked, and then I was standing in the village. And the best part was, I didn't feel a damn thing.

How about that? After I said nothing else would, there was still one more thing that surprised me.

"Holy shit!" I said in amazement. "How did you do that?"

"Magic, silly," she replied.

"Geez, Sam," Sartia added. "I'm surprised you didn't figure that one out?"

"I'm sorry. But I was a little busy being magically transported from one place to another," I replied.

"Follow me," Fayre said before leading us through her village.

. . .

Faeory was very similar to Ckrob. The only difference I noticed was that instead of living in huts, all the fairies lived in actual houses. I then remembered what Fayre told me about her species being all different shapes and sizes because the homes that they lived in were very much all different shapes and sizes. Hence why I saw very few buildings.

Some were two-story houses, and some were one-story houses. Others were about the size of a birdcage, and some were about the size of a regular house. Some were on the ground, and some were hovering in the air. The one thing they all had in common, however, was that they all had the same type of fairy dust emanating off of them.

The village square, or circle, as it looked to me, had a big fountain right smack dab in the middle of it. I kid you not, as the water came out of that stone fairy and shot up into the air, it gave off this weird, magical, bluish glow. As a matter of fact, everything on that planet gave off a sort of magical glow, depending on what color the object was. If it was a green tree, it gave off a green glow. If it was a stone, it gave off a grayish glow. But I think you get the picture.

Aside from the magical, fairytale-type setting, that place was as peaceful and tranquil as could be. Once we got past the village square, and I was done gazing at its magical charm, I noticed something odd.

While looking around at everything, I noticed that the planet didn't have many visitors and was curious about why.

"Can I ask you something?" I asked Fayre.

"What would you like to know?" she responded.

"I see a lot of fairies here but very few visitors. Why is that?"

"This planet is hidden from view when flying by it in space," she began. "It doesn't appear on any star charts, and no ships can detect it. The only way that you can see it and visit is if you're invited."

"So, when I saved your life and was granted a wish, I was automatically invited here?"

"Correct. And when you leave, we will disappear from your radar and view, and you'll never be able to find us again."

"What if I was to fly directly into the planet's coordinates?" I asked. "Would I still be able to see it?"

"No. You would simply fly right through us."

"How is that even possible?"

"Again, magic."

I just looked at her in disbelief while she looked back at me, only to smile and wink.

After a few more minutes of walking, we arrived at what I could only assume was the ruler's house. How do I know this, you ask? Well, I'll tell ya. I know this because the house I was now looking at wasn't a house at all. Nope. It was another fucking castle.

"More castles? Great," I sarcastically remarked.

"I can assure you, you'll find no danger in there," Fayre said.

That castle definitely wasn't as big as the one on Morgide. It was about half the size, was in the shape of a square rather than a hexagon, and didn't have any lava running underneath it. It did have a moat with water, though.

As I was now looking at this weird Hogwarts knockoff, another valid question came to mind. *Why would they have a castle and a moat if they were never in any danger?* There was only one way to find out.

"Why a castle?" I asked.

"What do you mean?" Fayre replied.

"Why do you have a castle with a moat if you're always hidden from view and never in any danger?"

"It just looks good."

It just looks good? Somehow, I wasn't totally surprised by that answer and just nonchalantly shrugged my shoulders in response before we all walked across the wooden bridge and through the front double doors.

• • •

Instead of us entering into a courtyard, we entered directly into the castle itself. There was no courtyard. Instead, it was just one big building with two floors.

We immediately entered a long hallway, and as we walked down it, I peered through all of the doors on both the left and the right-hand sides. While I was looking, I noticed all of the usual things that a castle would have: a galley, a meeting room, a dining room, and even a few bathrooms. The only difference was that instead of everything being made of stone, steel, and wood, all of the amenities looked modern.

At the end of the hallway, we could either go left or right up a couple flights of stairs, or we could take the elevator directly in front of us. Of course, we opted to take the elevator.

But on the ride up, a thought had entered my mind that was so ridiculous yet, made so much sense. Regardless, no matter how stupid it sounded, I just had to ask.

"Wait a minute," I said. "If you have magic, how come you didn't just whisk us up to the second floor of the castle instead of making us walk here all the way from the village gates?"

"Magic is forbidden within the city," Fayre said. "Only our queen is allowed to use it within its boundaries."

"More useless laws. How interesting."

No sooner did I say that, Sartia nudged my left arm with her right elbow while giving me a dirty look in the process. I mean, it's not like I was purposely trying to be rude. I was only curious. Oh well.

After a short ride to the second floor, the elevator opened, and we all stepped out.

"Another hallway?" I asked.

"This way," Fayre said.

Again, on the way down the hallway, I happened to take a peek through the doorways on both sides. But this time, I saw something different. I saw a bedroom, a living room, a kitchen with a table and a set of chairs, a bathroom, and an entertainment room. It almost looked like someone called the second floor of that place home.

When we finally made it down to the end of the hallway, we went through the last door on the left, or I should say, the last 'set of doors' on the left. When the wooden double doors opened inward, we walked in, only to now be standing in the castle's throne room.

A red carpet ran from the door that we walked through all the way up to the throne. The throne itself looked like it was made out of rose petals and also had a pair of butterfly wings attached to its back. Now, I'm not much for complimenting nature at its finest, but that throne looked ever so beautiful.

The rest of the room, which was about the same size as the throne room on Morgide, had all kinds of flowers, plants, and vines growing up the sides of the stone walls.

Butterflies and other miscellaneous peaceful critters flew around to complete the serenity type of feel. Candles also lined the walls, floating just a few feet away from them so as to not burn the plants.

We walked down the carpet until we were about ten feet in front of the throne. Fayre and Sartia both got down on one knee and bowed. After they did, I figured it was only customary that I do it too.

While I was kneeling and my head was down, I felt a burst of air hit the top of my head. When I looked up to see what it was, the ruler of the fairies was now sitting upon the throne, just smiling and staring at us. She was heavenly, to say the least. Like Fayre, she also had mocha-colored skin. But that was pretty much the only similarity they shared.

The woman sitting atop the throne had long, cloud-white hair that ran down to the middle of her back and beautiful, silver-colored eyes that were so bright, you almost needed a pair of sunglasses to look at them. She also had on a silvery, white, strapless ball gown type of dress that went all the way down to her feet. No other fairy that I saw looked like her, and no one was as beautiful as she was.

"There's no need to kneel," she said with a soft, sweet voice. "Rise."

After we all stood up, she did as well.

"Welcome to Faeory," she said. "Allow me to introduce myself. My name is Athena, and I'm the leader of this planet. Welcome, Sam and Sartia."

"It's a pleasure to be here," Sartia said.

"This place is incredible!" I blurted out.

"I'm glad you like it," Athena said. "Now, let's get down to business. First of all, we are grateful to you for saving one of our own. And, as you've already figured out, *you* have been granted a wish. Have you thought of anything you would like to wish for?"

"I thought I did," I said. "But I've been fighting with myself ever since I was told about my wish. The problem is, I just can't decide what I want to wish for."

"That's expected. People usually get overwhelmed when they know they can have anything their heart desires."

"Okay? So, do I just tell you what I want, and you grant it on the spot, or what happens?"

"Well, first of all," she said before turning to look at Sartia. "I do apologize, but Sartia will have to leave the room before you make your wish."

"Why?" I curiously asked.

"No one but you can know what it is. If she hears it, or you tell her afterward, then it won't come true."

As soon as she said that, I immediately realized where that whole 'don't tell anyone or your wish won't come true' theory originally stemmed from.

"Don't worry, I won't be long," I told Sartia.

"Take your time," she said before smiling at me.

Then, she got up, made her way back to the double doors, and exited the throne room.

"Now that it's just the three of us, what is it that you desire?" Athena asked me.

"Well, here's my dilemma," I started to tell her. "I love Sartia, and obviously, I wanna be with her. But because of the law forbidding Earthlings from being out in this sector, I can't."

"Yes. I can see how that would be a problem."

"So, with that being said, I think I'm ready to make my wish."

"And I'm ready to grant it. But before you tell me what it is, I must tell you something extremely important."

Important? Color me intrigued.

"What is it?" I asked.

"It's important to know that your wish won't come true until you are safe and sound back on Earth," she replied.

My eyes quickly narrowed in confusion. "Not until I'm back on Earth? Why?"

"We have laws of our own to uphold. One of them being that a wish cannot come true until the wisher is safely back on his or her home planet."

"But the second I step foot off the ship, Sartia will be gone," I pointed out.

"Let me hear your wish first. And then, if you'd like, I can give you my opinion about it."

"Fair enough." I then paused. "Okay. Here it goes…"

After weeks of racking my brain, thinking about all the things that I could possibly wish for, I was finally ready to make my wish. So, I tilted my head to the sky, closed my eyes, and took a deep breath before looking back at Athena. I opened my mouth to make my wish but then stopped. As I was about to tell her what it was, something inside of me clicked. Something had just popped into my head that I didn't even think about previously.

See, I originally planned on wishing for the law about Earthlings not being allowed in that sector to have never been made. But, thinking about all of the recent shit I went through and all of the people that were needlessly lost, I suddenly had a change of heart about my wish. Instead of thinking about myself, I thought about the people out there first.

I thought about the sphere, the treaty, and how much the sector has suffered over the past few thousand years. And even though I was never a part of it, I thought what life out there would be like if...

Damn my good intentions.

"I wish that the treaty between the Arnaxians and the Morgidians was never written," I said.

The moment those words came out of my mouth, both Athena and Fayre just stared at me with their eyebrows raised. Because of the utter shock now written all over their faces, I could immediately tell that they thought I would use the wish for myself.

"I wasn't expecting that one," Athena said. "Was that your original wish?"

"No. My original wish was to make the law about Earthlings being out here null and void," I replied.

"Then why did you change it?"

"I was hoping that by changing history, Del and Marok would never have conspired against each other and their planets. Sartia would never have met Harok, and the sphere would never have been lost."

"Do you even know why the sphere was lost on Earth in the first place?"

Another interesting question that I completely forgot to ask about.

"No. I never asked," I replied.

"Then how do you know it wouldn't have wound up there?" Athena asked.

"I don't. I was just assuming… what's with the third degree? I thought you were gonna give me some advice?"

"My apologies," she said, closing her eyes and nodding once. "With either wish, you're afraid that, once you step foot back on Earth, your wish will be granted, and you will never see Sartia again. Am I correct in making this assumption?"

"You're correct," I replied.

"In that case, would you care to hear my thoughts regarding your current wish?"

I shrugged. "What have I got to lose? Hit me."

"Patience," she said.

"You want me to wait for your advice?"

"No. That is my advice. Have patience."

Was she out of her mind? I mean, what the hell kind of advice was that?

"You are a good man, Sam," she continued. "I can see into your heart, along with all of the good things you have done, and all of the good things you will do in the future."

"Wait," I said, my eyes narrowed once again. "You can see my future?"

"That's not important. Now, are you ready?"

Knowing that she could see my future, I now had so many different questions I wanted to ask her. *How does my life turn out? Do I get married and have kids? Do I become rich?* You know, stupid shit like that.

However, I had an excellent feeling that regardless of what I asked her, she wasn't gonna tell me squat about what my future holds. I was also kinda glad that she wouldn't because I've seen enough time travel films to know what kinds of consequences knowing too much about your own future can hold.

So, the only thing I could do was just sigh and get it over with.

"I'm ready," I said.

Athena wasted no time as she pulled out her wand and waved it around for a few seconds while repeating some kind of strange magic spell. I also noticed that the more times she said it, the brighter her wand got. After a good solid minute, the wand was so bright that it was now as yellow as the sun. And that's when she pointed it at me and unloaded it.

The beam of light hit my body, and I could instantly feel a slight warmth engulf me like a cocoon. I was now glowing like an all-powerful being. And it felt good. However, as much as I liked it, it was very short-lived.

It only took a few seconds for the beam of light to surround me and then dissipate. Once it was over with, I was just standing there, looking myself over, wondering if that was it or not.

"Is that it? What happens now?" I asked.

"That's it," she replied. "Now, you may go home." She then held up a finger. "But before you do, and because you are a good person, I will give you a little hint of what's to come."

"But I thought you couldn't tell me anything?"

"Because you're a good man, and because of what you've done for this sector, we'll call this one a freebie."

But before I could get a word out edgewise, Athena leaned in and whispered something into my ear. Now, I don't know if it was the fact that she couldn't say it in front of Fayre or the fact that it was for my ears only. I didn't have a clue. And I would never know either.

Anyway, after she finished telling me what it was, my eyes opened really wide, almost as if I had just found out I won the lottery. What it meant, however, well, I had no idea. She said it in such a way that it was almost presented to me like a riddle. Whatever it was, I just knew I had to keep it to myself. That is until the time was right.

And, no. Now is definitely not the right time. So don't ask.

"I hope that satisfies you?" Athena asked.

"Oh, it does," I replied. "More than you know."

"Thank you for everything, Sam," Fayre said before giving me a hug. "And thank you for saving me. I will never forget you."

"You're welcome," I said. "And thank you for granting me a wish."

"It's what we do."

We then broke apart from our hug, and I was now face to face with Athena.

"Sam… we are forever grateful to you for saving the life of one of our own," she said.

But before I had a chance to reply, Athena did something totally unexpected. She leaned in close to me, grabbed both sides of my face with her ever so soft hands, and planted a kiss on me. Now, I thought that Sartia's lips were soft, but she had *nothing* on the fairy queen.

I don't know what it was, but a kiss from a fairy was, well, an experience all on its own. I never thought that anything could be so comforting, soothing, and sweet, all at the same time. The moment she pressed her lips firmly against mine, my legs instantly turned to jelly. I also think she anticipated what would happen because she had to use her magic to hold me upright while we kissed.

After a few magical seconds, she let go, and I was now standing on my own again.

"Thank you, Sam," she said with a smile. "You may go."

But I didn't say anything back to her. Instead, I just smiled, turned around, and started walking out of there, almost as if I'd been struck by Cupid's arrow. I felt like one of those cartoon characters after they got kissed by someone. You know, how they start walking around in some kind of a weird love trance or something? And even though I wasn't in love with her, it sure felt like it.

I stepped through the throne room doors, only to see Sartia standing in the hallway waiting for me. She took one look at me and could instantly see the elation on my face.

"Sam, are you okay?" she asked. "You look… different."

"Who, me?" I said, now sounding like I had just come back from an all-night bender. "Oh, I'm fine. How are you?"

"I'm good," she replied, a confused look now on her face.

She then leaned in close to try and read me a little better. When she did, she noticed something else that was different about me.

"Is that glitter on your lips?" she asked.

"Can you slap me?" I asked.

"What?"

"Please, slap me."

"Are you sure?"

"No. But, just do it before I change my mind."

She just shrugged. "Okay."

465

Sartia took her right hand, pulled it back, and whapped me hard across the left side of my face. In conjunction with me shaking my head, the sting from the slap allowed me to snap out of whatever trance I was in. It was mostly the slap, though.

"What happened?" I asked, my mind now clear.

"What do you mean, what happened?" she replied. "You told me to slap you."

"I did?"

"Yeah. Don't you remember?"

I paused to think about it for a moment before giving her an answer. "No."

"Yeah. You looked like you were drunk. You were bobbing your head back and forth while slurring your words."

"I was?" I asked, now more confused than ever.

She then got the most curious look on her face.

"What exactly happened in there?" she asked.

Of course, I just decided to make a joke. "Well, I could tell you, but then I'd have to kill you."

Thankfully, she knew I couldn't tell her anything about what had happened in there or what I wished for and just went along with it.

"Uh-huh," she replied, not believing me. "You're lucky you can't tell me. Otherwise, I might just have to beat it out of you."

"Ooh! I might like that," I replied with a smirk.

She also smirked and shook her head before leaning in and giving me a quick kiss on the lips.

"Let's go," she said before grabbing my hand and walking me back to the ship.

. . .

After we left Faeory, we only made a few pit stops along the way, as it took us a good week and a half to get back to Earth. During that time, we spent about 85 percent of it in the bedroom. After all, there was a strong possibility that we would never see each other again.

As much as I enjoyed our time during that last week and a half, one particular thought never left my head. I couldn't shake the idea of what exactly was going to happen the moment I stepped foot off of the ship. *Would my life be different? Would my time out in wild space change the whole dynamic of how I would live? What would Darius think about all of this?* Well, I really couldn't tell him because he'd most likely think I was insane.

As a matter of fact, I probably couldn't tell anyone, or else they might lock me up in a padded room or something. But most importantly, the question that never left my head was, *Would I ever see Sartia again?* That thought actually scared the shit out of me because I had just spent the last month or so with her, getting to know her inside and out… literally.

. . .

Sartia now had the ship cloaked, hovering above the river where I initially found the sphere. She thought it would be best to drop me off where she originally picked me up, hopefully, so we wouldn't attract any attention to ourselves when I disembarked.

So, there we were, standing at the side hatch, hugging each other while now saying our last goodbyes.

"I don't wanna go," I said.

"I don't want you to go either," she responded.

"Just, promise me that when you get back to Arnaxia, you'll try to convince the Coalition to eliminate the Earthling law?"

"Trust me. It'll be the first thing I do."

We just stood apart as we gazed deep into each other's eyes. As we did, a tear came down from her right eye. I took my left hand and placed it on her right cheek, wiping the tear away with my thumb. At that point, the waterworks started happening for me as well.

And that's when the last song I heard on that trip start playing throughout the ship. "Wicked Game" by Chris Isaak was now playing, and it was the perfect sad moment.

At first, I didn't care. I took my right hand and placed it on her other cheek while she now had both of her hands on my waist. I looked deep into her eyes again before planting a sensual, romantic goodbye kiss on her lips. That only lasted a few seconds because the music thing was now getting to me. The official 'last straw' had been pulled, and I just had to know… how in the hell through that whole trip was music from Earth playing on an alien ship?

"Okay. That's it!" I said, immediately breaking away from her lips.

"What's wrong?" she asked.

"I have to know something, and up until now, I've let it go. But where the hell is that music coming from? It's been playing throughout this whole entire trip."

She didn't answer me right away. Instead, she just put her left hand over her mouth and snickered, almost as if I was missing out on a funny joke or something.

"I'm so sorry," she said, laughing. "I completely forgot to tell you."

"Tell me what?" I asked.

"The music you're hearing… that's Zeke."

What the hell did she just say?

"Zeke?" I confusingly asked.

"Yeah. Zeke," she replied.

And that's when it happened.

I heard a voice emanate out of nowhere and say something to me. It's a voice I was very curious about and a voice that I know I've heard before. It also happened to be the very same voice that ruined my night with Nicky.

"How's it going?" the mystery voice said.

My eyes shot open, my jaw hit the floor, and I immediately backed myself up against the corridor wall in shock, as I now realized who that was.

"Holy shit!" I said. "You're the voice I heard in my apartment that night!"

"Correct," Zeke said.

I quickly looked around, hoping to get a glimpse of whoever the man was behind the voice.

"Who are you?" I nervously asked. "And better yet, where are you?"

"My apologies," he said. "I'm Zeke. And I'm invisible."

Wait a minute… was he serious? Did he really just claim himself to be the invisible man?

"Invisible? How's that even possible?" I asked, still looking around, trying to find him.

"I'm an invisible man who hails from the planet Invishia,"[12] he answered.

Still not believing what I was hearing, I immediately turned to Sartia to get a real answer.

"Is that true?" I asked.

"It is," she replied. "He really is an invisible man."

"Holy shit!"

And there it was. A real-life, walking, talking invisible man.

However, it didn't take me long to get over the few seconds of shock before I quickly thought about what had happened that night in my apartment and what he said.

---

[12] (Pronounced *In-vi-she-uh*)

"You ruined my night," I told him. "Why would you do that?"

"My species also has a knack for playing tricks on people," he said. "I didn't plan on ruining your night. I just happened to be in your apartment, scoping out the sphere."

"How do you think I knew so much about you?" Sartia added. "Since no one could see him, I sent him to find the sphere for me. That's when he informed me you had taken it and that you needed to come with me."

"Was that you in my room that night as well?" I asked him.

"It was," he replied. "Sorry about waking you up."

I still couldn't believe it. Not just one invisible man, but a whole entire species of invisible men. And women. That just made me even more curious about what else was out there among the stars.

Of course, now knowing that it was him playing all the music I heard, I was curious to know just how in the hell he got all of that, to begin with.

"Wait a minute, hold on," I said. "You mean to tell me that every time I heard music on this ship and in Sartia's apartment, it was you?"

"Guilty as charged," he replied.

"How did you get all of those songs, anyway?"

"While I was in your apartment, I looked through all of your stuff to get a good idea of what kind of music you liked. So, I stored a bunch of it on a memory box that I had brought with me."

"Holy shit! Wait, were you watching when I got attacked by the vampire?"

"Yeah," he answered before laughing. "You crouched into a ball like a scared little girl."

"You're damn right I was scared. And besides, how come you didn't help me out?"

"It was more fun that way."

I then turned back to Sartia.

"Is he always a dick?" I asked.

"That's just how he is," she replied. "I wouldn't let him get to ya, though. As a matter of fact, once you get to know him, he's actually a really nice guy."

"I bet he is. It's just a good thing he wasn't…"

No sooner was I gonna finish my thought, I realized that I had just answered my own question about all the 'other times' he could've been nearby without me even knowing. And man was that creepy.

"Were you watching us while we were having sex?" I asked him.

"Only a couple of times," he replied. "The rest of the time, I let the music play and just left."

"You sick bastard!" I shouted. "I couldn't believe you were the-"

But before I could finish yelling at Zeke, Sartia grabbed me and pulled me in for a long, gentle kiss.

"Well, I guess this is goodbye," she somberly said.

"I guess so," I replied.

She then pushed the button next to the side hatch. We just watched as the door swung open and the ramp extended all the way down to the shore.

"I love you," I said. "Don't forget that."

"I love you too, Sam," she replied.

"Damn! You two remind me of a cheesy love story," Zeke blurted out. "Will you just go already?"

With that one comment, I couldn't help but smile and laugh to myself.

"Take care of her, Zeke," I said.

"You have my word," he replied.

And with that, I gave her one more kiss before taking an almost somber walk of shame down the ramp.

But when I got down to the end of it, I stopped. I didn't wanna touch the ground because I was unsure what would happen the second I did. So, I waited just a few more seconds, took a deep breath, and then planted my feet firmly onto the grass. What happened next was something even I can't explain.

It was almost like it all happened at the exact same time. The moment my feet hit the ground, the ramp to the ship had retracted, which was then followed by a loud rumbling sound. I tried my hardest to keep myself upright as it shook the ground, but failed miserably.

The rumble knocked me down to the ground, and the second my ass touched that grass, the ship was gone. And that was the last thing I remembered. I honestly don't know what that noise was or what had happened, and I couldn't tell you either. But I did know one thing, though...

As I was still lying down, and after not being on Earth for the past month or so, it felt good to be lying down on home soil. My trip was finally over, and I was home.

Chapter 20

You know, it's funny. Those last few minutes with Sartia went by so fast, I didn't even get a chance to ask her who Zeke was, how she knows him, or even why he came across as a creepy, stalker dude. More importantly, what the hell does he look like? Well, I guess I'll never know.

I woke up sometime later and opened my eyes to see the bright blue sky staring me in the face. It took me a few seconds to recover from the disorientation, but I slowly made it to my feet before taking a look around. After I realized where I was, I hiked back up the hill to my car, but not before passing three piles of ash lying on the grass. I looked down at them and thought to myself, *I was gone for just about a month, and no one bothered to clean that up?* Of course, I knew that those were the remains of the three Morgidians that tried to kill me after I had found the sphere.

"The sphere!" I said out loud.

As soon as I said that, a bunch of radical thoughts started to roll through my mind.

Now, the whole point of making the wish I made was to have the treaty null and void. And if it were never signed, the Morgidians and Arnaxians would not have been as close as they were. And Sartia would never have come to Earth in the first place.

You see, if the sphere never made it here, then she wouldn't have come looking for it, and I would've never gone on my little adventure. Apparently, even after making my wish, I still found the sphere and went out into wild space. Or did I? I was so confused by everything that I was now trying to think of all the things I did in the past month. And you know what the weird part was? I remembered everything.

But none of that really happened, did it?

I only asked myself that last question because as I was now staring at the three piles of ash on the ground, they didn't look like they were a month old. As a matter of fact, they looked pretty fresh. And they were still smoldering. But that's impossible, right? As much as I didn't want to think about it, a completely different thought had now entered my mind. It was also probably one of the most ridiculous things I've ever thought of.

I thought that, along with my wish, I somehow managed to travel back in time to the very same day that I initially left with Sartia. Again, it was a ridiculous thought, because as we all know, time travel is impossible. I mean, there's no way those piles could still be that black after a whole month of traveling, could they? I won't lie. Seeing the ash and thinking about time travel made my heart race.

But, no matter how confused I was or how impossible it all sounded, I had to quickly calm myself. The only course of action left for me was to go home, take a shower, and get some sleep. I figured that by the time I woke up, I would feel refreshed and would be able to think more clearly. But when I got back to my apartment and stepped foot through my door, I couldn't even begin to tell you how wrong I wanted to be.

• • •

I quickly got out of my car and went up to my apartment on the fourth floor, hoping I would still live there and not be evicted. To my surprise, when I arrived at my door, it wasn't there. The door that the Morgidians had vaporized was still vaporized. I think I actually saw pieces of it still flying around. But, again, that was impossible, right?

After I walked inside, I noticed that my couch was still missing and that my TV was still on. The Blu-ray logo was now bouncing around the screen, just like it would if a movie had been paused for too long. So, I quickly found the remote sitting on the floor, picked it up, and un-paused it, only to notice that *King Kong* was still in there.

"What the fuck?" I muttered.

Now, I was curious. Was I really gone for a whole month? Did I really time travel back to the same day that I initially left? Or was I now officially losing my mind? Just to be sure, I pulled out my phone to check the date and time. Unfortunately, the battery was dead.

"Figures," I said.

So, I turned off the Blu-ray player and switched to the nearest news channel. When I did, I was both shocked and confused to see that it was, in fact, the exact same day I had initially left, but only a couple of hours had passed. Not believing what I was currently seeing on the TV, and in typical Sam fashion, I started to panic.

"How can that be?" I asked out loud.

I then ran into my bedroom, where I noticed the item that Zeke had knocked over was still lying on the floor.

"No. No. No! That's impossible!" I shouted.

After a few minutes of standing there with a confused look on my face, while trying to come up with some rational explanation of what could've possibly caused that, I ran back out to the living room, only to find the building's owner now standing there.

Alexei was a tall Russian guy with blue eyes, blonde hair, and was somewhat muscular. He could definitely take me down, that's for sure. He was also wearing his usual white, short-sleeve, button-down bowling shirt, tan khaki pants, and a pair of brown loafers.

The way he dressed, and other than his blonde hair, he kind of reminded me of Charlie Sheen's character from the TV show *Two and a Half Men*. Also, he looked none too happy.

"What the hell happened in here?" he asked using a deep, somewhat raspy tone, along with a perfect American accent.

"Alexei!" I shouted with excitement. "Thank god you're here! Look, I didn't do this. I swear."

"Well, if you didn't do it, then who did?"

"I don't know. But, look…" I started to say before running over, grabbing him by his shirt, and panicking. "Alexei, you have to tell me… what day is it?"

"Get your hands off me!" he said, slapping my arms away. "Are you out of your mind? Do you know how much damage you've caused?"

"Just answer my fucking question!" I yelled. "What day is it?"

"You're crazy," he said, now pointing at me. "I'm calling the cops."

"Look, man, it wasn't me, alright. Please, don't call the cops."

"I also want you out of here by the end of the day."

"You're evicting me? I'm telling you, I didn't do this."

"Then who did? The invisible man?"

Of course, with that last comment, he was officially starting to piss me off.

"That's not funny, Alexei," I said. "Look, it was the Morgidians, alright. They followed me here and then blew up the door."

"Who followed you here?" he confusingly asked.

"The Morgidians! You know, the big red aliens that come from the planet Morgide?"

"The who?"

"After I found their toy in the river, they followed me back here. Then, they blew up the door and tried to kill me."

Alexei paused before continuing on. "Do you need some help?"

"I don't need any fucking help!" I angrily shouted.

"You're insane," he said before pulling out his phone. "I'm calling the cops."

Okay. So, maybe I could've handled that whole situation a little better. But by that point, I had completely lost it. I knew that no matter what I said to him, wouldn't have mattered. I didn't know why or how, but my mind was definitely not where it should've been, and I was freaking out. At the time, I didn't fully understand what was going on and wished that Sartia was there to slap some more sense into me.

It didn't take long, however, because, within a few minutes of me prancing around my apartment, raving like a madman, both the cops and the paramedics showed up at my door. Or, my doorway, if you will.

The cops were there to try and keep the peace. As for the paramedics, well, they were there to either see if I had some kind of a mental issue or drug me and knock me out. But because of the disillusioned state I was in, they had no choice but to settle for the latter. As for the next part, well, I'm not proud of it, but it happened. It's also what ultimately led to my current situation.

Now, I won't tell you what kind of profanities I used or how many times I kicked and squirmed to get away from everyone because I'm not proud of it. Since my mind couldn't decipher what was happening (instead of what actually happened), it took both cops, both paramedics, and Alexei to hold me down. As they did, one of the paramedics managed to stick a syringe in my arm and inject me with something. But you probably already know what it was.

I remember looking up to see the cops, the paramedics, and Alexei standing there, looking down on me. Then, that was it. The next thing I know, I'm waking up sometime later, handcuffed to a hospital bed. The nurses, doctors, and police officers all came into my room to ask me as many questions as possible. They all wanted to get the whole story out of me, hoping to make sense of what the hell I was actually flapping my gums about. I mean, come on. What was I gonna tell them? Let's see...

I took a trip on a spaceship and went to another galaxy where I met many aliens, played weird forms of casino games, ate alien food, and even fell in love. Oh yeah! I also fought in a war and almost got killed. Yeah. That would've gone over really well.

As it turns out, no matter what I tried to tell them, whether it was the truth or not, they still wouldn't believe my story and still thought I was crazy.

Anyway, once I woke up, and even though I was perfectly sane at that point, I finally came to a realization about something. The time travel, my whacked-out, panicked mind, the confusion, and all the craziness that went on in my apartment (up until the cops arrived), was just a deadly side effect brought on by the combination of my wish and kiss that I had received from the fairy queen.

As you recall, right before I left, she kissed me and left me feeling 'drunk,' if you will. That's why I initially told Sartia to slap me. I knew I wasn't feeling right after that and needed to have some sense knocked into me. Once I stepped foot onto the grass by the riverbank, the rumble and shake that I couldn't explain was mainly the wish and the kiss both hitting me at once. It basically felt like I had just run full force straight into a brick wall. Unfortunately, I didn't realize what was going on or what had happened until after I woke up in the hospital. Like I said at the beginning of this story, all that was two days ago.

Now, I know what you're thinking. You're probably thinking that this story is complete bullshit and that you hate your job for having to sit here and listen to it. And for that, I'm sorry. Even if you don't believe me, that's fine. It's your prerogative not to. But everything that I've told you up until this point is the truth, no matter how crazy it sounds. Regardless, that's it. That's the end. My story ends today, here with you. I got nothing left to tell.

So before you give me your *expert opinion* on the matter, take a moment to think about everything I just told you. When, and only when you're finished, would I then love to hear what you have to say about it… Doc.

. . .

There is now nothing but silence, as the person that Sam's been speaking to this whole entire time just sits there with an intrigued look on her face while contemplating his story.

Apparently, he's been speaking to some kind of a doctor. The doctor in question is a dark-skinned female who has brown eyes, long brown hair pulled up into a bun, and is wearing a white lab coat, white pants, and black sneakers. She's also sitting in a chair next to a door, holding a tablet on her lap.

"Okay. Just so I'm one hundred percent clear on this," the doctor begins. "You were gone for an entire month and met aliens, flew in spaceships, visited other worlds, fell in love, met mythical creatures, fought in a few battles, had a wish granted, and to top it all off, time traveled?"

"Yes! That's exactly what I've been trying to tell you!" Sam replies.

"And, all of this was just two days ago?"

"Were you even listening to me?"

"Mr. Watson… as a professional psychiatrist, you don't really expect me to believe any of this, do you?"

"Take a look around you," Sam says, motioning to the room that he's in with his head. "I'm sitting here in a padded cell, tied up in a straitjacket, talking to a shrink. The cops, the paramedics, and even the other doctors wouldn't believe me. I mean, someone at least has to, just so I can get the hell out of here."

"And you really believe that someone is me?"

"It has to be. You're the only one left who will listen."

"I see," the doctor curiously says before picking up her tablet and typing in some notes.

"My phone!" Sam says.

"What about it?" the doctor asks.

"I have a ton of pictures on there that can explain everything."

"First of all, I took a look at all of the photos on your phone, and I must say those are pretty incredible. But you know, as well as I do, that photos are inadmissible because they can be photo-shopped."

"But, it's all true. You have to believe me," Sam says, a drop of sadness now in his voice. "Someone has to. I don't wanna spend the rest of my life living in a shithole like this."

"I don't blame you. Unfortunately, we'll have to pick this up again tomorrow. Our time is up for today," the doctor says before standing up and making her way to the door. "I think this was a good first session."

"Look, Doctor Bates," Sam says, also standing up. "What's it gonna take for me to get out of here?"

"Mr. Watson… I honestly don't know if you're crazy or if I should call a publisher to take all this information down and turn it into a book," she says. "I do know, however, that the only way you're going to get out of here is if you tell the truth. Then, after a little bit of good behavior, maybe they'll set you free."

The doctor then knocks on the door that leads out of the room.

"But that's the truth," he says, genuinely, hoping to change her mind.

"Mr. Watson, you seem like a nice person, so let me give you a little piece of advice," she begins. "And, by the way, you didn't hear this from me. But, if what you're telling me *is* the truth, and you do wanna get out of here to lead a normal life, then I would suggest lying."

Sam looks confused by her statement. "You want me to say that it never happened?"

"Yes. That's the only way they'll let you out of here."

"What do I tell people when I get out?"

"Simple… you tell them nothing."

Just then, the door to the padded cell opens up, and the doctor walks through it, stepping out into the hallway. But she doesn't leave just yet. Instead, she stops, turns around, and looks at Sam one more time.

"Just remember, I highly urge you to take my advice. It never happened," she says.

She then turns to her right and walks down the hallway, disappearing out of view. The only thing Sam can do now is stand there and watch the door to his room slowly close shut.

• • •

Day in and day out for the next two months, Sam stuck to his guns about his story and didn't falter or lie to free himself. He knew that what had happened to him was definitely not a dream, and he didn't wanna lie, just to prove a point either. However, even though he stuck to his story and didn't make anything up, he has now officially reached his breaking point.

The food is horrible, and by this point, getting time outside while wearing a straitjacket is no longer fun. Plus, having someone watch his every move and help him while he showers and goes to the bathroom isn't something he wants to continue doing either.

But, he's decided that today's the day. Today, he has no choice but to lie and tell the doctor that none of it was real. All that time he recently spent up in space was about to become complete and utter bullshit. After all, it is the only way he'll finally be able to get out of there.

The door to his room opens up, and not before long, Doctor Bates comes walking through it.

"Good evening, Sam," the doctor says, taking a seat in the chair next to the door.

"Hey, Lorna," Sam somberly replies.

"How did you sleep?"

"The same as I always do."

"That good, huh?"

"No offense, but can we just get this over with?"

"Straight to the point then," the doctor says, giving a nod of approval. "In that case, just like all the rest of our visits, minus our very first one, I'll start with this… do you finally have something to tell me today?"

Sam, who is currently sitting in the far right corner of the room, slowly looks up at her with his tired-looking eyes and his five o'clock shadow peeking out through his face.

"As a matter of fact, I do," he says.

"Okay, then. So, tell me… what really happened to you during those two days?" she asks.

Sam opens his mouth to say something but immediately stops. Apparently, even though he'd rather eat another bowl of Grefarian stew than be in his current situation, he still isn't sure whether or not he wants to keep telling her 'the truth.' However, he also knows that being in there is no picnic either.

"I…," he starts to say. "I…"

"Yes?" the doctor asks while leaning forward.

"I… I made it all up."

And there it is.

Now knowing that she's finally got the best of him and his story, the doctor immediately leans back in her chair, crosses her arms and legs, and smiles.

"So you mean to tell me that your whole story was nothing but a lie?" she asks.

"Ye… yes," he replies. "The aliens, the spaceships, other worlds, and everything else that I've been telling you is all a lie. I made it up strictly for the attention. It never happened."

Sam, who just lied to save his own skin and also knowing that he finally broke down to tell the doctor exactly what she wanted to hear all along, now feels like the world's biggest pile of shit. And because of it, he simply puts his head back down and continues to sulk.

"See? That wasn't so bad, now was it?" the doctor asks. "I'm glad you finally told me the truth. Now all I have to do is put this into my notes. And, hopefully, after a few weeks of good behavior, you can leave this place and never come back."

With his head still down, the sound of defeat rings out from Sam's voice.

"Thank you," he says.

The doctor then picks up her tablet and starts to type in some notes regarding their current session. Hopefully, Sam's journey can come now to an end, and he can finally go home. Well, whatever home he has left.

After a few short minutes of typing, the doctor stops and looks over at Sam, who is also looking back at her. They are only doing so because they can now both feel a rumble starting to shake the entire complex, kind of like when a tractor-trailer drives by a house, causing it to shake slightly.

"Is that an earthquake?" the doctor curiously asks.

But before anyone could answer the question, the shaking stops. The doctor listens for just a split second more before hearing silence and shrugging it off.

For the next few minutes, it's business as usual. The doctor continues to sit there, typing some notes into her tablet, while Sam just sits in the corner.

However, just as she's about to finish, she stops and raises her head. Sam also raises his head as both of them are now looking over toward the door. A small commotion can now be heard coming from somewhere on the other side of it.

"Is that gunfire?" Sam curiously asks.

The sound of gunshots immediately starts blasting on the outside of the complex. Within seconds, it quickly makes its way inside. The gunfire quickly gets closer and closer, making its way through the maze of doors and corridors, until finally, the door to Sam's room opens up, and in walks a female security guard.

She is just a little shorter than Sam and has long, blonde hair pulled back in a ponytail, blue eyes, and an athletic body type. She's also wearing a standard security outfit comprising a blue button-down shirt with a badge on the left breast, black pants, and black sneakers. She also happens to be pointing a gun at them. But it isn't any type of weapon that the doctor has ever seen before. Sam, on the other hand, recognizes it almost immediately and is now smiling from ear to ear.

"Darla?" the doctor asks, curious about why she's there. "What's going on out there? Is everything okay? We heard gunshots."

Without saying a word, 'Darla' walks right over to Sam as she continues to point the gun at the doctor. She then pulls out a knife and starts to cut Sam free of his straitjacket.

"Darla, what are you doing? You can't just release him like that," the doctor says. "I haven't cleared him yet."

While Darla cuts him free, Sam gets an up-close and personal look at the mysterious woman, trying to figure out who she is and what she's doing. But it doesn't take him long to figure it out.

"Holy shit!" he says, his eyes wide. "Sartia?"

"Hey, Sam," she says. "Sorry, it took me so long."

The shocked look on Sam's face says it all.

"But, where did you... how did you find me?" he asks.

"It's a long story," Sartia replies.

"I didn't think I'd ever see you again."

"Neither did I. But as it turns out, when I got back to Arnaxia, a few of the laws had suddenly changed."

Sam's eyes quickly narrow in confusion. "What do you mean changed?"

"Well, the treaty between Arnaxia and Morgide was never signed. And, for some strange reason, Earthlings were no longer off-limits."

"Gee, that is strange," Sam says, smirking.

"There. That ought to do it," Sartia says, removing the straitjacket.

Being able to move his own arms for the first time in two months, Sam immediately puts them up over his head, stretching them as far as he possibly can.

"I thought moving my arms would never feel so good," he says before turning to Sartia and smiling. "I missed you."

"I missed you, too," she replies.

And, just like two lovers who have been separated for what seems like a lifetime, they leap into each other's arms and begin to hug, almost as if it would be their last hug all over again.

All the while, the doctor just continues to stare at them, wondering what the hell's going on and why a security guard would go rogue to try and save a crazy person. After a long, few seconds, however, Sam and Sartia realize that they're now being watched like fish in a fish tank and immediately stop.

The doctor points to Darla. "I'll see to it that you never work here again!" she angrily says.

"I have no idea what you're talking about," Sartia responds. "Come on, Sam. Let's go."

"Wait!" he says, immediately stopping her. "What happened to all the staff?"

"I took care of them."

"You killed them?"

She laughs. "Of course not. I simply knocked them all out."

"Oh. Good."

"Now, what about her?" Sartia asks, pointing to the doctor.

Sam doesn't immediately respond. Instead, he just stands there and thinks about it for a couple of seconds.

He thinks about the last two months and how he's been trying to convince the doctor he's not crazy. She refused to believe him and also made him lie just to prove a point. So, he comes up with the only solution he can think of to finally show her that he's been telling the truth.

"Show her," he says,

"Show her?" Sartia asks, making sure she heard him correctly.

"Yeah. Do your thing."

"Are you sure?"

"I've been stuck in this hell hole for the last two months trying to convince *her* that I'm not crazy. When she sees you, either she'll think I'm telling the truth, or she'll wanna lock herself up. And I don't really think she wants to do that," he says, turning his attention toward the doctor. "Now, do you, doctor?"

"You're both crazy," the doctor says before attempting to run out of the room.

"Stop!" Sartia shouts. "You move another inch, and I'll shoot."

The doctor immediately stops dead in her tracks, turns back around, and is now facing them.

"There. Now, hold this," Sartia says, handing Sam her gun. "If she moves, shoot her."

Sam simply smiles. Of course, if she does try to run, the gun he's holding will only stun her. And because of that, he has no problem pointing it at her. He then looks over at Sartia, giving her a single head nod in the process.

Within a second, Sartia's skin starts moving around like jelly as she begins shapeshifting back into her original form. Sam can't help but smile as he watches the doctor's eyes practically pop out of her sockets. And because he's seen her change before, the whole minute is a piece of cake for Sam. But the doctor almost doesn't know what to make of it, as she just stands there, watching in shock and awe.

Finally, after the minute is over, Darla is no more, and Sartia has returned back to her original, beautiful, amethyst-colored self.

"There you are," Sam says with a loving smile. "Now, *this* is what I really missed."

Sartia smiles back before giving him a semi-quick, passionate kiss on the lips.

"Doc, I'd like you to meet Sartia. Sartia, my shrink," Sam says, introducing them to each other.

"It's a pleasure to meet you," Sartia says, extending her hand out toward the doctor.

But the doctor, now confused and shocked, doesn't say or do anything. She just stands there in a trance-like state, still trying to figure out precisely what the hell's going on.

"Doc?" Sam asks, hoping to get a response.

Short of smacking her, he tries almost everything in the book to get her to respond to him.

First, he snaps his fingers to no avail. Then, he tries waving his hands around in front of her face, which also doesn't work. He even tries yelling at her. But nothing works. And after a few seconds of trying, he just shrugs his shoulders before giving up.

"Are you ready to get out of here?" Sartia asks.

"I was ready two months ago," Sam replies.

They then smile at each other and walk over to the doctor, who just continues to stand there like a stone statue. Each of them gives her one last look before exiting the room and leaving the complex.

• • •

After navigating the confusing maze of corridors, they exit through the front door, immediately entering the courtyard.

The courtyard itself is about the size of a football field and has green grass all throughout. A ten-foot-tall fence, with rolled barbed wire on top of it, runs all the way around the entire complex to keep the criminally insane from escaping.

Once they reach close to the middle of the courtyard, Sartia activates the de-cloaking mechanism, and they watch as her ship appears out of thin air. Sam now has an odd yet, confused look on his face as to what he's currently looking at.

"Wait a minute," he says. "Is that your old ship? The one that got blown up?"

"Yeah," she replies.

"How's that even possible?"

"I'll tell ya later."

The side hatch then swings open while the retractable ramp comes down to greet them. Once it's fully extended, they walk up it and enter the ship.

But just as they are about to close the side hatch and take off, the doctor comes bolting through the front doors like a bat out of hell.

"Wait!" she shouts while screaming, waving, and running toward them.

When the doctor finally arrives at the base of the ramp, she stops and immediately hunches over to catch her breath.

"I'm sorry, Sam," she says. "You were right. You're not crazy. I know that now."

"I'm glad you finally see it," he replies. "But it's already too late. I have to go."

The ramp then retracts itself into the bottom of the ship. But just as Sam is about to push the button to close the door, the doctor stops him again.

"You can't go!" she says. "You have to tell me more of your story."

"I'm sorry, doctor, but that's it," he says. "This is where my story ends. Well, for you, anyway. But I thank you for your time. I really appreciate you listening to everything I had to say."

"Wait, Sam!" she says, putting her right hand out.

"Oh, and uh, doctor?" he says before slamming his fist against the button to close the side hatch. "I think it's best if you lie and don't tell anyone about this."

Just before the hatch slams shut, the last thing the doctor sees through the crack of the closing door is a satisfying Cheshire grin, spanning from ear to ear on Sam's face.

Within seconds, the ship's engines roar to life as it begins hovering just a few feet off of the ground. The doctor just stands there and watches with her hands covering her ears as the ship's engines get louder and louder. And before she can react, it blasts off straight up into the sky, causing the force from the takeoff to knock her backward onto her ass.

The doctor doesn't immediately get up, though. Instead, she just sits there, staring up into the sky. She can't help but wonder where they are going and what they would be doing. What alien planet would they be visiting next? What future battles await them?

As she continues to think about all the places Sam could be going to and who he would be meeting, the doctor feels a sudden sense of disappointment. Mostly because she now feels terrible for not believing Sam's story in the first place. Two whole months locked up in a padded cell for something that he was telling the truth about. But, can you really blame her?

Regardless, there was absolutely nothing that the doctor could do about it now. Because the moment that ship disappeared from view, Sam and Sartia left the atmosphere, never to be seen or heard from again.

Well, they did make a short pitstop at his parents' house to grab a few of his things. But after that, they were never seen or heard from again.

Actually, that's not true either. He did stop to see Darius, who ultimately freaked out like the doctor did, before coming to his senses and thinking that seeing Sam with an alien, was the coolest thing ever. Then, they were never seen or heard from again.

But we all know that's not exactly true, now is it?

Rob J. LaBelle

Epilogue

With this whole mess fully behind him, Sam has taken his place back on Sartia's ship, with not even a single thought of going back to Earth any time soon. Besides, why should he? The laws have changed, allowing him to be out there, and he now has everything he's ever wanted: a ship, an adventure (without being pursued by maniacs), and, most importantly, a girl.

But before Sam left Earth, though, he made a pit stop at his parents' house to gather a few of his things and to have a much-needed shower and shave. After getting admitted into the asylum, he was immediately evicted from his apartment, and all of his belongings were moved to their attic. Which also meant that he was kind of homeless.

Now, Sam's parents, who didn't fully understand why he was committed in the first place, finally did after he introduced them to Sartia. Of course, they had the same reaction that he and the doctor had when they first saw her. But, they eventually shook it off and were able to come to their senses.

After spending a couple of days at his folks' house and having Darius over to tell everyone his story, the roles kind of changed. Like Sam had mentioned earlier in the story, he was the big nerd, while Darius was always king of the castle. So, in a joking fashion, Darius was really impressed with what Sam endured, and therefore, had officially proclaimed him 'the cool one' ahead of himself.

Sam finally told everyone he wasn't staying and that he'd be flying off into wild space. He was a little surprised, though, because instead of trying to stop him, they actually thought it would be good for him. They encouraged him to get out there and see what the other galaxies had to offer. Just as long as he didn't become a stranger and visited from time to time, which he agreed to do.

Now, back to Sam and Sartia.

• • •

So, here they are, on Sartia's original and undestroyed ship, lying in her bed, of course. They now have two months of lost feelings to catch up on. Well, technically, it's three if you count the time travel bit. But it's really two. And because of the Earthlings no longer being off-limits, he and Sartia can finally be together wherever and whenever they want.

"God, I missed you," he says.

"I missed you, too," she replies.

"I didn't think I'd ever see you again."

"Why would you say that?"

"Because of what I wished for."

"Speaking of which…" she says, her interest now piqued. "What exactly did you wish for, anyway?"

"Well, I suppose now that it's done, I can tell ya," he says. "Instead of making a wish that benefitted me, I wished for the treaty between Arnaxia and Morgide to have never been signed."

Upon hearing Sam's answer, Sartia's eyes narrow in confusion.

"Why wouldn't you use the wish for yourself?" she asks.

"Well, I thought that if the treaty was never signed," he begins. "Del and Marok could never have conspired with one another against their own species. I also thought that the sphere would never have landed on Earth, and I would never have left, to begin with."

"But everything still happened the same way you and I remember it. Except for one small detail," she begins explaining. "Because the treaty was never signed, Del and Marok never got together, and instead of killing them both, Marok was killed in the war. His son, Harok, led the now peaceful Morgidians to a new home."

"I don't understand. If none of that happened, how do I still remember everything else?"

She shrugs. "Fairy magic, I guess."

Upon hearing Sartia's comment, Sam's eyes open as wide as they could possibly get, almost as if he just had a huge epiphany.

"That's it! Fairy magic!" he says.

"What the hell are you talking about?" she asks.

"It must have something to do with what Athena told me before she kissed me."

"What did she tell you?"

"She told me to make my wish, and then, after I did, she would offer me some advice," Sam begins explaining. "Her advice was for me to simply have patience. I didn't understand what the hell she was talking about until right before I left when she whispered something in my ear."

"What did she whisper to you?"

"She told me that 'patience is a virtue for those who await their true heart's desire,'" Sam continues. "Now, I had no fucking clue what that meant. That is until you showed up at the asylum. When you did, her advice, coupled with what she whispered to me, made perfect sense."

"Your true heart's desire was to be with me?" Sartia curiously asks.

"Yeah, I know. You probably think I'm corny and that this whole thing is bullshit. But, that's what I wanted above all else."

"I don't think it's bullshit."

"You don't?"

"No. As a matter of fact, I think it's really sweet," she says before leaning in and giving him a soft, sensual kiss on the lips.

"But that still doesn't explain the Earthling law," he says. "What happened with that?"

"Apparently, the Morgidians had a strong say in that law. But because they never signed the treaty, Arnaxia wasn't around to convince everyone else that it was a good idea, to begin with."

"Well, holy shit."

"My thoughts exactly."

"Does anyone else remember everything, or is it just us?" he curiously asks.

"It's just us," she replies.

"Good. In that case, I say we keep our mouths shut and bite our tongues. If I learned anything from being in an asylum for two months, it's to never open your mouth at all."

"I agree."

They then turn toward each other, look deep into each other's eyes, smile, and kiss once more.

However, that only lasts a few seconds before more random thoughts start popping into Sam's head.

"What about Harok?" he asks. "Does he remember you?"

"What do you mean?" Sartia responds.

"Like, does he remember why you were sent to get the sphere in the first place?"

"Well, *that's* another thing. You see, because I'm still a bounty hunter, he spoke with Del and asked who he could hire to find it. She recommended me, and soon after, I was on my way."

"And, what about sending everyone to hunt us down and kill us?"

"Marok had found out that Harok wanted to take control of the sphere so he could rule peacefully and overthrow him," she continues. "That's when Marok sent all of the other Morgidians and bounty hunters after us. Harok was then captured and imprisoned for treason. Luckily, we rescued him when we stormed Morgide."

"So, if Del and Marok weren't working together, why exactly did we storm Morgide?"

"One of Harok's followers got the word out that Marok had devised a new weapon and was planning on going to war with the rest of the sector. I think you can pretty much figure out that the whole idea of war didn't sit well with the Coalition."

"Makes sense," Sam says. "But what about everyone else? When exactly did the events that we remember start to change?"

"Everything happened to a *T*, right up until you saw me come out of the tube," she replies.

"Ah!" Sam says, nodding. "And because Del and Marok weren't working together, to begin with, we weren't forced to leave and have your ship get blown to bits."

"Correct."

"Wow. My head hurts so much right now, I don't even care anymore. I'm just glad I get to be here with you."

He then leans in and gives her another sensual kiss on the lips. Of course, that particular kiss turns into much more, but we'll just skip past that part. We don't need to know the graphic details.

• • •

A couple of hours later, and after they've taken a short break from 'catching up,' we now find Sam and Sartia sitting up in the cockpit of the ship, getting ready to cross the border and make their way into the Dromede galaxy.

It's now officially been two months since Sam has been out here, and at this point in time, he's like an excited kid finding out they're going on vacation to Disneyland.

"I can't wait!" he excitedly says. "I'm so happy to be back out here and visit everything without being hunted or running for our lives."

"Don't worry," Sartia says. "We'll have plenty of time to do anything you want."

Sam doesn't reply. Instead, he continues to stare out of the cockpit window, daydreaming about everything he plans on doing. However, after a few fleeting moments, he can sense two holes being burned into the side of his head. When he turns to look over at Sartia, she's just smirking at him, almost as if she has something on her mind.

"Why are you looking at me like that?" he asks.

"I wanted to ask you something, but I'm not sure how you'll feel about it?" she replies.

"You know you can ask me anything. So, ask away."

"I have two questions, actually."

"Okay? Shoot."

"The first one is… have you thought about what you're gonna do for work?" she asks.

"Shit. That thought never even crossed my mind," Sam replies. "I have no clue. I don't know, maybe, work for one of the corporations, or do some other type of business work? Why do you ask?"

"Well, just like back on Earth, you're gonna need some income to be able to live and afford things. And, I was thinking that, since you're gonna be out here with me, and since you already know how lucrative it can be, I was wondering if you'd be my hunting partner?"

Sam, now kind of taken aback by that question, just stares at her with a surprised look on his face.

"You want *me* to be your bounty hunting partner?" he asks.

"Yeah," she says. "But you can say no if you want. I just thought that you know, since we-"

"I'd love to," he replies, not even giving it a second thought.

"You would?"

"Of course. And, I know that when I was out here before, we almost got killed. Well, actually, you got killed, and I almost got killed. But that's not what I-"

"Will you just get to the point?" she demands.

"Sorry. Anyway, I know that I'm not very good at it. However, if I had the right teacher, I might be able to protect you for once."

Upon saying that, he can't help but look at her and smile.

"Don't worry, I'll show ya a thing or two," she says with a smirk.

"I bet you will," he replies with an even bigger smirk.

Silence engulfs the cockpit for a few short seconds before the conversation continues.

"So, now that we've gotten that out of the way, on to question number two," Sartia says before pausing. "Have you thought about where you wanna call home?"

"No offense, but after my last time out here and what my memories hold of Del," Sam begins. "I'd rather not live on Arnaxia. I couldn't come back out here and see her, knowing what she did, even though she now technically didn't do it."

"I understand. Besides, I've lived there my whole life. I think I'm ready for a change."

Upon hearing Sartia's comment, Sam is now a little unsure about what she means.

"Wait, a change? You mean, live where ever I live?" he asks.

"Well," she nervously starts. "I was thinking more along the lines of us moving in together."

"Really?"

"Yeah. I mean, if you want to. We don't have to-"

He immediately interrupts her thought process by placing his left hand on her right leg, letting her know that there's really no need to explain.

"I wouldn't have it any other way," he replies with a smile.

"Really?" she asks, not believing he would actually agree to it.

"Of course. I mean, to wake up every morning next to the hottest woman in all of space and see those beautiful violet eyes… I'd be a fool not to."

At that moment, he could almost see a small hint of red come out through her amethyst-colored skin.

"Okay," he says, clapping his hands together once and immediately changing the subject to something a little less mushy. "Now, I have a question for you."

"You do?" she asks.

"Yeah. Now, this has been bugging me since day one, and it's probably the nerd in me speaking, but… what the hell do you call this thing?"

"Come again?" she asks, her eyes now narrowed. "What do I call this thing?"

"Yeah. What do you call your ship?"

"I don't call it anything."

"Oh, come on. All captains have names for their ships."

"Not me," she says, shaking her head.

"Have you ever thought about it?"

"No," she responds before raising an eyebrow and realizing where this whole conversation is suddenly going. "Have you?"

"Actually, I have," he replies.

Sartia, now thinking that Sam is totally out of his mind for wanting to name her ship, doesn't exactly know how to feel about it yet, is completely intrigued by what he has to say.

"You've thought about naming my ship?" she asks.

"I have the perfect name, too," he says, grinning from ear to ear.

"I gotta hear this," she replies, leaning back in her chair and folding her arms. "Okay, let's hear it."

"I was thinking about calling it... the *Star Runner.*"

"The *Star Runner?* Where'd you come up with that?"

"I don't know. It just kind of popped into my head."

Sartia doesn't respond right away. Instead, she just sits there in silence for the next few seconds, nodding slowly. At the same time, she's trying to ponder how she feels about the name that Sam just suggested. In the passenger's chair, Sam can see this and now thinks that she may not even like it at all.

"Oh shit," he says. "You hate it, don't you?"

"Actually, I kinda like it," she replies.

"You do?"

"Yeah. Doing odd jobs and going from planet to planet... it works. I like it."

"I like it, too," Zeke blurts out.

Sam, completely caught up in their conversation, jumps a mile high in his chair, forgetting that Zeke was even onboard the ship.

"Zeke!" he says. "I forgot you were even here."

"That's kinda the whole point," Zeke replies.

"Yeah. Speaking of which…" Sam begins before turning toward
Sartia. "What's the deal with him, anyway?"

"What do you mean?" she asks.

"How did you two become friends?"

"Oh, that. Well, as it turns out, Zeke was one of my former bounties."

"He was a former bounty? And, you didn't turn him in?"

"I didn't have the heart to. You see," Sartia begins. "I was hired by the Mantillians to find Zeke and bring him in. The Mantillians are a race of insectoids that look very similar to a praying mantis back on Earth. Except that they're our height and intelligent.

"Anyway, Zeke, being the prankster that he is, accidentally caused one of their shipments of weapons to explode. Little did he know that, within some of the boxes, was also a highly toxic compound. Once the chemical touched his skin, within hours, he became invisible. Of course, he immediately went back to his homeworld of Grefar to try and have the chemicals washed off. Unfortunately, it infected about twenty-five percent of the population, causing all of them to become invisible.

"Now, in my quest to find him," Sartia continues. "I found out what had happened and knew that bringing him in would be pointless. So, I helped him and the rest of the invisible Grefarians leave the planet to seek out a new home. Of course, you already know that they now live on a planet called Invishia.

"I then went back to the Mantillians and explained to them what had happened. I also lied and told them that the chemical had melted all the Grefarians down into nothing, leaving no trace of them anywhere. Apparently, they're not that smart, though, because they believed my story and still paid me. The area on Grefar where it happened was then designated as a quarantine zone, allowing no one to enter.

"I eventually went back to Invishia and found Zeke. During our nice little chat, he expressed his gratitude to me for saving him and the other Grefarians. He then asked to travel with me and has been doing so for the last ten years."

Sam sits there in silence for a bit as he tries to digest the story that Sartia just told him.

"Holy shit. So, Zeke, you're from Grefar?" Sam asks.

"Originally, yes," Zeke replies. "Why do you ask?"

Sam immediately thinks back to when he was on board the Morgidian ship, challenging the chef before eating a bowl of Grefarian stew. Of course, with his wish having already been made and come true, none of that really happened. Well, at least, not to anyone else. For Sam, however, the thought still makes him want to hurl.

"No reason," Sam says. "However, I am curious about something."

"What's that?" Zeke asks.

"I've never seen a Grefarian. What do you look like?"

"Well, I guess you could say we're somewhat humanoid and stand at an average height. Our skin is either brown or green, and we have pointy ears, almost like what you would see on a bat."

"Oh shit. Tell me you're not a vampire?" Sam nervously asks.

"*Hahaha.* Not even close," Zeke replies. "Our eyes are brown, and along with having two arms, two legs, and a tail, our noses are flat, and our teeth are pointy. Other than that, there's really not much to tell."

"Thanks for the info. And, hopefully, one day, maybe we could visit Grefar so I can see where you come from?"

"Maybe one day."

"Does that answer your question?" Sartia asks.

"You know what? It does," Sam replies. "Also, I now feel much better knowing who I'm traveling with. I just hope that one day Zeke and I can become friends like you two?"

"We're already there," Zeke says. "Well, not quite."

"I can live with that for now," Sam replies.

"Well, good. Everyone's happy," Sartia says. "Now, going back to what we were talking about before… it's settled then. Once we all get situated, we'll throw on a nice new paint job and put the name right on the side of the ship."

"Thank you. I'm glad you like it," Sam says.

"Good. Now that that's out of the way, back to my second question. Any ideas on where you wanna call home?"

Now that Sam has the opportunity to go anywhere, do anything he wants (without being pursued by bounty hunters), and not having to worry about if he'll survive or not, he has a few places in mind.

But none of them compare to the one place that he can't stop thinking about. It's the one place that he constantly thought about for the past two months and ever since he left the first time. It's also the one place that, if he was ever able to get back out here, he knew, without a shadow of a doubt, he'd be calling it home.

"Hey, Zeke?" Sam calls out.

"What's up, Sam?" Zeke replies.

"Now that we're ready to go, and seeing as how all of my wishes have finally been granted," he says, before quickly looking over at Sartia and smiling. "What song do you got queued up for us in the old memory box?"

There's a slight moment of silence before Zeke gives him an answer. "I got just the thing."

Also, it's safe to assume that if they could actually see Zeke's face right now, he would be smiling too.

No sooner does Zeke give Sam a reply, music can be heard blasting throughout the ship. "You Make My Dreams" by Hall and Oates is now blaring over the ship's speakers.

"Perfect choice, Zeke," Sam says before turning toward Sartia. "May I?" he asks, pointing to the control panel.

"She's all yours," she replies with a smile.

They then get up and switch places, as Sam just plops himself down in the captain's chair. When he does, the harness automatically attaches itself.

After fiddling with the star charts and plotting a course, he places his hands on the glowing half orbs and is now ready to finally go home.

"Planaties..." he begins before turning toward Sartia and smiling. "Here, we come!"

Acknowledgments

First of all, I wish to give a very special thanks to one of my best friends, Eric Davidson, for reading through this and providing me with some valuable feedback, from a reader's perspective, as to what I should add or take away from this story. You know... so that people won't get bored and curse me out for writing a lame book. Which might happen, regardless.

Second, I'd like to thank my artist, Ethan, for doing a kick-ass job on the cover. If you like it and would like to see more of what he does, feel free to contact or follow him on Instagram, **@Roxniie**, to see more of his stunning artwork.

Third, I'd like to thank all of the great science fiction writers and filmmakers for inspiring me to write this. Without them, I probably wouldn't have.

Lastly, I would like to thank everyone who believed in me and supported me through all of the madness that comes with writing a book, especially one as long as this.

About the Author

Rob J. LaBelle lives in the middle of nowhere, Massachusetts, where he spends most of his time with his wife and two sons.

When he's not writing, you can find him doing a plethora of activities, including watching movies and TV, playing video games, playing his drums, spending time with his family, and working on computers (which he currently does to make a living).

For more information and upcoming works, please visit www.robjlabelle.com.

This is his very first novel.

CPSIA information can be obtained
at www.ICGtesting.com
Printed in the USA
BVHW050241010821
612841BV00007B/104